My other ♡ Half

My other half

A (HALAL) NOVEL

Neya B

ISBN Amazon paperback: 9798392804740
ISBN Barnes & Noble paperback: 9798369285800

Writing: Neya B
Editor: Fathima A.
Proofreading: Felicity Anderson
Cover: @/Kozukidbasma on Insta

بسم الله

Author's note

Please, before reading this book, understand that it's a
romance and doesn't represent 100% reality.

Trigger warnings

Body dysmorphia
Bullying/mention of bullying
Mention of self-harm
Miscarriage
Postpartum depression

To anyone who needs to reconcile faith and love.

Prologue

In a world where misrepresentation is dominant, where no one wants to separate conception and reality, where honesty is rare and lies spread faster than truth. This book will give you a brand-new image of Islam.

"*My other half*" will teach you the normal life of 1.8 billion people, a quarter of the world's population. You probably have an image of Islam – or Muslims – either mixed with culture or myths heavily infiltrated by the media. I'm not here to blame anyone. This is simply an attempt to give you a fresh set of eyes. It's an example of our lives, our work, our love life, our relationships, and our devotion to Allah سبحانه وتعالى.

With this story, you'll dive into a Muslim relationship inspired by the rules of Islam. However, it's not here to deny how Muslim women are often treated – and/or act – in marriages or relationships and also how Muslim men can act/or be considered in them too. Often, Islam gets caught in the web of culture. "*My other half*" will try to correct them and show you the beauty of love – and relationships – in Islam.

I want to bring a new representation to you.

As a Muslim, I can totally say: that's how we would like to be treated, respected, loved, and supported by our partners.

I hope this book gives you an opportunity to educate yourself beyond the surface. And most of all, men and women, RAISE YOUR STANDARDS! Do not settle for the bare minimum.

This was a special prologue for you and for me.

Have fun with Anas and Hayat! (*And Souhila too*)

Note: For every verse, you'll have only the translation with the source! (so everyone can read it)

Chapter 1

It was only seven in the morning, and Hayat was already mad at herself. As fast as she could, Hayat grabbed some clothes from her *wardrobe* chair. Even as an organization freak, she was late. Late on her plans, projects, and work. Though she had a very flexible schedule as a web designer, she needed to keep up those deadlines to maintain her place in the biggest firm in town. This job brought many things to the table; money, new opportunities, stress, and, most of all, responsibilities. Hayat was aware of its ups and downs. Nonetheless, she still had two more designs to work on before the end of the week for new launches prior to the start of the second semester this year. Luckily, Hayat could work from home, taking her time and doing her best in every aspect of her job. By the end of each day, Hayat was expected to send a report of her progress by email to her superiors.

Only there were two teeny *tiny* problems.

She hadn't started… Not even one.

The second one: it was already Thursday. Hayat needed to present them on Friday's first hour.

Why do I always do this? She thought as she took her keys.

Twenty-four hours left to produce two unique and new designs for two entirely different projects. She was late. Extremely late. Usually, she didn't let herself go, but Hayat deserved a short break after all the things she had to do in such a short time. Almost fifty hours a week for the past month, looking for a new place, and some side projects she had going on, Hayat was exhausted. So, instead of working a bit every day, she played, read, and had the time of her life during her "supposed" office hours.

And that, finally, led to this hectic morning.

It resulted in her frantically sprinting to her car this early in the morning, quickly peeking into the mirror one last time, hoping her outfit was loose enough to hide her curves.

Hayat rushed to do her du'aas while getting out of her building. To get back all the time she lost, she was going to grab an iced caramel macchiato – her favorite drink – at the nearest mall and then head to work.

The radio station started and played her favorite surah to listen to on bad days. Al-Sharh. She repeated after the reciter, appeasing her emotions a bit.

"Indeed, with hardship [will be] ease,"[1] Hayat muttered after the reciter in Arabic.

As the melody of the surah echoed in the car, her heart slowed down progressively to make space for a new sensation; peace. Her mind was now ready for a new mission: getting her coffee as fast as possible. It was so typical of her. This automatism challenged her with each action to achieve some goals so that her system was pushed through them one by one.

It was special.

It was *Hayat*.

---

[1] Verse of the Quran [94:5]

After exactly five minutes, she arrived at the mall. The parking lot was empty. It was strange for her to see. Hayat would usually come here when it was always full of people. Spending her time sitting on a bench watching them shop or clearing her mind after a long day of work. She would observe them and wonder about their stories. Why they were here, and why would they go in this specific store and not another. What attracted them in it? Just watching people she won't see anymore, analyzing them one by one. The thought pleased her in a way. Watching what they bought. This was a good strategy to acquire information on the market, and oftentimes, it helped her get over a creative block.

Hayat wasn't used to this emptiness. She felt like the main character in an apocalyptic movie, and she was the last mankind standing.

Weird.

Before getting out of her car, she rearranged her light green hijab, putting the rest of it over her shoulder before making sure none of her hair or neck was showing. It was one of her nightmares. Walking in the street, and then all of a sudden, a strand of hair was out to take some fresh air. She was unwell just thinking about it. Hayat looked twice in the mirror just to be sure. The young woman could see her big cheeks coming out through her face, hugging the jersey hijab. She sighed in disbelief but decided it was the last thing that should be going through her head. Hayat grabbed the handle and put her right foot out of her car, a small "Bismillāh" slipped between her lips. This was another habit for her to always draw Allah's blessing on her actions. She also checked everything in her bag, even if she already knew everything she needed was in there.

Again, another habit.

Out of anxiety, Hayat repeated the order in her head numerous times – while walking – to reassure herself in some way. She required everything to be perfect so that *she* wouldn't seem awkward or impolite. Even if her work forced her to present projects to a room full of people, her anxiety kept her awake the previous night. The thought of meeting new people put her at unease. Hayat was the kind of woman who *needed* to make a good impression. Her appearance was sometimes qualified as *dangerous*, *unsafe*… Therefore, Hayat was required to take into account these stereotypes. She appreciated being remembered as someone who was good and nothing else. Hayat wasn't concerned about people's opinions, but always wanted to be seen as a well-behaved woman.

The designer was walking fast enough to feel the fresh wind of spring on her skin. Somehow, it calmed her. Hayat took a deep breath of this benediction of Allah, and without losing a minute, she urged herself to the coffee shop on the second floor. She pulled her phone from her bag to keep track of time – as she had forgotten her watch before going out this morning. Seven-thirty. Hayat only got thirty minutes left to get a coffee and be behind her desk at work.

Easy, she thought.

Except when she was welcomed by a long queue of people waiting for their morning drinks. Her expression crumpled. Hayat was surprised when she noticed that many people were early birds. Normally, no one would be here at seven in the morning. That was what Hayat thought, but since she never came to the café this early, she wasn't aware of this detail. So, in typical Hayat fashion, she decided to wait. A new challenge to test her patience. After three minutes, the physical manifestations of stress started to appear; heart racing, fidgety fingers, and restlessness. Her whole body was moving for no specific reason.

Failure was right around the corner.

Please be quick, I don't have time…

Minutes passed, and only a few orders were taken home.

Time was flying, but not the people before her. Twenty minutes left. The designer was about to leave without it when she felt a light tug on her hijab. Her heart was about to burst out of her rib cage. Hayat tightened her grip on her bag, feeling her heartbeat accelerate in order to fight her assailant back.

Someone is trying to take off my hijab? At SEVEN FORTY in the morning?

A few seconds passed, and… Nothing. Her hair was still covered. No one was trying to rip the fabric off Hayat's head.

Everything was ok and normal.

Probably her imagination…

She felt the tug again.

Hayat quickly turned to face them, but all she saw was the mall. The quite *empty* mall.

"A'udubiLlah. Don't tell me it was a jinn." These words dripped out of her mouth due to fear. Hayat took a step back, hoping she wouldn't bump into someone, and that was when she heard it.

A small "oops," made by what appears to be a child. Hayat's eyes looked down, then locked with hers, big brown eyes on a beautiful baby face. The young lady put her hand over her heart in relief. After taking deep breaths, she crouched at her level, pulling the brunette in by the shoulders. However, the little one wasn't feeling it. She escaped the second she got touched. At this reaction, Hayat kept her hands to herself.

"You know that you scared me?" Hayat stated, waiting for an answer, but the brunette only stared at her for a whole minute. The oldest exhaled, her heart still on the edge of her lips, before adding, "What's your name?" While tilting her head to the side.

"Souhila," she responded immediately.

"Where are your parents? Are you here alone?" Hayat questioned while looking around. Her hazel eyes locked with Souhila again after a second. The girl blinked several times before speaking.

"No, I'm not alone. My baba is with me." She said while twisting her ankle a bit. Hayat observed that she was uncomfortable with what she was about to tell, so she made the decision to let her speak without pressuring her. "I saw your hijab, and I, I-"

"Souhila!" A loud, husky voice shouted her name.

"Oh, oh... I'm in trouble." The little one turned to face him. A tall man walked straight toward her. His appearance was imposing and calm at the same time.

That's probably her baba.

In a few strides, he was already at their level. Hayat stood up *fast*, letting all this man's attention on his little girl. He lifted Souhila with ease, a worried expression on his face – but for some reason, Hayat could actually see *noor* on his features. A strange emotion filled her body. Hayat made a fist and bit the inside of her cheeks to make this tingling sensation vanish.

"I thought I lost you too, baba, don't do that again, ok?" He pleaded while brushing her hair frantically. Souhila nodded, then he brought the girl close to him. The man closed his eyes in relief, accompanied by a loud sigh, finally feeling his baby in his arms. Souhila leaned in the embrace, still looking straight at Hayat. Her hazel eyes mesmerized the little one. Souhila hadn't seen anyone with

6

eyes like that. The father didn't even acknowledge the woman with all the emotions he was going through. "I only turned my back for one second, and you were gone. I already told you to stay by my side at all times when we are outside." He repeated firmly while brushing Souhila's hair with kindness. Hayat was, even now, looking at them; she didn't know if she was allowed to say anything.

So the woman stared blankly.

After a brief moment, the brunette tried to reassure her dad. "It is good, baba. I found her while you were looking for me!" Souhila pointed at Hayat bringing her father's attention to the person still staring at them, making the woman still for a second. Her eyes were wide open, her breath taken away, her cheeks flushed with embarrassment. Hayat felt an electric shock all over her spine, propagating side effects all over her body.

The surrounding air had grown heavy in a split second, making it hard for them to breathe.

Hayat didn't know what to do or say. Not only that, but she was just standing there, with his eyes scanning every inch of hers.

Why am I feeling hot all of a sudden?

She wasn't the master of her body anymore.

In Hayat's mind, time slowed down. Letting her print his face into her brain. To make it an everlasting memory, pleading that he isn't just one of the people she would see for the first and last time.

This sensation Hayat was currently experiencing was so pleasing.

She didn't know how to deal with it.

He's far too handsome to be real. Am I dreaming? I hope my outfit doesn't make me look too big. She thought. *AstaghfiruLlah Hayat, what are you thinking about?* She added, but her body didn't give any clue about what was battling inside her screaming mind. The woman was just paralyzed. That was it. It happened when she couldn't choose an option fast enough.

Say or do something. I don't know, but don't stand here looking at him like that. MOVE! Hayat screamed internally to make herself react.

His gaze was both mesmerizing and piercing.

She just couldn't budge.

He had that weird charm that probably left most people stunned by his beauty. If given a choice, she would stare at him as long as she was allowed to. But Hayat needed to get herself together; snap back to reality. She jerked her head, drifting her gaze since it was inappropriate to stare at a man, even if it was very tempting at the moment. She cleared her throat before speaking.

"Yeah," she said before swallowing loudly. "Hi. Thankfully, she found me." Hayat laughed, trying to make a joke out of the situation. Her voice dimmed when his piercing eyes met hers. She swallowed harshly once more, an odd smile printed on her face. Hayat waited for a reaction, but she only saw his jaw clenching, followed by the sound of his response.

"Salam a'leykoum, thanks for keeping my baby safe." He said firmly, letting his jaw's muscles appear again. She could see he was tense for no apparent reason. Hayat tried to be gentle and not let her discomfort show. After looking at him closely, she noticed he also had trouble swallowing correctly and that the tips of his ears were a bit red. The woman was about to ask him if he was fine, but Hayat internally restrained herself.

Was he in the same state as me?

"I, or rather *we*, won't take any more of your time. Barak'Allahu fiki." He stated. Hayat didn't have the opportunity to respond. The young man was already showing his back. She wanted to call him to ask his name, but it was beyond her limits.

So, the designer stood there, flushed, without understanding what just happened.

Souhila's voice interrupted her thoughts as she said, "Baba, why are you blushing?" and he was trying to get his kid to stop talking by saying, "I'm not."

Her question and his reaction got a chuckle out of Hayat's throat. The new sensation she felt left a mark all over her body. She was warm and red. Just by a look. It was the first time she had ever experienced that type of attraction. This meeting emptied all of her head.

Lost, that's how Hayat was feeling right now.

But then the real world came crashing on her, she remembered; work, time. She was about to be late. Hayat looked at the coffee shop and finally changed her mind.

Mission failed…

Hayat would have a million occasions to grab a coffee. However, she only had one job.

Chapter 2

While still in Anas' arms, Souhila made futile attempts to wriggle free of his hold for the rest of their time spent shopping. The father tightened his hold around her, warning his daughter with a burning look. Anas didn't need to say anything. She knew. A few minutes after her failure, the child used every little girl's secret weapon. The puppy eyes technique. But Anas didn't budge. The thirty-five-year-old man continued buying all the items his girl needed; a backpack, new pens, a new case, and brand-new supplies for her classes.

Which will soon start.

Souhila was getting impatient and wanted to walk by herself, she hated being carried everywhere. However, her father indicated his thoughts about this idea. The little one exhaled loudly, before putting her hands on each of Anas' cheeks, forcing him to lock with Souhila's adorable irises.

"Baba, please, I can do it alone…" He looked at her, taking off her fingers from his face and kissing them while putting them away. Anas' expression didn't change; closed and unhappy about her behavior. The man made it obviously clear.

"No, you ran alone in the mall. That's your punishment, benti. You won't walk until you're at school, which starts in less than thirty minutes. No more opposition about it. You misbehaved. You need to face the consequences, ghazaali." Anas put his lips on her brow to make her pouting face vanish. It didn't work, of course. He entirely understood that Souhila's reaction wasn't disrespectful. She was just a young six–year–old child learning how to deal with her emotions. In his childhood, Anas was treated very differently. He wished his parents would have acted toward him the way he chose to do with Souhila. When Anas came of age, he promised himself that this behavior would stop with him. The father had adopted a calmer way to make Souhila understand that for every action, there was a consequence; good or bad.

Even after all the special shopping she got, Souhila wasn't bearing her sentence. A gentle smile appeared on his face. With one hand, he opened the car trunk, still keeping an eye on his daughter's mood. Her mean expression made him chuckle. Souhila, a bit irritated, thought he was mocking her. The young girl stared at him, fisted hands on each side of her small hips.

"Dad," Souhila usually called him this way *only* when she was bothered by his attitude. "Why are you laughing? It is not fun!" Anas' laugh increased a bit. His daughter still confusing fun and funny, made him lose it. He knew it wasn't a way to deal with the situation, but he couldn't help it – she was so cute with her rounded cheeks and her eyes trying to appear threatening.

"I'm sorry, I'm sorry." Anas paused, kissing her again. "But your face was so cute, Sousou. Don't be mad at me, ok? I take you – and your feelings – very seriously, but you need to understand that being in my arms right now is the result of your actions." Souhila nodded, her pouting fading slowly. She understood at her own pace. Anas closed the car trunk before putting his daughter in her seat in the left corner – so he could keep an eye on her while driving.

The little one started playing with her fingers, probably thinking of all the things she was about to do at school today. Anas started the car, making sure everything was good.

"Are you ok back there?" He asked, looking in the rearview mirror.

"Yes, baba!" The girl responded immediately, still focused on her fingers.

Then, we are good to go!

From time to time, Anas gave brief glances at his baby girl since she was still a little overwhelmed, he needed to check on Souhila to get some peace of mind.

Still focused on the road, a flash of the young coffee shop lady came back to him. The man was so absorbed by his daughter that he almost forgot about this unexpected meeting. With only one look at the woman, he was able to rebuild her face in his mind. Anas remembered every little detail of hers; her hazel eyes, long lashes, ethnic features; large nose, pale skin, almond shaped eyes, and longue lashes. Her pretty red and round cheeks, and effortless beauty. The memories made his face flush with shyness – *again.*

Ya akhy, focus! Keep your head straight.

With a simple head shake, Anas attempted to remove all thoughts of her from his mind. Of course, it wasn't how the brain worked. The more he tried to forget, the more he will think about it – and, in this case, *her.* His wit was about to go wild again, but with a yawn, all of his attention returned to Souhila. She had develop a magical effect on him. With a simple movement, the daughter could captivate all of his thoughts and direct all his attention toward her. Souhila was so dear to Anas that he could forget anything just by looking at her beautiful face.

Today, his daughter woke up earlier than usual just to go shopping. It made her a bit sleepy.

"Already tired ghazaali?" He asked with a small smile.

The little one nodded slowly, looking at him through the mirror. "Aah baba, but I am ok." Anas hummed at this response, focusing back on the road.

After a while, they both arrived at the elementary school. Anas took the backpack out of the car, quickly adding all the important stuff, including her lunchbox. Souhila was still attached to her child safety seat, waiting for her father's signal to get down on her own. With his free hand, he opened the door to let her out safely.

"Can you do it alone?" The father questioned, only with his head in the car.

"Aah baba!" Souhila said before putting her small hands on her belt and pressing it with all her strength to snap it open. "See?" She exclaimed with glee, and – *finally* – a wonderful smile on her face. Anas chuckled. He put his hand out, so his little one could come down easily. Souhila took it to help her jump out of the car and landed on her feet.

"Are you excited for today's adventure, baba?" Anas asked, holding her small hand tightly.

"Baba," she paused. "I do not like school," Souhila added, looking at him while walking to the door of the establishment. The father nodded, agreeing.

"Totally understandable. Doing boring things and social interactions." He sighed dramatically, "Not for me."

Anas responded, a hand on his forehead. His daughter stared at him, squinting her eyes, doubting his sincerity.

"Are you mocking me again, baba?" The girl said.

"Of course not, benti. I'm just saying that sometimes you need to do things you don't like to have something better later." Anas explained at the same time as he lowered himself to her height. He gave Souhila the new backpack while she eyed him to make sure he wasn't making fun of her. "I made you a sandwich with tuna, lettuce, and tomatoes, plus apple dice on the side," Anas added before hugging her tight. The little girl inhaled her father's scent before running through the school's doors.

After a moment, he got himself back up while looking at her from afar. When Souhila disappeared from his sight, Anas looked at his watch while walking back to his car. His daughter was at school, so now he needed to be at work.

That was his journey.

Balancing his life between being a father and having a career was hard. Thankfully, being a estate agent helped a lot. It allowed him to be a full-time father. It was a lot of work, of course, but he will always make time for her.

Nine o'clock, I'm on time. He thought before opening his car door.

Anas brushed his hair fast enough to rapidly start the car. He – *as always* – made sure his Bluetooth was connected for his business calls on the road. As he was driving, he played a bit of Quran. It made him feel safe and protected. Today was a big day for him too. Anas needed to visit three new houses to decide which one he wanted to buy and then start a new project – his third one. He loved having a new house to rebuild. He loved creating something beautiful. He did it with so much passion and left a piece of himself in each project.

Suddenly, a phone call interrupted his recitation.

"Hello, Mister Saidi, it's Brittany Smith! Hope I'm not interrupting something?" The lady asked politely.

"Hi, Miss Smith. No, you're not. I'm actually on my way to your house. Is there something urgent you need to tell me?" Anas responded in the same tone.

"Yes! I'm going to be late, about ten to fifteen minutes, is that ok? I'm stuck in traffic." She said, "You know how Houston is." Brittany added jokingly.

"I know, I know. Don't worry, I will wait for you." He replied.

They both exchanged greetings before hanging up. His attention returned to the Quran and the road. After a bit, Anas arrived at the mansion. It was a large red brick house with a beautiful front yard. For a brief moment, he imagined that the sun was shining, and the birds were singing as Souhila played in the garden, running around, picking flowers and chasing butterflies, laughing and giggling. He also pictured a woman watching over her with a sense of wonder. A weird feeling bloomed in his heart. It was a peaceful moment, a moment of pure happiness and contentment as if nothing in the world could ever go wrong. Sometimes, Anas missed having a wife. Sharing his love, his daughter, his day, his deen with someone. However, he couldn't be selfish. Souhila needed him. Maybe, one day, they will be both ready to let a new person enter their life.

The man refocused on the house, which looked exactly like the picture. Anas observed every detail and nook. Especially if this one simple decision included a significant amount of money. He had already chosen three houses from personal ads on the Internet. They looked beautifully maintained, and adequate for the projects he intended to undertake. So, after five minutes of waiting, he started to walk around the house with his glasses all the way up his nose.

One specificity of his: taking mental notes.

Anas didn't need a physical Post-it to remember what he saw, what seemed to be good, and what needed to be fixed. He could close his eyes and imagine every single detail. Allah blessed him with a wonderful memory.

Inspection mode: *activated*.

Anas was hyperaware and never missed a single thing. The grass was so green and beautifully maintained. Not a single blade of grass was higher than the other, no spot of dry soil or a mysterious hole in the ground. It was what he considered perfect. After analyzing every aspect of the garden – to which a swimming pool could be easily added – a strange sensation started to take place in his chest. The outside was pretty clean and perfect, but what about the inside? Was it at the level with the outside? Plenty of questions materialized in his mind. Anas returned to his car, waiting for Brittany.

Twenty minutes passed, and still no sign of Miss Smith.

Leaning on his car door, Anas took out his phone checking if anything came up. His thoughts were interrupted by the sound of a parking Honda Civic.

Brittany was here.

Anas rearranged his hair and outfit before meeting the owner. Looking presentable was number one on his priorities list ahead of any type of appointment. To his face, Anas glued a polite expression, so he wouldn't seem rude. The woman got out of her car, carrying drinks.

Of course, it was coffee.

He hated this type of beverage. It wasn't tasty or useful. To him, it was a got, muddy puddle dumped with sugar that people drank for fun. However, refusing a gift –

to silence the fact she was *extremely* late – was disrespectful. Anas wasn't that type of person. It wasn't in his habits. His culture. He always accepted what was offered, even if he hated it.

"Hi, Mister Saidi! I'm sorry, I wanted to bring you something because I was late, but it just made me even more late." The gray-haired woman declared, running to give the coffee to him. Anas accepted it with a smile.

He let out a small "thank you" at the same time as letting her pass, so Brittany could open the door to show him the inside. She barely opened the door, and a light scent of flowers welcomed them. Anas inhaled every particle of it.

He *loved* flowers.

Before the man could speak about it, Brittany cut him short in his intentions. "The maid comes to clean every week. I, personally, can't do it alone. Too old, you see. My knees won't support it." The lady explained, walking – with her shoes – inside. It was a thing Anas noticed. Not many people took their shoes off before entering the house. This always ticked him off, and not in the right way. A wide corridor led them to the main room, very modern, where a television and a large sofa were waiting to be used.

"I see." That was all he said. Anas didn't come to chit-chat about silly things.

"Yes, of course, you do!" She added while getting deeper into the house. "So, here's the living room," Brittany announced, pointing to the space before them, "With the open kitchen I promised you. I remember you said you loved them," everything was just like the pictures. After so many years doing his job, Anas saw plenty of liars, scammers, and people wasting his precious time. Merely the idea of someone being honest in their ad made him happy.

"I also see that everything is contractual." He highlighted a smile on the corner of his lips.

"Obviously! I need to sell this house, so why would I lie," she paused, walking to the stairs. "Come on. You have more to see!" Brittany continued while emphasizing her words with a wave of the hand. With a joyful expression, Anas walked behind her at a respectful distance.

They went from room to room for about twenty minutes to finally arrive in the biggest chamber of this floor. The lady was still talking non-stop when she opened the door. At this moment, his earlier doubts practically disappeared as soon as his eyes landed on the main area.

Everything was organized perfectly. It was the perfect lighting, the perfect size, and the wardrobe was just stunning. Only the colors needed to be changed to match his taste but also the market's taste.

Anas loved this house.

Chapter 3

"Here you go! The master's bedroom," Brittany revealed. "This is the last room on this floor before we go to the attic, converted into a playroom. Do you enjoy your visit for now, Mister Saidi?" The owner asked, locking her joyful eyes with his. Anas knew what she was trying to do. Every seller needed to be friendly and make the buyer feel appreciated before *the* negotiation. Admittedly, she seemed honest in her ad, as well as during the visit, but would the price follow? Therefore, Anas simply nodded in response, still analyzing every detail of the area. His heart beat with joy. However, he couldn't give her the opportunity to take this as an advantage.

He had to look impassive.

They walked around the house once more and sat in the living room in order to discuss the price. Even after all this walk and talk, Anas never took a sip of his coffee. Not once. Luckily, the lady didn't notice it. Brittany was too focused on selling her beautiful house that she barely looked at him – except to catch a reaction or two. Which actually never came. Her heart was racing, hoping he would already make an offer.

"Mister Saidi, are you happy with the tour I gave you?" Brittany queried, a shy smile on her lips. Anas finally responded to it before letting out a proper answer.

"Yes, Miss Smith, you're a remarkable guide."

"Then, let's discuss the price, shall we?" She said while opening the book on her table. Anas only nodded while sitting himself correctly on the sofa before her. "Do you want to buy the furniture with it?" Brittany asked as she casually flipped the pages. Anas pretended to reflect on the question before giving her his answer, which he had already thought of beforehand.

"No, if I buy it, I will only throw them out. It will be a waste for you." The man answered while tilting his head to the side a bit.

"You're a hundred percent right, my friend." She wrote down his response before finally giving him the price. "If we take out the furniture, we are on a total of four hundred and ninety-four thousand and two hundred fifty dollars. For a house with one hundred and fifty square meters of living space, what do you think?" Brittany added, waiting for his approval. He only hummed, making her blood pressure rise to the top.

"This is a very interesting offer you've got here for me. I still have two other houses to see before accepting anything for now." Anas finally explained. "I'll call you tonight or tomorrow at the latest." He added. Brittany seemed a bit disappointed, but she understood his point. Anas couldn't buy a house or make a fair decision when he still had options. It was the law in this market. A very competitive one. House buying wasn't an overnight decision, either.

"Then, I will wait for your call, Mister Saidi." She uttered while standing up, letting out a loud and clear breath of deception. They exchanged greetings before parting ways. Anas' emotions were in total opposition to those of Brittany. He was smiling while getting to his car. A light heart in his chest and a clear mind.

The second one was about fifteen minutes away from his whereabouts. The instant he sat down in his seat, a new name appeared on his phone. Even though he had calls for his job, he hated them. Anas preferred either to speak face to face or to receive a message. In-person, his imposing physique was an advantage. Anas' commercial partners were – for the majority – intimidated by his presence, even if he got a very kind face or expression. Anas was thankful for this advantage. People generally didn't dare to trick him.

As always, Anas made sure to be in advance for his meeting. He wanted his work ethic to reflect in his actions. To portray himself as a trustworthy man. If he pretended to be perfect, no one could actually blame him for anything or be a burden to anyone. Therefore, the young man constantly made sure to be on time, nice, or meet the norm of society.

Blending in.

It made him feel *safe*.

Anas resumed his radio playing Qur'an, and a sense of relief filled him. He arrived at the second house exactly fifteen minutes later. When his eyes looked at the mansion, he was met with nothing but disappointment. Anas wanted to leave as soon as possible, to call off the appointment. The lifeless, neglected front yard and dirty windows made the hairs on the back of his stand-up in disgust.

Ya Allah, please, make it quick.

It was awful.

The owner, and Anas, went from room to room hurriedly with no attention to detail. It was unfortunate because the house had potential. However, it was extremely poorly maintained, and doing work in a house in this state could cost him a large amount of money. He had neither time nor money to waste in this domain.

And most of all, he hated *lies*.

"How did you find the house?" The old man asked, quite proud, making himself at ease on the sofa.

Silence…

Stephan cleared his throat, "Let's talk about the price!" Anas sat back, feeling his anger rising. The owner was talking, but all Anas heard was gibberish. His mind was a blank space, only reflecting his negative emotions. When he was in that type of mindset, his robotic side took advantage of the situation. His brain tried to catch some information to not lose track of the discussion while Anas calmed his worries progressively.

"I see." Anas mechanically responded.

"In this way, we are on a range of six hundred and five thousand dollars. For a house with ninety square meters of living space, what do you think?" Stephen said before putting his tablet away on the sofa. Anas, this time, didn't pretend anything. He wasn't losing his time. Honesty was the only option he currently had.

"To be frank with you, Mister Jones, I'm a bit disappointed about your property. In your pictures, you only show what's good about your house, and that's what we call a scam. There is a lot of work to be done here, and you hadn't mentioned the state of your house anywhere. If you want your house to be sold, make sure you don't lie in your advertisements or put it at an advantageous price, even if it means selling it at a loss." Anas pointed while standing up. "Of course, I'll post a review on the website.

Plus, I'm going to make sure everybody knows you're a scammer." He added, already at the door. "Have a nice day." Stephen was taken aback.

"I understand, but-" Anas continued, going through the door and closing it to the owner's face. The men were both irritated in some ways. Anas got in his car before almost slamming his door. His nerves got the best of him, but he knew how to overcome this feeling: by seeking help from Allah.

"A'udubiLlah mina sh-shaytani r-rajim." He blew, his hand clenching the steering wheel. Anger flowed out from him like a burning river of bitterness. It was a prayer to seek refuge from Satan. To make it disappear, he only said it twice more before regaining his composure. A hard breath came out of him while he looked at the clock.

Twelve o'clock.

Lunchtime.

The next visit was in less than an hour. He couldn't go home and prepare a meal for himself.

When he was finally in front of the last house, Anas lowered his backrest to enjoy his tuna sandwich in the best conditions ever. At the same time, he watched a live stream of a game he loved. Anas' favorite team was playing. He hoped they would win the tournament. A BO3 was hard to secure in that type of competition. They were almost at the same level. It was just a combination of timing, skills, mastery plus a bit of lineup and a lot of training. Anas was so absorbed by the round that he almost missed his meeting.

He got out of the car quickly after adjusting every detail of his appearance. Anas made sure his beard didn't have any rest of the food in it. He always had to make an impression. As an immigrant's son, he always needed to do extra efforts just to be seen as *normal*.

Therefore, doing more was only a habit now.

Peter Williams, the house's owner, came out at the same time. He was a man of the same size as Anas. Peter smiled at him while walking toward him before standing out a hand for him to shake. Anas automatically took it with a respectful expression on his face.

At first, the house seemed better than the first he visited this morning, but on close inspection, it had hidden wear and tear. Peter was a perfect guide, very kind, and able to answer his questions.

"And here is the terrace with an above-ground pool. It's up to you if you want to keep it after the purchase!" The middle-aged man explained, still having a big smile on his face. Anas was a bit impressed by this. On his new project, he really desired to add a pool to the house. It was a brand-new challenge for him. With his other three properties – two houses and an apartment – he still had no pool. His plans were starting to look a little too similar. It bothered him. That's why Anas directly searched for a house where he could add it easily.

Undoubtedly, Anas would not keep it in its current state. It wasn't attractive or pretty enough to rent it. They both discussed the price, before he left, his mind full of doubts.

- ☾ -

After resting for a few hours, it was time for Salat Istikhara. He already made his wudu for Salat Dohr. It wasn't necessary for him to do it again. Anas usually did it when a choice came his way, and he couldn't see yet the finality. In other terms, if it was a good or bad choice. It was a prayer for guidance. It was a way to seek Allah directly. Whenever faced with a dilemma of choices or a big decision to make, Anas did the Salat Istikhara with full sincerity. When he ended, if his heart was more attracted to one house than another, he knew which choice to make.

Anas was a man of faith and held Islam so close to him. He even designed an entire prayer room, only to worship his Lord in a more private place – when he couldn't go to the masjid. He wanted his prayer room to have the utmost serenity. Anas bought the furniture, chose the colors, and also the calligraphy that his ex-wife advised him. It was the only thing he kept from her. And it was enough, in Anas' opinion.

When he completed his duty as a Muslim, his duty as a father was waiting to be fulfilled: Souhila. It was time for her to leave school. So, he made sure to prepare her a snack, covering it with a towel. Then, he placed a teddy in the car in case she wanted to sleep.

Her school was only fifteen minutes from home. Anas had a little time to look back at the house's pictures, before Souhila's classes ended, his doubts still slighty present in his chest.

I think I will need two little hands to help me on this one.

Souhila was all joyful and jumpy at the end of the day. Her little backpack bounced with her every move, Anas loved to see her like that. He got down at her height to embrace his baby with a hug. She opened her arms widely, too, to welcome her father's presence. Anas held Souhila tight, feeling a sense of relief once she was in his arms.

"Salam a'leykoum benti." The man whispered.

"Salam a'leykoum baba!" Souhila responded, still as joyful as the beginning. After a moment, Anas let her go before leading her to the car and helping his daughter to get in her seat. "Teddy! You took him with you!"

"Yes, of course. You had a long day today, you probably need a nap on the road with teddy." Anas pointed while he fastened her seatbelt. Souhila nodded, holding the object in her hands. The father kissed her before closing the door.

As he started the car, Souhila closed her eyes instantly. When they arrived home, she was still in the same state. Anas smiled at this view. He just stood there for a while, looking at his daughter's calm face. After a few minutes, he took Souhila in his arms to put her in bed. Anas cuddled her a bit to make her feel comfortable during the change of environment. Then, when she was sleeping deeply, he sat on the sofa with pictures of the houses. He was about to make a decision, at the same time, a small voice came from the stairs.

"Baba! Look what I made!" Souhila almost screamed with a large piece of paper in her hand. Anas extended his hand to look at the paper his girl was delighted to display. He analyzed the drawing, pushing back his glasses. It was just a blending of colors and shapes. Nothing really recognizable. So, he just smiled, then praised his daughter.

"Wow, hbiba! You did so well. How was your day?" The father asked while picking her up to put her on his lap. She played with her fingers, answering at the same time.

"We read a new story, I liked it. And then, we," she paused. "We drew! But I was tired."

"Because you woke up earlier today?" Anas completed, Souhila confirmed with a nod. "Are you hungry?" The father added. Souhila nodded again. Anas put her down to bring her snacks to the table. As soon as he put them down, she grabbed them and let out a small "Thanks." Anas looked at her for a moment, waiting for her to say something before eating. And without saying anything, she added "Bismillāh," which made her father proud.

Anas got back to his files, still having no different feelings than before.

"Souhila benti, aji." *Souhila, my daughter, come.* Anas tapped the free place on his right. The girl immediately got up, took her food with her little hands, and kind of ran to her father's side. He took the house's pictures to show them to her.

"Aah baba?" She asked.

"I want to buy a new house for my work, and I don't know which one to choose. They are both very, very good, you see." He said, pointing at the plans. "But, for now, I can only get one. So, tell me, which one is prettier, ghazaali?" Anas explained, looking at his Souhila, totally focused on one of them. That was when he got his sign.

"This one!" The girl burped out, pointing at Brittany's house. The man smiled, agreeing with his daughter's choice.

"Excellent choice, then I will make a call, and after that, we'll do something together, ok?" Souhila hummed in response, so Anas got up and tousled her hair before he went to call the owner to share the good news.

Chapter 4

Nine thirty sharp, and Hayat was already passing the meeting's doors. Punctual, as always. She skimmed through the pages of her presentation one last time. Her speech replayed, in Hayat's head, while she was greeting everyone. The sound of the projector starting caught their attention, making some time for Hayat to take one last breath before displaying her PowerPoint. She checked if her hijab was perfectly done, then she took her papers and knocked them three times gently on the desk, capturing all the pairs of eyes in the room.

"Thanks, everyone, for coming today," she paused. "Mister, the CEO." Hayat added while lowering her head slightly. "I'm going to present, to you, the two designs for the next commercial operations." Merely a few words in, and the whole boardroom was mesmerized by her. The presence, the look, the charisma, and most of all, her eyes. All of these criteria made everyone, with a touch of envy, fall into her speech – and her presentation – so quickly. Hayat was only trying to impress the CEO, who was at his seat across the room's table for the first time in a while. He simply nodded from time to time on important information without giving any sign of what he was really thinking. Just a blank expression accompanied by serious eyes. Some people would already be destabilized by it. However, Hayat was pretty confident about her designs. She always made her best to respect the short notice her superior imposed while bringing a bit of her imagination into it. Until now, this method didn't disappoint anyone.

And she hoped it *never* would.

For a few minutes more, she entertained the people in the room before ending her speech with a beautiful conclusion. Her eyes were glued to her boss' face, inspecting every inch of him. Hayat's brain felt like something was wrong, but her heart was on the opposite side. The old man let a proud smile appear on his face, then sat back correctly on the chair. He cleared his throat while crossing his fingers, pretending to think about what he was about to say. Her heart was pounding, waiting for a sound from Mister Lopez's mouth.

"First, Miss Mazari, I want to thank you for your amazing work. I know it was a last-minute request, but you handled it like a pro." He finally said. "I noted some modifications to do before tonight, so we can start the operation on Monday." The CEO stared at his notebook before adding. "Moreover, I have a few missions to add to your planning. We are currently starting a new brand, and we need a new logo and a graphical chart." He closed his personal organizer, then looked at her for a moment. "As for the modifications and guidelines, I will send them to you by mail." Mister Lopez got up, so all the people did as well to show him their respect. When his hand was on the doorknob, he turned his head to speak again. "Also, Miss Mazari, I want you in my office in fifteen minutes."

All the eyes were on her at the exact moment. Everyone was wondering why he wanted *her* in his office. Even if the CEO was completely amazed by her work and her seriousness in every project, she was still an immigrant's child, a Muslim (and a) woman. Hayat also wore the hijab, and on top of all that, she was a plus-sized woman. She checked every item on the stereotypes list. Sometimes she'd catch people talking about her whenever she passed by. But, Hayat never let it slide and always stood up for herself. She understood, not the easy way, that if you didn't stop people from degrading you, the danger was right in the corner. So, at every opportunity, Hayat would put them in their place.

That's how she was.

That's how she *protected* herself.

Since everyone looked at her, she took her Mac and notebook and smiled at everyone. "Thanks for listening. I hope, next time, no one will feel threatened by my work. They are only *designs*, after all." Hayat threw her words at their faces. Some of them reacted with their head going backward, probably hurting their gigantic ego. She didn't care. Hayat left them behind the door while she was going straight to her success.

For a whole minute, Hayat stood up in front of her superior's door. Stress replaced her blood. The heat she was feeling started to change into a knot at the bottom of her stomach. A vague sensation passed through her, making her feel uncomfortable. Hayat knew she couldn't be fired this quickly, but having a last-minute meeting with her boss was always a source of anxiety. The million possibilities of what it could be made her sweat.

The unknown.

The lack of control.

That was *scary*.

Her hand was in the air close to the door, but not enough to make a sound. Hayat could feel every single muscle in her body straightening, just imagining him staring. She would love to hear what he had to say. However, Hayat usually preferred email. Not facing him was easier. More bearable. She took a deep breath and indicated her presence by a knock. When she heard Mister Lopez authorizing her to come into his space, the designer murmured a du'aa to protect herself and let her stress fly away.

The man was totally focused on the screen facing him. Hayat closed the door after her. This way, no one would overhear the conversation. She made a face of disgust due to the strong smell of cologne, for a few seconds before regain her serious. Strange, strong, and abrupt scents weren't her thing. The old man pointed at the seat in front of his desk with a rather friendly gesture. Mister Lopez took back his notebook in his hands, leafing through the pages one by one in order to find the subject he wanted to address. He closed it to face her again with another smile. Hayat was a bit confused about his intentions.

"So, I made you come here for a clear reason. I would rather not say this in front of everyone because jealousy could cause plenty of terrible things. But you're the best designer we got here so far, and I don't want you to miss out on this opportunity." He finally revealed. Hayat felt her heart being squeezed with pride and joy. She could jump to the ceiling. The designer simply smiled and nodded to thank him, containing her. "I know you're new here, and you barely know all the faces of this job. Nonetheless, your talent is wonderful. I really want to see your full potential, learn from my business and gain experience." Mister Lopez added while Hayat was listening closely. "That's why I would like to offer you a bonus mission system. Whether they're linked to the firm or not. I, personally, have numerous projects that need a designer,

31

and I think you are perfect for the job. It would add hours of work, but you can decline the missions if you can't do them on time. You will no longer be doing the usual missions; banners, graphics charts, and all. So, if you feel it's a lot at once, just tell me." He explained to make sure she would understand everything about this new work. The euphoria of the compliments earlier faded gradually. Of course, they would never come alone. They always required something in return; business is business. Hayat took a moment to think about everything; her organization, her finances, how she could fit every mission into her planning, and more.

"I don't know, sir. I need to think before giving you an answer." The old man was already prepared for this. He smiled again, understanding her doubts and her feelings.

"Totally fair. I knew you would say that. That's why I want to ask you to do a trial. Like a subscription trial that every application gets nowadays. You can try for a month, and see if this life suits you or not. What do you think?" He proposed. Hayat was pretty sure it wasn't his last card. Mister Lopez needed her, and he wasn't going to let her go easily. A smirk appeared on her face for a split second before going neutral again. The man obviously saw it since his eyes were glued to her face. Realizing that he was winning.

"How much for a bonus?" Hayat asked, without losing her focus on one thing: money. The CEO smiled again, but this time it wasn't a kind one. It was a proud one. He was proud of her. As if he saw himself in her. Only focused on her goals.

"It can go from five hundred to one thousand dollars." Hayat made the calculation. Adding this to her salary wasn't negligible. This could change her life – and also her family's life – forever.

"I see." She paused. "I think we got a deal here, Mister Lopez." The man nodded.

"Yes, Miss Mazari, I think so. I'll send you everything you need to know by mail, plus the NDA I want you to sign. Of course, this conversation and this new job are strictly confidential." He clarified, waiting for her response.

"Naturally." They both nodded in agreement. Hayat already imagined all the things she could offer to her family, friends, and the people in need just with this money. After parting ways with her boss, she thanked Allah for this beautiful opportunity. Feeling close to her Lord eased her daily choices. Even if she couldn't tell anyone, she was still joyful about it.

- ☾ -

In the afternoon, Hayat was waiting for her childhood friend – Kamila – in her apartment. The two of them were about to visit another flat downtown. The designer required a bigger place. Her room was getting too small to accommodate her work and gaming setup at the same time. Moreover, her wardrobe wasn't big enough for all the dresses, abayas, hijabs, and khumur anymore. So, Hayat and her friend, looked for a new place to live. After seeing a string of apartments in the surroundings, closer to Hayat's workplace, they came across a spacious flat, very bright, not expensive, but on the top floor of a building. With no elevator… It can't be all glitters.

Hayat hesitated to schedule a visit.

So, Kamila planned it for her.

Now, they needed to go downtown to meet with Mister Saidi. At three. It was already two-thirty. Kamila still wasn't there. Hayat had been waiting for fifteen minutes already. The youngest was getting impatient. She couldn't be late. Her brain was about to command her to call Kamila when a buzz brought Hayat to earth. A text appeared on her phone's screen.

Kamila was there.

Hayat took her bag and keys, checking if her fit was loose enough to hide everything, before disappearing through the door. Since she lived on the first floor, the main entrance wasn't far from her apartment. Kamila didn't park. The car was right in front of the building, waiting for her friend to come down. The woman opened the passenger door for her with a wide smile on her face. She patted the seat to indirectly urge Hayat to enter, so they could leave as fast as she came. Once in, at two thirty-five, they both took the road.

"Salam a'leykoum, how are you? You're late." The designer said, out of breath from running down the stairs.

"Wa'leykoum salam, good, el hemduliLlah." She responded, "I know. I'm sorry. My hair wasn't the way I wanted it to be, so I got frustrated. It's like you when you're in a rush, and your hijab doesn't go out the way you want." Kamila explained while raising a hand vaguely in the air to express her frustration – which was still there. "But that's not the point. Are you excited to see your new place?" Her mood totally changed in one split second. With her fingers, Kamila tapped the top of the steering wheel due to her enthusiasm for this change of life.

"This is not my new place yet." Hayat corrected, pointing at her with a finger. "It's a visit. I'm not signing anything. But yes, I'm excited about it. If the apartment is as beautiful as the pictures, I could actually rent it ASAP!" She added a smirk on her face. During the trip, they both chatted about their ups and downs recently. While talking, Hayat mentioned the coffee shop story. Kamila laughed at the first interaction between the little girl and her friend. The way her thoughts directly led to an Islamophobic attack was hilarious.

"So, you really thought someone was attacking you that early in the morning?" She asked ironically, laughing at the same time. Kamila couldn't contain her laughter. This was too funny.

"I was under pressure, ok?" Hayat responded hastily. Her friend hummed in response, letting her continue her story. She would rather not let one of the main characters out of the story. "Then, a pretty handsome man came to pick her up before leaving." She added.

"Did he have a ring?" Kamila asked frankly. Hayat wasn't shocked about her question. She hated beating around the bush. She only let out a chuckle, but before the woman could answer, Kamila parked in front of the building. A man was already waiting in front of the door. Probably the owner of the apartment she was about to visit. Kamila got out first, while Hayat took her purse and followed her steps

It was the beginning of a new chapter in life. It made her feel a certain type of way. Hayat couldn't describe it.

Excitement?

Joy?

Pride?

She didn't know.

Since Kamila was on the first line, she took the lead in the discussion. Hayat wasn't bothered, as her experience in this business. The brunette had a lot more knowledge in this area than anyone she knew. Since she was the first in line, Kamila greeted the man with a bright smile.

"Hi, are you Mister Saidi?" The man nodded, still hidden by Kamila's body. "Great! I'm Miss Bouzaz. We scheduled to visit your apartment." Kamila announced, before moving out of the way, showing Hayat to the man in front of her. "And this is Miss Mazari."

Hayat took a look and was stunned by what she saw. Her eyes were wide open, she almost gasped. It was him, the same man from the coffee shop. He wore a perfectly tailored suit, the fabric hugging his frame in all the right places, with a beautiful pair of glasses, which added something to his charm. Her face turned bright red. She tried to hide it, but the blush was impossible to ignore. For a long minute, the two of them were just staring at each other. Her eyes trailed the man's expressions. Hayat's heart skipped a beat as she noticed the tip of his ears going red *as well*. Nothing could come out of their dry mouths.

Body: *frozen.*

Mind: *blank.*

Temperature: *hot.*

Kamila's eyes were juggling between her friend and him, trying to figure out what had happened between them. The poke she gave to Hayat's shoulder brought her to her senses. Hayat blinked twice like she was in some sort of trance.

"Do you know him?" Kamila asked, pointing to the owner like he wasn't there.

"Hum, kind of. He's the father of the little girl I mentioned earlier." She responded, quite close to her friend while looking her straight in the eyes, avoiding any contact with him. The first time she saw him was already embarrassing, but now it was worse. The shame was taking over her body. Not knowing how she could control it, she just stood there looking at her friend, hoping this never happened. Hayat saw – in the corner of her eye – the man's expression changing for a moment, then gaining his seriousness again.

"Oh, so you talked about my daughter, I see." He finally said, the corner of his lip lifted slightly before lowering immediately. That's it. The young woman hid behind her hands, red from head to toe. Hayat wanted to vanish completely, to become liquid and flow down the road. To become a tiny, ridiculous ant running away from the tremor that the anthill had just undergone. Hayat felt silly. Talking about someone who probably already forgot the incident was absurd. "I hope it was in a good way, at least." He added jokingly, but Hayat couldn't detect it yet.

"Of course, she looks lovely!" She responded immediately, trying to explain herself with this compliment, which took a light laugh out of him. This lovely sound made Hayat's heart skip a beat again. Kamila was totally absorbed by this interaction, recording every word in her mind. They were definitely going to talk about it. With a smile, Mister Saidi clapped his hands to announce the start of the tour.

"Perfect, so let's get started."

Kamila took her friend by the arm, forcing her to go faster in her steps. The feelings she was going through weren't ready to go away. Her whole body was covered with a strange sensation of warmth. She barely listened to what Mister Saidi said while going up the staircase. Her mind was totally focused on how she got here.

What were the odds? Why now?

Mostly, why *him*?

"She is." Her friend said, interrupting her thinking.

"What?" Hayat responded, confused.

"He asked who was renting. I said you are." Kamila explained, frowning, realizing that her friend had been consumed in her thoughts for a while.

"Oh, yes, I'm seeking a bigger place not far from my work." Mister Saidi nodded again. He didn't seem like a very talkative man. Without noticing it, they were already in front of the apartment.

"Then, I hope this place will mesmerize you enough to sign the contract." He explained, showing her the key to her *potentially* new apartment. She smiled in response. The man stared at her for a while, completely zoned out. Her round cheeks, still flushed, pushed away by her smile, were beautiful. Hayat was beautiful. He cleared his throat before opening the door. Mister Saidi was about to say something but shut his mouth instantly.

They all entered the apartment. Hayat was a bit surprised by the light from the living room, illuminating the front door and the entrance. The place looked so clean she hesitated to enter with her shoes on.

"Sorry, but can we take off our shoes?" Hayat asked, praying it didn't sound weird.

"Of course, do what makes you comfortable." He said.

"Thanks." Hayat took them off, then her friend and Mister Saidi followed her lead.

As expected, every single picture taken was contractual. A poker face was hard to maintain when the place contained all the things she needed – and wanted. It checked all the boxes. The room she loved the most was the bedroom. Some changes will have to be done, of course, like adding a desk in front of the window, or trading the single bed for a king-size since she loved having space while sleeping. She was already imagining herself doing designs all day while taking breaks and looking out through the window.

It was perfect.

This place was her vision of *perfection*.

Even if she already saw the entire place, she did another tour of it since Hayat was very meticulous in her decisions. Just to analyze every spec of the apartment. Nothing was left out. Of course, it was normal for buyers to do a tour over again once the owner ended the visit. If he rented or sold a place, the owner made sure everything was regulated for the purchase. Kamila was in the living room discussing with Mister Saidi, waiting for Hayat to join them.

"Until she gets back, I want to ask you some questions." The woman started.

"Do as you please, Miss Bouzaz." A smile on his face, like she had just said something very interesting to him.

"You can call me Kamila. It's easier for communication." She replied politely. "Is there a community thing in here? Like a charge, she would have to pay in addition to her rent." The friend tilted her head, trying to see if this man was hiding something. In the ad, there were plenty of details about the apartment, as well as pictures – gorgeous pictures. And for that price, it was a steal deal. A place like this, in one of the safest areas of Houston, for only one thousand dollars a month?

It was obviously hiding something.

He got his serious face back on. "No, I don't hide this type of thing from the public. Every detail you need to know is in the ad I posted." Kamila felt the honesty dripping from his voice and his attitude. Therefore, she just kept going with the question.

"Perfect. So, Mister Saidi," she laid back on the armchair. "When did you start this?"

"Almost ten years ago, right after obtaining my degree in an entirely different field." He responded, crossing his fingers together, on top of his also crossed legs. His deep eyes focused on her expression. Mister Saidi was closed off. Kamila could see it. The gleam he had in his eyes was nothing like the one he had when he looked at his friend earlier. The lady scanned his hands; no ring. She smiled.

"This is impressive!" Kamila added, but his attitude earlier was too intriguing to let it go like this. "I only have one more question for you, Mister Saidi. This is not something linked to the apartment. Or actually, in some way, it is." Curiosity almost fell from her mouth, but she kept her composure. The man nodded with a puzzled look. "Are you interested in my *friend*?" When she eventually asked, she could hear footsteps approaching from behind her before they abruptly came to a stop. Hayat couldn't believe what she just heard from the mouth of her friend. Her hazel eyes were wide open, her lips slightly opened due to the surprise. She knew her friend was bold enough to do that, but she didn't believe she would say it to him *now*.

Both of them didn't know enough information about his situation to ask this question. He already has a daughter. What if he was still married? What if his wife was dead? Or something else along those lines.

It was inappropriate.

Mister Saidi's eyes slowly drifted to Hayat. His burning look wasn't bearable, she was too stunned, incapable to move. Like a bee who just came to inject venom into her veins, paralyzing her on the spot. Once more, she was embarrassed. Her body language became tense and awkward, she laughed weirdly to ease the tension in the room. Her mouth opened to say something, but a deep voice interrupted her.

"You know, it's not a question to ask a stranger, Miss Bouzaz." Mister Saidi stopped, his piercing brown eyes locked with a pair of hazel ones. "However, yes, I'm interested in her. *Very* interested."

Chapter 5

A strange feeling replaced Hayat's embarrassment, making her blood go directly to her cheeks. For a while, she just stood there, eyes still locked with his. This situation needed more than one blink to make her brain function again. Before Kamila could add anything else that could highlight her embarrassment, Hayat yanked her by the arm, leading them to the door. They both put their shoes on, while Mister Saidi followed them slowly and said something that they couldn't hear. Hayat had her hand on the door handle, ready to go.

"Thank you, Mister Saidi for this wonderful tour, I will give you my final decision in a day or two." She said, before fleeing. Hayat forced Kamila to run down, then to the car. The oldest anticipated what was going to happen and was ready to face it. "Start the car, we will talk about this at my house." She verbalized, only focusing her gaze on the landscape. Kamila didn't feel like she overstepped her friend's feelings, for her, it was the right thing to do. At least she wasn't trying to explain herself when Hayat was in this mood.

The youngest was silent, occasionally biting her nails, attempting to identify what she felt. It was a blur of emotions. Hayat *hated* that. There was surprise, a point of anger, but also… Happiness? All of this mixed together stressed her out. Hayat inhaled and exhaled several times to calm her heart, which was still racing at full speed.

Losing against herself wasn't an option, not again.

Once they arrived at Hayat's home, they both climbed the stairs in silence. The designer opened the door, letting her friend enter after her. She took her hijab off, letting herself drop on the sofa. A loud sound came out of her mouth, frustrated by the situation. Kamila stood before Hayat, waiting for a word from the woman. The friend patted her feet to make her react, but nothing. She pouted while sitting beside her.

"Don't give me the silent treatment." Kamila pleaded, but still nothing. Her head turned to face Hayat. She was looking at the ceiling with a blank expression. "Are you mad at me?" She added. Hayat sighed, squeezing the bridge of her nose.

"No, I'm not." She paused. "But, I'm frustrated because of what you did without asking me!" Her voice raised a lot, standing up with her hands over her head. Then breathed, seating again, zoning out. "And I'm thinking…"

"About what?" Kamila got up, to prepare tea for both of them.

"About what he said. I noticed you understood I was attracted to him, but I don't *know* him. And It wasn't appropriate to ask him that!" Hayat explained, joining her friend in the kitchen.

"Isn't that the point? Starting to know someone to marry them?" Her friend stated, glaring at her with an arched eyebrow.

"Yes, but he already has a daughter! And imagine-"

"You're trying to find excuses." Kamila cut her off.

"What?" Hayat raised her eyebrows, shocked a little. However, she knew that her friend was right.

"You're making up excuses! If you're not really interested, just say it. There's no shame in that." She explained, putting the cups on the counter. "If you're not ready, it's ok, you know?" Kamila added. Hayat nodded, sticking her brow to the cold counter. She wished she could understand what was going on within her head at the moment. This blurry sensation in her chest started to feel heavy. She averted her gaze, then Hayat began to enter her own head and attempted to express in words what she was experiencing. The designer was having trouble, though, because there were too many distinct emotions.

Hayat sighed once more. "I don't know…"

"Why? This is a simple yes or no question. Are you in or out?" Kamila asked.

"I don't know! Ok?" This time, Hayat could not hold her scream. She closed her eyes, breathed, then continued. "I'm sorry, I shouldn't have screamed at you. But, you know, I hate being pressured to answer." Her friend simply shook her head up and down, while patting the empty side of the sofa. Hayat put her head on Kamila's shoulder, not knowing what to say next.

For a while, they both stayed silent. It was very much needed.

"Let's make pros and cons to help you." Kamila proposed. She spoke like a true businesswoman.

"Ok, pros, a Muslim man. Very attractive, honest, and frank." Hayat said, her body getting hot at the memory of him saying he was interested in her. "Cons, most likely a facade, he's the owner of my future apartment, and his wife, or ex-wife – since he doesn't have a ring, we still don't know, and he has a daughter." She added. Her eyes got wild, thinking about something. "Kamila, imagine if he's looking for a *second* wife!" The emphasis on the "second" gave away that it was a definite no.

"Probably, and why is the daughter a con? I thought you didn't hate children?" Kamila asked, sipping from her cup, aching a brow.

"It's not like that. Entering the life of a grown child is not easy. It's going to be so hard to deal with the sudden change. I don't know anything about her. What if she absolutely hates me? And what if she has trauma? It's not something you can neglect." Hayat explained, taking a sip from her cup of tea – still hot. Kamila agreed with the look in her eyes. "I'll pray, and see if he still wants to talk to me after what happened at his apartment earlier." The designer finally said.

"So you're taking it?" Kamila asked, her voice going in high pitch.

"Of course! Did you see it?! It was precisely what I'm looking for. And, the rescission date of the lease to this apartment is coming to an end soon. So, I need to move out as soon as possible." The two friends continued their discussion, looking back at the picture of the apartment on the website. Completely excited about the idea of having a desk where she could work, and a whole room where she could read and play as much as she wanted. This was a dream coming true. A smile glued to her face. Hayat was sure about this decision; she was about to take this apartment. Now, she needed to think about the preparations to move out all her furniture, the biggest task of all.

Or can't I just give them to my mom, if she requires them? She thought, still looking at all the pictures with Kamila.

The talking stopped after two hours, and five cups of tea. Hayat accompanied her friend to the door, letting her go home after a big, deserved, hug. Once the last barrier was closed, she was practically alone with her thoughts again. To avoid overthinking the rest of the day, and all night, one solution; pray and talk to Allah. She started to bite her nails again, not knowing what she would ask or speak about. Hayat made her wudu and put her prayer mat in the direction of the qibla.

HE says: *"Do not be afraid. I am with you: I hear, and I see.*[2] She thought, reciting this aya to herself.

It was a way of reassurance.

A way to escape her mind.

A way to feel protected.

To feel *heard.*

- ☾ -

Light streamed through the blinds of her window when a loud noise woke her up from her morning nap. Hayat had fallen asleep on her prayer mat. Startled by it, she immediately stood up, becoming lightheaded as she made her way to the window of her room. It was only one of those big trucks making too much noise early in the morning. Someone was moving out from here. Soon it will be her turn. She will start a new chapter of her life. Happiness took over her. With a smile on her face, she went to her kitchen to brew a fresh cup of coffee. There was something so meditative about the ritual of measuring out the coffee grounds, filling the water reservoir, and pressing the button to start the brewing process. Hayat loved the way it filled her entire apartment. The vibration from her phone attracted her gaze. Faudel was written in big bold letters on her screen. It was her older brother, probably to inquire about her house hunting. Too lazy to

---

[2] Verse of the Quran [46:20]

text back, Hayat pressed the call button. Instantly, a voice responded to her.

"Hayat! Salam a'leykoum, how are you?"

"Wa'leykoum salam habib galbi, good el hemduliLlah and you? How's work?" Hayat asked with an extremely joyful voice.

"Good, good! El hemduliLlah. So, tell me, about the apartment, is it what you wanted? Any visible or non-visible problem?" The brother was worried his baby sister was being scammed. Hayat sighed at his reaction.

"Yes, we checked it with Kamila, I wasn't alone. Don't worry!" Faudel shrugged at the name like she was some kind of joke.

"Yeah, of course." Hayat could sense in his voice a touch of bitterness. She knew her brother wasn't feeling her, only Allah knew why, but she wasn't going to let that slide.

"Faudel, she's my best friend, remember? She always helps me when you can't. So be a little nicer." He sighed, reluctant to start an argument over his personal feelings.

"You're right, I'm sorry." He paused, "Are you going to send me some pictures? And why didn't you call me yesterday? I also wanted to see it for the first time with you…" Her brother pretended to be sad, making Hayat chuckle.

"Yes, I have some. I was about to call mama and baba today to let them know I'm going to move. I didn't tell them yet. Just wanted to make sure I was moving first."

"As you should, so they won't worry too much." A loud sound cut the talking. "I need to go, there is a patient knocking at my door like it was made of steel." Faudel blew a kiss through the phone. "See you, Hayat, I love you."

"Love you too, bye." She hung up, happier than before. Now, she needed to speak to her parents and announce the big news.

Hayat frantically crossed the room, from left to right, her thumbnail within her teeth, biting it. Her stress was hitting. Hard.

The bookmarked apartment ad page was still on her computer. Her lips turned dry just thinking about the embarrassment. Sending him a message was a real trial. Mumbling incomprehensible words between her lips, the designer sat back down behind her computer. Nothing came to her mind.

Literally *nothing*.

"Hi, how are y-…" She whispered while writing it. "No, no." She quickly pressed the delete key.

"Hello, Mister Saidi. This is my answ-"

Deleted, once more.

"Argh! No!" Frustration started to grow inside of her. "Ok. Let's make it simple." Hayat paused, biting her lips, and started again.

"Hello, Mister Saidi. I hope you're doing well. As I said after our meeting, I'm sending you this message to give you my final answer." That was how the words came to her after a moment of hesitation. Her fingers typed fast enough to make her complete her message in one second. Hayat's mind already knew what she would answer, but the embarrassment misted her thoughts. After sending it, in less than a minute, the owner answered her. It was a Saturday, after all.

From: *saidiagency@gmail.com*   ***1 minute ago***
To: *mazari.h@gmail.com*

Hello Miss Mazari, I'm well, thank you. I hope you're doing well too.

I'm glad to hear – or more read – a positive answer from you.
We can sign the papers today if it works for you.

Sincerely yours,
Anas Saidi.

     Anas, that's his name.
     A faint smile appeared on her face, due to the tint of humor in his message, and on the other side for his fast response on a weekend morning. She replied in a few seconds, making an appointment. After she hit the send button, Hayat took her phone and called Kamila.

- ☾ -

     "*That's* where he told you to meet him?" Kamila wiggled her finger toward the coffee shop's sign. They both looked at each other for a moment. Mister Saidi gave Hayat the address of one of the fanciest coffee places in town. This man knew how to treat people. They were both confused, seeing him through the window.
     "I think so because he's right here." Hayat pointed. Their eyes landed on the man holding his drink in one hand while reading something on his phone. As soon as they spotted him, they hurried in and joined Anas at his table. A waiter accompanied them to his table.

"Hello ladies, do you want to drink something before talking business? It's on me." Anas suggested them, going straight to the point – as always. The two friends looked at each other, hesitating on taking something. It was rude in their culture to deny a gift coming from good intentions. Thus, out of respect, they took an iced coffee and an iced caramel macchiato. A few minutes later, the waiter came with their order. Anas waited for them to drink from their beverages before getting the papers out of his suitcase.

"Here is the contract, you can read it carefully with your friend. And I'm right here if you have any questions." The man explained, with a strange look on his face. His expression was unreadable, but it didn't make Hayat feel uneasy. It was quite the opposite, she felt… Safe? An awkward feeling bloomed in Hayat's heart, pushing her to only smile in response to his words.

About two hours into the meeting, Hayat and Kamila asked all the questions they felt needed an answer. They were, of course, supported by documentation. When Anas got up to pay the bill, Kamila took the opportunity to talk with Hayat.

"Ok, so, are you sure you want it? Even with this weird situation going on between you two?" Kamila asked, a bit worried. Without hesitation, Hayat nodded.

"I need a new place, and if it keeps being weird, I will just ignore it until… I don't know. We will see. Kheir In Shaa Allah." *I wish everything will be fine, in God's will.* The woman added.

"In Shaa Allah." Her friend whispered.

Once Anas was seated, Hayat asked for a pen to sign the contract. In less than a minute, all the papers were signed, and the owner handed Hayat the keys to her new apartment.

"Here they are, for your new home. Congratulations." Mister Saidi said. In one motion, he carefully put them in the palm of her hand without taking his eyes off her. Redness tinted her round cheeks. Hayat tried to hide with a smile.

Mission: *failed*.

He noticed, his expression was distinctly showing it.

Kamila, still watching their scene, cleared her throat to catch their attention. It worked. They both said their goodbyes and left as fast as they could. Outside, Kamila pinched Hayat's arm to tease her.

"You were *staring* at him, hbiba. Are you hypnotized, or something?"

"No, I'm not-!" Hayat was about to deny everything when a deep voice cut her out.

"Miss Mazari!" The two turned around, surprised by the call. Mister Saidi trotted up to their level as if they had missed some important thing. "You forgot your phone." He has given it to her. "Can I also ask you something?" His voice was like a breeze on her skin, which made her freeze in place. Not of embarrassment, or discomfort, no. Hayat just didn't know how to react to this kind of spontaneous request. Kamila sucked her lips, before heading to the car – still keeping an eye on them.

"Yes."

"I know it's going to sound weird, and all. But, I feel *drawn* to you." Anas stopped for a second. Taking the breath away from Hayat's lungs. "I want to do things right. So, can I have your mahram's number?" The woman's jaw almost dropped at the question. Her heart stopped, as much as her brain. Nothing was going through. Just a blank space. She glared at him with her wild, open hazel eyes, trying to figure out if it was some kind of joke.

Why would a man like him be attracted to a woman like me?

Anas wasn't pressuring her to answer. He let her take all the time she needed, while the tips of his ears were turning red. Finally, after blinking several times, she came back to her senses.

"Of course, I would love to."

- ☾ -

"I gave it to him." Hayat exhaled, putting her head on her friend's thighs, confused by her own behavior.

Kamila patted the top of her head, "You gave it to him."

"I *gave* it to him." She repeated, just to be sure.

"You gave it to him because *he* asked for it." The oldest highlighted.

"Kamila, do you imagine *my baba* receiving a message – or a call – from a perfect stranger to speak about *me*?!" Hayat almost screamed at her friend, while walking from side to side.

"First, calm down. Two, why did you give it to him?" Kamila asked, in a gentle tone.

"I'm attracted to him? I think…" She awkwardly said, raising her shoulders.

Her friend arched a brow. "You *think*?"

"I mean, Kamila, this is surely not a coincidence if I met him a second time for him to own my new apartment." Her weight dropped on the sofa next to her friend. "It has to be a thing, and I want to see where it goes." Hayat paused for a second. "And, I also felt something since the first time I saw him." She whispered, almost not hearing herself saying it.

52

"So, what's the problem?" The brunette questioned, not sure of her response.

"I'm scared." Kamila didn't say anything, waiting for Hayat to continue. "I'm a twenty-six-year-old web designer, who's fat and a hijabi. I have stretch marks, scars, and I have fat everywhere on my body. I'm like a kinder surprise of deception. Not only that, but I have an apartment on my own, and I have – always will – put my career before anything. I never let a man enter my life because I was so scared to be disappointed. Men are new to me."

"Fair enough," Kamila said with a hint of pride in her voice. "And stop talking about yourself like that. You have much more to offer than your appearance, and you know that." Hayat turned silent for a moment, nodding in agreement.

"Still is. I'm still scared of the disappointment I could feel if this fails. However," she turned to face her friend. "I want to know what it's like. I want to experience the changes that love can bring into my life, and how it would impact my vision and conceptions of it. But, if it doesn't work, I think I'll be *ruined*?" Hayat said unsure, still trying to come to terms with her feelings.

"Then, you know what to do." Kamila simply answered. The woman looked into the space, walking into her mind. She put her head on Kamila's shoulder, sighing.

"Yeah, I kno-…"

A familiar sound cut her short. Hayat took the phone out of the back pocket. Her blood froze. It was her father. She could guess it, just by the personalized ringtone. Hayat got up again, sweat trickled down her spine. Her parents didn't call often. So when it was them, she knew it was an emergency. Like now. Hastily, she took it out of her pocket to put it on Speaker.

"Salam a'leykoum, henunna, how are you?" The old man said with a neutral tone. Hayat inhaled, deeply.

"Wa'leykoum salam, baba, I'm good el hemduliLlah, you? I'm with Kamila." She answered, almost shaking because of the stress.

"Salam a'leykoum, khali!" The brunette said. Hayat inhaled, deeply. She knew why he was calling, for the first time in her twenty-six years of existence, a man pursued her. It was new for her, and Hayat didn't know how to handle the situation. She thought her father would brush him off, like every protective dad would do. However, she was a bit surprised by his next sentences.

"Wa'leykoum salam, benti, I'm good el hemduliLlah." Salim paused, "I know you already know why I'm calling." Her father stated, letting her respond with a humming noise, before letting him continue. "He called me to meet me later this Monday, but before it happens, I want to make sure that you're interested and *ready,* henunna." He paused for what felt like an eternity for Hayat. "If he pushed you into this, you can tell me." Outlining in a serious tone.

"No! No, he did none of that. He was, in fact, very polite and asked directly for your number." She felt her father smiling on the other end. "And, yes, I'm also looking forward to getting to know him, baba." She added, her cheeks flushed with red.

"Then, I will meet him. And as you know, we will contact his family and friends to know what they have to say about him. After that, we will do a sort of mulaqat to start the right process, benti." He answered in a lighter tone, before hanging up. Hayat looked straight into her friend's eyes, letting her weight drop in front of Kamila. This was huge. It felt like an earthquake. Kamila gave Hayat an understanding smile, the calm on her friend's face made her believe that everything will be alright. The youngest sighed in relief.

Time to try new things.

Chapter 6

Souhila welcomed her father with wide open arms, jumping on him like he represented her favorite person in the world – and he *was*. Anas lifted her with ease, only with one limb, while thanking Houria – his older sister – for keeping his daughter. Two other children, two boys, with giant smiles on their faces, came running down the stairs, greeting their uncle. He clearly was a favorite among kids.

"Khalou!" The twins screamed at the same time, grabbing each one a leg to hug. In return, Anas petted their heads slowly.

"Habayeb!" He said going down to face them. "You're already this tall, soon you will be both taller than me." He teased. For a moment, he spoke with the two of them, before continuing with his sister.

"Thanks again, Houria, I'll see you soon." He started to walk away, almost forgetting the big news. His lips formed a big "O" ahead of turning back to his sister. Houria's door was almost closed, he stopped it with one hand. She frowned in confusion, not understanding the flip of the situation.

"Achnou?" *What?* "Do you need something?"

"I met someone. I'm going to speak with her father on Monday, In Shaa Allah, I'll soon tell mama and baba about her. So keep it a secret!" Anas explained, bringing his finger to his lips.

"Why did you tell me, if you want me to keep my mouth shut, Anas?" Houria asked, putting both of her hands on her hips.

"Because you're the oldest and I can't keep a thing from you." He paused, thinking, "And also, I know you would scream at me if I didn't tell you beforehand." Her brother added, a contagious smirk on his face. His sister smiled in return, knowing it was all true. Without a word from her, he got back to his car, Souhila still in his arms. Right before he closed his car door, his sister shouted.

"Anas! Take things slow this time!" A warm expression was his only response to his sister's worries. Souhila settled in her seat.

"Baba, were you talking about the lady we saw the other day?" Anas smiled with pride at his daughter's choice of words.

"To whom?"

"'Amtou!" The father nodded.

"Yes, that's my little clever girl. You guessed it right." His smile got bigger, happy to see how quickly she could catch the hints.

"Is she going to be like a new mama?" In a second, Anas' expression shifted. He gripped the steering wheel tighter, flexing his jaw. At this exact moment, the father wasn't worried about him. All of his thoughts were only directed to Souhila. She was still too young to get attached to someone, without knowing if they were going to stay long in her life. Anas could handle it, erasing people from his world was easy for him. However, it wasn't Souhila's case. Getting to know a woman, and introducing her into his daughter's life, was a risky game after how his ex-wife left them three years ago. The little one was still waiting for an answer. Souhila tried to focus on something else. Anas noticed.

"Not really, ghazaali. She will be like a motherly figure if you want to, but she won't be your real mother. Do you understand?" Souhila nodded, trying to catch the subtlety of her father's words. "And, if we get along with her, you will have a new friend. However, ahead of that, I need to do some things. Are you ok if you wait a bit before meeting that woman again?" The father looked through the rearview mirror, raising his brow, waiting for a response. Souhila stared back at him, nodding. Anas smiled again, feeling relieved.

Without knowing, Anas was already at a restaurant waiting for Mister Mazari. Monday arrived in a blink of an eye. The young father was so invested in his schedule, he didn't even notice the time passing by. Right before going to his seat, Anas was already showing signs of tension. Even if he was once married, making the request to know someone to their mahram constituted a stressful moment. He wanted to leave a good impression, but Anas also had second thoughts about his actions. Is he being selfish? Is he being a good father? He tried to keep his composure, naturally, however, his racing heart and uncontrollable moves showed his discomfort. As a habit, Anas took the table next to a large window, giving him access to peaceful views. Anas loved having things to watch while eating, it occupied his workaholic mind. Calm, and movement, brought him some tranquility. Even if these two ideas were entirely opposite, for Mister Saidi, that didn't prevent them from complementing each other.

It was all about balance.

After several minutes, Anas started to wonder if a simple call was good enough to schedule a first meeting.

He wanted to do things according to Islam, going by the back door to pursue a woman wasn't his type of behavior. Going straight to the point was easy, nonetheless the most stressful method. The only solution was to stay there and look for him through the window. He noticed that the sky was already getting darker.

It 's probably going to rain.

For over twenty minutes, Anas only declined the waitress once before an old man arrived, passing the door to scan the room, fate had ensured that their eyes would be the first to meet. Instantly they both knew. Just by this look. Anas saw a large smile appear on the father's face. He did too, in response. The man came and sat in front of him like they already knew each other. Out of respect, Anas stood up, letting him be the first one seated. In synchronization, the two of them nodded.

"Salam a'leykoum Mister Mazari." Anas greeted him with a shy smile.

"Wa'leykoum salam weldi, you can call me Salim." Once the old man was seated, he continued. "Anas, right?"

"Yes." He answered, before rearranging himself on the chair and clearing his throat. "I know I already told you the point of this meeting. Nonetheless, I want to say it again. I'm here to get to know your daughter for the purpose of marriage. You can ask me all the questions you want, of course." Salim smiled once more. Anas couldn't interpret the emotion he saw on his face. However, it didn't give him a feeling he should be alarmed.

It was tender.

"I want to be honest with you, weldi. I'm glad to see that a man is interested in my daughter." He was about to continue when the waitress arrived to take their drinks and dishes. One double hot espresso, and a tea. Obviously, Anas let Salim say his order first. When they ended, the father of Hayat continued. "As I said, I'm happy. However, I won't be less harsh on you, Anas." His tone was serious and harsh. Salim's words sank into him. This sentence totally made sense, and Anas would never dare question this type of warning – or neglect them. If it was his daughter at Hayat's place, and him at Salim's; Anas would have done the same.

"Understood, sir." It was the only suitable answer. Salim nodded, mentally noting every answer and action of Anas. It was his job to protect his daughter and make sure he was worthy to know Hayat, in the first place.

"Then, let's start." The two men discussed various subjects in order to get to know each other. When the pastries arrived, both of them were already laughing. In fact, the atmosphere got lighter right after the drinks. Since it wasn't their first time, they both knew what kind of subjects they were going to discuss. Anas felt less stressed after the first few questions. It went from his age, his job, his first marriage, his daughter, and the vision he got for the future, before tackling lighter subjects such as his hobbies and interests.

It was, of course, easier than the first time.

When the waitress brought the bill. Both of them tried to pay. However, in Anas' mind, it was obvious who was paying for the meal. Salim insisted on splitting the bill. Anas refused. After setting up the meeting, it was unimaginable for him to let Hayat's father pay. Anas had to. That was his law. To avoid getting into an argument, Salim let him do as he pleased but insisted on it being the first and last time. Once outside, they exchanged a last handshake while saying goodbyes.

"Before we plan the mulaqat, can you give me your baba's number?" Salim asked, looking for his phone.

"In fact, I haven't told my parents about your daughter yet. Since I wanted to meet you first, and then talk about the situation with them." Anas confessed, a bit embarrassed, scratching the back of his neck. "I would be pleased to give it to you, however, can you wait a few days before contacting him? I will obviously give you a call and let you know when everything is settled on my side." The youngest added, staring at Salim. Anas felt a gentle hand pressing on his shoulder in a friendly gesture. Hayat's father genuinely understood his situation. Engaging the discussion with your parents on a second marriage, while having a little girl, was certainly not an easy move to make. Anas was entirely ready financially, physically, and mentally for this new step. This type of event wasn't only implying him alone, nonetheless. And that's what made it all the more complicated

"Sure, weldi. I will wait for your call then." Salim simply responded, his hand still on Anas' shoulder. The suiter took his phone out to send him the number in a text message.

"Thanks, I just sent it to you. I will call you soon." Once again, they both shook hands before parting ways. Anas felt at ease.

The hardest part wasn't done yet.

Once he was in the car, tiny droplets fell on his windshield. Anas smiled, seeing that his guess was correct. It had started pouring by the time he settled. He joined his hands together, "Allahumma soyyiban naafi'an."[3] *O Allah, make it a beneficial rain.*

- ☾ -

---

[3] Source: Sahih Al-Bukhari 1032

Right before three, Anas was already in front of Souhila's elementary school. Rain was still pouring, so he brought an umbrella to wait for his daughter outside the car. Luckily, before dropping her off for school today, Anas gave her a coat – just in case. He thought right. Less than five minutes later, the bell rang. In a blink of an eye, the entrance was full of children screaming and laughing. Anas wasn't bothered by all of this. His only preoccupation right now was his daughter.

A few minutes after the first wave, the father spotted a little brunette wading through the student tide. A smile appeared on his face, he got down to her height for her to jump easily into his arms. Anas loved the warmth he felt every time his daughter was close to his heart and sometimes, it was hard for him to let go.

"Salam a'leykoum ghazaali, how was your day?" The father asked while taking her backpack on his shoulder.

"Wa'leykoum salam baba, it was good el hemduliLlah! I did another drawing of you and me, I will show it to you." Anas nodded. Even if he didn't express it verbally, the father was, in fact, very excited to see her artwork.

Every time he got his daughter from school, some people were looking at him with strange emotions on their faces. Anas got used to it. It was unusual for them to see a man pick up their child. Some looked at him with compassion, while others wondered why they had never seen the little brunette's mother. He didn't give any thought about them, but he was concerned that his daughter might be picked on. His daughter's happiness and education were all that mattered to him. Thus, Anas continued his way to the car, protecting Souhila with the umbrella he was holding even if his shoulder would be soaked by rain.

Once home, he prepared her snacks before getting back to work. Until now, he hadn't been able to focus on it with everything that was going on. Anas' mind was caught in an uncontrollable whirlwind of thoughts, between the meeting he had this morning to his daughter being safe at home with him. Work automatically passed after all the recent advances in his life. Anas put the snacks on the living room table. Souhila came down running, a huge smile on her face, followed by a paper in her tiny fingers. She held up her brand-new drawing. His eyes softened at the moment he saw a crayon drawing of them holding hands, with their house in the back. Internally, Anas was so proud of her progress, even if the drawing was clumsily done.

"Wow, benti, you did this? This is wonderful!" Souhila's smile widened even more.

"See?" The little one pointed to a point on his face, trying to make him notice something. Anas didn't budge, waiting for her to continue. "I even made your glasses!" They were done badly, but as a dad, he needed to agree with her. So, he put on his best acting to make her feel validated.

"Oh wow, you did so well! I'm proud of you." His daughter hugged him. To this, Anas simply added, "I will put it on the fridge, so I can see it every day before going to work. Thank you, baba." A cute laugh of happiness came out of her, before she sat beside her father, eating her snacks. Anas, entirely full of love after this adorable moment, petted her after leaving a kiss on the top of her head. He then opened the laptop, and instantly his expression thoroughly changed. Seriousness as its climax. Work made him behave this way. Closed, cold stare, and glasses on the tip of his nose. As soon as he opened his work files, a string of messages appeared under his eyes.

Anas pinched the bridge of his nose, above his glasses, regretting not opening it sooner. However, what was done, was done. He needed to focus on the present and go forward.

He decided on his schedule.

He needed to face the consequences.

After hours of emails and calls, it was now time for dinner. Fortunately, some leftovers from yesterday were still in the fridge. While Anas was cooking, he rang his father – Hakim – so he could meet with him and Faiza - Anas' mom. One ring was enough for him to pick up.

"Salam a'leykoum baba."

"Wa'leykoum salam Anas." Hakim only said to him, in a cold voice.

"I called you to meet you and mama, when are you two free to talk?" His son responded, trying to hide his irritation. Since he got divorced, his parents acted strangely with him. It ranged from mean comments to dubious insinuations as if they didn't know their son. This situation made him uncomfortable, nonetheless, he needed to tell them.

"You can come at the end of the week to the house, it's been a while since your last visit." And that was one of these comments he hated. An uncontrolled rolling of eyes passed through him, making him regret it immediately.

AstaghfiruLlah. I need to control myself on those things.

"Ok then, I will see you there." He said before hanging up. Emptiness was the only feeling flooding his heart whenever he spoke to his parents on the phone. It saddened him to see that this was their relationship. The father sighed at the realization. Souhila came up to him, a smile on her face, and instant happiness replaced any

64

negative remains of that episode. She was his boost of serotonin. His heart was warm again. With his hands finally free, he picked her up to hug her tight.

Anas needed it.

A big, homely hug from his daughter.

"This weekend we will see grandma and grandpa, are you ready, 'azizati?" Souhila nodded in response. A smile appeared on his face before he patted her back. They both stayed this way, for a time.

Chapter 7

The air was so clear today, not a single cloud obstructed the view of this gorgeous blue sky. There was complete silence around the street; just the sound of his own beating heart could be heard coming from the car he was sitting in, in front of his parents' home. Seeing his parents' faces after six months of strictly texting, excuses of not coming home to see them, of avoidance… Anas felt trapped.

He wished the reunion would happen differently.

Anas unbuckled Souhila's belt, before helping her to get out of the car. In a second, the father rearranged her dress and hair before going toward the door. His heart was pounding in his chest. Nothing troubled him more than seeing Hakim and Faiza since what happened with his ex-partner. The look of disgust and shame on their faces deeply disturbed him. Unconsciously, the pressure around Souhila's hand grew. She looked at him with an understanding smile, before putting her free hand on Anas'. In a split second, his heart was feeling at peace. The connection he had with his daughter was a blessing from Allah. Anas picked her up with one arm and knocked on the door.

An old woman opened it, before greeting Souhila with wide open arms. The little one gripped on her father's shoulder, waiting for a sign from him. He gently tilted his head, letting her go in her grandma's arms. Hakim was standing still behind his wife, at that moment he only had soft eyes for his grandchild. Anas felt like his parents did everything to make him feel outcasted. It hurt him. Making it easy for him in front of his girl wasn't an option. A knot formed progressively in his throat once his mother took his only support from him.

Breathe. You're not alone.

Then he finally entered the house. Houria ran out of the kitchen, welcoming her little brother. Anas instantly hugged her back. Although he was a tall and grown man, he was still a baby in his sister's eyes.

"Welcome home, Anas," she moved away a bit. "We have missed you here." Houria added while patting his shoulder. Surprised by her words, his eyebrows raised. He pointed his chin in the direction of his parents, who were playing with his daughter in the living room.

"They don't look like they did." A ghost of an understanding smile passed on her face, before joining her husband – Mohamed – back in the kitchen. Anas was now alone. Facing his demons. He wanted to bring bright news, to outshine the commentary of his parents – as much as their attitude. Still, he was just standing there. Not capable of facing the situation. Unable to predict their reactions.

Once he felt a bit ready, he joined his family in the living room. One foot was enough to gather everyone's attention on him.

All of them were here, looking at him. *Staring* at him. Unease started to envelop Anas' body. He never liked being the center of the family's attention. An awkward smile appeared on his face. Anas' second older sister,

Hafsa, almost dropped her glass of *atay* when she noticed him in the door frame. On the other hand, his two younger brothers, Nourdine and Sofyan, almost jumped in his arms to embrace him. The middle child instantly welcomed the warm gesture.

"Welcome back, kho!" *Brother,* "It's been so long since we saw you," Nourdine paused. "Did you go to the gym? You seem bigger." he put a hand on Anas' biceps, pressing them lightly to feel the new muscle under his touch. It made him chuckle. Before Anas could respond, three little kids came running too.

"You're talking about me getting bigger, Nourdine, but look at your kids! They grew so fast." All of them started to laugh, except for his parents. When the middle child entered the room, they both turned silent. Souhila noticed the change, so she slipped from her grandma's hand before going into her father's arms. Without any reflection, he picked her up to play.

In a hot and cold ambiance, they all tried to enlighten the room.

After a while, Houria finally came back to the living room with her husband, their hands full of delicious traditional Moroccan pastries; jawhara, sfenj, briouates, ghryiba. Discreetly, she smiled at her little brother as she walked to the table and came beside her mother. Like a big family, they all sat down at the table, waiting for *the* topic of the day. Anas was back home, it obviously intrigued everyone. He felt it. Even during other discussions, everyone was expecting something from him – except Houria, who was, in fact, already aware of the reason for his arrival.

Out of the blue, Hakim asked him *the* question… "*Why* are you here?" His father really emphasized the first word, as the old man was growing impatient. Anas and

Houria almost choked on their sfenj, Faiza sent an inquiring glance at her daughter, but she remained silent in the face of the situation. The middle child pinched his lips together, feeling his pulse increasing. Once again, every pair of eyes was on him.

"Hum," Anas cleared his throat. "I'm here to tell all of you that," he paused again.

"Ya kho," *hey brother,* "Don't make us wait any longer!" Sofyan said, while everyone was gripped by each of his words.

"I'm going to pursue someone in marriage."

Silence.

Then a gasp came from his second sister, bringing back to life all the people around the table. Hafsa jumped from her place, before rushing to her brother. Nourdine and Sofyan also started to cheer him up, filling the room with happiness. Houria smiled at him, joyful to see Anas having a bit of a smile on his face again. Only laughter and praise were audible in the room.

"What about Zahia? Why aren't you trying to get her back?" Faiza said coldly, making all of them freeze. Especially Anas and Souhila. The little girl hadn't hear her mother's name in a while, and it was rubbing her father in the wrong way. These simple words cut out every single thought in Anas' mind. He was about to snap back at her. However, before he could say anything, Houria stepped in.

"Mama, what are you implying here?" She asked harshly.

"Benti, this is not your business. How could he see another woman, when Souhila already has a mother?" Faiza stared at her son, disapproving of his choice. Anas wasn't having it. He could clearly see the change in Souhila's attitude. He didn't bring her here to make his daughter feel this way. Anas knew his mother was bound to make horrible comments, but not in front of *her* – and certainly not like that. In a second, he gathered his daughter in his arms. Insults formed in his throat, and Anas barely kept them in his mind. His siblings were too stunned to say a thing after their mother's words. Nourdine got up to protest, but his older brother stopped him while shaking his head. Reluctantly, he sat down, not wanting to make the situation worse.

"Chokran," *thanks*, "Now we will leave." Not letting any responses affect them, they both walked out. His steps were fast enough to create a large distance between them in a few seconds. Anas had his hand on the handle of the back door when a fatherly voice came to him.

"Weldi, wait!" Hakim almost came down running. "I thought I wouldn't catch you, with your mama trying to stop me." He added with an odd smile. Anas didn't laugh or respond. He felt too disrespected for that to happen. "I'm sorry for her, I will talk to her." Hakim paused. "I know we have been harsh on you, and I regret it. I just thought it was the best for you. But when I saw your expression while saying you will see someone new, I knew I was wrong." He put a hand on Anas' shoulder. "Could you forgive me? I would be glad to meet her family." Instinctively, Anas escaped from the touch of his father holding a still expression.

"I'm not ready to forgive you." He paused, putting some distance between them. "For three years. Three years. You just stayed there, listening to mama bash me for absolutely no reason. And moreover, you were adding some mean comments. I'm *your* son too, baba. So don't try to pretend your passiveness was naive." Anas added, a burning sensation at the end of his throat. "Now I told you my intention, and what I'm about to do, I just want the two of you to let me go forward in life." He paused, before letting his daughter go in her car seat to close the door. "I'll be coming back when I need to, and when things get better on my side. For now, I just want to be away from all this. Salam a'leykoum." He opened his door, before looking at his father for the last time today. He didn't let him respond, slamming the car door closed on him. In an instant, Anas and Souhila were far away from this house.

Anas regretted bringing Souhila with him. Not in any way, shape, or form has he once imagined his mother would be speaking that way in front of her. Guilt bloomed in him. Anas failed to protect her from Faiza's mean comments. The thought wouldn't leave his mind. Once in a while, he looked at Souhila only to see her being lost in her thoughts. Guilty, that's how he felt. Whatever it is, he was unable to fill the gap her mother left her. Playing two roles in one will never be enough, although he always tried to accommodate all of her needs. When Souhila was younger, she always used to ask why.

"Where is mama?"

"Why she left?"

"Why?"

"Why?"

"Why?"

Until, Souhila partly understood that she will never be like the other children in her school. The simple thought made Anas' heart tingle. Sadness. Sadness took place in his entire body, making him tighten his grip around the steering wheel a little harder, while all of these memories took place in his mind. Confusion was a normal emotion for her to feel when one of her parents would rather not stay, and sorrow was also usual for the one who decided to bear all the responsibilities. Almost choking as he tried to swallow the knot in the middle of his throat, he finally broke the silence in the car.

"Are you ok, baba?" Souhila looked back at him, and Anas could clearly see the fog in her eyes.

"Yes." She was lying and it made him even sadder. To ease the both of them, he played some Quran in the car, letting her sleep for the rest of the road.

During his daughter's nap, Anas watched her sleep leaning over the door frame. She seemed so peaceful in her dreams. Since the time of prayer was already here, Anas left her alone before going to his special room. It was a room he made for himself and his ex-wife, so they both could pray together. As he opened the door, he instantly thought about changing it. He needed to create a new memory with this place, and it was starting now. After praying one last time in this old decor, Anas immediately took everything off in boxes. Occasionally, he stopped on religious paintings Zahia made. He thought about sending them back to her. However, he didn't know anything about Zahia's new life.

In an hour, the room was bare of any color, or personal touch, like a blank canvas. A new start. His chest felt less heavy. Anas felt a new breath passing through him. Souhila came up to his room, rubbing her still sleepy eyes, intrigued by all the sounds and moves.

"Baba, what are you doing?" Noticing her, Anas got to her before taking Souhila in his arms.

"Nothing, baba, I'm just changing things here. It was well-needed." His daughter leaned in the embrace, feeling his warmth. She obviously needed it after this day. "Are you hungry?" He asked, pressing his head to hers. The little one nodded, not getting away from his warmth.

"Ok, let's get something into this stomach." He added, pointing to her belly, making her laugh loudly. The sound flowed in his ears like honey. Happiness was back in her mind, as his own.

Chapter 8

Hayat almost landed on the ground when she saw her best friend sitting on the sofa. Kamila was just enjoying some of her leisure time while reading a book, a cup of *atay* in her free hand. She greeted a sleepy Hayat with a wide smile, before rushing toward her. This wasn't the first time she forgot the spare keys she gave her years ago.

Note to myself: I will not give her the ones for the new apartment.

"Kamila, what are you doing here? At six in the morning?"

"Just checking. So," her friend paused. "Did he call you?" Her brows almost met her hairline.

The young woman blinked several times before having a coherent response on the tip of her tongue. "Who?"

"Your baba! Wasn't he supposed to meet *him* at the beginning of the week?" After these words, everything made sense in Hayat's mind. Kamila was simply curious, as always. "Did he call you?"

"No," she pointed at the door with her thumb. "I'm going to see him at home. Do you want to come?"

"Can I?" The oldest asked, making a *Puss in Boots* face.

"Of course, you're family." Hayat patted Kamila's shoulder. "Just to let you know, my brother will be there too." A sort of protestation came out of her friend, who was rolling her eyes.

"If I need to bear his presence to have my curiosity fulfilled, I'll obviously come with you." She finally stated before crossing her arm with Hayat and going straight to her room.

For what seemed like an eternity, Kamila waited for her friend to come out of the bathroom. After thirty minutes, she still wasn't done. Locked in, the brunette could hear whines coming from the other side of the door. Intrigued, she knocked on the door three times. Kamila had an idea of what was happening in there, nonetheless, she wanted to make sure her friend was ok.

"Are you ok in there?" More whining, and sighs. "Hayat?"

No response.

Kamila opened the door. When her eyes landed on her friend, she almost burst out laughing. Hayat was there, struggling with her hijab, not knowing how to put it correctly – even though she has worn it for ten years. All of her pins were put on the side of the sink, both of her hands trying to form something on her head. Nothing looked good enough for her.

"Bad hijab day?" Kamila leaned on the door frame.

"Yeah…" All of her strength left her before she pouted, looking at her friend. "Every time I put a pin in, it's sliding or making some sort of bump." Kamila walked up to her, sticking out her hand for Hayat to drop whatever was needed to fasten her hijab. Without hesitation, she put her pins and let her do the magic. Only a few moves were enough to fix everything in place. A ghost of a smile appeared on Hayat's face, watching her friend meticulously planting the pins in her cap – ensuring to not hurt her with them in the process.

"I'm so excited to see you in my place one day, Kamila." She only whispered as loud as a blow. Once done, the friend took one last look before staring at Hayat frowning.

She shrugged. "Which place?"

"Struggling with your hijab, so one day I could help you as you did today." Kamila's features bend under an expression filled with longing. She put a hand on Hayat's shoulder.

"You will, In Shaa Allah, you will."

- ☾ -

At the exact moment Faudel saw his sister, the young man jumped from the couch to hug her. When his dark brown eyes met a pair of green ones, his expression of joy and happiness instantly dropped. Kamila was standing behind his sister. With a false grin, he greeted Kamila.

"What are *you* doing here?" He wiggled his index finger in a circle, "It's a family meeting." Faudel added without breaking his fake expression. Kamila was about to snap back at him, to let Hayat's brother know about every thought she had. But when her mouth opened, an old woman interjected.

"Faudel!" Lamia slapped her child's hard chest, letting a muffled sound come out of him. "Goutlek beli familtna hedi." *I already told you that she's like family.* The old woman explained. With a warm embrace, the mother welcomed both of them happily. Emotion dripped from her touch. She was so thrilled to have them home. "Everything is almost ready for lunch, and babek is on the road. He will be here in less than five minutes."

It was enough for all of them to release the tension, and let their feet guide them to the living room. Salim arrived exactly five minutes later and greeted all of them with a "Salam a'leykoum" before sitting between his wife and daughter. Automatically, the youngest leaned on her father's shoulder to feel more of his comfortable warmth - Salim did the same in response. They both stayed this way until Faudel came into the room with the main dish; couscous. Saliva drooled from Hayat's mouth, she hadn't eaten one since her last visit months ago. Leaving your parent's house to study – and later work – four hours away, wasn't an easy choice to be made at only eighteen years old. However, this situation did not prevent her father from supporting his daughter in this choice. Salim always pushed his children to pursue their dreams within the rules of Islam. It put Hayat at ease to know one of her parents was here to support her projects.

A cup of *atay* in their hands, Hayat and her father were both seated on a sofa swing in the garden. Cuddling in silence. They enjoyed their father-daughter moment. Since they don't see each other that often, even if silence filled their discussion, they will always cherish this type of moment. As Salim used to say, "It's you and me against the world, Hayati." every time he got the chance. He never missed an occasion to show his love to his children. An affectionate yet strict father. Certain rules have been established, and his children had to respect them. That was his only command.

"What do you want to know, benti?"

"Everything he told you."

Salim arched an eyebrow. "Don't you want to discover it by yourself?"

"Yes, I do. But, I need to know what he told you. Just in case he's lying, I would know." Hayat explained.

"Smart," he nodded proudly. "Then, I'll tell you."

"I also want to know what you discovered about him."

The old man turned his head to look his daughter in the eyes. "I didn't do any research yet."

This time, it was Hayat's turn to frown. "Why?"

"Because he asked me to wait until his parents were in the loop. And-" Salim was about to continue, but a phone call cut them both in the middle of the discussion. The old man looked at his phone.

"Subhaan'Allah" A slight smile on his face, showing his phone screen to his daughter. "It's him."

Hayat's expression froze. "Talk to him like I'm not here."

A chuckle came out of her father, accompanied by a nod. The man put his phone right in his ear, before speaking.

"Salam a'leykoum Anas, how are you?" Salim let him respond before continuing. Hayat's curiosity took over her. She got closer to the phone, but Salim gently pushed her away, moving his finger to say no. To make sure Hayat wasn't dictated by her vicious feelings, the father got up. A few minutes later, Salim came back.

"Didn't you say you wanted me to talk like you weren't here?" Her father reminded her.

"Yes, but I still wanted to listen."

"You know that's spying, right? You can't do that. If you wanted to listen, I would just have to explain you were with me." Salim said with a severe expression.

Hayat ashamed, lowered her head."Na'am baba."

"Mlih." *Good.* He patted her head slowly. His hand shifted to her shin to lift Hayat's face. "You know I'm proud of you, Hayati." The daughter pinched her lips together with a smile. Salim did the same in response. His hand dropped before he sat next to her again. "Anas only called to inform that his parents were now in the loop, and they know his intentions. I'm going to call his baba, to talk to him." He paused, "After that, do you want me to meet them first? Or all together, here?"

Hayat started to think about it. She almost forgot; a man, asking for courtship, needed to visit her father's house. If she chose the second option. Anas would come here, with his family, to only ask her if she still would like to know him after all. Her face flushed thinking about it. She covered her mouth and turned away in an attempt to hide it.

"Let's meet them here, together."

Salim smiled at her, nodding in agreement. Once they both settled on the time and date, the father started talking about every single detail he noted about Anas; from the way he was dressed, to the small smile he got while talking about his daughter. Hayat was curious to know if her father liked him or not. His daughter tried to analyze his body language and expression, but, all in vain. Therefore, Hayat simply decided to wait to make her own opinion.

Chapter 9

"Why can't I come with you, baba!" Souhila protested, stomping her feet on the ground. Every time his daughter made a fuss, Anas kept his composure. However, today was not one of those days.

"Listen to me," he said with a steady, calm, and firm tone. "Today, you can't. That's it. We can't bring the children with us for the first family meeting." Anas got at her height, studying her pouting face. With a softer voice, he added, "I'll drop you at 'amtek Houria. A babysitter will be there for all of you. I know you're upset, but you will be with your cousins, having fun. And when everything ends, I'll come get you." He brushed a strand of hair behind her ear, "Understood baby?"

In this situation, Souhila didn't have a choice. Frustration dripped all over her face. Souhila nodded, still a bit sad. A no-word answer made him a bit worried. To reassure her, Anas opened his long arms to welcome his petite daughter. Still mad, she jumped in them. All she needed was a tight embrace to calm her emotions. Feeling each other's warmth and love made them both cool down. Anas understood it was hard for Souhila to stay away from him, even for a small amount of time. The father made sure to always reassure her and know that he loved her before each goodbye.

"I know ghazaali, it's ok. I'll be back before you even notice." Anas said, rubbing her back. Some more pressure was applied on his neck in response. He smiled against Souhila's shoulder, before picking her up while standing.

Anas parked in front of Houria's house, praying everything would go perfectly. Souhila, by herself, jumped from her father's car. He followed her, trying his best not to dirty his suit in the process of getting out. His little girl, who totally switched moods, waited for him in front of the door. Anas smiled at her, knocking only three times for his sister to come open and welcome them. Houria was stunning. No makeup, a lovely beige hijab coupled with a light orange traditional dress.

Marvelous.

"You look wonderful, Houria. They would certainly pick you instead of me."

"Oh, thanks, this dark bluish tuxedo looks good on you too." She responded, chuckling, by patting his shoulder and inviting them in. "The babysitter will be here in five minutes. Nourdine already dropped his children, baba, mama and Sofyan left with him. Hafsa is still getting ready upstairs" Strangely, a sensation of ease passed through him.

"Good," he said firmly, clenching his jaw. Having Houria with him made Anas feel at ease. "Also, Nourdine's wife couldn't make it. She had an urgent matter at the hospital today."

"Oh no, I hope it wasn't something serious."

"I don't know, her beeper rang right before they came here. They were probably short-staffed." Hafsa looked really saddened by her sister-in-law's absence.

"Yeah, I'll see her next time!"

Only a few minutes later, the bell rang; the babysitter was here.

Houria welcomed her, letting Mohamed explain everything the children needed. Anas hugged Souhila one last time. However, he knew she wouldn't let go that easily. To make her ease her grip, he kissed her cheek before going.

All set in the car, stressed and nervous. Houria noticed his legs shaking in anxiety. She glanced at her sister, who also noticed. Both of them touched a part of his arm to calm him.

"You look like a dead body, smile a little, or I will take your place." The oldest stated. With these simple words, Anas chuckled and started the car. It was ten o'clock, and now they have four hours to go.

- ☾ -

Straightening his grip on the steering wheel, only a few miles away before parking in front of his final destination. On the road, with the advice of his older sister, he bought a flower bouquet. It was a wonderful mix of cold colors; altheas, myosotis, and magenta lilacs. Houria had an instinct on this specific one. As always, Anas took her suggestions *very* seriously. Of course, they didn't only bring flowers. Nourdine, and his mother, got all the Moroccan traditional pastries.

For a first meeting, extravagance wasn't necessary.

In a few minutes, he will have the chance to see the woman he hasn't stopped thinking about lately. The one he managed to free his schedule for, just to look at her. Once more. Anas had a mixed feeling blooming inside his chest. A part of him was stressed, and the other excited. When he was in her street, Anas could see his brother's car. It was packed with his family. He waved at them before parking, too. Sofyan, the last child, jumped out of the car just to hug his biggest brother. He gave him two big pats on the back, strengthening his grip around Anas.

"You're good?" He moved away a bit.

"Yeah! A bit stressed, but I'm ok." His brother paused, "You?"

"Same, just excited to meet her!" Sofyan turned his head to Nourdine and his parents, "We all are, actually." Anas followed his gaze, gazing into his mother's eyes. He wanted to greet them, but the sour sensation in the back of his throat wasn't gone yet. So, Anas only pinched his lips together, waiting to greet them all at once. Hakim tried to get close to him. Automatically, he stepped back, holding his hand out for him to shake it. Hakim stared at it. Sad, but he respected his wishes. However, stepping back didn't stop Faiza from hugging him tight. Anas, pushed her gently, a neutral expression on his face.

"Salam a'leykoum mama." The woman frowned.

"Wa'leykoum salam Anas, you don't kiss me?" She brought his head down, to whisper in his ear. "Don't push me back, they're probably looking." Faiza scolded him right in his ear, a fake smile on her face. Of course, she wanted to paint a perfect figure in front of them. Again, Anas pinched his lips together to suppress a sigh. All of them could feel the change in the air. Houria and Hafsa shared a look. To ease the tension, Hafsa stepped in, parting them. Anas automatically went to his safe space, Houria. She gave him the flowers before pushing him toward the door.

A moving curtain attracted his attention, and at the same time, his hand dropped to the doorbell.

That was it.

He was about to see her.

He *wanted* to see her, to *know* her.

Now, Hayat was all he had in mind.

Once the door opened, they were instantly welcomed with joyful greetings. Salim shook hands with Anas once he gave the flowers to Lamia, to salute one another with respect. Of course, he also shook hands with Hakim, who was directly standing behind his son. The father led the way to the living room, letting everyone greet each other. As Anas entered the spacious place, they were welcomed by the warm and inviting ambiance of Hayat's family home.

The walls were adorned with colorful tapestries and intricate Islamic art. The air was fragrant with the spicy aroma of Algerian cuisine. A tray of steaming *atay* with mint and a plate of numerous Algerian pastries; msemen, ghrayef, zlabia, dzariat, mashagaq, were placed on the coffee table, ready to be enjoyed. Anas and his family inhaled this delicious scent simultaneously, already feeling at home. They were welcomed by beautiful gold and red *sedaris*, arranged perfectly to make the room bigger than it really was. When everyone was inside, Faiza gave the Moroccan pastries to Lamia. With one glance at them, Hayat's mother already guessed the ethnicity of Anas' family. She smiled in return before sending them to the kitchen with Faudel.

Anas sat nervously on the edge of the sedari, with a pounding heart and sweaty palms. Hakim sat on the right, letting his son face Hayat's father. For this meeting alone, they were all in the same room, but men and women were on different sides. In that sense, both parties had different discussions. The room was filled with the warm glow of the sun, which came through the large window, casting a soft light that illuminated the faces of the gathered family members. Despite Anas' nerves, he could sense the genuine warmth and hospitality in Salim's gaze.

"So Anas, tell me more about yourself," Salim began, his voice deep and melodic. "New projects? How does your daughter feel about this?" Anas took a deep breath and then began to speak, his voice slightly shaky at first but growing more confident as he found his footing. He spoke about the new house he was about to buy, his love for art, and his passion for raising his child as a single father. He could feel the tension in his shoulders easing as Salim nodded thoughtfully, his gaze never leaving Anas' face, seeming to take a genuine interest in what he had to say. The suitor felt a sense of respect and admiration for the man.

"In that sense, I would very much like to get to know Hayat, and In Shaa Allah marry her if everything goes well." Anas finally expressed, proposing officially to Salim, loud enough to let every member here witness the statement. Hayat's father leaned forward and placed a hand on Anas' shoulder.

"Anas, as I already told you, I appreciate your honesty and sincerity," he said, in a warm and welcoming tone. "You have my blessing to pursue a relationship with my daughter, plus she also wants to get to know you better." Anas felt a rush of gratitude and relief wash over him. Once they shook hands, Salim got upstairs to bring the main character of the event.

Chapter 10

Earlier that morning.

"Sbah el kheir ya benti!" *Good morning, my daughter!* Lamia screamed while opening her curtains. "Aya, nodi! Lezem tdewwshi, telebsi w koulshi!" *Get up! You need to shower, get dressed, and all.* Her mother stripped her from the bed.

"What time is it, mama?" Hayat asked, covering her head with the pillow.

"Setta w nos." *Six thirty.*

The daughter jumped up, to glare at her mother, the morning sun gleamed into her eyes. "You wake me up, at half past six in the morning, when they arrive in the afternoon?" She paused, "'aleh, mama? 'aleh?" *Why, mom? Why?* Hayat pleaded, trying to gain some minutes of sleep.

"Barkay matahadri flfragh, mabqash el waqt." *Stop talking in a vacuum, we don't have time.* Lamia pulled the cozy blanket closer to her chest. She simply left Hayat fighting with the sudden intrusion of light – with no cover.

Last solution: getting out of bed.

With a protestation, to let her mother know she wasn't happy about the situation, Hayat got up.

"I have no choice then…" The brunette muttered under her breath, "Time to start the day." She slammed her door behind hard enough to make the walls tremble a bit. A grimace appeared on her face, hoping Hayat's irritation wasn't too audible. Lamia's muffled scream made her wince a bit more. "Sorry!"

As the cold water hit her puffy face, she started to see things clearer. Now that her soul came back to her body, she was overwhelmed by her emotions. For a moment, she froze over the sink to process what was going to happen today. Anas and his family were coming to her – *for* her. Her face was red and hot. A new wave of cold water came crashing on her face.

Everything felt better.

It was not even seven in the morning, she was already greeted by the smell of different Algerian pastries when she opened her bathroom door. Lamia seemed to have spent the whole night in the kitchen, working her hands off on every little snack they were going to serve and offer. Every North African mother was more excited – *stressed* too – than their daughter when days like this came around the clock. Her heart sank. She knew her mother couldn't handle stress, and got easily overwhelmed by her emotions; and generally, her daughter was the one paying the price. This mixed feeling made her guilt bigger. She imagined the word "ungrateful" appearing on her forehead when she gave a last glance at her reflection in the mirror. With one hand, she tried to brush away this unwanted emotion, letting it sit in this room waiting for her to come back and look at her *broken* self.

Once she collected herself, in the staircase, Hayat was welcomed by a wonderful scent of coffee. This strong smell was the last blow to really wake her up. With a smile on her face, to cover her internal disaster, she came down the stairs fast enough to almost trip on the last one. Salim stuck out his head from the kitchen, worried about the noise. A chuckle escaped him when he saw his daughter, half asleep, holding on to the stairs' handrail as if it was the last thing keeping her alive. Hayat glared at the laughing noises, thinking it was Faudel, but her eyes softened when they met Salim's.

"Sbah el kheir Baba." She said while hugging him.

"Sbah el noor sleepyhead. Yemmek woke you up early today, huh?" Hayat sighed when they both sat on the sofa.

"Yeah… I believe she needs some reassurance, but it's understandable." Instinctively, she leaned on him, "This is the first time a man comes for me. And, you can add that I'm the youngest, plus the only girl she has." Salim slightly nodded, keeping his warm close to her. He noticed a tint of sadness in her voice.

"Tell me more, how do *you* feel, henunna?"

"Stressed, happy, anxious and guilty?" Hayat sighed once more. "I wish she would just be there for me, you know…"

"I see, you can't handle her emotions while erasing yours. Over again."

"Exactly. I want today to be my day… Is that selfish?"

"Sometimes you need to be a bit selfish, and it's ok. You just can't be an ass because this isn't correct."

"Baba! Language."

He giggled, it was a sentence he used to say when she learned how to talk. "You're right. AstaghfiruLlah. But you see my point benti, be selfish. Today *is* about you – and Anas. Mostly you, nonetheless."

"Saha baba." *Thank you, dad.*

"Now get up, and go take a coffee too. You can barely open your eyes properly. Nobody wants the sleepy bride." Shocked, she just left her mouth open before laughing with him.

- ☾ -

A warm breeze came from her window. Hayat already felt every inch of her outfit stick to her body. In less than ten minutes, they would be here. Anas would be here. She was excited and stressed at the same time. She was lost in her emotions, completely spacing out while looking at herself in her mirror. The hijab Hayat was supposed to wear was still hanging on the chair where she was seated. A light tap on her door brought her back. Salim got closer to her in a few steps.

Only with a look, she was at peace.

"You're not ready yet?" The father sat on her bed. Hayat turned to face him.

"I got caught in my thoughts, I just need to put my hijab on."

He held out his hand in her direction, "N'awnek?" *May I help you?*

"You know how to do it?"

"Of course! I was the one doing ta' mamak when she struggled with it." Hayat smiled at this thought. Now collected, she gave her light lilac hijab to him.

"I'm proud of you, benti." Salim whispered when he ended. A glimpse of emotion was hiding in his eyes, letting Hayat see it for a slip of a second. A tear filled the corner of his eye. The old man tried to hide it out of pride. Hayat let herself be taken by all these emotions, before hugging her father from his back. A new step in life was right in front of her, and Hayat was ready to take it. Salim knew that. Realizing his little girl was now grown hurt him, a *lot*. Once they both got back on their feet, he showed his face to her before kissing her on the forehead. They shared one last look, making sure they were both good.

"I love you, baba."

"I love you too, Hayati." He was about to add something when the doorbell rang. Salim pinched his lips in a smile. "Here he is!"

In a second, the colour drained from her face, due to the stress, leaving her white as snow. A chuckle from her father made the youngest glare at him with bitterness. Salim put both of his hands on her shoulder, absorbing a part of her chaos.

"It's ok, benti, we're here for you." He paused, getting his eyes at her height. "*I'm* here for you. And to be honest, I was paler than you the day I asked for mamak's hand." This simple joke made her smile. It was what she needed; a distraction from all of her own intrusive thoughts. With a movement of the head, she let her dad go down to welcome them. For the first visit, according to tradition, the woman waited upstairs until the suitor asked directly the father to court his daughter. It sounded old-fashioned, but she loved the idea and felt protected. Knowing that whoever would stand before her father had to go through all these steps just to get to know her, made Hayat happy.

It made her feel *worthy*.

Trapped in her mind, the loud celebrations and numerous voices brought her back on earth. They were officially in her home. Anas was here. A warm feeling took over every fiber of stress. Her muscles, once tense, relaxed just like the tension in the air. She felt the weight over her shoulder vanish. After turning around in her room, Hayat sat on her bed with a mind filled with questions she wanted to ask. It was an opportunity for her – and for him too – to know if they *still* wanted to start the talking phase.

Hayat's mind was fuming, looking at the blank note on her phone. When you don't know what was appropriate to ask, it was hard to form questions out of nowhere. As a last resort, Hayat typed several subjects: "*10 Islamic questions to know your future husband*" or "*Questions to know someone*". Google would probably help her on this topic more than herself. Obviously, she knew what she was looking for in a man, but she would rather not make it obvious. People of her generation were too vicious to trust their words. If she made her points too obvious, how would she be aware if this was his real face?

Trust wasn't given, it was *earned*.

In that sense, she needed to ask very specific questions, study his comportment, and watch his moves without blowing up her cover. She was on a mission for herself. For her future. Starting from now. Hayat will be meticulous with everything; answers, choices, and the list continued. She felt a bit paranoid about some subjects. Her mother even called her a control freak, but how can you feel safe in a place you don't know anything about? What if he had a secret family elsewhere? To let go of the paranoia, she needed to collect information.

Three knocks on the door brought her mind to the real world. Her father was there standing in the door frame, a massive smile on his face. Salim led out a hand for her to hold. Eventually, she did with a shaky one. At the top of the stairs, Hayat could already perceive the strong and masculine scent she already smelled once. Her gaze found Salim's and they both nodded in silent agreement.

"Bismillāh," they breathed out at the same time.

Chapter 11

Anas and Hayat couldn't dare to look at each other with their family around, the two were submerged by shyness. *Haya*. A beautiful sight, that made Salim slightly smile. Her cheeks were tinted with redness as much as the tip of his ears. A light breeze entered the room, brushing their hot skin, and making them shiver with an unknown feeling. Both pretended to look around in order to get a brief glance at each other. This indiscreet technique made Anas and Hayat blush when their eyes finally met.

They looked beautiful, breathtaking even.

Hayat put a hand on her heart, which was racing like a horse, while Anas tried to keep his composure, focusing on Salim's lecture on what a man should be like and how he should act with his family – and particularly, his wife. It was a chance for both families that Salim studied in one of the best Islamic schools in Egypt. Listening to his lecture was, for Anas, a necessity. Islam was a key point for both families, therefore a little reminder of the good behavior of a believer was mandatory.

As everyone settled in, Lamia asked Faudel to bring some more *atay* since the teapot was already empty. Hayat's mother tried to push her daughter to serve Anas something to drink – or bring him something to eat – but she refused. Hayat was too shy to show him some sort of interest in front of everyone. When Salim ended his speech, Hayat's family members began to ask questions to one another. At some point, Lamia hid her face with one hand discreetly pointing at Anas, winking at her daughter with a thumbs up. It made Hayat redder than a stop sign. Her mother's excitement was a bit *too* visible.

Faudel, on the other hand, was having a very animated conversation with Anas, his brothers, and father. The suitor kept looking back and forth at Hayat, sometimes distracted by the sound of her laugh when his sisters made jokes about his younger self. Hafsa and Houria, both extremely excited, sat on each side of her, encircling the young woman. On their side, Lamia and Faiza were having a pretty calm conversation.

This hubbub of discussion left an opportunity for Salim to prepare a private area outside for Hayat and Anas to have a conversation. The old man stole some *atay*, mint, and a couple of pastries from the kitchen before putting them on the outside table. As a perfectionist, he checked the cushions and every detail in the process of creating a very welcoming ambiance for them to feel at ease while speaking to each other. Once finished, Salim went to get his daughter, leading her outside while holding her hand, before nodding discreetly to Anas to follow them. Without hesitation, he greeted everyone politely, his ears still red with shyness.

The two of them sat side by side on the swing, in a way that Salim could still have an eye on them, their bodies slightly angled away from each other out of respect. The gentle creaking of the wooden frame filled the quiet afternoon air, punctuated by the occasional tweedling of birds. Even under the eyes of her mahrams, this felt intimate to Hayat and Anas. The space Salim gave them permitted the tension to flow out of their bodies. Anas cleared his throat to finally break the ice.

"So, Hayat, tell me about yourself. What do you like to do?" Hayat smiled shyly, rearranging her lilac hijab, reminding Anas that Houria was right about the choice of the flower bouquet.

"Well, I'm a web designer, so I spend a lot of time on my computer. But I also love to read books of all kinds. I enjoy art, video games, and spending time with my family and friends. Basic stuff, I guess." Anas nodded thoughtfully, his gaze fixed on Hayat's face as he listened intently to her every word. He found himself drawn to her gentle demeanor and thoughtful words. He felt a growing sense of connection between them. "And you?" Anas got caught out off guard since he was only listening to her. He directly turned his head to the beautiful garden, not bearing to look at her anymore. Anas scratched the back of his neck, embarrassed by his lack of restraint.

"Probably going to need your help to change my online site," he laughed, taking Hayat with him. "I'm pretty basic myself, by the way." Anas looked back at her. "As you most likely guessed, I'm a estate agent. I buy houses or apartments, renovate them, and put them back on the market, so people can rent my properties." In one smooth movement, he pointed his chin at her. "Like you!" Hayat agreed, her hazel eyes catching his brown ones. For a second, he saw something passing in her look. However, he didn't understand. Admiration? Interest? *Attraction*? He couldn't guess it. Anas' eyes got back to the garden. His throat felt dry, almost cutting him in an attempt to speak. "I do like video games too, but now that Souhila is getting older, I can't play as much as I did before. She needs a lot of attention, I don't want to deprive her of that because of my hobbies." Anas stated, keeping his gaze on the flowers in front of him.

Hayat smiled, leaning her head on one side, "I guess you'll be thrilled once she'll be old enough to play with you." Anas chuckled at the thought. A sight of Souhila's tiny hands on his keyboard, and mouse, trying to understand what was going on before her eyes. In fact, Anas *was* excited to see this moment happen.

"Do you mind if I ask you questions about your faith?" Hayat continued, wanting to have a more serious discussion. Anas instantly shook his head. "Are you a Sunni?"

"Yes, like you, I guess?" Hayat nodded to his question. "On a scale of one to ten, ten being the highest, where do you put your relationship with Allah?"

"I would say seven, and you?" For a solid minute, Anas really thought about this question.

"I will be around five, five and a half." Hayat nodded understanding that everyone has their own struggles. Their own journey. It made her remember this aya: "*Allah does not lay a responsibility on anyone beyond his capacity.[4]*" Knowing that one day, probably, they could both get closer to ten.

"Which habits do you want to break? And some you want to build?" The woman asked, remembering the question she saw online.

"Read more Quran, be more patient on my breaking points – if I can even call them that, stop being a workaholic because sometimes I tend to miss things with Souhila... Earn more science in Islam, so I can be a good teacher for her. That's all I can think of for now."

"For me, it would be praying more often on time, doing dhikr when I can't pray, stop playing too much, and

---

[4] Verse of the Quran [2:286]

reading more about Islam." On some points, they partially completed each other.

As the conversation continued, Anas and Hayat discovered that they had many common interests and shared values. They spoke about their families, their hobbies, and their hopes for their future. Though they were unable to touch, their eyes met frequently, and they both felt a growing sense of comfort and ease in each other's presence. After a time, Salim came back, and both didn't realize the time fly. Sadly, the afternoon was already coming to an end. Lamia told her husband to bring them since she was going to serve dinner before letting Anas and his family go. They smiled at each other as they walked back to the living room.

Once everyone sat again, the conversation flowed easily, with laughter and anecdotes filling the air. Hayat's mother, a skilled cook, brought out a piping hot *tajine* filled with tender lamb and vegetables, served with fluffy couscous. Anas' family enjoyed every bite, savoring the flavors of Algerian cuisine. Despite the initial formality of the situation, the room was filled with an undeniable sense of warmth and hospitality, and Anas felt his heart swell with a sense of belonging. He knew that Hayat's family was not just welcoming him. They welcomed each member of his family, even the ones who weren't there to witness the event.

As the night wore on, Anas stood up and turned to his family, who were gathered nearby. "It's getting late, we should probably be going," he said, his voice tinged with reluctance. They exchanged warm hugs and kisses – men and women apart – with Hayat's family, expressing their gratitude for the warm welcome they had received.

On the porch door, Salim was accompanied by Hayat, who received a tight hug from Hafsa before walking away. This sudden act of affection didn't make her uncomfortable, it felt welcoming. As if she really wanted this to work. Hayat rested on the porch with a sense of excitement and hope, feeling as though she had just met someone truly special.

Anas was the last going toward the car, he seemed hesitant to say or even do something in front of everyone. After two seconds of hesitation, Anas approached Hayat, under the eyes of every family member gathered on or in front of the porch, a small smile rose at the corners of his lips. "Thank you for this wonderful evening, Hayat. I had a great time getting to know you." Hayat blushed, returning the smile. Even though the air was getting cold, it wasn't the cause of her shivering under her dress.

"Thank you, Anas. I enjoyed our conversation as well."

Anas felt a sense of sadness mingled with hope. He knew that this was just the beginning of their journey together, and he was eager to see where it would take them. With a final wave and a last look at Hayat, he turned and walked away with his family, feeling grateful for the respect and incredible welcome that he and his family received.

Anas climbed into the car, he was greeted by the excited chatter of his two older sisters. They didn't wait for him to get comfortable, they simultaneously bombarded him with questions.

"So, how did it go? What did you guys talk about?" Their curiosity was palpable. Anas chuckled softly, feeling a mix of amusement and shyness at their persistent inquiries.

"Relax, I'll tell you everything another day. For now, let's just enjoy the ride," he said, flashing them a small smile. Houria and Hasfa exchanged glances, sensing that their brother was holding something back.

"Come on, Anas, you can tell us. We're your sisters, we won't judge you," Hasfa said, a mischievous twinkle in her eye. Anas shook his head, his expression firm.

"I would rather not share any details yet. I need some time to process everything that happened this afternoon. Besides, it's not just about me, it's also about Hayat and her privacy. There are probably things she doesn't want me to share yet," he stated, his tone gentle but firm. His sisters fell quiet, recognizing the wisdom in his words. As they drove through the quiet streets, Anas tapped his fingers on the steering wheel, lost in thought. He knew that his sisters were only trying to be supportive, but Anas also knew that he needed to take things slow and be careful with his words. For now, he was content to savor the memory of the evening and to let his heart guide him as he navigated this new and exciting chapter of his life.

Hayat stepped through the door, with her father patting her head with pride in his eyes. She was greeted by the mischievous grins of her mother and Faudel, who were lounging in the kitchen, sticking their head through the door.

"So, how was it? Did he ask for your hand yet?" Faudel teased, a playful glint in his eye. Hayat rolled hers and chuckled.

"No, he didn't ask for my hand yet. It was just a casual meeting to get to know each other," she said, trying to keep her tone casual. Her mother smiled knowingly, sensing that there was more to the story. Lamia giggled, getting closer to her, almost hopping with excitement.

"Come on, Hayat, don't be shy. We're just curious about what happened. What is he like? Did you *like* him?

Did he like you?" she prodded with a gentle but insistent. Hayat blushed, feeling her cheeks grow warm.

"Yes, I appreciated the discussion with him. He seems like a kind and respectful man," she said, her voice barely above a whisper. Faudel whooped in delight, grinning from ear to ear. Joining his mother to physically tease Hayat.

"I knew it! You totally have a crush on him, don't you?" He said, nudging her playfully. Hayat sighed, feeling a mix of frustration and amusement at her brother's teasing.

"I don't have a crush on him. We just had a nice conversation, that's all," she said, trying to keep her tone firm. Faudel and Lamia exchanged knowing glances, sensing obviously that she wasn't telling everything. But they also knew that Hayat was a private person and that she needed time. Therefore, they let the matter drop, content to enjoy the warm and comfortable silence that surrounded them, cut by cute giggles, savoring the memory of this afternoon and the promise of what was yet to come.

Chapter 12

Hayat sat at a small table by the window, sipping her favorite drink and watching people's lives. She loved watching how people acted behind a tinted window. Some rearranged their hair, their outfits, or tried to see what was on the menu. The waiter brought the second coffee Hayat ordered for Kamila. She had arrived early, eager to enjoy the peaceful atmosphere of the coffee shop alone. The soft hum of chatter and the clink of coffee cups blended together into a soothing melody, and the smell of freshly brewed coffee and occidental pastries filled the air.

As she sat there lost in thought, Hayat noticed a familiar figure walking toward the coffee shop. It was Kamila, she could recognize her simply by her long and powerful stride. Her friend had just come out of work and was still wearing her business suit and heels. But even in her formal attire, she exuded a sense of grace and confidence.

When she was finally at her level, Hayat stood up to greet Kamila, a smile spreading across her face.

"Kamila! It's so good to see you, hbiba," she said, giving her friend a warm hug.

"Babe! It's great to see you too. Sorry, I'm late, work was crazy today," she explained, gesturing toward her business suit. Hayat waved off her apology, happy just to be in her friend's company. They sat down at the table, and Hayat ordered a fresh slice of cheesecake for Kamila. That was their ultimate comfort food, a slice of creamy cheesecake and freshly brewed coffee. As they sipped their coffee and caught up on each other's lives during these past few days. Kamila was her closest confidante, and she felt comfortable sharing her thoughts and feelings with her.

"So, tell me, how was your meeting with Anas and his family?" Kamila asked, a playful glint in her eye. Hayat blushed, feeling a mix of excitement and nervousness at the mention of Anas' name. "Give more details on the Anas part," she added, tapping the table with the top of her nail. Hayat chuckled with the straw between her lips, taking a sip of the cold drink.

"It was… Intriguing. He's a nice guy, very respectful, I know baba already likes him a little. We have a lot in common, too." She paused, thinking about what she could add next, "Oh, and he looked so adorable every time he spoke about his daughter," she said, her voice trailing off. Kamila leaned forward, her eyes sparkling with curiosity.

"Intriguing? What do you mean by that? Was there any chemistry between you two?" Hayat nodded, feeling her cheeks grow warm.

"Yes, totally, and a good point, he's a good listener, not once did he interrupt his interlocutors." Hayat stated, looking at Kamila agreeing with her with a simple nod, bringing a piece of cheesecake to her mouth. Her friend let a little *hmm* slip between two bites, enjoying every flavor of it. Hayat smiled at this view, she knew Kamila had a big sweet tooth, and would welcome a little pastry after a stressful day with open arms.

"We will see if he can remember the details we spoke about in the future, that's all for now," Hayat said, trying to keep her tone casual. Kamila raised an eyebrow, sensing that there was more behind this. However, this time, she wouldn't dig too deep. So, she let the matter drop, happy to enjoy the warm and comfortable coffee shop's melody that surrounded them, savoring the end of this afternoon and the promise of what was yet to come.

- ☾ -

With a sigh of relief, Hayat took off her hijab before dropping onto the sofa. Her eyes lingered on the numerous boxes in her apartment. She was finally home, alone. For a second, it sounded amazing, but in a heartbeat, this thought consumed the last bit of of energy she had left. Her now empty mind gave space to all the thoughts muted by her daily activities. In the silenced room, her thoughts were loud enough to paint the walls with words and questions she would rather avoid. The padded cushions felt her body grow heavier and heavier, as if each letter of those words added a kilo to her weight.

Was I doing the right choice?
Do I really want to leave this place?
Am I ready?
Will he like me? My body?
Am I not too broken for a relationship?

Hayat knew she needed to do something to not get consumed by her thoughts, but every limb of her body was glued to the sofa, impossible for her to move and make them disappear. Closing her eyes was a big mistake. Now her unanswered questions materialized before her, hitting her every time they got the chance. Hayat wondered how she would find the strength to overcome them, and whether she was on the right path.

He already has a child, what if he wants more?
Are you capable of being a stepmother?
What if she doesn't like you?

She felt defeated.
Incapable.
Weak.

Hayat wanted to scream, to be freed from herself. She couldn't. Then, slowly, she started to drop the matter, letting the thoughts consume her. Feeling like she just fell into a rabbit hole.

A black and deep rabbit hole.

The gravity bringing her down never felt heavier.

Suddenly, the *adhaan* brought her back.

This melodious call to prayer made Hayat remember her master, Al-Muhaymin, the controller of all things. She gathered all her energy to reach the sink. The first wave of cold water aggressively washed off any thoughts. Each time it touched her face and limbs, it made her feel clean.

Protected once again.

While she was getting dressed to pray, her mind was loud. It drained her. For the first time in a while, Hayat didn't feel like praying in her tiny, overwhelming room. She took her prayer mat and placed it in the middle of her living room. Hayat stood in her quiet apartment, ready to perform her sunset prayer. She took a deep breath and closed her eyes, just for a second to focus and mute her thoughts.

Then, after her Takbeer[5] she whispered, "Glorious You are O Allah, and with Your praise, and blessed is Your

---

[5] Stands for "God is the greatest" (Allahu Akbar)

Name, and exalted is Your majesty, and none has the right to be worshiped but You." She began by reciting the opening chapter of the Quran, seeking refuge in Allah's words. Hayat also recited another chapter, the words flowing from her lips. As she recited, she could feel the tension in her shoulders slowly dissipating, and a sense of peace spreading through her body. Next, she performed a series of physical movements, each one representing a different aspect of worship. She stood up straight, bowing down and placing her hands on her knees. A gesture of submission. Then, she stood up again, saying "Allahu Akbar."

Hayat repeated this cycle several times, each movement accompanied by a specific phrase. The familiar words and movements of the prayer seemed to transport her to a different realm, one where her fears and doubts didn't have the same power over her. As she recited the words, she felt her heart opening up, the barriers she had built around herself crumbling away. She focused on the words, allowing them to penetrate her consciousness and soothe her troubled soul. Hayat could feel her body and mind slowly relaxing as if a weight was being lifted from her shoulders. She placed her forehead on the ground, the pressure of the floor against her skin grounding her in the present moment. Above all is Allah. Hayat recited a few final phrases, then sat back up, at that particular instant, she felt a deep sense of peace and serenity.

For a few moments, she was completely lost, the past and future slipping away. As she emerged from the prayer, she felt that her problems were now manageable. Hayat felt a renewed sense of purpose and strength, and a conviction that no matter what lay ahead, she would find a way through it.

Hayat finished her prayer and sat quietly for a few moments, relishing the sense of calm that still lingered within her. But before she could fully savor the moment, her phone rang, and she saw Faudel's name on the screen. Hayat responded to her brother with a wide smile on her face.

"Habib diali," she answered, trying to keep the peace she had just found within herself.

"Gazouza, when are you moving out of your current apartment?" Faudel asked, without any premise. Hayat sighed inside. Faudel could be blunt and straight to the point, but she knew he meant well.

"I'm still working on it, I'm currently looking at the boxes," she said, trying to keep her tone even. "It's not as easy as it seems, you know."

Faudel grunted. "You've been saying that for days now. You need to get it done, Hayat. You can't keep living in that place forever." Hayat bristled slightly at her brother's tone. She knew he was trying to be helpful, but it felt like he was pushing her.

"I know, Faudel," she said, her voice a little sharper than she intended. "I'm doing my best. It's not like I enjoy living here." There was a pause on the other end of the line.

"Sorry, I didn't mean to sound harsh," Faudel said, his voice softening. "I just want you to be happy and comfortable. You know that, right?" Hayat felt a twinge of guilt for snapping at her brother.

"Sorry, I know. And I appreciate your concern. I'm just a little stressed out right now." Hayat tried to explain, pinching the bridge of her nose. She could hear her brother smile on the other end of the phone.

"I get it, Hayat. You've got a lot on your plate. But don't worry, we'll figure it out together. You're not alone in this." Despite their occasional clashes, she knew that Faudel had her back, no matter what.

"Thanks," she said, a small smile tugging at the corners of her mouth. "You know I love you, right?"

"I do." They chatted a bit more, she explained to him that she was looking for a moving company to help her with the furniture at the end of the week. Faudel offered his help. Hayat felt grateful for her family's support and thanked her brother. As she hung up the phone, she took a deep breath.

She couldn't wait to start fresh.

However, she also felt a pinch of sadness at the thought of leaving behind the memories of her old apartment. She remembered the times she spent with her friend, the peaceful moments she had during her daily prayers, and the feeling of warmth and comfort that filled her home. But she knew that it was time to move on and make new memories in a new space. Hayat walked around her apartment, she continued to pack up her belongings, feeling a sense of nostalgia as she came across old photos and mementos. She took a moment to sit down and reminisce, allowing herself to feel the emotions that came with this transition. Hayat knew that it wouldn't be easy adjusting to a new space, but she was ready for the challenge.

Chapter 13

Souhila came running down the steps of her school toward her father. The little one jumped into his arms, giggling with excitement, lighting his face up with a big smile. He was always happy to see his daughter, especially after a long day of work. Souhila was his little princess and the center of his world. Her bright eyes sparkled with joy, and he could feel her tiny body quivering with energy.

The father held her close enough to notice the pink paper she clutched in her hand. It was a picture of her and him, drawn in bold strokes of crayon and marker. The childlike artistry of the piece only made it more endearing to him, and he couldn't help but grin at the sight of it.

"Salam a'leykoum, benti," he said, returning her embrace. "How was your day at school?"

"Wa'leykoum salam, it was good, baba," she replied, her voice filled with excitement. "We did a project on the solar system and I got to be the sun!" Anas chuckled.

"Wow, that's wonderful! I bet you were the brightest one there." Souhila giggled, still holding a piece of paper behind her.

"What's behind your back, baba?" Anas asked, waiting for his daughter to show him what she was holding. With a wide smile, she proudly held up her drawing.

"Ta-da! The teacher also asked us to draw our families today." Souhila explained. "It's me and you, baba!" Souhila exclaimed, beaming up at him. "Look, we're holding hands!" Anas took the paper and looked at it, admiring his daughter's creativity. The sun was shining, and the sky was blue. It was a beautiful picture that depicted the love between a father and his daughter.

"That's beautiful, benti! You did an amazing job. I'm so proud of you," Anas said, ruffling her hair. Souhila beamed with pride, happy to have made her father proud. While they walked back to their car, Souhila chatted away, telling her father about her day at school. She talked about her friends, what they learned, and what they had for lunch.

Anas listened, smiling as he watched his daughter's enthusiasm. He felt a lump form in his throat as he looked at his daughter. The man felt guilty. Seeing what family meant in his daughter's eyes. Anas knew that Souhila had been struggling with the absence of a mother in her life, and it broke his heart to see her feeling different. He had become a single father when Souhila was just a three-year-old baby, and he had struggled to raise her on his own. The little one was his pride and joy, his reason for waking up every morning, and he wouldn't have it any other way. As they drove home, Souhila chatted excitedly about her day at school, telling her father about the games she had played with her friends and the snacks she had eaten at recess. Anas listened attentively, nodding and smiling as she spoke.

Suddenly, Souhila's tone changed, and her face turned serious. "Baba, why don't I have a mama like my friends? They all draw one in their family." She asked, looking up at her father with innocent eyes. Anas felt a pang in his heart as he realized that he couldn't protect his daughter from the sadness she felt.

"Well, ghazaali, some families have a mommy and a daddy, and some have just a mommy or just a daddy, some even don't have parents. Everyone has their differences," he explained gently. "And in our family, it's just me and you for now, and we love each other very much." Souhila was quiet for a moment, taking in her father's words.

"But why can't we have a mama too? I want my mama to love me and take care of me like my friends have," she said softly, her voice breaking slightly. Anas felt his heart clench as he heard the need she expressed. It was, in fact, a recurring question she had. However, every time he could distract her from this emotion, but never gave her a satisfying answer. Anas parked in front of their house and turned to face his daughter, taking her hands in his.

"Souhila, I know it can be hard sometimes, but you have me, and I love you more than anything in the world. And you know what? You have lots of people who love you, like your grandma and grandpa and your aunts and uncles. And one day, if Allah wills it, we might find someone special to join our family." Souhila looked up at him, her eyes wide with wonder.

"Really, baba? We might find someone special?"

Anas smiled. "Yes, really. But until then, you and me, we're a team. We'll take on the world together, ok?"

"Ok, baba," Souhila said, sniffling slightly. "I love you."

"I love you too, my little sunshine," Anas said, kissing her hands. "Now let's go home and have some ice cream!" Souhila jumped from her seat in joy. Anas knew it was one of his distraction tactics working again.

Once in the kitchen, Anas added the drawing to the collection using a magnet. A lump formed in his throat at the sight of the two stick figures on the paper, their hands clasped tightly together.

- ☾ -

Anas sat in front of his computer, tapping away as he worked on some spreadsheets. He could hear the soft hum of the fridge and the distant sound of his daughter playing in the living room. It was a peaceful moment, one that he cherished. Suddenly, his phone rang, interrupting the silence. Anas picked it up, curious as to who could be calling him in the middle of the day. It was the moving company that he had hired to help him move to his new home.

"Mister Saidi, I'm sorry to inform you that we won't be able to make it until next week," said the voice on the other end of the line. "We're experiencing some logistical issues, and we won't be able to come until then." Anas felt a wave of anger wash over him. He had planned everything out perfectly, and now this unexpected delay was going to ruin his plan. He had taken time off with his daughter, and he had made sure that everything was in order for the move.

"What do you mean you can't make it?" Anas said, trying to keep his voice calm.

"I'm sorry, sir, but it's out of our control," the voice on the phone said. "We'll be happy to reschedule for next week if that works for you." His grip tightened around the phone, he felt more frustrated than ever.

"I can't wait until next week, I called workers to come because the house was supposed to be empty *tomorrow*." He couldn't believe that this was happening. "I'll ask your boss for a refund, and call another company to do the job." Anas hung up the phone without waiting for an answer. He had been looking forward to the move, and it wasn't a matter he was going to drop. Anas paced back and forth in the living room, his mind racing with thoughts of how he was going to manage this delay. Anas knew he had to find another moving company that could come and transport the furniture on short notice.

"Best company in the whole town, huh..." He whispered to himself before sitting back, tapping angrily on his keyboard, looking for a new company to call. After a few uneventful calls, he got up from his desk, with frustration evident on his face, and joined his daughter in playing with her toys. She looked up at him, sensing that something was wrong. He had been waiting for weeks for the moving company to transport furniture to a depot nearby, so the owner can have them back, and now they were telling him they couldn't come for another week. His schedule couldn't wait. A sense of hopelessness wash over him, how was he going to manage this situation? He needed to start the renovation as soon as possible since the workers were already booked for that. Anas had invested so much time and money into it. After a little break, he got back to his desk ready to find a solution.

As he was about to give up, he stumbled upon a moving company that had an opening for the next day – it was twice the initial price due to the extremely short notice. Anas felt a glimmer of hope and quickly booked them, relieved that he wouldn't have to wait another week. He went back to his computer to resume his work and added it to his schedule. His mind kept going back to the delay and the added stress it was causing. He took deep breaths and closed his eyes, focusing on them. Slowly, but surely, he felt the tension in his body begin to ease. Anas thanked Allah for showing him this solution to the problem and that everything would work out in the end. Souhila came over to him, sensing her father's distress was still a bit present. She crawled onto his lap and hugged him tightly. No words needed to be said. Anas felt a surge of love and gratitude toward his daughter. She had a way of making everything seem a little less stressful. He kissed the top of her head and thanked her for her kind gesture.

"What's wrong, baba?" Souhila asked. Anas took a deep breath and tried to pass over the matter while explaining it.

"Oh, it's nothing, ghazaali," he said, forcing a smile. "The moving company can't come until next week, that's all." Souhila frowned, sensing her father's disappointment. She knew that the move was important to him, and she wanted to avoid seeing him upset.

"Is it ok, baba?" she asked, her big brown eyes looking up at him. Anas sighed.

"It's ok, benti," he said. "I found a new company to do the job. I'm just still a bit on edge," Souhila nodded. Anas pulled her into a new hug, holding her close to him. The father was about to add something, but his phone rang again, interrupting them in that father-daughter moment. An unknown number was on his screen. While Souhila was still in his lap, he answered.

"Hello?" he asked, unsure.

"Salam a'leykoum Anas! It's Faudel, Hayat's brother. Sorry to call you this late, I just want to know if you could be here when my sister will move into the apartment you rented her." Faudel bluntly said.

"Oh, wa'leykoum salam! When does she move in?"

"At the end of the week, but she doesn't know I'm asking you yet." Anas narrowed his eyes suspiciously.

"Why?" Faudel chuckled on the other end.

"Because I'm not a hundred percent sure to be with her, and I know she won't ask for help apart from her friend." He explained, "So if you have time, you could help her if I can't make it." Anas thought about it for a moment.

"Yes, just send me a message to confirm the day and hour." He could hear the brother smile on the other end.

"Perfect, thank you, Anas." Faudel before hanging up. With a smile at the corner of his lips, happiness washed over him. If helping meant seeing Hayat one more time, Anas was in. Since the first official meeting, Anas really wanted to see her again but was too intimidated to ask for a new muqabala. He would rather not seem like a man desperate to see a woman once more, but he wanted to avoid appearing underinvested either. So, Anas let a small period of time pass by before seeing her again. The top of his ears got hot in a second, thinking about her eyes looking at him. This hazel color had something over him, but he couldn't describe what – or even how.

However, Anas was sure about something: he really wanted to see her.

Chapter 14

Hayat had been looking forward to this day for weeks now. She had spent countless hours packing her belongings and getting everything ready for the move to her new apartment. The sight of the numerous sealed boxes and furniture made her feel like she won a marathon. When she first came in, she was a scared, barely functional adult, taking her first apartment alone, partially paid by her parents for the first three years. Now, she's an independent woman, renting by herself. Years had passed in the blink of an eye. It was impressive, and a big step for Hayat. Her brother kept his word to help her move everything, and she was grateful for his assistance.

When she stepped out of her building and looked around, she couldn't help but feel a bit nervous. Moving to a new place always came with a certain amount of uncertainty, and she wasn't sure how she felt about it. But as soon as she saw Faudel waiting, her nerves began to settle. He had always been her rock and she knew he would be there for her through thick and thin.

"Hey!" Faudel exclaimed, his arms open wide for a hug. "Ready to move into your new place?" Hayat smiled and hugged her brother tightly.

"Yes, I am! I can't wait to get everything set up and start living in my new apartment." As they waited for the moving company to arrive, Hayat and Faudel chatted excitedly about all the things they were going to do once they got to the new apartment. "You didn't forget anything up there?" The big brother asked, his protective side showing.

"Nope, but *you* look as if you forgot something with your frowned brows." Hayat explained, pointing at the middle of his forehead.

"Probably, I feel like something is missing, I can't remember..." He paused, "We will find out eventually." But as they stood there looking at the moving company taking all his sister's boxes and furniture, Faudel couldn't help but feel bothered.

Thirty minutes later, they were at Hayat's new building, ready to get all the stuff in her new home. A knock on the passenger side window scared them both. It was Kamila. Her friend was already here, waiting for them, a gigantic smile on her face and a sparkle of mischief in her eyes. As if she knew something that Hayat didn't. The silence was shortly cut by Faudel's almost inaudible whisper.

"Oh, that's what I forgot..." He looked, from the corner of his eye, at his sister that was totally confused.

"What?" Faudel turned to face her, an uncomfortable smile on his face.

"You'll see if I tell you now..." He paused, "You're going to scream at me." The oldest added before jumping out of the car. Hayat followed him instantly.

"Faudel, comeback he-!" Her voice dimmed when she met his eyes. Anas was standing at the door of her building. Waiting. His arms crossed, his glasses all the way up his large nose, back against the wall, finally waving at them with one hand after a second of staring. Kamila put her hands on Hayat's shoulders, both watching Faudel run to Anas. Her friend tapped on her chin playfully.

"Close your mouth." Kamila said, chuckling.

Hayat turned to her friend, fire in her eyes. "Don't tell me you knew about this?" She raised her hands, proclaiming her innocence.

"WAllahi I didn't," she was still laughing. "When I arrived, he was already there, standing at the door," Kamila pointed at him, still talking to Faudel.

"You don't have to swear for this, but why is he here?" Hayat asked in distress.

"Don't ask me," she forced the youngest to watch the two men laughing with each other. "Ask Faudel." Kamila patted her shoulders, "Now let's go, they are waiting."

When the two women arrived at their level, his dark brown eyes instantly met her hazel ones. Redness spread all over her body, tinting her white cheeks with it. She smiled awkwardly at him, but he didn't seem to let any emotion show. As they came closer, they both could hear the end of their discussion.

"Again, Anas, I apologize for not telling you I was able to come." Faudel explained, as Anas was about to respond, Hayat interjected into the discussion.

"Salam a'leykoum, Anas." she exclaimed, surprised. "What are you doing here?" Anas smiled, his eyes glued to hers.

"Wa'leykoum salam, I'm here to help. Faudel called me in case you needed someone if he wasn't there, but then, he forgot to tell me everything was ok." Hayat couldn't believe it. She narrowed her eyes at her brother, mouthing a thing that only Faudel could understand. He was dead. He brought the man she was seeing, not to mention the *owner* of the apartment, to help her. All behind her back. She felt betrayed. Faudel made himself small, waiting for his sister's fury to pass.

"I'm so sorry for the inconvenience. Thank you so much for the help, Anas," she said, feeling a lump form in her stomach. "I really appreciate it." Anas smiled and nodded.

"Of course. Anytime." As they waited for the moving company to park, the four of them chatted and laughed together. When the moving truck finally pulled up, they all sprang into action, charging off boxes and furniture out of the truck with speed and efficiency. Despite the hard work, Hayat felt her spirits lift with each passing moment. This was her new beginning, and she was going to make the most of it. Hayat felt a sense of pride as she watched her belongings find their way home in the new apartment.

She had done it.

She had made it to the next chapter of her life.

This was it. Her new place. It wasn't much to look at yet, but she knew with a little time and effort it would be perfect. While they started moving in Hayat's furniture, Anas couldn't help but notice the strong bond between Hayat and her brother, as they joked and laughed together, even though just a moment ago she was prepared to murder him. While they were moving the last boxes labeled "heavy objects", Anas and Hayat started to chat, using the opportunity to get to know each other better. They had a pleasant conversation about where she wanted to hang all of these beautiful crafts and projects of hers. While they worked together, Hayat and Anas continued to talk about their interests and passions. At some point, the discussion led to a video game they both played and their competitive side came out instantly.

"One versus one," she pointed at her soon-to-be gaming desk. "When I'll have my setup back, I'll win every one of them." Anas laughed, putting the last box down.

"You wish you could win even one against me." He chuckled, towering over her, making Hayat look up from where she was standing.

"We'll see, Anas." She threw at him, fire dancing in her eyes. He loved what he saw before him. A woman sharing his hobbies, and his competitiveness. This was too intriguing for him. Sadly, Faudel interrupted their little moment with his whining, completely slumped over the sofa. Hayat instantly ran to him, worried that he injured himself. Kamila, on the other hand, sighed because her favorite show got interrupted.

"What's the matter, habibi?" She got to his level, "Are you hurt?" Faudel only whined more.

"No," he exhaled. "I'm just tired," the brother explained.

"You brought two boxes in," Kamila shot his foot hard enough to put his hand on the contact. "Get up."

"First of all, I brought three, ok." Faudel frowned, "And, did I ask for your opinion?" Kamila opened her mouth, ready to snap back. Hayat rolled her eyes, seeing the two of them fight all over again. She returned to her activities; putting away the light objects first before taking the larger ones. When both ended with their little argument, they joined her.

Once it all finished, Hayat turned to all of them, her eyes resting on one specific person, a grateful smile on her face.

"Thank you both so much. I couldn't have done this without you." Kamila and Faudel exchanged a knowing look, and then Anas spoke up, not letting them respond first.

"No problem at all." Hayat felt a sense of joy washing over her. "I'm sorry to leave you now, but I need to go. My daughter is waiting for me." While Anas walked away, Hayat felt a pang of sadness. She was already thinking about the next time Hayat could see him. Faudel followed shortly after, kissing his goodbyes before leaving Kamila and Hayat all alone in this new place.

"Let's go, babe, we need to finish this." Kamila said, patting Hayat's back.

Chapter 15

Monday marked a new week for Hayat. For the last few days, work didn't even cross her mind. Since she was focused on the move-in, she took days off and put her projects on hold. But now she needed to get back on track with five more projects on her to-do list, totaling ten. Thanks to Kamila, her work equipment was already placed in front of the window. With her coffee in hand, she enjoyed the view for a short time, then focused back on her work before getting lazy. Hayat took her digital pencil and started several projects all at once. She'll probably have to stay here all day to only finish half of it for a first draft. So, she got started with the least recent, sending the first version as soon as she finished it, and seeing if any modifications would be needed.

Hayat was sitting at her desk, multiple windows opened before her, trying to come up with the next design. But no matter how hard she tried, she couldn't seem to find the right inspiration for the remaining seven projects. She had been working for hours unceasingly, and the exhaustion was starting to take its toll on her. Hayat felt overwhelmed by the number of projects she had, and the pressure to meet her clients' demands was starting to weigh on her. This clouded her imagination, leaving no space for inspiration.

Exhausted, she decided to take a break and go for a walk, hoping to clear her mind and find some peace. But even as she stepped outside, she found herself unable to shake the anxiety that was gnawing at her. Even the warm wind landing on her face wasn't enough to wash her thoughts away.

After a few minutes of walking, she noticed a small mosque on the corner of the street. She had never been inside yet, but she felt a sudden urge to seek solace in prayer. She took off her shoes, walked inside, and found a quiet corner to pray. Hayat had always felt a strong connection to her faith, but she had been neglecting it lately. While she was praying, she felt a sense of calm wash over her. However, the thoughts were still buzzing in her mind. Her anxiety didn't let her go.

Her prayers were now finished, Hayat walked back through the streets, her spiraling mind not giving in until she found herself standing in front of a small park. She hesitated for a moment, then decided to enter, hoping that the quiet surroundings would help her find some clarity. While she walked through the park, Hayat noticed a group of little children playing together, their giggles filling the air. Watching them made her feel like adulthood wasn't worth it. Hayat wished to be as little as them. Running, smiling, and screaming as much as she wanted, and no one to ask. No worries about responsibilities, and no anxiety about the future.

This feeling of serenity.

She felt *free*.

Hayat just stayed there for a while before going back home.

With the fourth mug of hot coffee in her hand, Hayat sat back at her desk, sighing at the sight of her monitor with countless windows opened. For a solid minute, she just blankly looked at it. The melancholic feeling, that washed over her earlier, inspired her for her clients' projects. The freedom she wanted to claim back stimulated her brain in a way she couldn't explain. Without any further hesitation, Hayat took her digital pen to start.

- ☾ -

As the day almost came to an end, Hayat got startled by three succinct knocks on her door. She almost knocked over her mug as she turned toward the door. Who could that be? Her eyes were on the clock to check the hour, it was too late for a casual visit. Until now, she didn't move, pretending she wasn't there to open. But the person knocked again. Harder this time. Hayat tiptoed to the door, to look through the peephole. A sigh of relief escaped her when she saw the face of her brother. In one fast motion, she unlocked the door and made Faudel come in.

She turned to him furious, "What are you doing here? You know you scared me!"

"Salam a'leykoum to you too, Hayat!" His sister was fuming, turning all her stress into anger.

"Wa'leykoum salam, Faudel, but what are you doing here? Don't you have work tomorrow?" Unbothered, he simply sat on her sofa, waiting for her to join him.

"Yes, I do have work tomorrow. Thanks for asking," he paused, looking at how Hayat arranged her decorations and furniture. "But I still wanted to visit you. Can you give me some water, please?" Faudel asked, watching his sister go to the kitchen and grab him a glass of water. Still angry, she came back.

122

"Here." Hayat handed him his full glass, "Why did you make two hours to only stay for a few moments?"

Faudel pretended to think, "Because. Does your brother need a reason to see you?"

"No," Hayat sighed, putting her head on his shoulder. "Of course not."

"And I wanted to complain about the patients I had today. I don't know why, but they were all crazy in the waiting room." His sister laughed, before preparing some snacks for their little siblings' moment.

While Faudel was talking to Hayat, his phone rang, interrupting them in their vivid discussion about Madam Sehal, and her issue to marry her oldest son. He picked it up from the table, frowning at the caller ID. Anas was calling. Very late at night. She verified the time; eleven forty-five. Faudel excused himself and answered the call, and Hayat went back to the kitchen to bring something else to eat. But a few minutes later, Faudel approached her with an excited expression on his face.

"Anas just called me," he said, almost jumping.

Hayat gave him a suspicious look, "Yeah, I saw that. But why?"

"He wants to have a muqabala, at the coffee shop nearby. On Friday, after jumu'ah. He really wants to talk to you." Hayat looked up from her cutting board, surprised.

"Really? What about?" She shook her head, focusing back on the knife near her fingers.

Was he thinking about me? Or does he want to stop everything already? Hayat thought for a second, before forgetting the stupid idea.

"I don't know, but he sounded pretty insistent." Hayat hesitated for a moment. Why would he call to see her, this late at night? It made her doubt a little, but she decided to go along with it.

"Ok, I'll go. But just for a little while, I have a lot of work to do." Faudel smiled.

"Of course. However, baba will be with you on Friday. I can't be there." Hayat smiled, happy to see that her father cared about her protection as much as her brother did. They always did.

"It's ok, just make sure that baba can make it that day. And if not, just tell Anas that the timing wasn't working for us and to arrange another time." Faudel nodded, ready to continue their conversation. Hayat was still cutting the fruits, but her mind stayed on the previous discussion and the inconsistency of the hour. The thoughts of it made her stop her brother in his monologue.

"Isn't it odd for him to call this late?" Hayat asked, desperate for another opinion. Faudel's head tilted back a little, startled by the question.

"Kinda, but why are you bothering yourself with this detail?" His sister shook her head, thinking she was just being dramatic.

"Forget, it's nothing." She said, dropping the matter as fast as it came. Faudel frowned, holding her hands to get her attention.

"No, no, no, no," he paused, looking straight into her eyes. "Tell me what's on your mind, Hayat." Defeated, his sister decided to spit it out because she knew her brother wasn't dropping the matter.

"I…" She hesitated, "It simply doesn't sit right with me, that a man will call at almost midnight just to set a sort of… Date with *me*." Faudel had a reassuring expression while putting his hands on her shoulders.

"It's ok to be taken aback," he tilted his head to the side, trying to whisper to himself, "And actually, I'm pretty relieved to see how you react to this call." Then looked back at her, "You don't *know* him, Hayat, and it's ok to

doubt people when they still haven't earned your trust."
She smiled at his words, which echoed her thoughts.
"Thanks. I needed that."
"Always," he simply said before hugging her tight.

Chapter 16

Anas was standing in front of the mirror, examining his reflection in the blue-navy qamis, with white stitches all over it, he had chosen to wear for jumu'ah and his meeting with Hayat and her father, hoping to make a good impression. Then, it was time for him to apply some musk on him before going. Just the simple act of not making the person next to you in prayer uncomfortable was a good deed. As he was doing so, his daughter Souhila walked into the room, and her eyes widened in awe.

"Wow, Baba! You look so handsome!" Souhila exclaimed, a broad grin on her face. Anas smiled at his daughter's compliment.

"Thank you, baba. Do you think this outfit is good enough for my meeting with Hayat and her father?" Souhila tilted her head to the side, looking thoughtful for a moment.

"Hmm, you're pretty, but I think you should wear your brown shoes instead of the black ones." Anas chuckled, impressed by his daughter's eye for fashion.

"Ok, let me go get them. Thank you for your advice, ammura." Following his daughter's opinion, Anas and Souhila got the shoes in front of the door before waiting for the babysitter to come. She could be there any minute. He couldn't be late. Anas needed to honor his commitments.

He was a man of his word, a tiny tug on his qamis made him come back to reality.

"Yes, baba?" He asked, getting to his daughter's level.

"Why can't I come with you?" Souhila said, a wave of sadness washing over her adorable features.

"I can't take you to meet her yet," he explained gently once again. Touching her shoulder lightly, tugging her in his arms.

"But I want to come. I want to see her too." Anas softly caressed the top of her head, understanding her needs.

"I know, baby, I know." He hugged her tight, "I will make you look pretty next time, ok?" With a sulky face, she replied reluctantly.

"Ok..." Anas was about to add something, but someone knocked on the door. The babysitter. He greeted her, before giving one last kiss on his daughter's forehead. Then, with a smile on his face, he grabbed his keys and headed out the door, ready to meet them.

- ☾ -

Hayat was biting her nails off, waiting for Kamila to answer her FaceTime. She was still thinking about the subject she brought to her brother; why did he call so late? Nervousness dripped from her face, stealing every color from it. Her dad was waiting for her downstairs – and Anas probably at the coffee shop, too. It was the second official meeting, and this meant a lot of stress. After a few calls, she finally answered. Her shoulders, once tense, were now released from all the stress just by seeing her best friend's face on her phone.

"Kamila! What do I wear?" Hayat screamed at her, putting the phone down on the bed.

"For what?" she said, plugging her headphones in.

"I'm seeing Anas, in like fifteen minutes, and I don't know what to wear." She explained, looking through her wardrobe.

"Excuse me!" Kamila gasped, "You're seeing Anas and you did *not* tell *me*?" Hayat turned to see her, an apologetic expression on her face.

"I forgot?" Her friend sighed, feeling betrayed.

"Yeah, yeah… You'll have to pay me dinner for that." The youngest smiled, trying to mix and match an abaya to a hijab. After several tests, nothing was convincing.

"Try the green khaki abaya in satin with the white hijab, it will match," Kamila suggested. She was sure about her call. Hayat instantly followed it. She took her clothes, after tying her hair up in a low bun. A few minutes passed before Hayat returned. She was stunning, these two colors looked wonderful with her light-toned skin, and the hazel of her eyes. Kamila's jaw dropped. Her friend was stunning. Modesty made her look spectacular.

Hayat spiraled on herself, before staring at Kamila, waiting for a word from her. "So, what do you think?"

"You are stunning," she said instantly.

"Really?" Kamila vividly nodded to support her answer, "I don't look too big?" As she looked back at her reflection, old memories came to her mind, hurting her one by one.

A bunch of children surrounding her, laughing and pointing their finger at her younger self. This sickening feeling locking her words into her throat, making her unable to defend herself. An innocent fall on the ground

*after one of them pushed her, caused her to be the new
main attraction to this circus of horrors. Her vision was
fogged by the numerous tears that she accumulated,
ten-year-old Hayat was trying so hard to not shed any.*

They did not deserve it.

They did not deserve to win.

*"Look at her, she can't even get up because she's
fat," and just like that, all the laugh increased around her.*

She felt humiliated, miserable.

*"You're just a cow. A big fat cow." The leader of the
crowd got closer to her. "Next time, don't come in my way.
You take so much place that even the thinnest of us can't
stand by your side in the hallway." Without any warning,
she felt something hot and viscous on the top of her
head...*

Hayat was so caught up in her memories, that she
barely noticed the deadly stare as a response that Kamila
gave her. "You look amazing. Go before I come and take
you by the hand."

Her friend chuckled, "Then let's go." Hayat blew a
kiss to her friend, before hanging up and rapidly got down
to meet Salim – who was still waiting in his car. She was so
late, and Hayat knew it. This wasn't playing in her favor.
Father and daughter stared at each other knowingly, it
wasn't time for chatting.

They both walked fast to the entrance, acting as if
their delay wasn't so critical – internally hoping he wasn't
already there. Obviously, they were mistaken. Anas was
sitting, alone, at a table in the back. Salim entered first,
Hayat didn't want to be the first to be seen. A shy smile
appeared on Anas' face when he saw Salim. Then his
eyes locked with a pair of hazel ones, and he literally froze,
stunned by Hayat's beauty. Green never looked so

graceful. Anas blinked several times, hoping no one noticed the second of weakness. Feeling the air getting warmer, he just drank three successive sips of water.

Don't let yourself go like that, Anas said to himself. *Be a man. Have some respect for yourself and for her.*

Hayat felt embarrassed walking toward him. She had a habit of always being on time, but today was one of those unfortunate days. Hayat didn't want to look like she wasn't invested in this *relationship*. She was, in fact, genuinely interested in that man, but showing up late at a muqabala, wasn't giving the right impression. When they arrived at his level, they both apologized. Anas, however, greeted them warmly.

"Salam a'leykoum, Anas. We're sorry for making you wait." Salim said while sitting across from him, letting enough space for his daughter to come to sit next to him.

"Wa'leykoum salam, Salim. It's ok, I didn't wait too long." He responded politely. Even if he waited for an hour, Anas wouldn't complain. Then, his gaze landed on a shy woman, not willing to look him in the eyes – yet. "Salam a'leykoum, Hayat." She automatically raised her head, already having red all over her face. A mix of embarrassment and shyness washed over her, making her hands slippy.

"Wa'leykoum salam, Anas." For a second, they were all in a sort of awkward silence. She couldn't add anything. No subject came to her mind. The waiter came in to save the day holding three different drinks – an espresso, an iced caramel macchiato, and a tea – and a snack. Anas had ordered them for Hayat and Salim. They thanked the waiter, then looked straight back at the man before them.

"Sorry, I ordered for you. I didn't want you guys to be waiting too long. I hope you like them." Anas explained, pushing back his glasses. He arranged everything in front of them. A simple cheeky smile revealed a small little dimple on his right cheek. It was adorable.

"It's very nice of you, Anas. Thank you." Hayat said, stealing the strawberry pie from her father. He smiled at the view. Anas started to think about Souhila while seeing this, it had him missing her. Usually, when Souhila could, on Fridays, he brought her with him, to pray together at the local masjid. Then, they had a father-daughter date wherever she wanted; the park, on the sofa watching Rapunzel – or any other Disney movie. Anything she asked for, Anas would do. However, today, his daughter couldn't come. That's why he'll redeem himself this weekend by doing whatever she wanted. Souhila deserved, and *needed*, this moment in a full week of school.

"It's nothing," Anas finally said, coming back from his thoughts. "Well, I hope the snack suits you both." Hayat bit her underlip, since she was the only one enjoying it at the moment. They chuckled at her reaction, sensing the ease filling the atmosphere. "I want to avoid sounding cliché, but what are you looking for in a marriage?" With this simple question, the ambiance switched. Shyness took over Hayat, who slightly looked at her father. Salim nodded, giving her the confidence that she required. She cleared her throat.

"To be honest, I'm looking for what I have now. Respect, a roof over my head, financial stability, and security, to share with a partner – who I can connect emotionally with. I look at marriage as a situation always in motion." She paused for a moment, "It is like a game, the outcome will be good or bad depending on what you choose." Hayat stated.

"I see it the way you do. For me, marriage is like a new home that needs to be built, and depending on the foundation that you're using, the home can stay still or crumble." Anas instantly responded, without hesitation, echoing Hayat's answer.

"Do you mind for your wife to work?" She wasn't ready, risking her career for a marriage.

"No, if it's halal, and she's having fun, I don't mind. It would be a waste for both of us. This means," he stuck his fingers out to count for his points. "Less money, less fun stories to share about our work, less happiness when we find each other alone. And the list goes on." Hayat laughed at the last point. For her, every point was valid, and it reassured her a bit. They were both so invested in this discussion, they didn't even touch their drinks. Salim, on the other hand, was silently enjoying his espresso and the last part of the strawberry pie. Unless he was solicited, by his daughter or Anas, Salim wasn't interfering. Internally, the father was very pleased to see this happen before his eyes. Being a witness to good behavior was an honor for him.

"What if your wife doesn't want to work? Can you take care of her needs?" Once launched on the subject, Hayat was going to explore all the facets of the dice. Checking her pros and cons list, in her mind.

"I think I can if she stays righteous in her needs. El hemduliLlah, my hard work bears fruit, and I can afford to live comfortably." He slightly paused to drink from his tea, planting his gaze in hers. "I do not marry to seek a new source of income, but marry to find the person who will bring me peace, and love my daughter as much as I do." Hayat almost gasped at the response. He was checking too many pros, it started to make her doubtful again. In fact, she remembered, he did call really late at night on a Monday.

"You have only one daughter?" Anas nodded.

"That's right, she's my little princess."

Hayat kindly smiled, "Do you want more?" For a second, he paused, genuinely thinking about the question. Anas knew what parenting was, and also what postpartum depression could look like. But was he ready to live this once again? Twice? He couldn't tell.

"I don't know," he simply said nervously, not ready to disclose more about his past life. "And you? Do you want children of your own?" Hayat sensed that Anas was hiding something, but she wasn't going to push him.

"Having children, for me, is not a need. Either way, I'm happy." A wave of reassurance washed over him, making Anas feel at ease again. "I'm totally changing the subject, but just out of curiosity, why did you call my brother at past eleven, on a Monday?" He blinked twice, in surprise about this question.

"I just came home late. I'm on a project to renovate a new house, and on Monday I had the workers all day for the first time. It was almost dinner time when work was done." Hayat's mouth formed an "O" understanding more about his schedule. Since he was on his own, he could only count on himself. "Did this call make you scared?" Anas asked, intrigued.

"A bit… It's unusual for me, I'm sorry."

Anas frowned, "You don't have to apologize, it's ok. I called late, it was weird, and it made you feel awkward. It's normal." Hayat felt understood, it was pleasant. She simply smiled at him, and he kindly returned the gesture. For a moment, they both looked at each other, feeling a sort of electric shock running down their spine. A clearing of the throat brought them back to reality, making them blush with shame. Salim laughed inwardly, he knew his role could make them shameful sometimes, but it was necessary. He was a reminder of *haya*. After a few sips of their drinks, the discussion flowed again. They talked about their work and their interests. Anas was impressed by Hayat's passion for her work and her creativity, and she was charmed by his kindness and intelligence. Salim was happy to see them getting along so well.

"You made this ad?" Anas pointed at her phone's screen, totally thrilled by her work.

"Yes, I did! I also did this one, my boss was very pleased – his words, not mine – by my work." Her suitor, impressed, simply showed it by his expression.

"Wow, you have so much talent! Guess I have found a new designer for my ads." Anas chuckled. He, too, showed her his last renovations, and future projects. Both were amazed by each other's work.

When it was time to leave, Anas looked like something was on his mind. Slightly hesitant to say what bothered him. Anas walked Hayat and Salim to their car, still looking troubled. When they exchanged goodbyes, he finally spilled it out.

"Before I let you go," he cut them in their walk, looking back at Hayat. "There is an exposition in a museum an hour away from here, in two weeks, do you want to come?" Anas said fast, almost not articulating it enough. The woman tried to hide her smile, while excitement washed over her. "Souhila will be there too." He added.

Hayat's smile got even bigger, "Then, if she's here, I will join you." Once again, they said their goodbyes. Hayat couldn't help but feel a flutter of joy as they drove away. Anas could really use something cold for his hot ears.

This could be something good, Anas and Hayat thought as they drove back to their respective houses.

Chapter 17

Hayat and Faudel waited patiently in front of the museum, looking regularly at the entrance to see if any silhouette was familiar. The sun was out today. Warming their bodies under the cool wind. Sadly, they will have to stay inside despite the beautiful weather. It saddened Hayat a bit since she usually stayed either on her computer behind closed doors and windows, or on her desk at work. She used every opportunity she got to enjoy the sun. Faudel was about to call them when a gravelly voice came behind them. Hayat jumped a little, surprised by the sudden sound. She smiled at them, a hand on her heart, trying to calm it. Anas was standing behind them, with his little girl holding his hand. Souhila was adorable. The white bow in her curly light-brown hair made her even cuter.

"Salam a'leykoum, I hope I didn't make you wait too long." The father explained, happy to finally be able to bring his daughter with him. It was a considerable step. Letting Souhila, his precious treasure, bond with a new woman was bold – and *scary*. Now it wasn't only implying him, but also her. He thought about this for a long time, before actually proposing this muqabala.

"Wa'leykoum salam," Faudel responded, Souhila looked at her father, waiting for a reaction from him first, with a movement of his head he encouraged her to speak. However, the little one only responded with a smile.

"Wa'leykoum salam Anas!" Hayat said, with a little too much excitement in her voice. "Salam a'leykoum Souhila, do you remember me?" The child stared at her, too shy to respond with her voice.

"Don't be mistaken, Souhila is actually very excited to see you. She just needs some time to get used to you both." They genuinely understood. It was a normal reaction for children. Without waiting for more, Anas, Souhila, Hayat, and Faudel walked toward the museum.

The two siblings started to grab their wallets to pay for their tickets, but Anas has already planned everything. They thanked him, even though Hayat and Faudel were a bit embarrassed. Together, they started the tour through the museum, admiring the various artworks on display. Hayat was particularly thrilled to be there, as she had always been passionate about art and design. She was pointing out various pieces that caught her eye, and asking Anas and Faudel what they thought of them. Hayat tried to include Souhila in some jokes, or discussion to make her feel at ease, and she noticed a smile for some of them, but she wasn't totally into it yet.

While they walked through the museum, Souhila couldn't help but notice how much Hayat resembled her mother. She had the same way of wearing the hijab, the same pale tone, and the same infectious smile. Souhila doesn't especially remember her voice, or her affection toward her, but seeing Hayat today made her think about Zahia.

A few moments later, Souhila was alone with Hayat while Faudel and Anas stood inches away. The young woman took her chance, waiting for the little one to speak first. A minute alone with her did the trick.

"Yes, I remember you," Souhila said out of the blue.

Hayat was taken aback, slightly forgetting what she responded to. "You do?" She asked, looking at her big brown eyes while Souhila was nodding. Hayat got to her level, thinking it would help her be relaxed. "Then why aren't you speaking to me? Is it because of me?" Hayat asked softly. Souhila hesitated for a moment before answering.

"Yes," she said. "You look like mama." Hayat was touched, understanding the longing of Souhila. Her vulnerability was visible, so she simply got a few inches closer to her.

"I understand," she said. "However, I'm not your mama, but I would love to be your friend." Hayat paused for a second, "Only if you'll let me." Souhila smiled at Hayat, feeling a warmth spread through her chest. She was adorable, the sparkle in her eyes returned and made the oldest happy.

"I would love that!" Before returning to the men, Hayat lent her hands for the little one to hold, and she instantly took it.

Her small hand in hers, chatting happily. It was a delightful view for Anas. While talking to Faudel, he noticed the empty space at his side. Therefore, he briefly checked around him to find Souhila. The tension built in his shoulder, in a few seconds, instantly vanished when he saw both of them discussing near them. Something twisted in Anas' chest, but he couldn't clearly understand this feeling yet. Seeing her almost on her knees just to be at the same level as Souhila while speaking, made him smile – and blush. When he saw them come back, he pretended not to notice, continuing the discussion with Hayat's brother.

As a group, they continued their tour of the museum, Souhila and Hayat were now inseparable. They chatted until the end. Hand in hand, pointing at different paintings, and laughing together. Anas found himself drawn to Hayat's infectious energy, enthusiasm, and care for his daughter. This sight made him feel hopeful about a future with her. Faudel was also enjoying himself, discussing different subjects during the tour. He could sense the connection building between Anas and Hayat - but also between Hayat and Souhila. This comforted him that his sister was probably in good hands. Faudel gave Anas a knowing look, happy that his little sister was able to find common ground with someone else.

After the visit, they all sat down in the museum café to discuss their favorite pieces and grab a bite to eat. This time, Hayat insisted on paying the bill. Reluctantly, Anas let her pay. In their culture, men were the ones who paid – a woman paying could be taken as an insult to the men. So, he silently noted that he will pay her something back soon. When they were back at their table, Souhila and Hayat continued to talk and share stories, and Anas and Faudel joined in.

As they left the museum and walked back to their respective cars, Souhila took Hayat's hand in hers and gave it a gentle squeeze. Interrupting them in their keen interest, Faudel heard a call from his replacement for an emergency at work, he had to leave as soon as possible.

"So you're coming home with us?" Souhila said, understanding the matter. Hayat smiled at her, before looking at her brother. He seemed reluctant to this idea, but he had to be at his office. This will prevent Faudel from making a detour to return home to drop off his sister.

Anyway, they weren't going to be in the car alone. He exchanged a look with Anas, inherently signing a deal to keep Hayat safe. This innocent proposal from Souhila had to remain so.

"I would love to," she replied. Anas and Faudel walked ahead, chatting. Before going, Hayat's older brother hugged her tight.

"Be careful, ok? I know you're not alone, and I would love to bring you home. I'm sorry," he whispered in her ears. The youngest tapped his back lightly to reassure him. Faudel left at a trot, wanting to get to his workplace as quickly as possible. At the same time, Hayat and Souhila climbed into Anas' car, Hayat sat with the little one in the back. A sense of nervousness washed over her. Even if she wasn't alone, being in a closed space with a non-mahram man was strange to her. She distracted herself with Souhila. The little girl looked so precious in her toddler seat. Her bow was still at the top of her head, even with all the jumping and running in the museum today.

Looking at her closely, she could clearly see the resemblance to her father. Same big brown eyes, curly light-brown hair, and tan skin. Earlier, Souhila said that Hayat looked like her mother.

It stuck in her mind.

The sound of a slammed door made her come back to her senses. Anas was now behind the steering wheel, looking straight at her in the rearview mirror. A lump formed in her throat, making it hard for her to swallow. Her eyes went back to Souhila, still sensing this burning look on her.

"Baba, is your seatbelt well done?" His sudden question almost startled Hayat.

"Yes, baba!" Anas didn't start the car yet, waiting for something. After a moment, he spoke again.

"Hayat?" She turned to him, planting her eyes in his. The woman could feel her heart go faster, and faster every second passing looking at him.

"Yes, mine is done as well." Hayat finally said, freeing herself from this game she would rather not fall in.

"Then, let's go."

On the way back, only Souhila started conversations. Both of them knew they couldn't casually talk to one another, to know more about the other person, especially when they internally knew they were mutually attracted. This game that hung in their face was far too dangerous to even, *only*, venture. Both reminded themselves of that fact with the temptation they felt.

Do not even approach fornication, for it is an outrageous act, and an evil way.[6]

This aya stuck to their skins, shielding them from any tension, until they parked in front of Hayat's building. She kindly thanked them, before almost running to her apartment. She needed to breathe, after suffocating this whole time.

The ride was definitely a test, and she barely passed it. Even Anas had a hard time, it was a very bold and dangerous proposition, but Hayat was safer with him and his daughter than a taxi. For a moment, Anas watched her partially run to her building and left when she was in, his attention now only on his daughter.

"Did you enjoy your day?" He asked, wanting to know if Souhila liked Hayat.

"Yes, baba, it was very fun!" Seeing her wide smile in a reviewer mirror appeased his worries. He internally wanted them to get along, and have a good relationship.

---

[6] Verse of the Quran [17:32]

"Was Hayat nice to you?" He anticipated the answer with a hint of fear in his chest.

"Very! She also looks a bit like mama." Shocked by the insinuation, Anas almost stopped the car in the middle of the road. He forcefully swallowed the pill, not wanting to tell his daughter of his vulnerability. What if this resemblance would disturb her? What if it wasn't going to have a bad consequence on their relationship? Worry was starting to take up space in his mind. "Baba?" Souhila asked, getting his attention back. Her voice could dissipate his problems without her even realizing it.

"Yes? Sorry, I was focused on the road." Anas bluntly lied, he wasn't going to share his worries. He'd rather not be responsible for the seed of doubt that might plant itself in her mind.

"Do you think that too? That she looks like mama?" The little one asked again. For a solid minute, Anas waited and thought about it.

"Why do you say that?" The father was actually intrigued.

"Because she looks like her! She has the same skin color, and the hijab is the same." That's when he understood. The fact that Hayat was a hijabi woman, speaking with her father, and having a pale skin tone, for a child; they do look alike.

"You're right, in some way they do look alike, but you need to remember that they are not the same person, baby." Souhila simply nodded, taking his statement as advice. For the moment, he was simply going to stop there, before refocusing on the road.

Chapter 18

The warm rays of the sun were a pleasure to feel, unlike the number of defeats Hayat saw on her screen. Seven lost games. One more and she will derank, and probably be hard stuck for a while – *again*… She was, as her duo called her, *salty*, or more simply irritated by the defeat streak. Her duo could literally feel the anger pouring out of her expression. Hayat would rather stop here than risk her rank today. Resilience was her new way of thinking. It was hard, but she chose to leave and get tea before going back to her designs.

The bell rang, startling her. She almost burned her hand with the hot kettle of water. On tiptoe, she got to the door – as if she didn't make any sound while putting down her tea – Hayat put her eye to the peephole. She only saw what looked like flowers, roses to be exact. Before opening the door, she grabbed the nearest hijab and covered herself. The delivery man gave her the bouquet, she didn't even have the time to thank him for his service, he left Hayat with a lot of confusion and questions in her mind.

Did Anas send me flowers? Was it ok to give such a thing? I will ask my dad later.

Hayat was taken aback by the unexpected delivery of flowers. She smiled at the sight of them, admiring the beautiful arrangement of vibrant colors, but even these wonderful flowers couldn't brush off the sensation inside her. It felt wrong. Was this authorized to receive a gift from a man in the courtship phase? Was this halal? She sent a picture to her father, asking if this was a correct behavior. Three little dots appeared on her screen, then disappeared again. Hayat started biting her nails. Nothing was more stressful than waiting for an answer. She closed her screen, unable to tolerate the wait, and got back to her kitchen. Sipping her hot tea made her feel better. The screen of her phone lit up, notifying her that her father had responded.

Baba

> It's ok, benti. He asked us first, and you two are getting to know one another to probably get married. The context is halal, and we – your mahrams – didn't see any evil intentions in this gift. So, we said yes.

A feeling of relief washed over her, but this tint of nervousness was there. Still confused, she read the attached note, and her heart skipped a beat. Anas really had sent them to her, it was *real*. He was asking for another muqabala with her. She couldn't help but feel a mix of excitement and nervousness at the thought. With the approval of her brother, Hayat quickly agreed to the invitation. She was eager to spend more time with Anas and see where their connection could lead. Their muqabala was set for the following Friday afternoon, and

Faudel was already in the loop. Anas had planned a special surprise for Hayat, but wouldn't reveal what it was. She tried not to get too excited, but couldn't help but wonder what he had in store for her.

This time, she instantly called Kamila, who arrived in a blink of an eye. Her friend was just as excited as her. The soft cushions of the sofa absorbed all the jitters of Hayat. Her impatient friend didn't bat an eye at the tea and the snacks. Kamila was only focused on her friend – who was partially trying to pass over the matter and made this gift disappear. Hayat couldn't take her hazel eyes off the flowers.

If he sent this when I wasn't promised to him, what would he do when I will be? Red tinted her cheeks, then her face. She gave herself a few taps to come back down to earth, she couldn't start making scenarios for simple flowers. Hayat was about to send Anas a message – through her brother – asking him to not give her gifts, but Kamila prevented her from it.

"Wow, what are you doing?" She frowned, not understanding this reaction.

"I was about to explain to him that it makes me uncomfortable to receive a gift when this could actually not work after all." Hayat said trying to get her phone back.

"Oh no, you're not doing that." Kamila hid her friend's phone behind her, making it impossible for Hayat to get it back.

"Give it to me." She landed her hand with a burning gaze.

"No," she ate a cookie, looking at her in the eyes. Hayat was fuming, she was about to jump on her, but her friend's voice warned her. "Now, tell me, do you think you want more with him?" She shutdown. This question was like the second surprise of the day. But the first response in her head was: *Yes.*

She wanted more from him.

Of him.

"Maybe?" Hayat gobbled a cookie, trying to hide any trait that could betray her real feelings.

"So you do like him!" Kamila jumped off the sofa to do a little victory dance. "I knew it, I knew it, I knew it!"

Hayat quickly attempted to brush off the subject, "Yeah, I like him. So what? I still don't know him." With a sigh of annoyance, Kamila got back on the sofa, already her motherly speech in mind.

"Hayat... You can't know someone fully before marriage, that's impossible. Muqabalas aren't only there for you to wait for the red flag and run. They are here to help you, to know what you really want so you can tell yourself: yes I want that, no I don't want that, I can live with that flaw, and the list goes on. Marriage isn't about 'I know him, so I want to marry him.'" Kamila paused for a second. "Do you like him?"

Blush flushed her round cheeks, "Yes."

"Does what he shows about his deen satisfy you?" Kamila pinched her lips together, waiting for her answer.

She nodded, "Yes."

"Are you attracted to him?" The oldest said while raising her brows multiple times.

Hayat smiled at her silly action, "Yes."

"Can he take care of you? Financially?" Kamila looked at the flowers, "Emotionally?"

This time the response took longer to come. "Financially, yes. Emotionally, I don't know yet."

"Ok, so that's a point you need to figure out." Kamila thought about her last question, "Can he protect you?" Hayat's face turned red once more. A flash of his physique passed through her mind, even if she knew Kamila didn't imply this, her mind started playing tricks on her.

"Yes, physically, for sure. But in terms of secrets, defense of my honor, and reputation, I don't know." Her friend smiled at her response.

"Then, you know what to look for in the next meeting! Put him in a situation, challenge him. Anas is interested and seems to be a man of his word. Test him while you still have the chance. Your mahrams are with you, to protect you. Take it." Hayat stayed silent. Thinking about what she said. Kamila was right on every point. She spoke clearly. This discussion made her highlight the last points she was looking for. It was one of the last steps to know if all of this was worth it, or not. She was ready to face the final answer.

Yes, or no.

These were the only two options for this situation.

As the conversation flowed again, Hayat and Kamila were sitting more comfortably on the sofa, enjoying a cup of hot tea. Hayat talked about how she was still adjusting to her new surroundings. Kamila shared about her job and how much her clients were driving her crazy. The conversation that was once about Hayat was now about Kamila.

"So, we talked about me and Anas but what about you... Do you have someone in your life?" Hayat raised her eyebrows, hoping her best friend was finally interested in someone. Even if it was for a split second, she noticed a change in Kamila's demeanor.

"No, not yet." Her friend looked away.

"I know you're lying to me. Even if you won't tell me now, I will find out myself." Her friend laughed genuinely.

"You can try, but since there is no one, you will find nothing." To make her spit it out, Hayat jumped on her friend, tickling her all over her body. Kamila's stoic face didn't last long, in the silence she burst out laughing. After a few minutes of torture, Kamila pleaded Hayat to stop. Not convinced by her technique, Hayat stayed on top of her hoping she would speak, but once again Kamila had the same statement; no one was in her life that way.

Defeated, the youngest got back to her place, laughing. Before they could even notice it, it was late and Kamila had to head back home. They hugged each other tightly, promising to catch up soon. Hayat sat back on the couch, looking at the flowers that filled the room with their fragrance.

Chapter 19

The reflection in her mirror made her smile. Her loose floral dress with long sleeves made her look wonderful. She looked cute and elegant at the same time. The style of her hijab was more suitable for the weather, letting her feel the wind while hiding her *'awra*. A twirl was enough to make her feel like a princess. Hayat checked the clock in her living room, she was perfectly on time today. No rush or delay. Faudel was already in his car waiting for her to come down, and drive her to her surprise. Anas' surprise was a well-kept secret, neither Faudel nor Salim were aware of the details. Excitement and nervousness washed over her the moment she stepped out of her apartment.

Half an hour later, they both arrived at a beautiful park.

They could see Anas waving at them, while Souhila was running around him with a toy airplane in her hand, miming its flying movements. Her little floral dress was almost a match to Hayat's one. She could watch her little curls bounce with her every movement. As they arrived at their level, Hayat could see a small basket, surely filled with several things to eat and drink.

It was a picnic muqabala.

Hayat was so thrilled to, finally, see the surprise. Faudel was the first to greet them, for the first time, she was seeing her brother shaking hands with Anas while giving him a tap on his back. How did she miss the bond they started to have? Her family was so implicated in this, and she was starting to realize it. A part of her was very pleased to see that, but another part felt anxious that if this wasn't working, they would probably be affected too.

Souhila distracted her from her thoughts with light tugs on her dress, making her look down. Without hesitation, Hayat bent down to Souhila's height, simply to greet her.

"Salam a'leykoum, Souhila! You look beautiful today, I'm jealous! Your dress looks better than mine." She said jokingly, pointing at Souhila's dress.

"Wa'leykoum salam, Hayat! You are?" To make her even more envious, she spun around intentionally. They both started to laugh together, when a deep soothing voice came to interrupt them, causing Hayat to almost fall in the process of getting up.

"Salam a'leykoum, Hayat." He said, looking her straight in the eyes, "So you're jealous of her dress? I can give you the address." Hayat bit her bottom lip, a bit embarrassed that he heard what she said. He watched her move meticulously. She was stunning in her summer dress. The sunlight kissing her features made her look even more breathtaking.

Hayat is such a beauty that I feel guilty looking at her. He thought for the spit of a second, before hearing the melodic sound of her voice.

"Wa'leykoum salam, Anas. I would actually love to have the address." Anas smiled so wildly that Hayat could see his dimple. Every time this little detail about him made her melt inside.

150

"Perfect, because I made it." The father stated, slightly tilting his head to the side, "This could be a new reason to take a step further into our relationship." The young woman gasped, looking at the man towering over her, while hearing her brother almost choked on the fruit he was eating.

"Excuse me?" Hayat tried to say something else. However, she was too baffled to add anything.

"Isn't it the point of it all?" The response was hard to form since her mind went completely blank. A mix of hot and cold sensations passed through her. She was taken aback. Surely, the point of talking to him was to see if this could go further. However, Hayat felt like it was a bit too soon. They both needed to know more about each other, their strengths, and their weaknesses, their defaults, their characters, their habits, and more. Her mind started to go off again, but the wise words of Kamila echoed into her. Reminding her that it was totally normal, she couldn't control the future even if she knew him better. Hayat gathered herself, muting her loud thoughts.

"Yes, but why?" Anas pretended to think while easily carrying Souhila in his arms.

"I like you," he pointed at his daughter. "She likes you, we have plenty of common ground, you're a Muslim as I am, we share the same values, and I can sense this feeling between us. You're what I'm looking for, I don't understand why I shouldn't ask to go a step further." He replaced a strand of hair behind his daughter's ear, looking for any objection from Hayat, but nothing. Anas was right. If she was what he looked for in a partner, why would he waste any more time? It has already been more than a month since they had been talking to each other, apparently he didn't need to wait any longer.

"You're right, but to be honest, I'm not ready for this step to be taken on my side. I need a bit more time." Disappointment pinched Anas' heart, he wanted more than what they shared now. However, he respected her choice.

"Ok, my little girl and I will wait for you to be ready." Hayat smiled at his reassuring response. Not pushing her into doing something she wasn't ready to do, he made her feel safer around him without even realizing it. Faudel, on the other hand, was still enjoying his fruits, casually listening to their discussion. They joined him, getting everything out of the little picnic basket. It was getting windy, but the warmth of the sun made it bearable. Her hijab was struggling to resist the strong wind, and she was fighting with all her life to keep it on her head. It was funny for a moment before she decided to secure it with more pins. Anas asked if he could hold them, to help her, Hayat was happy with the thoughtful gesture. They spent the afternoon chatting and laughing, enjoying each other's company.

After a while, Faudel almost got dragged by Anas's daughter to play ball near their picnic place. The sound of laughter, the scene of a still lake, and the birds around Anas and Hayat created an intimate cocoon, pushing them to talk a little more about themselves. They gazed at the surrounding beauty, mesmerized by the shimmering lake and the lush green trees that surrounded them.

"I want to ask you something, but please don't make it too embarrassing." His grave laugh almost resonated, with her fast heartbeat. This sensation made her feel some type of way. Euphoric. She smiled to herself.

"Me? Embarrassing? Never. Go ahead, I'm listening." Anas opened his posture, genuinely welcoming the next question. Hayat knew this subject was important for a couple, and wanted to talk about it, but the taboo around this specific subject made it seem *haram*.

"What's your way to ask consent before initiating something intimate with your wife?" Hayat asked, sensing her cheeks grow red. The young man, discovering what was the embarrassing subject, struggled to hide his smile.

"First, I want you to know that's not embarrassing. It actually pleases me to know that you're comfortable enough with me to ask about it." He paused, rearranging himself on the ground. "I usually come with direct intentions, with my moves, I would say." Hayat nodded, agreeing with his words. "And you, how do you imagine it? With words? Actions?" Hayat thought about it for a solid minute, as an inexperienced woman, she was clueless.

"I don't really know. I never did something like that. Probably the moment would indicate to me if I need words or actions." Now, it was Anas' turn to nod. "Hum, how do you see intimacy? It can go to only some touch from time to time, or particular practices you would like to do with your wife?" Her face was as red as a stop sign, and the wind wasn't enough to make her cool down. She could sense a change in his posture, but also his look. As if the simple mention of this part in a couple could activate some dormant hormones that fogged their senses. Anas cleared his throat, feeling hot himself, and drifted his gaze to the side, incapable of looking at Hayat in the eyes again.

"Intimacy is a whole, from the cuddle to the intercourse. All of this, for me, is intimacy. And yes, I do have desires that I would try with my wife." The speech was abnormally fast as if every word about this subject was burning his tongue. His ears were almost as red as Hayat's face, who was trying to hide it behind her fingers.

"I see, we have the same vision. Next question!" Anas instantly joined in.

"Great Idea, what do you expect from me financially and emotionally?" Hayat was happy to see that he was on the same page.

"To support me. You already know, I have my own job, my own money, so on this part, it depends on where we live. If we go to a new house, I will help you with the bills, paying furniture. If we move to your home, I could send you money, I don't know. On the emotional level, I need a patient man who can deal with my anger issues. I can get overwhelmed easily. I want someone to understand me and can listen when I require him to, I need a partner, a shoulder I can lean on and be peaceful." Anas nodded, agreeing with her points.

"First, even if we change houses, I will never ask you to pay anything. I wasn't raised that way. I have the money to take care of a family, I won't take your money. If you want to help, I'm fine with that, but your money is your money, and my money is my family's money – including my wife." He paused for a second, letting Hayat process all of this. "Second, to be honest, I can handle that. As much as you'll find peace with me, I hope I can find peace with you." She smiled at his words.

And of His signs is that He created for you from yourselves wives that you may find tranquility in them; and He placed between you affection and mercy. Indeed, in that are signs for a people who give thought.[7]

Earlier, her resilience was high, but now after a few hours of talking, she could picture them together. The golden color of the sun hitting on Anas' skin was a pure delight for Hayat's eyes. His dark skin returned the rays of the sun, making a golden halo around him. He was

---

[7] Verse of the Quran [30:21]

wonderful. Every time the wind passed over him, it made her smell the small atoms of his perfume.

As Faudel and Souhila came back, Anas and Hayat were still sitting on the cozy blanket. Souhila was bragging about the number of wins against Faudel, and he played his part; pretending to be annoyed.

While the sun began to set, they packed up their picnic and took a leisurely stroll around the park. The golden sun dipped below the horizon, casting a warm and fiery glow over the landscape, and the sky was painted in shades of orange, pink, and purple. Anas and Hayat stood together, watching in awe as the colors of the sunset filled the sky, creating a breathtaking masterpiece.

"Subhaan'Allah," they exclaimed under their breath, appreciating the magnificence of their Lord. At that moment, everything felt perfect and serene, and Hayat felt grateful for the beautiful surroundings, for Anas' company, and for all the effort he made to make her feel special today.

The moment she opened the door of her apartment, Hayat made her wudu to pray Salat Istikhara. With all the occasions she had to talk to him, she still didn't see anything wrong. It was a bit weird at first, but Anas was possibly the one. Therefore, Salat Istikhara was her only way of knowing what was best for her, only Allah could guide her. Hayat already did this Salat several times, and now Anas was proposing to her. She felt the necessity to do it again before taking a step further. Then, she'll be waiting for signs.

Chapter 20

Even though she left very early in the morning, Hayat still ended up in traffic. A week had already passed since her picnic with Anas, and she was supposed to go home this weekend. To see her family, and spend some time with them. But with the roads completely blocked, she was surely not staying awake long once she arrived.

Now that summer had arrived, many people travelled for weekends. Hayat, herself, was one of them – whenever she had the chance. These past few weeks were intense. Between work, muqabalas, the moving, and all the worries that came with it, she no longer knew what to focus on. She almost lost herself in this. Being with her family might help her occupy her thoughts, and give her some space. Hayat just needed to be at peace and focus on new things.

The horns all around her gradually faded the further she went down the road. The farther the city was, the more she let go of those thoughts. The road was long, longer than usual due to traffic jams. She somehow needed to pass the time for the long journey ahead, so to occupy herself, Hayat considered the latest events.

What if she missed something?

What if she was mistaken about him?

Thinking about it, she realized that marriage was scary and a bit contradictory on some points. Linking your life to someone else's just with the idea that she had, not completely sure if the image he gave her was just that, or who he truly was. Of course, Hayat watched how he spoke, how he acted with his family and hers, how he acted with his daughter, and mostly how he acted with *her*. Since day one, he had been respectful, listening, and remembering details about her – like the coffee she ordered the first time with him. Even with all of this, there was this *what if* that bothered her.

Still lost in her thoughts, the sight of her childhood home brought her back to earth. Hayat arrived at her parent's home. Salim was the one welcoming her with open arms. He had been waiting for her since morning, so the instant he heard the car parked before his house, Salim got up to hug her. He missed his little girl – *old* little girl. Hayat didn't even have the time to get her luggage out of the car that Salim tucked her in, inhaling her scent like he was deprived of oxygen since the last time he saw his daughter.

"Salam a'leykoum, Hayati! You arrived late today, traffic?" Hayat returned the embrace immediately, nothing was worth more than a hug from the first man in her life. When she was in his arms, all the worries went away like old times. The time when she used to run to her father's room, crying her eyes out, fearing the monsters under her bed. This protective feeling never went away.

"Wa'leykoum salem, Baba. Yeah, the sun is out and they all take weekends." Ear on his heart, she could hear his laugh, through his chest.

"I see, let's go inside, mamak is waiting for you." Before she even could put her hand on her suitcase, Salim grabbed it. It was truly a Father thing. On the way, she was fighting with him to have her luggage back since it was heavy, but he pretended she wasn't even there. Hayat internally knew the bag was now a no-go zone. The moment her father put his hand on it, the luggage became his property. She had already lost this non-existent fight.

One foot in the house was enough of a signal for Lamia to bombard her daughter with questions about Anas. No greeting, no hug, just questions and curiosity to welcome her daughter. Hayat ate the inside of her cheeks to release the imminent stress. With a weird smile on her face, she put her hands on her mother's shoulders, hoping it would help her to cool down.

"Salam a'leykoum, mama! Wesh raki?" *How are you?* Lamia wasn't even listening, she wanted to know.

"Wa'leykoum salam, benti, mliha, el hemduliLlah. Weqtesh tzewwejou?" *I'm good. When will the two of you get married?* Her daughter was about to say something, even if her expression was already getting signs of annoyance. Salim stepped in, interrupted his wife gently by taking her to the living room, freeing the way to the stairs. Lamia tried to escape from his grip, but he was firm enough to make her understand without any word. The father gave a look to his daughter, who thanked him with a grateful smile. In one smooth motion, she took off her hijab before running to her room. After closing her door, she jumped onto her bed, feeling her anxiety getting soaked into her mattress. Hayat felt saddened all of a sudden. She actually knew why, but she ignored this guilty emotion. Hayat passed out in the clothes she had on because she was so exhausted.

- ☾ -

The door suddenly getting open startled Hayat, making her almost jump from her bed. Faudel showed no consideration for her sleeping sister. He stood with, a regretful expression. In his defense, he didn't know she was asleep before opening the door. With a wide smile on her sleepy face, she opened her arms waiting for him to snuggle with her while Hayat woke up slowly. Faudel slid between her arms, happy to see her. Occasionally, when she had him there, she remembered the time when they couldn't even bear each other's presence in the same room. They were like most siblings and fought for silly things like most siblings; him, opening her door for no reason, because he breathed too close to her, Faudel just teasing her because he felt like it, and the list was long enough to make an encyclopedia. Then, Faudel needed to leave for college. They both realized the emptiness of their heart when one of them wasn't near. Therefore, when they would be around one another, they fought less and less.

Expressing her love to her sibling took a long time.

They stayed this way for a solid five minutes before going down together. Her nap completely messed up her hair. She didn't notice it until she passed in front of the mirror at the entrance. Hayat rearranged them to, at least, not look like the pillow just blew up on her. The mission failed when her mother saw her. Lamia laughed a bit when Hayat entered the kitchen, trying to make herself a coffee.

"Tartqet 'lik el mkhada?" *The pillow exploded on you?* Quickly, Hayat brushed her hair back with her hand, hoping that her spikes were all gone.

"Yeah, kind of," she said before trying to get a hug from Lamia. Feel some love. Her mother welcomed the embrace for a second, before going back to her previous activity: cooking. She loved to do so. The sound of the coffee machine filled the room, accompanied by the bubbling sound of the sauce. Lamia was cooking *rechta*. A wonderful smell was coming from the pot, and Hayat inhaled it without hesitation. It was one of her favorite traditional dishes.

The coffee mug in her hand, she thanked her mother for making it before leaving the kitchen and joining her father on the outside swing. Salim smiled at her sight, happy to know she slept a bit after this long road.

"Rqeti mlih hbiba?" *Did you sleep well, my dear?* The father asked, moving a bit to the left to give her more space to sit.

"Na'am, but Faudel scared me when he opened my door." Hayat put her head on his shoulder, as she usually did. They both welcomed the silence of nature to accompany them during this father-daughter moment. After a while, they started to talk about what had happened recently.

"A friend fell while praying last jumu'ah, we all got scared for a second, but then he raised his thumbs up to let us know he was ok. He only stepped on his robe." They both started to laugh. Hayat couldn't relate more to this case. How many times she almost fell – or actually fell – during prayer when she got up from sujood? She wasn't able to count them. They continued laughing and having fun. However, without knowing how, the conversation drifted to a more serious tone, and how it was going on with Anas.

"Did you enjoy the flowers he sent you?" Hayat smiled at the remembrance of the vivid colors and smell they left in her apartment. She was already picking up the fallen petals to dry them and make them into cute little objects. Memories of this gift were going to be with her for quite a while.

"Yes, I did love them. Even if I felt a bit of unease receiving a gift from a man who isn't my mahram yet." Salim raised an eyebrow at the last part of her sentence, a smile at the corner of his lips.

"Yet? You imagine him being one, one day?" Red stole the place of the colors on her face. Eyes wide, her gaze fell onto Salim. She didn't expect to blow her cover so fast. A stutter stole her words, making Salim laugh. "It's ok, henunna, why are we doing all of this then?" Her gaze softened, he was right. They were all right about this; Kamila, Salim, and Anas. The point of this was to know if they were compatible. And, el hemduliLlah, it was doing great for now. "You don't have to be embarrassed to tell me that you like him. Actually, I'm happy that you finally found someone who deserves you." Hayat chewed the inside of her cheeks, a specific question in her mind.

"But how do you know he's the right one for me?" In a smooth and affectionate motion, Salim's hand slid from the top of her head to her cheek. Hayat had intentionally snuggled up against his touch.

"I don't know, but he asked for me first. Isn't that right?" His daughter simply nodded, "He wanted to meet me, then the family, just to talk to you. He didn't even try to bypass us." Hayat only listened to his point, like she needed Salim to list them to have no doubt anymore. "Did he once try to touch you? Disrespected you in any way? Did you find anything that you couldn't live with?" At first, Hayat stayed silent, thinking about these questions.

"No, he did nothing to make me think he wasn't a good match." Then Salim continued.

"Mala 'lesh raki khaifa baba?" *Then, why are you scared, baby?* For a second, Hayat was hesitant, but the softness of her father's tone and touch allowed her to speak.

"I don't know…" Her words weren't louder than a whisper, "Imagine this is all a masquerade, and he isn't the man he pretends to be?" That was when Salim understood where his daughter's heart lay.

"Did you ever think about what he felt?" For a split second, she frowned, not understanding his point. "Let me explain. When you're a man, you have responsibilities, the moment you take the daughter from a father. It's like having a death threat up your head until the day you die. In fact, even after you die… You need to shelter her, care for her, be patient with her, love her, and the list goes on. It's scary." He paused for a second, "The day I married mamak I was so scared of failing her. There is nothing more scary than a woman leaving you to go back to her parents. In the eyes of the two families, the man failed. This doesn't happen everywhere, but when they are a righteous family, a woman going back to her father's house is the worst insult you could ever have. Because you failed to do your duty as a man and as a husband." Hayat stared at him, understanding more about the place of a husband between the linked families. "In his mind, Anas already failed once. Then, imagine him trying for a second time, and he already has a little girl. This man is probably as scared as you are." At first, the daughter wasn't realizing this part of the deal. Hayat was so focused on her own emotions and worried that she wasn't seeing the bigger picture.

"Saha baba." *Thanks, dad.* "Since he never showed a weak side, I never imagined this from him." Salim tucked her in for a hug.

"You're welcome, henunna. I'm here whenever you need to." A little chuckle escaped her. They stayed here for a while before getting called to eat dinner. Hayat almost ran to the living room. She was so excited to have her favorite dish. She helped Faudel to put the table in order to eat as quickly as possible.

The sounds of cutlery, with some discussion, filled the room. There were only laughs, and pleasant subjects when they were at the table. But when they were nearing the end of the meal, Lamia launched the hot topic of the moment: Anas. The mother didn't want to drop the matter. She absolutely wanted the two to go further in their relationship, she could already see herself welcoming her numerous grandchildren into the house. Hayat laughed oddly at her mother's requests, wanting to avoid the subject as much as possible. Her brother and her father exchanged a knowing look, understanding the situation. They tried to change the subject but in vain.

"'lesh rakoum tbeddlou lmodho'?" *Why are you changing the subject?* Hayat tried to contain her sigh, so she wouldn't sound disrespectful.

"Because there isn't any wedding yet, mama." Lamia laughed, thinking all of this was silly. Her daughter looked back at her plate. The change in the air was weighing on everyone's shoulders, except Lamia's.

"Don't say things like that, you will get to know him after the wedding. Just give me a date, so I can send the invitations." Hayat bit her cheeks so hard they almost started to bleed.

"Mama, it's ok. She will tell us when she's ready." Lamia's gaze drifted to her son, who was still not married at thirty years old.

"You're not even married, you don't know what you're talking about." It was too much. Hayat was about to call her to order, she could take the remarks for herself, but she couldn't see her brother dealing with the backlash when he was just trying to defend her. Salim saw the tone rise, so he took his daughter's hand before speaking.

"Lamia, khlass." *It's enough.* "She said she wasn't ready." Distraught, his wife protested.

"But Salim-" Without any hesitation, or being mean.

"I said, khlass Lamia." His tone was cool and low, so he didn't sound too harsh. He hadn't intervened to hurt his wife's feelings, but only to protect his children from her insistence. Without any further protest, Lamia changed the subject, and the once palpable ambiance became lighter and joyful. Even though Hayat still had that pressing feeling on her shoulders, she tried to blend in.

Acting as if nothing had happened.

Chapter 21

Anas took his daughter in his arms to get to the car as quickly as possible. In two hours they were to be at the family meal. Sofyan, had asked them to come because he had something to announce. Anas almost missed going as the family WhatsApp group was indefinitely muted after his divorce, but his brother had the decency to mention him and to send him a private message. Sofyan specified that they needed to look classy for this meal. So for the occasion, Anas put a pretty little sky-blue dress on his daughter, which matched perfectly with his shirt, and his black pants. He also braided her hair, adding a red bow at the end. Souhila was adorable with the strand of hair framing her face perfectly. Anas thought he already knew what Sofyan was about to announce, but he still wanted to give him a chance to do it himself.

Occasionally, the blinding sun disturbed his driving, but even if he seemed slightly late, he drove carefully on the highway. Casting a few glances at his daughter, making sure everything was fine on her end. She was so taken by the landscape that slipped by her side, that she didn't even realize the stress that emanated from her father. Certainly, he had already stated his boundaries, but he knew full well that it was not enough to protect them –

especially his daughter. Hakim said he would try to be better and Anas believed him, slightly, but he needed to prove himself. Anas couldn't swipe under the carpet three years of remarks, and humiliation, and pretend like it never happened.

Naturally, he was a little anxious to see them the day his little brother had an announcement. He hoped not to steal any attention and make a scene and ruin his moment. The warm rays of the sun gave him a soothing feeling, lightening his heavy heart. Anas thanked Allah for this moment of peace and quiet before he had to face the storm. During the last part of the trip, Souhila took a little nap, as if she recharged her batteries before joining her cousins to run, scream, laugh, and jump around. Sometimes, Anas was relieved to know that Souhila wasn't too affected by how her grandparents treated him. He sincerely wished to see them have a good relationship.

Anas parked in front of his parent's house, breathing one last time before gently waking up Souhila. Once they were both ready, they headed for the house, but before he had the chance to knock, Faiza had already opened the door to welcome them, especially her granddaughter.

"Salam a'leykoum benti!" Faiza said, opening her arms for Souhila to jump in them. She instantly did. Anas smiled at this view, he was a bit relieved.

"Wa'leykoum salam jaddati!" The little one responded automatically, happy to see her after a long time.

"Salam a'leykoum weldi!" Hakim greeted his son, trying to hug him. A little reluctantly, he returned the embrace quickly, before expecting something from his mother, but nothing. She had already gone to the living room, holding Souhila's hand.

"Wa'leykoum salam baba. Is mama still mad at me?" Hakim pinched his lips together, already knowing the answer. He tried to talk to her, but she wouldn't listen. In his mother's eyes, Zahia had been the best match for him Faiza chose her for him, and she couldn't accept the fact that she was wrong. A discussion between the two and they could remarry tomorrow if her son made the effort. At least that's what she believed.

"I'm sorry, I tried my best, but your mother is harder than a rock. Only Allah, and you, could make her see the light." Anas thanked his father before following him into the living room, and almost everyone was there, except for Sofyan.

The young man greeted them one by one, before sitting down between his two big sisters, who until now still pampered him like the little boy he once was, and he loved every instant of it. When they were younger, his sisters were much more present in his life than his parents. Often they prioritized those after him to his detriment. When he had a school event, the people present were more frequently Hafsa and Houria than his own parents. It made him sad, but Anas knew for a fact that his parents loved him unconditionally, even though they had a hard time showing it. This was one of the reasons he had sworn to care for his children equally. For now, he only had Souhila, and that was enough for him.

He was happy.

Sometime later, Sofyan finally entered the living room. Everyone was waiting for him, drinks and snacks in hand. After greeting them, he appeared in front of them, a big smile on his face. They looked at him impatiently for his announcement.

"So, I know you are all waiting for my announcement, but before that, I want to thank each one of you for coming here today, even with your busy schedules." Sofyan paused for a second, "I think some people already have their suspicions about today's subject since it's still a fairly recent topic that we had in this family." Hafsa and Houria stared at each other with open mouths, almost already screaming for their little brother. "I met someone! I wanted to wait a bit before saying anything, but I really want to take things further with her." In an instant, the silent room was now filled with loud celebration, *zagharit,* and screams of joy. They all surrounded Sofyan to hug and kiss him. But the happiness could not stay long, not with Faiza and the fact that she had not yet digested the divorce from her first son.

"Fortunately, this one won't be a fail…" Everyone shut their mouths. They were too stunned to speak. No one believed what Faiza just said, luckily no kids were in the room with them. Anas sneered while pushing his cheek with his tongue, totally irritated by his mother's behavior. He was about to break loose on her.

Sabr.

Patience.

That's the notion he used to calm his anger, but this was his last straw. Faiza has allowed herself to spoil the wonderful announcement. And now, when today should have been *his* day, Sofyan had an expression far too sad for Anas' liking. He knew that his little brother felt guilty since he was the one who had *forced* him to come.

"Three years. Three years! And you can't move on!" Anas almost screamed at Faiza. Hasfa came to his side to calm him down, but he refused to be touched. He was way too angry for that. Tears burned the corner of his eyes, "I waited for you, patiently, to change your mind. To face the fact that you were wrong, but you can't, can you?" His voice broke on the last word.

"I'm not wrong, you just need to go get Zahia back. But you're too busy running after a little girl far too young for you." Anas couldn't stop laughing at the hypocrisy.

"Oh yeah? What about khaltou then? Didn't she marry a man ten years older than her? Or does this rule only apply to me?" Faiza was unable to let that offense slide.

"As-skout! Hayawan." *Shut up! You animal.* She scolded him, "It was another time, you need to get back with your wife, end of discussion." Anas swallowed his emotions, knowing he was talking to a wall.

"There will be no end of discussion because you know what? Souhila and I *like* Hayat, and she's going to stay. Thebi we tkhrhi." *Whether you like it or not.* Faiza was about to snap at him, but Hakim stopped her. He knew his son took a step back. Something had to be done to get the pressure off, so Hafsa pulled Anas aside and led him out into the garden.

Thanks to a few walks, soft words from his sister, and a few caresses on his broad back, Anas felt the muscles in his body relax. They sat down on the garden chair, face to face, to discuss and change their minds. But Hafsa did not forget the words he had said before about Hayat.

"So, you like her?" Her little brother hoped she would have missed this information in all the chaos. The mere mention of Hayat could make him smile as he did back then. It was so nice to see.

"Yeah, we do. We do like her." The way he instantly included his daughter in the response made Hafsa smile too. Anas was a man, but a father at the same time. His choices directly impacted his daughter. It made her joyful to see her little brother have a new person who could bring him what he lacked in his life.

"Are you planning on marrying her?" Hasfa asked out of the blue, unable to hold back.

Anas chuckled at the sudden curiosity, "Yes, but she doesn't seem to be ready yet. So, I'm waiting. I will still see her, though, so she can decide soon enough." In a few movements, Hafsa brought her chair closer to her brother's, in order to take his hand in hers. She wanted to make physical contact with him, certain that it would be more comforting for Anas.

"You're doing the right thing, don't let mama's words change your mind. You're doing great, and we are here to support you." She paused, rearranging her posture in her chair. "I, personally, hope you will have a summer wedding, I want to take pictures outside, not in a gloomy room because it's too cold outdoors." Anas laughed at her suggestion. It was true that summer weddings were more pleasant than winter or fall because the temperature often left to be desired. However, it was not up to him to decide, since only Hayat could.

For a while, they continued to chat in the garden before returning to the living room. There was pin-drop silence as he stepped into the room.

Nevertheless, Houria tapped her husband on the shoulder so that they all resumed the discussion as if nothing had happened. Anas had chosen to stay for his little brother, but he didn't want anything to do with his mother at the moment. Sofyan had even come discreetly to apologize, his big brother scratched the top of his head, explaining to him that none of this was his fault and that he was eager to meet the woman Sofyan had chosen

After the meal, Anas picked up his daughter, greeted everyone before leaving to hit the road. Tomorrow Souhila had school, like her cousins, so she had to get up early. She had played so much that once in the car, she fell

170

asleep. The mere sight of his daughter in the rearview mirror made him forget everything he had just experienced. This event made him realize that he was really ready to take another step with Hayat. He liked her a lot already, and it wasn't just stubbornness against his mother's suggestions.

In complete silence, he drove back home, thinking about the next time he might see her.

Chapter 22

The house was filled with the sound of drills and sledgehammers. Each worker had his position and carried out their work under the sharp eye of Anas. He had a very specific plan, and he was going to make sure that it was going to be followed to the inch. Yesterday, they started to dig into the perfect garden to start the plan for the in-ground swimming pool. Seeing the trucks come and go to transport the dirt, and the workers working passionately to coordinate their movements, was actually his favorite moment. He imagined it as a big anthill where each ant had its post and knew exactly what it had to do. Anas looked at his watch, before seeing that the time had passed much too quickly. In twenty minutes, he had to be in front of his daughter's school to pick her up. Rapidly, he went to find the project manager to remind him of his instructions and that he had to follow the plan, except if there was a problem during the execution. In this case, he had to call him to offer him a solution.

Anas arrived in front of the school right on time. Luckily the kids weren't out yet, he would feel guilty for leaving his daughter to wait even a minute outside unprotected. As soon as he got out of his car, the school gate opened, allowing the numerous children to run to their parents. The air was filled with screams, laughter, and excitement, when a familiar little brown-haired child ran in his direction, before jumping into his arms. Anas inhaled her scent, welcoming her with warmth and love.

"Salam a'leykoum baba!" The little girl almost screamed in his ear. She was more excited than usual.

"Wa'leykoum salam benti." Anas said calmly, hugging her tight. Unfortunately, he knew he had to go back to work for a while. He had no babysitter, and he knew that his sister was already, at this hour, overwhelmed by her children. While she was beneath his arms, he thought of an idea, but it was far too daring to propose before being certain. Souhila began to tell him about his day in the smallest detail when he thought of a solution to his problem. He picked her up easily, then he put her in her toddler seat. Anas sat in the front, watching her in the rearview mirror. "Souhila, I need to make a call for a moment. Can we continue this after?" Anas asked nicely, waiting for her reaction. She responded positively to the request, patiently waiting for her father's attention again. Anas took out his phone, and dialed Faudel's number, hoping that he would answer directly. He bit his lower lip, before hearing a voice on the other end of the wire.

"Salam a'leykoum Anas! How are you?" Anas was partially relieved. The solution might be right in front of him.

"Wa'leykoum salam Faudel! Good and you?" He could hear the other smile at the other end.

"Do you want to set another date for a muqabala?"

Anas scratched the back of his neck, "No, no. Hum, I need a little service from Hayat."

"Which one?" The father looked at his daughter for a second, who was playing with her belt, partially listening.

"I need someone to keep Souhila today, and I can't bring her with me to the renovation site. It's too

173

dangerous." Faudel stayed silent for a moment, thinking about it.

"Let me call her, and I will call you back in a few minutes." They agreed and waited patiently for Hayat's brother's call. His heart was beating so fast, waiting for Faudel's response. It was his last hope. A few minutes later, Faudel called back. Anas was a little afraid to answer because he would rather not disturb her, but also he wanted to avoid exposing his daughter to danger.

"She said she was at home. You can drop your daughter off and come get her back after. She has nothing to do, except some designing." The father was so relieved. He thanked him, before hanging up.

"Baba, I still have important things to do at work. You will stay with Hayat for the rest of the afternoon, ok?" Anas said slowly, anticipating her reaction. For a few seconds, the little girl remained stoic, then her smile became even bigger than usual.

"Yeah!" Relieved, Anas drove off toward Hayat's apartment.

- ☾ -

In the silence of her room, all you could hear was the tapping of her digital pen on her tablet. Nothing could disturb her concentration. Or at least that's what she believed. Hayat was adding the finishing touches to her design, and her signature, when the doorbell rang, breaking her absolute silence. Was it the surprise his brother had mentioned earlier?

What did he deliver to me? The sibling thought, believing her brother ordered something for her.

What was her surprise when she looked in the peephole and saw Anas and Souhila waiting on the other side of the door. Completely taken aback, she took a hijab, covered herself, and in one movement she opened the door to a father completely desperate to have his daughter looked after by someone he trusted.

"Salam a'leykoum Hayat! How are you?" The tone of his voice was irregular, showing him the worry he had inside.

"Wa'leykoum salam Anas." She responded by trying to hold steady to hide her surprise. Her gaze got on the beautiful little girl at his side, "Salam a'leykoum Souhila!" She looked back at Anas, "I'm good! How about you?"

"I'm fine, thanks for keeping Souhila." That's when it all clicked in her mind.

That's my delivery... She said to herself, awkwardly smiling at Anas.

Souhila was the surprise.

She was going to be a babysitter for a few hours.

With the most grownup face possible, she ushered the little one into the apartment.

Anas continued. "I will be quick, I just needed to drop her to someone I trusted enough to keep her for a few hours. Again, thank you!" No response came from her mouth, that he was already gone. Hayat was a bit stunned at the moment. But she closed the door and looked at the little girl balancing her feet on the sofa. Hayat now had to think of things to do for a little girl her age, the problem was: she had none. Her gaze drifted to her last tablet, still showing her last design. And that's when she got an idea.

"Souhila, do you want me to show you something cool?" The petite brunette stopped her foot movements, thinking.

"Yes!" At this response, Hayat told her to follow her, which she did. The oldest took a second chair and put it beside her so that Souhila could look at her screen without having to come on her lap.

"So, what you see here is what I do for work." The little one looked at her, a smile on her face.

"You draw for work! I love drawing too, can I do the same when I am older?" Hayat chuckled, finding her reaction most adorable.

"Yes, you can." The woman pointed at her head, "You can do whatever you want if that big brain of yours is determined to do it." Hayat chuckled, finding her reaction most adorable. After a few minutes of discussion, Souhila and Hayat were laughing and trying funny things on her tablet. She left the child the freedom to draw whatever she wanted under her watchful eye, an accident quickly happened even sitting at a desk. Souhila had fun mixing colors, even if sometimes they didn't go together, they managed to find it pretty.

They spent almost an hour drawing funny figures before they both got hungry at the same time. Hayat had got up to prepare a small snack, and Souhila absolutely wanted to help her, but she had no chair for children. Thus, she gathered everything she needed to cut fruit and make small sandwiches, and went to the coffee table to prepare it.

"I will cut the fruits with the big knife, and you will have the spoons and make peanut butter and jelly sandwiches. Ok?" Souhila vividly nodded, accepting her dear mission. Hayat put a towel around her neck, hoping not to see any stains on her clothes when finished. The fruits were cut, and the sandwiches made, Hayat brought orange juice and apple juice, leaving her the choice between the two.

"Apple juice, please." Hayat smiled at Souhila, serving her a glass.

"Excellent choice!" After her glass was full of juice, the youngest began to talk about her day at school. How she got her first A, and how super happy she was with that grade. She had also started playing a new sport: dodgeball. The little girl had found it so fun to run around with a ball in her hands, with her friends, and shoot it at people. Hayat listened carefully, taking in every detail and mentally noting the names of her friends.

"And Sarah ran with the ball, threw it at me, and it almost landed on my head! Luckily, I was quick, and I avoided it." Hayat dramatically gasped, as if she was in her place. The two continued their discussion, unaware of the minutes passing. Souhila began to rub her eyes regularly, indicating that she was beginning to get tired. It was time for her to take a nap. Exceptionally, Hayat put her in her bed under her blanket, before leaving the door slightly open to keep an eye on her from afar. She made herself a coffee before sitting down at her desk, the hot mug in hand, she saw Souhila's drawing and decided to save the draft and pick up where she left off in her work.

When she pressed send, she was so focused that she didn't even notice the presence of the young girl at her side. Her heart raced for a fraction of a second, and she put her hand over her heart to calm it down.

"Hey, did you sleep well?" Hayat asked, still a bit shaken. Souhila hummed, her eyes fully opened. "Good, good." She checked the clock; seven half past. Anas should be here soon. Hayat put her hair in a bun, covered herself with a hijab, waiting for the bell to ring any minute. And the woman was right, only a few moments after that, someone was at the door. Souhila ran to it, put on her shoes, waiting for Hayat to open the door. As soon as she did so, the little girl jumped into her father's arms, happy to see him again. With one arm, he picked her up with it, without showing any signs of effort. Hayat felt a weird sensation washing over her, sending an electric shock down her spine. She weirdly smiled, trying to brush it off.

"Thanks again, Hayat, you really helped me. You can't even imagine." The woman nodded in return, while he rearranged a strand of hair behind his daughter's ear. "Did you have fun?"

"Yes! She drew all day for work, I want to be like Hayat. I want to do that too." Anas and Hayat chuckled at her response, finding her adorable. They exchanged a knowing look, before saying goodbyes.

The look he gave her every time he put his eyes on her was so mesmerizing. She couldn't look away. Warmth spread all over her body, making her speechless. The moment they were down the hall, Hayat closed the door fast behind her, feeling her cheeks burning. Slowly realizing she liked him more and more with each passing day.

"I'm screwed…" She breathed out.

Chapter 23

Today, Hayat was the one asking for the muqabala. She invited Anas, and Souhila, to a retro restaurant. 70s theme. With dim lighting and vintage decor. The walls were adorned with framed black-and-white photographs, and old vinyl records were displayed on the shelves. Hayat always wanted to eat in that specific type of restaurant, even if she only ate fish at the end. She loved the vibe, and how it looked. With Faudel, she was waiting for them at a table near the window, watching the passers-by, hoping to see them before they entered. After about twenty minutes, she saw them arrive. Hayat noticed that they still had matching clothes. It was so sweet. She made sure she had nothing on her face, or between her teeth, by asking her brother for help. He sneered when he saw his sister stressing out. Only a warning look in response was enough for him to get serious again. He rearranged a strand of hair, and it was enough.

As usual, she looked *wonderful*.

In just a few minutes, they had arrived at their table, with radiant good humor on their faces. While they sat down at their table, Anas and Souhila faced them, greeting them with a wide smile. For the first time since the beginning of the muqabalas, Hayat felt much more stressed than usual. They didn't even discuss yet that her heart was already racing so fast.

Subconsciously, she already knew the subject that gave her all these feelings: marriage.

She still had doubts, but after her last realization, she wanted to go a step further, *too*. However, Hayat didn't know how to approach the subject. Therefore, she let the discussion start and then go on for a while because there was one last question Hayat wanted to ask him before making her decision. At some point, Souhila asked to go play in the kid's area not far from the entrance, Faudel accompanied her, leaving Anas and Hayat alone for a moment.

"Last time we spoke about children, I forgot to ask to have a Genetic Compatibility Test, so we could see if we're compatible for a child." She explained, with a serious expression. Anas nodded without hesitation.

"Of course, I will book an appointment for that." Hayat smiled at him, thinking about another question also linked to intimacy. Last time she was too shy to continue on the subject, however now, she felt a bit more comfortable speaking about it.

"And a test for any disease, sexually transmissible, we wouldn't know about. To be safe, at least." Again, he agreed in an instant. "I also wanted to ask you something. I think it's probably still a sensitive topic for you, and you want to avoid disclosing more to me for now, but I still *need* to ask." She explained. Anas' features changed for a split second, wondering what she was about to ask. "Why aren't you with your ex-wife anymore?" Hayat dropped out of the blue. This was a question stuck in her mind since she discussed it with her father a few weeks ago. She could see vulnerability slip into his beautiful dark brown eyes.

Anas sighed and cleared his throat. "Hum, let's start with the beginning, then." He paused, thinking of how he could respond correctly. "As you know, I'm the first man in my family and to set an example, my mother tried to marry me off very young. When I was around nineteen years old, she started looking for a wife on my behalf, but I declined every time since I had no degree or even money. A few years later, when I was twenty-four, I had my degree and then my first job, so she presented me to a woman around my age. Zahia. The feeling was good, she was a woman on the deen, and we were on the same page. Anyway, these are the details. Within two weeks, we decided to get married and start our life… " Anas felt his throat go dry, so he took a sip of his drink before continuing. Hayat didn't interrupt him, thinking that if she did, he wouldn't find the strength to tell her more about it. "Zahia wanted to have children, so much. We tried, for a long time. She had five miscarriages, until Souhila. She is our rainbow baby. You can imagine the impact of those miscarriages on her mental and physical health. As a husband, I tried my best to be there for her. Comfort her, love her. To be the rock she needed at that time." He paused again, eyes drifting to the window, remembering all the bitter memories. Hayat felt guilty to inflict that on him just out of curiosity. "When Souhila was born, she was the sun in our life. For the first few months, Zahia looked tired and exhausted. At that time, my business was the most flourishing, so I was able to be at home more often, and be there for her and the baby. Then Zahia seemed to do better, she was more active. She would go out, go for a walk, and take care of the baby more regularly. And a few days after Souhila turned three, I was coming home from kindergarten with Souhila, Zahia told me she couldn't pick her up, so I did. When I came back home, she disappeared. The only thing I could find was an envelope, with divorce papers in it." Anas pinched his lips together.

"I'm so sorry, I shouldn't have asked you this. You're not obligated to continue." With a weak smile on his face, he still decided to go through. Even if you pass this type of experience, diving into these memories was still hard.

"No, it's ok. You have the right to know, so you can understand me and my situation a bit more. After she asked for a divorce, I felt my world crumble under my feet. My wife disappeared, and I'd probably lose my daughter in the process. Obviously, I tried to contact her and make her come back to me, but I found nothing. Months passed, and I decided to go through her stuff, since I was clueless about why she left. That's when I found a letter for me, and signed papers where she renounced her rights over Souhila. Zahia was explaining why she left. She had postpartum depression and was unable to love our daughter – the way she wished to. She was tired all the time and was unable to meet the demands of motherhood. Zahia suffered, for three years, each time she looked at what she dreamed of having, and it made her almost hate her. The irony of the situation killed her. So, she left. Obviously, I never told Souhila why she really left. It would break her into pieces. So I burned the letter when I finished reading it." The saddest thing about all of this was the fact that Anas was not sorry for him, but for his ex-wife and for his daughter. With one breath, Hayat recollected herself, not wanting to appear more moved than him when it was not her story. Thanks to this explanation, Hayat understood more about the man before her. The bond he had with his daughter, the way he smiles when he talks about her, or whenever she was mentioned. Anas was emotionally wrapped around that little girl's finger, but not in a bad way.

He didn't blindly grant her every wish. What she saw behind this story was a man capable of empathy, not ashamed to show emotion.

"Thanks for telling me, I feel so sorry to make you reveal this and relive it again." They exchanged a knowing look, before taking a bite of their dishes, as if it would brush off this weird feeling they were sharing. At some point, it worked, but when Faudel and Souhila came back they could sense it in the air.

Faudel tried to break the ice, "Why do you look like you both received bad news? Did something happen?" For a second, Anas and Hayat looked at each other, not knowing what to say in response. Then, he came up with something.

"No, don't worry. Everything is going perfectly, right, Hayat?" Hayat got lost in his gaze. He was indirectly asking her to follow him on this one. She looked at her brother, with a big smile on her face, putting a hand on his shoulder.

"Yes, it's all good habibi don't worry." Hearing this nickname, Anas had a peculiar reaction, somewhat. His ears turned pink and warm. There was a part of him that wanted to hear her use it to call him. Uncomfortable with that stupid thought, he cleared his throat before continuing the conversation with them.

For dessert, they shared a slice of homemade apple pie, topped with a scoop of vanilla ice cream. When she looked at Anas, Hayat finally had her answer. She finally knew that she wanted to continue her journey with him and try to build something together. She looked at him intently, the answer burning her mouth. Hayat didn't want to interrupt them, but she had to tell him before she left. The warmth of her body began to become more and more important, giving her a feeling of a second skin. Once the discussion seemed calmer, Hayat took the opportunity to finally free herself from this subject.

"Anas, for the proposition you made last time." His attention got back on her, making her even hotter. "Yes, I would love to have the address for the dress." Anas' eyes widened in surprise. Understanding was instantaneous on his side, but this was not the case for Faudel and Souhila. Both were completely lost. Why would she talk about dresses after a drastically different discussion? The dismayed laughed loudly among themselves. "I'm saying yes to his marriage proposal." Faudel's mouth formed a wide "O" and then the news hit him with a second wave.

"Wait! We need to tell everyone." Faudel was getting ready to take out his phone, while his sister was laughing. She cut him off, taking it from his hands.

"We're going to tell them, but in person." Hayat looked at Anas with a big smile on his face. This growing bond between them was seen more and more and was a pleasant sight to witness.

Chapter 24

The sun slowly kicked in, warming every being awake at this hour, coloring the sky with orange and yellow tints. Hayat enjoyed the sunrise, a coffee in her hand, sipping from it the hot and dark brown substance slowly on the outdoor swing. She was trying to relax before the imminent stress she was going to receive today. The ambient air as well as her coffee did her a lot of good considering the events planned. Anas and Hayat are going to make it official. They will start planning a wedding. A *nikkah*. They will start preparing *the* contract to seal their union. Just thinking about it, Hayat was already feeling all the stress that was about to fall on her shoulders. A small wedding, that was her wish. Friends and family only. Without music or gender mixing. Hayat knew it would be hard to convince her mother.

Lamia was fond of big events.

For her, the events were to be shared, the more people there were, the more witnesses could spread the news. But also, there was this cultural rule – which Hayat found very irritating: if they invited you to one of their weddings, you *must* invite them to yours. It was no longer a choice, but an obligation. When she was younger, she managed to end up at weddings she had no clue about.

She would rather not have people she had only seen once at the most important day in her life. Even if it meant her community would complain about it later.

It was her day and Anas', no one else's.

So, Hayat gave herself a little strength to challenge the proposals for invitations, ballroom, or even caterers that wouldn't even serve something good or suitable for everyone. Hayat, lost in her thoughts, barely noticed the weight that was added to the swing. Salim had just sat down, too, to watch the sunrise. He put a hand on her shoulder, to make her realize his presence.

"Sbah el kheir benti." *Good morning, my daughter,* "Ready for today?" Anxiety flashed in her eyes.

"Sbah el noor baba, I hope so. At least…" In a movement filled with compassion and warmth, Salim brought her closer to him. He knew full well the worries that crossed her mind. The father, too, had been there before.

"Kheir In Shaa Allah, we're here to help you overcome this feeling benti." At these words, Hayat snuggled up against her father, this simple gesture melted her worries. A kiss on the top of her head was enough to make her heart feel at peace.

"Do you think we will make a good couple?" The question came out of nowhere, but she still wanted her father's opinion.

"Allahou a'lam." *Only God knows.* "What I think does not matter, Hayati. If Allah made you get this far, He got His reasons, and it's on you to discover them." Salim paused for a second, admiring his daughter's beautiful face. He brushed the hair from her face, before pinching Hayat's big cheeks. "If you called for Him throughout your decisions, and you came to this day, then you have your answer. There are no coincidences, hanunna, and you know it." It wasn't really the answer she expected, but her father was absolutely right. For a time, she remained silent, slowly accepting his words.

"True, thanks baba." He kissed her one more time before she left. The hennaya was soon here to get her ready for the day, Lamia insisted her daughter should get something on her hand to make them look good. The mother was taking this as an engagement party when Hayat wasn't on the same page. She wanted to keep it simple.

Therefore, Hayat made a deal with Lamia: it will simply be the families, and Kamila – and her family – but there will be no party, nothing grand. By accepting this agreement, she avoided taking weeks of preparation, wasting money, and time for merely formalizing the relationship socially.

In terms of attire, Lamia, who was expecting a party, had prepared a traditional Algerian outfit for her: a red and gold Karakou. It was *stunning*. Hayat was a little embarrassed to see the time she had invested in preparing this surprise, so she put it on to please her mother, even though she thought it was too dressy. Lamia helped her put on this sumptuous outfit, the mother gave her a soft smile, admiring the final result on her daughter. Under the emotion, she had a few tears in the corner of her eyes. She wiped them away instantly, not wanting to sound too emotional. Hayat was going to console her when the hennaya entered the room, her father must have opened the door for her. The hannaya, who was surely younger than Hayat, introduced herself to them.

"Salam a'leykoum! I'm Rahma, your mother called me to do your henna today. Are you ready? Did you think about models?" She smiled, delighted to do this service. Lamia left the two together, in order to add the finishing touches to Hayat.

"Wa'leykoum salam. Thanks for coming today, and yes, I'm ready, but I didn't think about anything for today. Do you have suggestions?" Rahma came to sit in front of her, with her little bag in hand, before taking out her phone, offering her several models that she had already performed before and brand-new models that she would like to try. The two agreed on a photo, and the hennaya got to work.

When one hand was finished, Kamila stormed into the room out of breath, half-prepared with a small case in hand, ready to put on makeup before putting on her outfit.

"Salam a'leykoum! Wow, your hand looks so nice." She looked at the hennaya, "Good job!" Kamila said, a thumbs up to Rahma, who smiled and greeted her back. Hayat laughed softly at her friend.

"Wa'leykoum salam hbiba. You arrived early. Why didn't you come with your family?" Kamila stared at her for a solid minute, wondering whether this was a real question or not.

"Babe, you're my best friend, and you thought *I* would come with everyone? Did you lose your mind?" The oldest looked slightly offended, making her friend chuckle.

"No, but look, you're not even prepared yet. You brought all this makeup, and they are coming in less than an hour." Kamila pointed at her with a brush, warning her with a burning look.

"Don't underestimate me hbiba, watch me doing my makeup, my hair, get dressed, help to put your hijab on, *and* help your mom in less than an hour." Hayat was thrilled to see her friend succeed in the little challenge.

"Bet." Kamila raised an eyebrow, accepting it. This simple sentence signaled the beginning of a race against time. Once the other hand was finished, Kamila was already down to her hair. Hayat thanked Rahma, who was about to leave, but her client offered to let her stay a bit if she had time. She couldn't go without enjoying some snacks that Lamia had taken her evening to prepare. Rahma gladly accepted, staying with Hayat and Kamila in the room. A warm and friendly atmosphere was born between them. Rahma told them how she had come up with the idea of doing hennaya on weekends, to pay for her studies. It reminded the older ones of the lives they had led a few years ago. Studying and working at the same time.

There were only a few minutes left before their arrival, and Kamila succeeded in her challenge. She looked breathtaking in her emerald green *jebba*. It went perfectly with her simple golden makeup, her brown hair, and her matte complexion. She helped Hayat put on her red hijab properly, before going downstairs to help Lamia in the kitchen. Once again, Hayat was going to have to wait a while before introducing herself to the families downstairs. Before leaving, Rahma gave her some advice to accentuate the color of her henna. They greeted each other, and Hayat now found herself alone, facing her concerns and her many questions.

- ☾ -

This morning, Anas woke up Souhila very early, unlike usual on weekends. For a good half hour, he had to cuddle her so that she would wake up slowly, without being in a bad mood afterward. The day before, they had both chosen the outfits they were going to wear. Once her stomach was full, Anas put her in front of the bathroom mirror. Souhila was reading out loud the new book her father bought her last Monday. Anas let her hair curl in its natural form, adding only braids on top of the notch, keeping her locks out of her face for the day. He added a small purple bow to her that went perfectly with her dark purple *caftan*. For the occasion, Anas had cut his hair and trimmed his beard. He, too, had his midnight blue *jabador* waiting for him in his bedroom. He couldn't wait to see what Hayat looked like today. See what she had picked to wear. Once he dressed his daughter, he hurriedly dressed himself before going to get the flowers he had ordered.

A bouquet of white roses.

He knew very well what message they conveyed.

On the road, Souhila fell asleep several times, since she had woken up way too early today. This time, Anas was not going to pick his siblings up. They were all going on their own, not forgetting to pick up all the gifts and cakes for the future bride. Before going, he added a personal gift (among the others) that he just got last afternoon: a dublah. That matched a wedding ring with his, and hers, initials on it. Anas was positive that it was the right size, since he secretly asked Salim if he could borrow one of her rings to match it. The closer he got to the destination, the more he was stressed.

He was going to do this again.

Sharing his life with someone new terrified him.

Was she also going to disappear overnight? He thought, looking at Souhila sleeping in her seat. *Will I be able to make her stay? To love her enough to keep her?*

With a quick shake of his head, he made these questions disappear, far too heavy for such a day. He should only have joy and good humor, no bad thoughts were allowed. To change his mind, Anas started listening to the Qu'ran – at a low volume, since Souhila was still sleeping – to ease his worries. The sunlight hitting his face, combined with the beautiful recitation, was so pleasing. It made him feel a bit more confident. They were only a few minutes away from Hayat's childhood house.

His palms were *sweating*.

Heart *racing*.

Temperature *rising*.

He could already see his brothers' cars parked in front of the house. Sofyan was with their parents and Nourdine was with his wife and his kids. The only ones missing were Houria, her husband and children, and Hafsa. They should be there soon. Anas woke Souhila up slowly, making sure she was ready to walk. As soon as he parked his car, and opened her door, Souhila jumped to join her cousins. This was perfect, he had his hands free to get the bouquet out and take the little gift in his other hand. When he was also out, he joined his family, waiting for the rest of the family to come. He greeted them, before getting cheered up by his brothers. Anas was about to call Hafsa when he saw a car park next to them.

They were here.

Everyone looked so beautiful for a little formality, it made him wonder how they'd look at the wedding itself. They all wore traditional outfits, the men, and kids too. It was heart-warming to see that they all made an effort for him and Hayat.

Right before he knocked at the door, his sisters held his arms to give him a boost of confidence. Like the first time, he rang the bell, notifying his presence.

It was time.

He will soon be engaged to Hayat.

She will soon be engaged to Anas.

Chapter 25

The bright sun added warmth to the wonderful ambiance they were in. The joyful celebrations, applause, *zagharit*, were loud enough for the whole neighborhood to hear. Once in, Anas scanned the room, hoping his eyes would lend in a pair of hazel ones. However, she wasn't there.

A bit of gloominess washed over him.

Gently, he gave the flowers to Lamia who took them to Hayat's room. Her eyes got wider when she saw them. A warm feeling spread into her chest, turning her white cheeks red and kindly matching the colors of her outfit. Hayat looked at her hands one last time, the henna was so beautifully executed, it made her smile. Right before they arrived, she added press-on to her nails, since she hadn't done them in a while. Now Hayat seemed perfect from head to toe. Before leaving, Lamia kissed the top of her forehead, giving her confidence. Earlier, her brother and father did the same.

Downstairs, the discussions were getting increasingly energized when it suddenly fell silent a while later. Hayat therefore suspected that Anas had proposed and that Salim would soon appear in the doorway of her room. Her heart started to beat faster, and faster, each second passing.

It will soon be *official*.

They will soon be official.

Salim appeared a few seconds later, looking as beautiful as ever. With a wild smile on his face, he came for her, and she knew it. Instantly, she got up, took his arm, and walked down the stairs with him. Anas heard them coming, and his heart was ringing in his ears, its drumming was so strong it would probably come out of his chest anytime soon. The words stuck in his throat as his eyes fell on Hayat. The *karakou* she wore suited her to delight. The moment she stepped into the room, and her gaze met his, time seemed to slow down. *Zagharit* started to fill the room. Making this moment more memorable.

Second seemed like minutes, minutes like hours, and hours like days.

He was totally mesmerized by her. By her eyes, her features, her beauty. This time dilation only made the view more pleasant. She was so beautiful, he couldn't look at her any longer without feeling guilty. Sensing this hot sensation spread into his body, and betraying his stoic face. Anas drifted his gaze to his sisters, who had a gigantic smile on their faces. Everyone knew she was gorgeous. Salim accompanied her to the women's side, making sure she couldn't see the garden, before returning to the men's side. Kamila looked at her friend for a moment, feeling proud – she also sensed a look on her, but she was too busy hyping Hayat up.

While the men continued the discussion, the women began to hand-deliver the gifts to Hayat. All wrapped up beautifully with satin ribbons. She thanked them one by one, feeling far too spoiled for the situation. Exceptionally, they had the right to walk with the shoes in the house. Souhila came twice to Hayat, just to tell her how beautiful she was and show her the dress she was wearing.

The little girl was *adorable*.

The afternoon continued and Salim announced that the buffet outside was ready. To her surprise, Hayat looked at her mother, who shared a sly smile with Kamila. The two had organized this little surprise, there was even a cake with the initials of Anas and Hayat. She wanted it to remain a mere formality, but these two together sure knew how to turn it into extravagance. The garden was decorated with home-grown lilies and chrysanthemums. Though Hayat had clearly specified her wishes for the day… Deep down, she appreciated the gesture, because she knew full well that they were doing it in a way to please her and make this day memorable. Small groups formed in the garden, each had taken what they wanted from the buffet. How had she missed this organization? Hayat must have been far too absorbed in her preoccupations not to notice such a setting.

The afternoon was going wonderfully until Hayat found herself chatting with Anas' mother. Ever since they met, Hayat felt something unusual from looking at her. Admittedly, she hadn't interacted with her much, but the little she saw made her doubt her goodness and her investment in this relationship. The more the discussion progressed, the more uncomfortable she felt.

"Ah! Benti, Anas told me you worked. Are you going to stop after the marriage?" Hayat frowned, not understanding the statement.

"We already discussed the matter together. And he's ok with me working. Why wouldn't I?" Anas' mother gave her a fake smile. Preparing her answer.

194

"Because his ex-wife did." She answered, laughing. With each chuckle, Hayat's muscles tensed little by little. "You need to be better than Zahia if you want to keep him." Hayat's mouth dropped open in shock, fully understanding the innuendo behind her words. For a second, she was silent, considering an appropriate response to this out-of-place interaction. Hayat was about to snap, feeling her anger winning the best of her when she sensed a presence behind her that towered over her even more. Then a silky, hoarse voice caressed her ear, making her shiver like never before.

"Can I know why *you* are mentioning the name of my *ex*-wife to my *future* wife, mama?" Anas had apparently heard his mother's words and decided to intervene before Hayat did something she might have regretted. Hayat didn't even dare to turn around to look at Anas, she could feel the warmth of his body emanating from him in a way she didn't really appreciate. She persisted in her displeasure.

Faiza opened her eyes wide, raising her eyebrows. "Future wife? Anas we know it's only a phase, and you will soon realize that your only match is Zahia." Hayat's mouth opened furthermore. Her heart was aching. She could hear Anas contract his jaw, as he noticed the twitch in Hayat's mood, before speaking again.

"Hayat, could you please excuse us for a moment?" His fiancée didn't even have time to answer. Anas took his mother's hand before forcing her to walk away and go where the cars were. This action drew attention, and Kamila joined her best friend.

"Hey babe, what happened?" She put her hand on Hayat's arm. She was still in shock when she explained to her friend what had just happened.

"His mom just compared me to his ex-wife." Now it was Kamila's turn to be in shock. She was about to go there and scream at her to leave, but Hayat held her back. A weak smile on her face, she would rather avoid making a scene, and her friend instantly understood.

Anas, in front of the house with his mother, was trying to calm his emotions. "Why? Why mama?" He pinched the bridge of his nose, hard enough to leave a trace. "You're going too far." Faiza chuckled in her son's face, irritating him even more.

"Anas we both know you still love Zahia. She's the love of your life. She is the mother of your child." With these simple words, Anas saw red.

"Stop! Mama, please stop!" His tone was loud enough for Hayat and Salim to come running, seeking to investigate the situation. They both came to his side, slightly bothered by her behavior. When he saw her face, Anas calmed down. Salim put a hand on Anas' shoulder, capturing his full attention. His heart, once filled with anger, found himself more peaceful in their presence. This time it was up to Hayat's father to impose his boundaries.

"You have two solutions here. Either you respect my family, and my daughter, or I will make you leave with your husband. Who's actually coming to you right now." Not believing him, Faiza turned around and witnessed Hakim walking to them, fuming from his wife's behavior. Before she could even add anything, her husband took her, bringing her behind his back.

"Salim, please excuse my wife. I'll talk to her, and keep her with me for the rest of the day. Let us stay until the end, you won't hear from her anymore." Hayat's father thought about it for a while, before giving his final decision.

"I forgive you, but your wife needs to apologize to my daughter. She disrespected her." At these words,

Hakim pushed his wife to regret her actions. Like a child who was punished, she apologized quickly before returning to the buffet under her husband's dark gaze. Salim moved away to give space to Hayat and Anas. He turned to his fiancée, a sorry expression on his face.

"I'm so sorry for what my mother said, I never thought she would be bold enough to say this to you..." Presently, Hayat wanted to take him in her arms in order to erase this unbearable expression off his face. But she couldn't – at least not yet.

"Anas, you don't have to be sorry for someone else's behavior. You stood up for me against your mother, this alone proved a lot. Thank you." The two young people looked at each other for a while, as if in a single gaze, they were saying much more to each other than the words heard before. A throat clearing called them to order.

"Let's go back to the not-party party." Salim said, laughing. They joined him with this simple joke.

Once they were back in the garden, they saw that Hakim had kept his word. He had taken his wife to a corner, making sure no one spoke to her but him. She hung her head down in shame. Kamila called everyone to stand around the table where they were going to cut the cake, Anas had planned to give her his personalized gift before the cake-cutting ceremony. Hayat was once again the last to know about the plan. Once behind the table, and at a respectable distance from each other, Anas handed her a small box, which she took hesitantly. Words failed her when she saw the count. A simple, yellow gold ring with today's date engraved inside. She hastened to put it on, a smile on her face. Congratulations and cries of joy filled the silence that surrounded them. In reality, Hayat had liked the surprise. Maybe she will actually listen to her mother's suggestions for her marriage. Each with a knife in hand, both began to cut the cake at the same time. With shared joy, the cake was distributed to visitors by Anas and Hayat.

Hayat's gaze lingered on each of them, a smile on her face. The smaller events were always the best. For a second, she noticed that her brother's gaze lingered on one person, but he looked away before she could see who it was. Hayat would certainly ask him about it later.

In her thoughts, she stared at the ring around her finger, indicating her new status to everyone looking at her hands. A new feeling came over her, but she couldn't describe it.

All she knew was that she felt good and relaxed.

From the moment Anas gave her the ring, he couldn't stop staring at her. Hayat was beautiful and wore a ring to indicate that she would become his. Soon they would have to meet more frequently, to plan their wedding but also choose his wedding ring. A ring that also signified to the world that Anas had his heart taken. She smiled at the thought of seeing a ring around his finger.

Anas approached Hayat, still at a certain distance, before whispering to her, "I just know the other ring will look wonderful on you." In other words, Anas was already calling Hayat *his*. This simple thought made her blush, so hard, that she was now matching with her karakou. Seeing her change color, he chuckled a bit before receiving a scorching glare that silenced him instantly.

Now they were laughing together.

Everyone could witness that this union would lead to something unique.

Chapter 26

Anas and Hayat were finally committed after months of muqabalas, and they were on cloud nine. He and his daughter were waiting at the jewelry store, so they could finally choose the ring. They both agreed on a date in a month and a half, and they needed to get everything ready together before then. Sadly, he couldn't match Hayat's ring to the color of it, since men aren't allowed to wear gold.

The Messenger of Allah ﷺ said: "Gold and silk have been permitted for the females of my Ummah, and forbidden to the males."[8]

A few minutes later, the young woman arrived with her brother by her side. The smile on her face gave him butterflies. Since the engagement, Hayat – in Anas' eyes – seemed much brighter than before. The reflection of the light on her ring caught Anas' eyes, which made him smile a little. Arriving at their level, Hayat had kept her broad smile, ready to pick her future husband's wedding band.

---

[8] Narrated from Abu Musa, Reference : Sunan an-Nasa'i 5148, In-book: Book 48, Hadith 109, English translation: Vol. 6, Book 48, Hadith 5151.

His fiancée already had an idea of what she was going to pick for him.

"Salam a'leykoum! How are you doing?" Hayat greeted them, a tint of excitement in her tone.

"Wa'leykoum salam, Hayat. We are good, how about you two?" Anas answered, before shaking Faudel's hand, who was standing a little behind today, his phone glued to his ear. Probably an important call.

"Good too, let's go inside, I already have an idea for you." She told him before setting foot in the jewelry store. In reality, Anas was a little excited to see the materialization of her idea. Hayat had waited so long for this day that she had taken the time to draw the design she was looking for; a simple silver signet ring, to carry on the thumb, with the engraving "H & A" on it. She only needed his size.

This will be one of her wedding gifts to Anas.

The jeweler greeted them with a broad smile, before presenting him with a string of samples so that she could find the starting model. Not finding the design she had imagined, she asked if it was possible to create the model from another. The designer showed him her drawing, so he could have an idea of the final result she wished.

"Miss Mazari, we don't have this model in stock at the moment. We can add you to a waiting list for this model, or we could create the model custom-made for you. It will be a shorter process, but pricier." Hayat seemed a little disappointed not to find her happiness. Anas noticed it.

"How long is the waiting list?" She started biting the inside of her cheeks, scared to see it would take too much time.

"Let me check," he kindly said before tapping on his keyboard. "Eight weeks." It was too long of a wait, and they both knew it. She looked at him for a second, unsure of what to do. Hayat was about to speak, but Anas preceded her.

"How much?" he asked, staring at the jeweler.

"For the custom-made one?" He nodded, "Three thousand dollars." Anas considered the price on his side, while Hayat was already thinking about taking another model. They exchanged a look, checking if they were on the same page. Her fiancé took the initiative as if he had a plan in mind as well, but she was still uncertain.

"Perfect, when can we come get it?" The jeweler smiled at him, pleased with this choice. He noted in his notebook, the name of the buyer then looked back at him.

"In two weeks. You must make a deposit of fifty percent of the amount today." Hayat looked at her brother before signing the deposit. She wasn't sure of this decision, but she still wanted to give him a wedding gift as symbolic as this one. As they were about to leave, Hayat noticed that she had forgotten her bag inside. The youngest told them she'll only take two minutes, before pushing them outside. The jeweler handed her the bag, before returning to his activity, but she requested the jeweler to add a little detail to the ring.

"On the inside of the ring, I would love to add the name "Souhila", is that possible?" He nodded, sure that he would make it happen.

"No problem, is that a surprise?" Hayat smiled at him.

"Yes, it's his daughter's name." He did the same before giving her the new price, and she paid him instantly. Before it got too suspicious, Hayat came out with her bag in hand, a smile on her face to not blow up her cover. After picking out the perfect wedding ring at the jeweler, they decided to head to a nearby coffee shop to spend the afternoon together.

They took a seat at a table, and Hayat couldn't help but notice her sparkling engagement ring. Since his fiancée returned, she had a grin on her face, and all signs of dissatisfaction vanished from her features, leaving Anas beaming with joy. The group ordered some coffee, tea, and sweets, while Anas and Hayat began to chat about the wedding plan and Faudel was playing with Souhila. Before them, a pile of wedding magazines and papers. They were planning their small and intimate *nikkah* ceremony, and Hayat was excited about all the details that needed to be considered. Anas smiled as he watched Hayat flipping through the pages of wedding magazines, pointing out different ideas for the decor, and the cake.

They started suggesting menus, themes, and even guests. The fact that the two were on the same page when it came to arranging was quite pleasing. A small nikkah, with friends and family, an open menu so everyone could eat, and no music. Hayat proposed signing the contract at her local masjid, since her father was very close to the imam. Anas took notes of every one of her suggestions, occasionally pushing back his glasses, in order to present them to his family later. Both knew very well that two details were going to disturb their parents – especially their mothers; the music and the fact that the party was limited in terms of guests.

This wish simply went against their culture.

However, the future bride and groom preferred a small wedding with the *baraka* of Allah even if it meant being criticized by the community, than pleasing the community and not having the *baraka* of their Lord.

"So, what do you think about the beige decor? I was thinking about keeping it simple and elegant," said Hayat, looking up at Anas.

"I think it's a great idea," replied Anas with a soft smile.

"Ok, what about the guest list? I only have my family and Kamila and her family, what about you?" asked Hayat, looking at Anas for his guest list.

"I have my brothers and sisters, and their families. I will specify that I only want the close family to come since I'm pretty sure my family has probably already invited the whole town…" Hayat smiled, laughed even, thinking it would be a small inconvenience, then she remembered how Faiza acted the day of their engagement. Her facial expression dropped.

"Will it be easy for you?" Her tone had more worries in it.

Anas continued eating his pastries, "I don't know, I shall see." He huffed lightly, like extracting pressure from his shoulders that he didn't want to add yet. Noticing this, Hayat then moved on to another, much more important topic that they still hadn't touched on. Dowry. *El Mahr.* The right that was truly hers as a Muslim woman. She had thought about it for a long time, even before she met Anas.

"There is a point that we still haven't addressed, and that was totally out of my mind until now." Hayat stated, sipping from her drink. His interlocutor nodded, waiting for her point. "El Mahr." She paused, waiting for his reaction, but he wasn't going to bat an eye. "I thought of doing this as a sort of palm tree, and I know you can afford that expense given the work you do and how flourishing it is. I have already taken that into account. Thirty thousand dollars if you don't incur any expenses for the wedding, twenty-five thousand dollars if we make fifty-fifty, and

fifteen thousand dollars if you pay absolutely everything."
When Hayat announced her way of thinking, she thought
that Anas would be reluctant to the idea, but this one
seemed to agree with this reflection. As if it seemed
logical, not extravagant.

"I see, pretty fair if we are being honest. Can we
agree on the thirty thousand dollars? Even if I intend to pay
a part, I think that thirty thousand dollars is still a
reasonable amount for my situation." Hayat's eyes got
wilder, confused. This wasn't how she conceived the
discussion around that topic.

"But, how is it fair for you to pay thirty thousand
dollars, and be invested financially into the wedding? I
know we said a small wedding, so small expenses.
However, I'll feel bad if you pay this much." Anas looked at
her sympathetically, wanting to reassure her on the
subject.

"I made my choice, Hayat. For me, it seems fair
enough to give my wife the first amount she had in mind if I
can pay it. It is within your right to ask for a just amount,
and by seeing the method you thought about, you actually
took my situation into account, so I'll take your thoughts
into account, too." Hayat was now faced with a dilemma,
how could she accept such a sum when she had already
thought about her system – in the first place? It didn't seem
fair to her, yet Anas seemed determined to make her
understand that it wasn't going to be a question or even a
debate. Hayat sought her brother's gaze as if to comfort
herself with the idea that it was nothing, but the chaperon
was much too busy playing with Souhila. She knew full well
that she had already lost against him, so she gave up on
the idea of continuing her opposition.

"Ok, then let's go for this amount. Also, I want to
have a civil wedding." Anas looked at her.

"Do you want to do a contract or not?" Hayat now found herself surprised. Anas was again so easygoing on these subjects.

"Yes, I do." He, for his part, noted that he would soon have to arrange an appointment with the notary in order to prepare the formalities. They continued to discuss their nikkah plans. Anas and Hayat were excited about the big day and couldn't wait to celebrate their relationship with their family and friends. Anas loved how excited she was about everything and couldn't wait to make her dreams come true. For a while, they continued discussing the preparation, but also the vacation they could go with Souhila. They wanted to choose a place where his daughter would like it too. Both had agreed on Malaysia; a Muslim country with magnificent landscapes, and the culture was also to be seen and experienced. It was the best choice they had presently in terms of a first sitting. Souhila was also thrilled to benefit from this new destination, she will soon be on a school break.

It was perfect timing.

As the afternoon drew to a close, they all finished their drinks and their sweets. While discussing upcoming events, and things they would like to see together. Faudel even suggested a new release soon, but Hayat and Anas were far too busy for that at the moment. Until the details were perfect, or at least thought out and prepared, they couldn't afford to be distracted. The outfits still had to be checked, the caterer with a menu also had to be called and scheduled, the contract also had to be prepared and then styled, and the list went on and on. Everything still had to be done, so the time for small distractions was not allowed.

Anas and Hayat exchanged a look, completely thrilled to have their soul linked for what, they hoped, would be *forever*.

Chapter 27

One month left from their nikkah, and Hayat's mother was still trying to convince her daughter to book a ballroom for a bigger party. On this point, Hayat was adamant she didn't want a big party, music, or guests she barely knew. It was her day. Not her mother's. Lamia had a hard time accepting the absence of music, but the guest issue was the worst one for her.

"Ya Hayat, khoudi salla!" *Hayat, book a ballroom!* "How can I invite them if we only do this in the masjid, and our garden? It won't be enough. You don't want a henna, you don't want music, and now no guest? You can't do that." Hayat pinched the bridge of her nose, annoyed to have this discussion for the fiftieth time since her engagement. This was Lamia's technique from day one. Talking about the same matter, over and over, until she had what she wanted. Brainwashing her daughter till she became the blank canvas where Lamia could paint her *own* outlook of Hayat's future. The only person it never worked on was Salim. Until this day, his daughter was still wondering how he managed to endure this.

"Mama, here's the plot twist: you won't! Goutlek shal men khetra?" *How many times did I already tell you?* "I can't even remember. So, madabik," *please,* "Mama,

Neya B

don't make me say it again. If I see one person I don't know that day, I will ask Faudel and baba to make them leave. Fhemti?" *Understood?* "We only need at least two men witnesses, not fifty." Her daughter got up, irritated by this discussion, she no longer had the head to continue making calls all afternoon to find a suitable caterer. Lamia was about to follow her, but this will only fan the fire. Therefore, Salim intercepted her to make her sit back where she was. With this simple action, she stayed there pouting like a kid.

Hayat swung her feet to ease her anger, even though it was already at the top. Her mother only added her stress when she needed comfort and peace. As always. While he sat down, Salim disrupted Hayat's regular rhythm, causing her to raise her head.

"Wesh sra?" *What happened?* His daughter sighed, lining on his shoulder.

"Once again, mama is trying to make it happen like *she* wants when I already said no several times." She paused, trying to cool her tone when she was speaking to her father. "And I want to avoid being mad at her, but she makes it hard on me to keep my cool when I have thirty calls to make a day." Hayat breathed in and out, sensing her anger rising once more. Salim nodded, understanding her point.

"Ok, let me talk to her. She will come and apologize to you, I'm coming back." Before she could even answer, Hayat's father got up, going back to the living room where his wife was. She heard their voices talking – her mother trying to convince him – but then a few minutes later it was silent again. Lamia, with an annoyed look on her face, came in front of her. Salim was standing behind her, waiting.

"Semhili benti," *Excuse me, my daughter,* "I will not ask you to do things you don't want to." A sensation of relief washed over Hayat, as she smiled at her mother. When her punishment was done, Lamia got back inside, and Salim sat back with his daughter on the swing.

"Thank you, baba." His only answer was a kiss on top of her head. This simple thing made her feel valid and listened to.

It was easy.

For a moment, they both enjoyed the fresh breeze, talking about what happened in their week. Summer started not long ago, and it was already so warm during the day. They had discussed so much this afternoon, they could both see the colors of the sky changing little by little, announcing the coming of the prayer. Seeing the hour approaching, Salim offered her to join him. It had been a long time since they had prayed together. She accepted immediately. Hayat knew full well that it was one of the acts of worship that, until today, had allowed them to have such a close relationship. Praying with her father gave her a new vision at this moment. This feeling of sharing that she felt following her father during prayer was unique, and nothing can replace it. It was as if she connected with him through this act. It was special, and she appreciated every second of it.

After the prayer, Hayat and Salim were sitting in the living room, sipping on their cups of *atay* that her father made – he *always* made the best ones. It was a quiet start to the evening, and the golden sun was shining through the windows, casting a warm orange glow on the room. As they sat there, Salim put down his cup and looked at his daughter with a warm smile.

"You know, Hayat, I am so proud of you," he said. Hayat looked up at him, surprised by the sudden praise.

"You always tell me you're proud of me, but why, baba?" Salim leaned forward, resting his elbows on his knees.

"Because you've grown into such a strong, independent, righteous woman. Seeing you today how you want your nikkah to be, and how you manage your relationship with Anas. It feels like I have succeeded. You're my key to heaven. The daughter I have dreamt about, Allahuma barik fiki ya benti." *God bless you, my daughter.* "And even with your career! You've pursued your dreams, even when they seemed impossible. That's not an easy fit, and I admire you for it." He paused for a second, "I'm so proud of you." Hayat felt her cheeks turn warm at her father's words.

"Allah y barik fik, ya baba. This is all thanks to you." Salim smiled and reached over to take her hand.

"You know, I remember when you were just a little girl, always drawing and painting. You had such a talent for it, even back then. I always knew you were destined for great things." Hayat chuckled at the memory.

"I remember those days too. You always hung my drawings on the fridge, no matter how terrible they were." Salim laughed, nodding his head.

"Because I was proud of you! And look at you now. You've turned that talent into a successful career." Hayat smiled, feeling a sense of gratitude wash over her. She was thankful to have such a supportive and loving father.

After a few moments of silence, Salim spoke again, bringing her close to hug her.
"N'habek bezef henunna diali." *I love you so much, my darling.* Hayat looked at him, understanding the significance of his words. "You're growing so fast, and I can't help but think you're still my little girl running around

the house." Salim squeezed her enough for her to ask for air, while tapping his shoulder slowly.

"I know. Ana tani nmout a'lik baba." *I would die for you too, baba.* Reluctantly, he releases a little pressure, so that Hayat could breathe.

"I love you, Hayat. And I will always be there for you, regardless of what could ever happen." Hayat felt a lump form in her throat at her father's words. She knew he meant every word.

"Thank you baba," she whispered, feeling grateful for this special moment with her father. As they pulled away from the embrace, Salim looked at her with a twinkle in his eye, they continued to chat and laugh, and Hayat felt a sense of love and warmth surrounding her. She brought back the discussion of the masjid, and whether everything was good for D-Day. Salim reassured her by explaining that everything was fine, he had reserved the place between two prayers so as not to disturb anyone and to do this in the most total privacy.

- ☾ -

As Anas sipped hot tea and nibbled on homemade cookies, Houria set his drink in front of him. Anas was conversing enthusiastically with his brother about their childhood tales. The moment he noticed her presence, he thanked her, continuing the conversation with Nourdine. He was waiting for everyone to come, so he could explain at once the details of his nikkah. Anas spoke eloquently and passionately about how Nourdine was the type of child to run around and scream all over the house when Anas was quite the opposite. They would argue about which was who, but they all knew the truth.

Houria patted his back, wanting to get his attention. He looked at her confused, then she pointed a small mace at the sedari. Lina was sleeping peacefully, shifting a little from left to right at the noise. Both of them calmed down, not wanting to wake the little girl. Souhila took this opportunity of silence, to sit on her father's lap, where he could hug her the easiest.

After a while, all of Hakim and Faiza's children were in the living room, enjoying every little snack they had in front of them. Souhila was still in her father's lap, a towel around her neck, so she won't get dirty while eating. Once everyone was sitting in the room, Anas started talking about how the nikkah will go; the theme, the menu, how there will be separate sections for men and women, and certainly, no music and no strangers. Hayat and Anas mutually agreed on that, but they knew it would be difficult to make them understand. The more he spoke, the more he realized he was approaching these points. He felt the nervousness growing inside of him and started sensing a lump in one's throat. He chased away this unbearable feeling with a clearing of the throat before arriving at the sensitive points of the discussion. To bear himself, Anas decided to kill two birds with one stone.

"Since we decided to have an intimate nikkah, we don't want people we don't know, and also no music." He stated. Everyone kindly agreed to his terms, but Anas was only waiting for the reaction of his parents. Hakim also nodded, taking a weight off his shoulder as he did so. One left. Faiza. Was she going to be passive? Or to be as tough as old boots? Facing silence, Anas thought he won. However, Faiza was only thinking about how she could hurt him more.

"S'herhetek?" *Did she do black magic on you?* She asked, genuinely worried as if she didn't recognize her child. "Klit chi haaja? Chrabt?" *Did you eat something? Drank?* "You changed, what did she do to you?" His anger rose, but he was so used to her ridiculous questions, not finding it useful to waste his energy on trivialities.

"You know what, mama?" Anas said his tone completely blank of emotions. "If you're not happy with how I want my nikkah to be, don't come. You already had two nikkah, yours and *mine*. You decided for me, and it was a disaster. Not only that, but you invited the whole town, in one ballroom, with music killing everyone one's ears. So 'afak," *please* ", stay out of it." Everyone was speechless at the courage Anas had shown by standing up to their mother, but also at the calm he demonstrated. She was about to snap at him when Hakim took the lead.

"Habsi." *Stop it,* "You already said enough. He told us how he wanted his nikkah to be and as his parents we need to respect that." Hakim looked at his son. "Is he transgressing the laws of Islam?"

Faiza glared at her husband, "No." He looked back at her with a smile.

"Then, we don't have anything to say against this ceremony." This is how the discussion ended. As time passed, Anas became more and more aware of his father's growth as an individual. Nevertheless, his mother did not move an inch in terms of behavior.

It saddened him.

Houria, with a big smile on her face, tried to hide the awkwardness and asked her brother about the organization of his nikkah. Gradually, this uncomfortable feeling went away, giving way to a most pleasant union. The soft glow of the surrounding light created, adding to the beauty of the scene. The sound of the distant adhaan echoed through the air, providing tranquility for their conversation. At the hearing of it, they all got up to pray together.

While doing so, Anas prayed for his mother to understand how he felt, and asked Allah to give her wisdom and change her mind.

Chapter 28

The beginning of this lavish day was heralded by the hurry of joy, the constant comings and goings, and the noises of the suppliers who were arriving one by one. Since this morning, Lamia and Faudel had already covered a distance of at least a kilometer just going up and down the stairs. For the past few days, Hayat's family has been acting like an anthill. They had moved the furniture to create a space inside for the women. They also installed a barnum outside, a white one, so it could match the theme. Therefore, the men had a space in the garden. Rahma came back today, but this time for the whole day. She booked her services to do the henna on the female guests since Hayat was satisfied with her past services. Thus, Rahma came early to do her hands and feet first. This time, Hayat already had a design for each part.

Kamila was only going back and forth between the bedroom and the bathroom. She wasn't able to find which light flattered her best for her makeup. Hayat looked at her while she still couldn't move. It would ruin her henna.

"What's the problem?" She asked, a smile on her face. Kamila sighed, exhausted to go and come back, still hesitant about the color.

"My eyes are green." She looked at her friend, totally distraught, not finding the right color to achieve the look she imagined.

"Allahuma barik fiki, Ma Shaa Allah, you have beautiful eyes, yes. So, again, what seems to be the problem?" Hayat said while laughing a bit. Her friend glared at her with fire in her eyes.

"I can't find a matching color that goes with my eyes and the cream of my tarayoun!" The youngest stayed unfazed by the matter.

"Then, don't wear makeup." Kamila blankly looked at her.

"What?" She nodded, sure about her statement.

"Don't wear makeup. If you can't find the right color, don't torture your mind and don't wear it. It's probably a sign for you to stop…" They both looked at each other, and Kamila felt like she had a point on this one. The oldest smiled at her before coming close and pinching her chubby cheeks.

"You know I love you?" Hayat laughed at this sudden action, which made her cheeks red afterward.

"I do." After half an hour, they finished getting ready, even Kamila had the time to ask for a simple pattern on her hands. Thus, it would dry quickly before the afternoon started, since the nikkah was going to take place between 'Asr and Maghrib.

It was still the morning. They had *time*.

With each passing second, Hayat felt the excitement rising within her. She no longer dreaded this moment, but she wanted to live it. She wanted to touch him, take him in her arms, and feel him close to her. There were only a few hours left, but it seemed so long. The last month had passed in the blink of an eye.

For this day, everyone was invited to show themselves in their best light and to proudly wear the colors of their country with a traditional outfit. Hayat will have two dresses; a beige *badrun*, with gold work on top and a white cap over all, and a white and gold *chaouia* dress for when they will come back home. The young woman was a little moved to see herself in her outfits. It reminded her of those that Lamia wore during her wedding. The moment she saw herself in the mirror, it was as if she saw her mother. They looked so alike. Sometimes, it scared her that she was turning into her. She was afraid to reproduce the same actions as her when, in reality, both were entirely different. Obviously, Hayat loved her mother. However, she didn't want to be her. There were some points where they were not on the same page. And it was those differences that could make their relationship a bit more difficult at times.

Hayat breathed out, taking over all her emotions, looking at her ring. She smiled at the sight.

I will soon be his wife.

- ☾ -

Houria came to wake Anas up, who jumped when she put her hand on his shoulder. With the door ajar, Anas could see the comings and goings in the hallway of his family members. He stretched on the bed, dropping the pillow on the empty side of the bed.

"What time is it?" Houria looked at the clock, then back at her brother.

"Tmeniya," *Eight.* Anas wanted to take advantage of the few minutes he had.

"Thanks. I will be there in a minute." Houria patted his chest, then left him. His vision was only a blur of colors

216

as he rose from the bed and caught his glasses. Anas stretched again, slowly recalling what day it was. He quickly brushed the thoughts of his groggy state aside and jumped out of bed with a gigantic smile on his face.

Today was the day of his nikkah.

He took a deep breath, inhaling the joyous air around him. While he left the room, he also remembered that he had rented a house, two nights and one day, for himself and his family so that everything could be there, close to the event. The gifts, the traditional pastries, the outfits, and the list continued. Since they were initially four hours away, they collectively decided to be in one home, only an hour away from Salim's house. However, when he woke up, Souhila was no longer by his side. Probably, already with the others eating breakfast. Before joining them all in turn, he went to wash his nose in the bathroom and remake his wudu. Once downstairs, he saw them all in a corner of the living room with different drinks; coffee, tea, and hot chocolate for the children. Hafsa handed him his tea and sandwich, which she had carefully prepared with peanut butter and jelly. He thanked her before joining his brothers, who still seemed to emerge from their sleep. Only the children already had a lot of energy to spare when the day had barely begun.

Everyone was getting ready, and Anas was still afraid of what his mother could do today. He knew his father was going to have an eye on her. However, since the men would be separated from the women, Anas feared that her tongue would loosen. Thus, Anas took his sisters aside to ask them to keep Faiza away from the other guests or stay with her whenever she went to talk to someone. Of course, they accepted, reassuring him that she would be in their care. On one hand, his fear was now attenuated, but on the other hand, how can he be sure that

Faiza wasn't going to do everything to ruin his day? Certainly, she was not going to miss her son's nikkah. But, was she going to be able to hold her remarks toward his future wife? She was only going to be surrounded by people who loved Hayat. Anas didn't want Faiza to be shunned.

In a way, he asked his sisters to protect their mother from her *own* demons.

It was almost one o'clock when they all finished getting dressed in their outfits – which matched the theme perfectly – and putting on the finishing touches before leaving. Anas chose a particularly strong perfume, pleasant to smell so that Hayat will be able to remember their first hug every time she smells it. The young man smiled, already imagining her in his arms. His heart skipped a beat at the image of this intimate moment they were finally going to share. Anas was also eager to see what she looked like without her hijab. Souhila once said, "She is so beautiful with her hair." He was a bit jealous that his daughter saw her first without it.

During their muqabalas, out of respect, he had not asked her once for details about her physique. Because for him, the most important thing was to know if, on the religious, future, and emotional levels, Hayat was going to suit him. He found her face attractive. That was enough. Anas didn't have to know or see more. He looked at himself one last time in the mirror, arranging the last details of his appearance before joining his daughter, who must surely be prepared by Hafsa.

Souhila was on a chair in the living room, having her aunt do her hair, dangling her feet as she waited for Hafsa to finish. He arrived at before her, smiling, to show her and his sister his outfit.

"How do I look?" He said, turning on himself. The two exclaimed in fascination that this outfit suited him perfectly.

"Nta zwin baba!" *You're pretty daddy!* Souhila exclaimed, her eyes filled with stars. Hafsa instantly agreed, still styling the little girl's hair. Anas wanted to carry his daughter just to decrease the agitation he had inside him, but for the moment, it was impossible. Therefore, he took a chair and put it in front of her before playing with her little hands to calm himself. His daughter's laughter was a medication he could never live without. She was the cure for his sorrows, his worries, and this mind of his that was far too uncontrollable.

Gradually, the members of his family gathered one by one, all ready to leave. Phone, charger, keys in hand, he had to drive for an hour before this wonderful day really began.

The shining sun accompanied them through the road. It was a perfect day for an *intimate* ceremony. Anas hummed a cheerful tune as he looked at his daughter playing with her dress. He felt like the happiest man alive, and his heart was full of love and joy. Anas couldn't wait to see his bride, dressed in a beautiful traditional Algerian dress, signing the nikkah contract with her hands covered in henna. He could already picture her, with her white hijab, smiling at him as the pen ran the ink on the paper in front of the imam. Even if the imam's presence wasn't mandatory, they were still doing it in a masjid where the religious representative had to be present. He felt a wave of emotion overwhelm him, knowing that today was when they would be united in front of Allah.

Anas was filled with a sense of anticipation. He couldn't believe that the day he had dreamt of for so long had finally come. It was finally his choice to be made. The ceremony, the bride, the schedule, it was all *his*. Eventually. Anas chose this one in every aspect. Relief washed over him. He was confident that the ceremony would be perfect and that they would have their moment. He could hardly contain his excitement as he drove to Hayat's childhood house. His heart was beating fast, and his hands were sweating, leaving a stain on the wheel.

While coming out of his car, Anas could already see the few decorations at the entrance, the balloons, and the mirror with their names printed on it. A small path led them directly to the entrance of the house. He smiled at the sight. With one hand, Anas helped his daughter to get down the car, but the moment they set foot on the green grass, the exclamations of joy, the screams, the applause, and *zagharit* were here to welcome Anas and his family. With that, he could no longer hide the smile that he had been trying to hold back. There was too much joy in him not to show it and share it with his family. As tradition dictated, Anas went to fetch Hayat, who was sitting in the living room with her cape covering her face. Only her hands were visible. At this sight, Anas felt his heart skip a beat.

She was sublime.

Breathtaking *even*.

The colors she wore suited her so well. She was a work of art. Anas could no longer take his eyes off the magnificent painting in front of him. Noticing his presence, Hayat caught his gaze, making this man even weaker than he already was. Her hazel eyes stole the last bits of force he had left. Anas could find himself on his knees in front of the woman who sat before him as he found her *magnificent*. The purity that emanated from her hypnotized him. Hayat's heart accelerated, seeing him out of himself.

Not moving or telling her anything.

He received a tap on the shoulder from Salim, snapping him out of his trance. The latter nodded at him to push him to move on or say something, but the breath stuck in his throat prevented him from doing so. He cleared it, ready to be the man he was supposed to be.

"Are you ready?" His husky voice hit her ears, making her heart skip a beat, and her body temperature rose a few degrees. Neither could take their eyes off the other.

"More than ever," Hayat said, her eyes hidden by her smile, making Anas feel hot under his clothes. She looked so perfect today.

Since they were not married yet, they only walked side by side until they arrived at the car under the sound of the families who were there to celebrate them. For the duration of the drive to the masjid, Salim and Hakim had replaced Souhila in the back of Anas' car. The procession began its journey under the sound of horns and the disorderly movements of cars, as the North Africans knew so well how to do. Cars passed through the streets, displaying the Algerian and Moroccan flags, greeted by passers-by once passed. This journey was all joy and eagerness to arrive at the final destination: the masjid.

Once in front of it, Anas and Hayat waited for a while, letting the guest and the photographer surround them before coming out.

They exchanged a knowing look, ready to finally seal their union in front of Allah.

Chapter 29

Since there were only a few women, they were all on the lower floor, separated by a fabric wall so that everyone could enjoy the ceremony in the same way. In their center, Salim and his friends had arranged a table covered with a light beige cloth to be viewed by either side. So that it would be more intimate. The empty place added a layer to that sense of intimacy they all shared. Hayat moved forward, holding a microphone in hand, on a chair, unlike the other women who were sitting on the ground. She was waiting for her turn to sit on the chair next to the imam. Anas was already on his left, patiently waiting for the microphone to give his consent.

Once everyone was seated, quiet, and well settled, the imam began to make his lecture ahead of the ceremony. Throughout the entire speech, Hayat and Anas were just staring into each other's eyes. Both knew what it meant. Their souls would finally be bound forever.

They couldn't look away from each other.

"Anas Saidi, son of Hakim Saidi and Faiza Tahar, do you agree to marry Hayat Mazari, daughter of Salim Mazari and Lamia Badani?" The imam asked in Arabic, looking at him, waiting for his answer. Anas, with his eyes still deep in Hayat's hazel ones, took the microphone and brought it to his mouth.

"Yes," he stated, maintaining his gaze. Under the emotion, Hayat smiled, ready to give her agreement too.

The imam took the microphone again to ask the same question to Hayat after asking her father, who only took a few seconds to hold the suspense, and with a laugh, she said, "Yes."

Once the agreement of the two was given, the hearts were appeased and filled with happiness. *Zagharit*, clicks of the camera, and applause filled the holy place. Those sounds didn't stop until Hayat sat in her father's place to sign the nikkah contract. Before letting her, Salim felt obligated to hug her and kiss her forehead, adding a few words discreetly to her.

"Farha diali," *my pride*, "Nmout a'lik ya benti." *I would die for you, my daughter,* he whispered in her ear. Turning away from her, Hayat could see that her father's eyes were shining with emotions. She then took his face before kissing his cheek with tenderness.

"Ena tani baba," *me too, dad,* she said back before letting him go, his eyes filled with tears. Hayat knew Salim cried under emotions. It was endearing. She will never be used to seeing a man like him, completing all his duties as a father and husband, and still got teary eyes when he watched Disney with his only daughter. His pure heart was something she would always protect.

The imam gave a new lecture before the newlyweds took the personalized pen specially made for this event – with *Anas & Hayat* written on it. These two names looked beautiful together. Both exchanged a quick look when the paper was in front of them. The photographer was waiting for them to sign and take beautiful pictures.

Anas and Hayat were now officially *married*.

Once the signatures were done, the two looked at each other as the masjid once again filled with joy. After the imam left them to rejoice a little, the formerly-quiet guests started to chatter once more before they arrived to congratulate the newlyweds. Hayat and Anas were now face to face. Time had slowed down, and everything in the room faded, and suddenly it was just the two of them.

For a moment, they looked at each other, their hearts pounding, their hands sweating, their brains clouded with the happiness of this union. They only wanted one thing; to feel close to each other for the first time. Anas opened his arms, which Hayat immediately placed herself in. As a reflex, she inhaled his strong scent, easing her stress a bit. She usually hated them, but on him, it had a different effect. The way they complemented each other, as if their bodies were meant to be close.

Like two puzzle pieces that fit together.

Taking the opportunity in his hands, Anas approached her ear, making Hayat shiver with a new emotion. Gripping her tightly under the emotion. He was afraid of letting go of her and having her fade right in front of his eyes. Being this close to a man for the first time was oddly satisfying. They could hear their hearts beat with nervousness. It reassured them to know that they were both in the same state.

"You're finally mine," he stated in a whisper, maintaining firmly his grip around her waist. Hayat could feel her cheeks getting hotter as he stayed this close to her. She wasn't able to add anything, so Hayat hid a little more in his arms, accentuating the exclamations of the guests looking at them.

She was *his*, and he was *hers*.

Anas kissed her forehead as Hayat chuckled while
haya washed over them, making both of them shy. They
were in their bubble of happiness that got popped by the
new wave of joyful celebration. To make this moment even
more memorable, Anas called his daughter to come and
share the hug with them. The little girl laughed loudly when
she found herself squeezed between her father and her
stepmother. Under the cheering sounds, Anas, Hayat, and
Souhila walked together to the car to go back to Salim's
house for the final part of the nikkah.

When they arrived, Kamila made sure the entrance
was free and that they should be the first to enter the
home. As a sign of respect, everyone moved to the sides
of the path, showering them with celebration. The two had
to go through the living room to get to the garden in order
to open the sideboard. Once this was done, the newlyweds
parted ways reluctantly so that each one could stay on
their assigned side; men and women.

Before going up to change, Hayat put on her
chaouia dress with a much lighter and open veil while
adding a few touches of make-up and perfume – since it
was only women now. Kamila looked at the result of her
work on her friend. She was delighted. Rahma also added
some details to her henna before she joined all the guests
downstairs. Now that men and women were separated,
women could dress differently. At first, they were a little
reluctant to the idea, but Hayat reassured them because
she had already planned everything.

"Don't worry. I've made sure no men can enter the
living room while we're here. Faudel has put the tables in
front of the window curtains, and the front door is closed.
And since the little ones are already with us, you don't

have to look over your shoulder." Hayat explained to ease her guests. But even with those words, Houria looked around the room. "Houria, your twins are now big boys. They can't stay with us. They are in the right place with their father and uncles." Houria looked at her, genuinely understanding the meaning of Hayat's words. Lamia arrived a few minutes later to bring the tea, as well as small desserts and finger sandwiches.

The women discussed their lives and sent remarks regarding the wedding arrangements. Suddenly, Hayat felt a weird sensation in her gut. Her gaze swept around the room, lingering on Faiza, who was just staring at her with a smug look. A drop of sadness tingled her heart. She wanted Anas' mother to enjoy the day. Still, she couldn't change Faiza's feelings toward her. Hayat smiled at her before redirecting her attention to something else.

Meanwhile, Rahma was doing henna on whoever wanted one. Even Souhila asked for one. The hennaya specifically said she couldn't play for at least an hour, or her outfit would get dirty. Therefore, when she finished, the little girl stayed seated until an hour passed, so she could wash her hands. Occasionally, a child would cut them off in their discussion, however, no one was really bothered by their attitude – since they were children.

At one point, Hayat looked at her friend, Kamila, who had a rather worried look on her face. The bride approached her, wanting to know what was troubling her fiend's mind.

"Hey babe, what happened?" The bride put her hand on her shoulder to get her attention since she seemed to be in another world.

"Huh?" Kamila blankly looked at her, "Oh, sorry. Nothing, I'm just a bit worried about Imran." Hayat gave her an understanding look. "I'm scared he would get overstimulated by the environment, even with his headphones on. Weddings and events make him overwhelmed, and it's hard for him to keep his cool." In a few seconds, Hayat found a few words to comfort her friend.

"He is with your father and little brother. Don't worry about him. He is in good hands. And if he has a crisis, my room is empty and far from the noise." Kamila leaned into her touch, finding comfort. With a light heart, her friend resumed the discussion so as not to draw more attention.

The sun was starting to paint the sky a new color. The time of prayer will soon be there. Salim arranged prayer mats for every guest, so each side could pray peacefully – if they could do so. They locked the door of the living room; thus, the men could go to the bathroom and do their wudu. Looking back, it was exactly how Hayat and Anas envisioned their nikkah.

They felt blessed.

Even the children seemed to have a good time with the little activities Hayat and Lamia prepared for them. After the prayer, the bride took off her hijab, and added her cap over her dress. Anas would come any minute, so they could exchange the rings. She knew it was the perfect time for him to see her without. Kamila helped her to prepare, and fixed her hair. She looked wonderful. They screamed out of excitement. Hayat wanted to have his honest reaction. She asked her friend to film discreetly in a way we could only see him, in case she wanted to share the video. A light knock on the door signaled the presence of Anas on the other side. Once passed, Salim – who was aware of her surprise – closed the door behind him, so that no one would sneak in during this time.

The newlywed entered the room, a happy smile on his face, to finally give her the ring that she will wear

227

proudly from now on. Hayat sat on the sedari, the hood of her cape hiding her features. For a second, he thought she was just hiding out of shyness, but when she got up and took it off, Anas froze. His heart skipped a beat. The tops of his ears turned red, as did his cheeks. He was all flushed by his shyness. Her hazel eyes captured his dark brown ones. Hypnotizing him. Anas cleared his throat under the persistent eyes of all the women present.

"Wow…" He breathed out. His gaze lingered on her features. They stayed like this for a solid minute, looking at each other. Hayat's temperature started to rise too. "I can't stop looking at you," he confessed, relaxing every muscle in his body as if the words were weighing on him. In one smooth motion, he opened the tiny box to get the ring. Anas landed a hand for her to hold. Hayat shyly smiled and put hers in his.

It fitted *perfectly*.

The bride also took out his signet ring. Before putting it on, she called Souhila to make her read what was written inside. Her little eyes widened the moment she read her name on it. The little one jumped into Hayat's arms.

"It's my name!" Then, turned to her father, "Baba, it's my name here!" With her little fingers and a wide smile, Souhila pointed at the inside of the ring. Anas got, too, to her level.

"It's so beautiful," he paused, drifting his gaze to his now wife. "You really wrote her name in it?" Hayat nodded, a smile on her face, happy to finally see his reaction. For a second, he studied it, euphoric to see that he had probably made the right choice. He gave it back to her, waiting for Hayat to put it around his thumb.

When she finally did, in one quick, gentle motion, he pulled her closer to him. Under the gasps of the other women, who all looked away, they were only a few inches apart. However, he only came close to her ear to whisper something that only she had the right to hear.

"If I was alone with you right now, I would have kissed you until you wouldn't be able to think straight anymore." All her thoughts left her mind. The blush on her cheeks intensified. At the limit of breaking the rules, Anas kissed her forehead before taking her daughter in her arms and standing up, easily. Hayat was unable to move for a second, before her husband held out a hand, so he could sit up. He put her hood back on her before giving Hayat a last hug. He took the opportunity to slip a tiny kiss into the crook of her neck, before disappearing through the door with his daughter in his arms. She touched the kissing spot with the tips of her fingers, completely frozen, but also by the desire she felt blooming inside her.

Kamila arrived, a little worried to see that her friend was quiet.

"Are you ok?" The oldest said, putting her hands on Hayat's shoulders.

"I'm very much ok." Hayat confessed, looking at her friend as if she was transparent. "Too *much*, even."

Chapter 30

All the boxes in her apartment were looking back at her. In a few months, her life had totally changed, the improvement in her work, she met Anas, then they got married, and now she had to move again, or rather move in with Anas and Souhila. One last time, Hayat walked around her apartment, not wanting to forget anything. As she looked into her room, she heard light knocks on the door. Hayat covered herself with a hijab to open the door as quickly as possible, assuming the movers had arrived. She looked through the peephole and was surprised to see that it was actually Anas, her *husband*, who was standing behind it. With a big smile, she welcomed him inside.

"Salam a'leykoum, Hayat." Her husband said, towering only inches away from her, closing the door behind him.

"Wa'leykoum salam. I thought it was the movers," she stated before going back to her room, removing unnecessary layers of clothing. Anas stood there, expecting to receive something more than a simple greeting. He looked back at his thumbs to make sure all of this wasn't just a dream – or a wish. He was certainly married to the woman who was going back and forth in front of him. Hayat was too busy with her thoughts. She didn't even notice him staying too long in front of the door.

Without waiting any longer, he began to help her, seeing if everything was good on her side. Each time he approached her, stood behind her, and watched her, Hayat could feel herself getting hot. Even without touching her, she could sense him all over her body. Several times, she tried to brush this sensation, but something in his gaze made this sensation envelop her in a cocoon of desires she wasn't ready to explore. As if nothing was happening in her mind, the young woman started to run around the house faster. While she was in her thoughts, Hayat didn't feel Anas coming up behind her to look over her shoulder. She jumped in surprise, almost falling. Anas caught her by the waist, looking into her eyes. Eyes wide open, her cheeks turning red, she was stunned by the sudden closeness. Unlike Anas, its effects could be seen directly on her face. His husky voice cut her off from her thoughts.

"You know," he brushed back a strand of her hair behind her ear, trailing his finger down her neck. "I'm glad to be the one coming in here to help you." Hayat swallowed hard at this revelation.

"Why?" She responded, in a soft tone. Anas analyzed her features, a crooked smile on his face.

"Because," he simply said before kissing her cheek and straightening her correctly. Then he went back to move the boxes in front of the door. Hayat blinked several times, confused. She had absolutely no idea what had just happened. Without dwelling on the situation any longer, Hayat joined him in moving his boxes. Sometime later, they rang.

It was time.

Time to finally move in with her new *family*.

- ☾ -

On the way, Anas had a new emotion blooming in his chest. Every so often, he would glance at her to make sure she wasn't bored. Admittedly, it wasn't very far from Hayat's home, simply, he couldn't find a topic to discuss. A sudden urge to take her hand crossed his mind, but he pushed the thought away, returning his attention to the road. There were only a few minutes left before arriving home, their home. Anas smiled at this thought. Sharing his life, his routine, his daughter, his emotions, his bed, and his desires with someone new.

In a way, Anas was as excited as his *wife*.

When Souhila and the babysitter heard the car park in front of the house, the little one almost ran out, followed closely by her guardian. The father quickly got out of his car before crouching down to grab his daughter in his arms, lifting her from the ground easily. Almost every time Hayat met the little girl, she was all giggly and always had a big smile. Her attitude was contagious. *Extremely* contagious.

"Salam a'leykoum, Souhila. How are you?" Her stepmother asked, seeing her raising her head from Anas' shoulder.

"Wa'leykoum salam, Hayat! I'm good!" Hayat smiled, happy to see this little girl again. After this warm welcome, they went home, waiting for her furniture to come. There were countless boxes to move, but the most important thing will be to make sure everything fit in the house. Luckily, Anas had enough room to provide space for her things.

While moving Hayat's stuff, he made sure the right boxes were in the correct room to ease his wife's task. Tomorrow they will make sure to build the furniture she had brought because it was far too late to do so this afternoon. When Anas put down the boxes for her desk furniture, he was already thrilled to watch her work on her designs. Already imagining her, her long light-brown hair tied in a high bun, with some strands of hair coming on the sides of her face to frame her features. The light from her digital tablet enlightening her traits. Anas already wanted to move on to this stage. His heart skipped a beat at the sight, but it actually scared him a little. He remembered his big sister's words and about taking his time in this relationship.

However, he couldn't help it.

His *heart* couldn't help it.

Hayat caught him daydreaming in the middle of the room. Slowly taking away the box from his hands, "Anas? Are you ok?" He blinked several times, taken aback by the sudden question. Then, cleared his throat, embarrassed to have been caught red-handed.

"I'm good," Hayat smiled at him, putting her furniture on her future desk.

"Good. The babysitter is waiting for you downstairs, so she can leave." Anas nodded, a red tint on the top of his ears. Hayat chuckled at how fast her husband ran downstairs to be freed of this embarrassment. After nearly two hours of movement, Hayat decided to take a good shower before getting dressed in much lighter and more comfortable clothes. Yet, looking at herself in the bathroom mirror, grabbing some fat all over her body, she hesitated to go out. Her clothes were far too revealing – for her taste – for a first night here. Although it was usually the kind of clothes she wore at home when she was alone, Hayat was not mentally prepared to put them on in front of her husband. Slowly, she passed the type of her finger onto the old scars she made herself. They gradually faded with time, but they were still slightly visible if you looked closely.

Locked in the bathroom, her brother loudly speaking downstairs with their parents, Hayat ran the hot water from the shower to hide her next actions. She was exhausted. Every day for the past five years, Hayat had a lump in her stomach before going to school. Not a single one of her complaints had been taken into account by her school. So she had given up talking.

The more she talked, the harder the consequences were to bear.

Words turned into threat, threats into hits, hits into pain, and pain into scares.

For the past five years, every time she needed to express her sadnesses, she locked herself up, either in her room or in her bathroom. Alone. Alone with her thoughts, and her own mind, rewinding the humiliate comments she had during the day. The years. She had looked for help, but nothing worked.

So, she took the blade and marked her body for life with a past heavy with filth.

Each red trace was freeing herself from this unbearable pain. Hayat felt euphoric. Lighter. That was what she needed, what she looked for. Sometimes, when she had no more place to write her story on her arms, she attacked her legs. Going deeper every time the blade touched her skin.

This deep pain she felt was symbolized all over her body.

Her deformed body that she never thought she could appreciate…

Hayat sighed, thinking about her past. She wasn't ready to display it. So, she swapped the shorts for longer pants, all covered by a loose long-sleeved t-shirt, hiding her figure.

Her damp hair framed her face once she walked into the kitchen alongside Anas, already busy preparing a meal for tonight. Souhila was playing with a puzzle in the living room since she finished her homework with her babysitter. Her father avoided letting her watch television before she went to sleep or even after she had finished school in the afternoon. From his perspective, a child had much better things to do than to sit and watch images that were far too stimulating for their brain. He believed it hampered their natural curiosity and creativity.

Hayat watched Souhila assemble piece by piece, delighted to see that she was blossoming the way a child should. Being totally focused on the small being, she didn't notice the large hands that gently circled her waist. Getting her closer to a hard chest. From this distance, she could feel all his muscles against her back, squeezing her as if his hands already knew her every curve.

As if his body was made to welcome hers.

In an intimate motion, he placed his head on her shoulder, also desiring to watch his daughter. Being half hidden by the kitchen island, the youngest couldn't make out what was going on in the kitchen. Anas inhaled her scent, drunk by the sweetness of it.

"You smell so good, Hayat." He dug his nose a little further into her neck before moving closer to her ear, whispering, "Is it a way for you to seduce me?" Slowly, the heat weighed on her body, forcing her to face him. She put her hands on his chest as she wanted to keep a sort of distance. Her gaze grew cloudy as desire took place in her brain.

She *wanted* him.

More than ever.

A glimpse of arousal slid into her look, making him want her even more. Nonetheless, Hayat wasn't quite ready to feed the monster that was locked down for a long time now. Thus, she tried to ease the tension.

"I think so, probably." For a moment, they stood there, their eyes fixed on each other. Then, she pointed to the pan on the fire, "You should look at the food before it burns." Anas sniffed to be certain, and she was right. The food has started to burn. He turned quickly before removing it from the fire. Hayat chuckled.

"Do you need some help?" Her husband looked over his broad shoulder to make eye contact.

"I would love that." Hayat answered him with a smile before coming to his side to help him prepare the meal.

With two more hands, it was going to be much faster. Only the laughter, and chatter, were audible. The meal was almost ready when little Souhila came into the kitchen, showcasing her brand-new puzzle in addition to an adorable drawing. It was a wonderful representation of Anas, herself, and Hayat, all holding hands in front of the house. With bold letters *"Welcome home Hayat!"*, it was adorable. Hayat went to her level before taking the drawing in hand, her eyes shining with joy.

"Oh, thank you! It's the best welcome gift I have ever received," she looked at the little one for a second, holding the drawing close to her heart. "Can I give you a hug?" She asked, opening her arms, ready to welcome the little one at any moment. For his part, Anas watched his daughter think about the question. After a time of reflection, Souhila immersed herself in them under the relieved gaze of her father.

El hemduliLlah. Anas thought.

The first hug was always a little challenging for children, and it was nice to know that Souhila seemed comfortable enough to give her one. Ready, Anas tapped on the edge of the pan, indicating that it was time to prepare the table.

- ☾ -

Hayat's heart skipped a beat as she stepped back into the room, followed closely by Anas. She didn't know what to expect from him. Since their nikkah, he has been very adventurous. It did not displease Hayat, far from it, but now she found herself completely alone with a man, between four walls, and did not know what to do. Thus, she stood in the middle of the room for quite a long time. Hayat felt his hands on her shoulders, sliding to her waist before he spun her to face him.

"Are you ready, Hayat?" He breathed as if he was lacking oxygen presently, with her between his hands. His wife looked back at him, unsure of what she desired.

"I don't know…" She replied in the same tone, almost inaudible to his ear. Anas seemed confused at this response, thinking she was ready.

"Why? It's supposed to be time." Fear started to grow inside of her guts. She felt trapped. One afternoon. Only one afternoon was enough for him to change. She felt his hold tighten around her, only accentuating this unpleasant feeling, telling her to flee the room. Hayat was getting ready to protest before seeing him run a hand through her hair. Confusion made her freeze. "Your hair is dry." His wife blinked, not understanding his point. Her shower had been taken a while ago, it was obvious her hair was going to be dry.

"Why wouldn't it be?" Anas frowned.

"Because it's time, we need to pray. It's 'Ishaa." All her fears instantly faded away. If he didn't act, she would have made a fool out of herself.

"Oh…" Anas side-eyed her for a second, unsure about the topic that was in her mind.

"What were you thinking, Hayat?" She escaped from his grip before heading to the bathroom connected to the bedroom. However, Anas wasn't done with her. He caught up to her, blocking her way.

"I-…" She sighed. "I had no thought. Can you please let me go to the bathroom?" Her husband crossed his arms, understanding what she was hiding from the red that tinted her cheeks, but also from the fleeting gaze she had. He grabbed her chin, forcing her to meet his eyes.

"Look at me." She obeyed. "Were you thinking I was going to force you to have sex with me, Hayat?" Her hazel orbs juggled between his as her cheeks grew redder and redder. Then, she nodded. Anas chuckled, rearranging a strand of hair behind her ear, "Oh habibti, don't ever think such a thing about me again. Would you?" He breathed, her heart skipping a beat at the nickname.

"Sorry." She said as he left a kiss on her cheek, "But why did you say it like that?" Anas looked back at her, his hand still holding her face in place.

"How?" Hayat pinched her lips together.

"As if you had trouble breathing." Now, it was his turn to turn red and avoid her gaze.

"You make me weak, Hayat. The mere sight of you drives me mad. I wasn't ready to have a woman like you." She raised a brow at his statement.

"Like me?" Almost losing all his strength to resist the desires fogging his judgment, he got closer to her.

"Yes, like you." His face was merely inches away, his gaze completely focused on her lips. He ran his thumb

238

over them, "They call me." Anas looked back at her, "Your eyes undress me." His hand slid to her collarbone, "Your heart claims me." In one smooth motion, with his hand on her hips, he brought her close enough to make them one. "Your curves were made to match my body." Anas hid his head in her neck, inhaling her. "Your scent drives me intensely crazy." He paused before leaving some kisses on his path. "Every second you spend before me is torture. I would love to undress you and claim you completely as my wife. But I can't, yet, since you're not ready. However, believe me, Hayat, when you are," he paused, locking his dark *burning* brown eyes into her hazel ones. "These clothes won't stand a second between my hands." She was out of words, hot, and completely needy. He left another kiss on her forehead, before separating their body. Hayat felt the cold hitting her limbs, giving her shivers all over them. Anas pushed her through the bathroom, so she could do her wudu and join him in prayer.

Each wave of fresh water made her steamy thoughts go away.

Once she finished, she joined him in the blank prayer room. It saddened her for a moment to see this place lacking personal touches. Since it was the first night alone as a couple, Anas and Hayat didn't have to honor it yet. After 'Ishaa, both prayed two additional rak'ats to celebrate this union. Then, they sat together, silent. Enjoying this pure and intimate moment. A feeling of satisfaction passed through them before he placed his hand on her forehead and recited the following du'aa.

"O Allah, I ask You for the good in her, and in the disposition You have given her. I take refuge in You from the evil in her, and in the disposition You have given her."[9]

Hayat did the same for him. Feeling like a bond strengthening between them. They both felt blessed, as if this simple action took any devilish thought out of their bodies. After a while of just looking at each other on their prayer mat, they slid under their blanket. Their hearts light and serene.

It was their first night together, and they felt blessed to spend it this way.

اللَّهُمَّ إِنِّي أَسْأَلُكَ خَيْرَهَا وَخَيْرَ مَا جَبَلْتَهَا عَلَيْهِ وَأَعُوذُ بِكَ مِنْ شَرِّهَا وَمِنْ شَرِّ مَا [9] جَبَلْتَهَا عَلَيْهِ

Reference: Sunan Abi Dawud 2160
In-book reference: Book 12, Hadith 115
English translation: Book 11, Hadith 2155

Chapter 31

The sound of her alarm coming through her ears suddenly woke her up. Hayat remained on her side for a moment, feeling a heavy weight on her body, holding her down. For a moment, she forgot where she was. Unable to recognize the decor of the room or even the arrangement of the furniture, Hayat tried to turn around, but something prevented her. After several attempts – all failed – she heard a rather masculine protest close to her ear.

Then she remembered where she was, the confession of last night, and especially who was hugging her against his strong chest.

She squirmed, so she could face him, not being able to free herself from his tight grip. With her finger, she pressed his cheek to wake him up. Nothing. Hayat tried another time, but still no improvement.

"Anas…" His wife waited for a reaction, "Wake up." Anas' sleepy face stared back at her with partially opened eyes.

"What time is it?" His voice echoed through his chest.

"Five," she said after checking back on her phone. He turned around, releasing his wife in the process.

"Coming." With this simple confirmation, Hayat got up to go to the bathroom to start her morning routine. A few minutes later, Anas followed her, eyes half-closed and a face swollen. This was the first time she saw his non-businessman self, all real. Hayat chuckled at the sight but took a moment before noticing that her husband was shirtless a few centimeters from her. Realizing the situation, Hayat hastened to do her wudu. With an almost sure step, Hayat went to get her things to pray and waited for her husband in the prayer room. Looking at the white walls, Hayat thought to add some paintings and decorations to make the room warmer and more pleasant. She suddenly had an idea as a surprise for her husband. She will have to do it discreetly and quickly. A moment later, Anas came in wearing his night-blue thobe. He looked so good in modest clothes. A yawn escaped him, when he stood on his prayer mat. Her husband looked at her, a sleepy smile on his face.

"Ready?" Hayat nodded, standing to his side.

As they prayed together, both felt a sense of fulfillment that lifted their worry from their shoulders. Once it ended, they sat there, a feeling of ease in their heart. In the most complete silence, after the du'aa which sounded much louder than their whispers, Anas looked at her with an indecipherable emotion in his eyes. Peaceful, Hayat rested her head on his shoulder as he took her hand to do dhikr. At least ten minutes passed before they finally ended. However, a presence was missing at their side.

Souhila.

"When does she wake up?" Hayat looked at Anas, wondering if the little one was about to join them.

"Usually, she gets up at six, so in less than an hour." He met her gaze, "Why?" Hayat thought about her answer for a second, looking hesitant. Anas leaned his head, intrigued by the sudden doubt.

"I don't know if it's my place to ask you that, but I think it's a major subject to discuss again." He stayed silent, waiting for more. "Has she already prayed with you?"

"Yes, not a lot, but already did. Why?" Hayat pinched her bottom lip, not sure if she should give him advice on his way to educate his daughter.

"Are you going to introduce her to salat more regularly? So, she could start a routine around it." Anas smiled at her, pleased to see that she was actually involved in Souhila's bond with Allah. With his hand, he caressed her cheek fondly.

"Yes, I already have ideas. Since this is her first day of summer break, I will ask her to pick between the day salats and start from there. On the side, I'll give her some classes, explaining the importance of each one of them." Hayat was about to respond, but Anas continued. "I want her to feel connected to her deen from the beginning. I don't want her to struggle as I did." His wife put her hand on his back, wanting to make the gesture loving and comforting.

"Why do you say that?" A glimpse of sadness brightened in his gaze as he remembered some heavy memories.

"When I was younger, my parents forced me to pray. No explanation, no bond, no *feeling*. I prayed only because I needed to. And growing up, not seeing the point, I walked away from it for a long time. I pretended to pray for them, locking my room and playing video games. I had to rediscover Islam myself…" He paused, leaning in her embrace. "There are other things that they justified in the name of Islam, which damaged my relationship with it. But now, prayer remains the major subject." Hayat understood him, and his experience was a reminder of how lucky she was to have a father who raised her with compassion without repressing the feelings he felt while being fair in his decisions. They stayed like this for a moment, not wanting to break the bubble Anas and Hayat were in. Slowly, they could see the sun gradually rising through the window of the room, prompting them to start their morning. The little one was going to wake up soon. However, breakfast wasn't ready yet. Together, they went downstairs to prepare the meal so that the youngest can wake up with something waiting for her on the table.

While cooking, Anas told her his daughter's favorite fruit and what she usually had in the morning. In about ten minutes, Anas would go up to her room so that he would already be there before Souhila realized she was alone. Mornings were quieter and easier when he showed up before she became aware of her loneliness. Every morning, Anas sat on the edge of her bed, waiting for her to wake up on her own before taking her in his arms and cuddling her until she slipped out of his embrace to go downstairs. Each awakening was like a little challenge to take up, to see if her daughter was going to have a good day.

After barely a few minutes of waiting, Souhila opened her eyes.

"Sbaah nnour ghazaali." Anas greeted his daughter, a puffy and sleepy face welcoming him.

"Sbaah nnour baba." Souhila crawled into his arms. As he hugged her tight, he left plenty of kisses on the top of her head. Like his heart needed as much gesture to make it lighter. He required his daughter far more than she did. Birdsongs outside were the only sounds that lulled them into that intimate silence they shared. Even if this

244

moment was a part of their routine, it felt unique each time. Unlike the other mornings, today was a bit longer than the others. It didn't worry him that much. She was just a little more tired than usual.

- ☾ -

Hayat was putting away the dishes when her phone rang, displaying her mother's name on the screen. She wiped her wet hands, a smile on her lips before picking up.

"Salam a'leykoum, mama. Wesh raki?" *How are you?* Hayat held her phone with her shoulder, putting the rest away as she could.

"Wa'leykoum salam, benti. El hemduliLlah, w entia?" *and you?* "How is it going?" Her daughter knew that the question had a hidden meaning.

"It's good, first day here. I still have my furniture to unpack and build, since I didn't have the time yesterday." Lamia hummed at this statement.

"Mlih, mlih." *Good, good.* "But, did you do it?" The daughter pinched her lips together, dreading the real subject of this conversation.

"Do what?" Her anger began to rise. This change was so fast that she had to stop her activity to try to take control of her emotions. She took one breath.

"Did you consummate the marriage?" The bite on her lip was much more pronounced this time. Second breath.

"Mama, with all due respect, this is none of your business." Third breath.

"How am I supposed to have grandchildren, then?" Fourth. It was enough for her.

"I'm going to hang up, mama. See you this weekend for la'sha. Bye." Before she could add anything,

Hayat ended the call with one click. She was so close to throwing her phone on the wall. How, with all the decency in the world, could she ask such a thing? It was inappropriate, unnecessary, and disrespectful. She felt insulted.

As if her only role was to bring her mother grandbabies.

A crackling sound behind her made her turn fast. She was faced with a puzzled Anas, looking at her with a perplexed expression on his face.

"Are you ok?" Fifth breaths. Pretending nothing happened, Hayat got back to her main activity: emptying the dishwasher. Her back turned, and she steadied her voice before answering.

"Yes, I'm perfectly fine." Sixth breaths. And it was still not working. Her heart was still racing with anger. Anas got a step closer, sensing something was wrong.

"You sure?" Seventh breaths. Silence. Probably, if she stayed that way, he would just drop the matter and leave her alone. She grabbed the last knife from the dishwasher, still with her back to him. "Hayat?" That was it. His wife snapped.

The knife firmly gripped in her hand. She rotated to face him, fire dancing into her eyes. "What?!" Sensing the danger inches from his face, he took a few steps back, showing his hands as if he meant her no harm. He mimed the movement of breathing in and breathing out. She followed him. And each time he did, Anas got closer to her until he had a hand on the knife.

"First, Hayat, we are going to put this away." She relaxed, already feeling her heart calm down after the physical contact Anas had made. To keep her that way, Anas rested a hand on her shoulder, feeling her tense muscles gradually relax. "Now, you'll tell me what's

happening." Hayat looked at him with a regretful
expression on her face. Anger had clouded her judgment,
and she no longer knew how to control it.

"I'm sorry," she rested her head on his chest. Anas
looked at her doing so while stroking her back gently.
"Mama just called me, and as you can see, she knew on
which nerve to hit."

Her husband frowned, "What did she tell you?"
Hayat met Anas' dark brown eyes, hesitant. However, he
raised his eyebrows, waiting for the subject.

"She asked if we had sex." Hayat bit her underlip,
guilty of what she just revealed. For a second, he sucked
his cheeks before putting both of his hands on her
shoulders so that she stands up to her full height. Even like
that, she needed to raise her head to meet his eyes. His
comforting and welcoming eyes.

"Hayat, you're going to listen to me, ok?" She
nodded, silent. "Firstly, we'll work on your anger
management. Because I don't want you to hurt yourself or
anyone else. Understood?" Again, a nod, "Then," his
hands slid to her waist. "If she is worried about
grandchildren, you can say she already has one. Even if
she is not biologically hers, she can satisfy herself with
Souhila until you say so." He brought her closer in one
smooth motion, his face inches away from hers. "No one is
entitled to command your body or make wishes upon it. If
you want children, I'm on it, and if you don't want any, I'm
on it too. The choice is yours." Anas got even closer,
mixing their hot breaths. "Did I make myself clear, Madame
Mazari?" As if by reflex, she wanted to get closer and give
him the most effective non-verbal response. But she still
didn't feel confident.

"Yes," she breathed unevenly.

Anas kissed her nose, "That's my girl." In the blink of an eye, her husband was already on another task. Hayat almost instantly folded with the unexpected praise. A strange feeling built up inside her. She was incapable of understanding it yet. Then his voice cut her, "Are they coming this weekend then?"

Hayat cleared her throat, "I hope so. I told them, and I reminded her before hanging up." Anas nodded, before pouring water into a glass. In reality, he had come here to bring a glass of water to his daughter, who was playing in her bedroom upstairs. Nevertheless, he witnessed a scene far more important at the time. Before leaving, he kissed her forehead, giving Hayat a feeling of peace and calm.

Both thought that the marriage would allow them to be a little quieter. Yet, in reality, this was only the beginning of a long and tumultuous road.

Chapter 32

There were many comb strokes on Souhila's curly hair before Hayat could finish her hairstyle without hurting her. Their families would soon be here for dinner, and the Mazaris were staying for the night. Hayat was going step by step with Souhila. And she felt honored as she asked her stepmother to do her hair today. A warming feeling bloomed in her chest, inflating it with pride. It was a way for her to accept Hayat slowly.

Once they ended, the oldest landed her hand for a high five, and Souhila hit it with a giggle. Influencing Hayat to do so. They were both ready to welcome them for dinner. Unfortunately, today, it was only going to be Anas' and Hayat's parents. The respective brothers and sisters could not move this weekend.

When they went downstairs, Anas was delighted that the two were already getting along well. It took a stitch off his shoulders. However, he knew that this relationship was fragile. He was also a little apprehensive, knowing that it could explode overnight. But he reassured himself that all this could not happen.

After a few seconds of relief, Anas saw himself sweep away when he saw his mother's name appear on his phone screen. A new feeling took over him. He was afraid. Scared, even, to hear what nonsense she had ready to hurt his wife.

Anas watched Hayat and Souhila checking if everything was on the table as he answered the phone.

"Salam a'leykoum, mama." The sound of the moving car was resonating into the phone, accompanied by the echo of his own voice in the car, indicating to him that he was indeed on the loudspeaker.

"Wa'leykoum salam. Qrib ouslna." *We'll be there soon.* Her cold tone made him shiver with uneasiness. Anas nodded as if they could see him.

"Perfect, we're waiting for you." He looked over his shoulder, checking if his wife was watching him. "And please, mama, be nice." Silence. Even if each time his mother deceived him, he always expected a change from her. As if Allah was going to make her resonate one moment or another.

"Waakhaa, waakhaa." *Ok, ok.* Anas sighed in relief, hoping she would keep her word. With a half-reassuring, half-uncomfortable smile, he returned to see his wife and daughter, who were now waiting for him in the living room. Everything was already ready; the dishes, the desserts, the drinks, and even the fruit after the meal was prepared.

For the occasion, Hayat made sure that the table was well presented, with new table linen and cutlery. Anas thought that was a bit over the top since it was only his parents coming. However, he let her do as she wished. Since it was her first marriage, she probably wanted to make a good impression. Hayat was most likely stressed by this dinner. Thus, he made sure to share that weight with her by not telling her about it. Anas sat next to Hayat and Souhila, patiently waiting for everyone to arrive.

"It was mama. They'll be here soon. Where are your parents? Do they need us to prepare anything else?" Hayat shook her head.

"No, they got everything." Hayat looked at him as if she wanted to add something, but she restrained herself from doing so. Anas noticed it. Then, with a gentle movement, he brought her closer to him, planting his eyes in hers.

"Tell me what's troubling you." She seemed surprised that he instantly guessed.

"I'm afraid my mother is going to ask questions that are too intrusive…" He stroked her arm gently, reassuring her.

"It's ok. We're in this together. Right?" Hayat smiled at him before lining into his embrace, feeling this sense of comfort washing over her. In saying these words, he was not saying them only for her but also for himself. He intensely wished that this meal, but also this weekend, would go well.

The doorbell rang, signaling the beginning of a very long evening.

- ☾ -

The sound of knives and forks completed the silence between conversation. Until now, nothing to report for the couple. The parents seemed to get along well and hadn't said anything disrespectful to them so far. They were all having a good time. Even if they had to stay on their guard about everyone's actions, Anas and Hayat exchanged a knowing look, being a little more peaceful about the course of the evening. Then, a fateful discussion reignited the flame the couple were trying to keep extinguished.

"Are you planning on having children?" Faiza dropped, side-eying the couple, before looking back at her granddaughter. "Do you want to have brothers and sisters, hbiba?" Hayat nearly dropped her fork in surprise at the sudden change of subject, while Souhila was clueless on the subject.

Anas sucked his cheeks, afraid of any hurtful words from her, then said in a cool tone. "Children aren't our main worry yet. We're actually looking forward to a family holiday." He took Hayat's hand under the table, squeezing it gently. "Right?" Anas' gaze drifted to his wife. The young woman looked lost for a second, then remembered the discussion they had on it.

"Yes!" She responded, smiling, "We decided on a fascinating destination. We plan to go there in a few weeks." They both smiled oddly, hoping this would bring up a new topic to discuss. The pole was now taut. Someone just had to grab it. They waited half a second, breathless. Waiting for someone to do so.

Salim did.

"Can we know the destination, or is it a surprise for the little one?" Hayat thanked his father with a look, ignoring the two women, who were not very fond of the sudden change of subject.

"East of Malaysia, it's a perfect destination for us and less expensive than the Maldives." Once reassured, Anas released his wife's hand. They had perfectly avoided the sensitive topic. The rest of the evening went perfectly. Anas was happy that his mother had kept her word, giving him hope for a change. However, the weekend was not over yet, and Hayat dreaded her mother's questions. She knew Salim was going to make sure that didn't happen, but a moment of inattention would probably allow her mother to intrude.

When the evening ended, everyone greeted Anas'
parents. He took advantage of this for something he hadn't
done voluntarily for years now; a hug. He took his mother
in his arms on his own accord. The gesture surprised her
somewhat, but she accepted it with pleasure.

"Chokran mama." *Thank you mother.* Anas
whispered into her ear, his heart light, hoping she could
finally accept her wrongs, and one day probably apologize
for it. In a motherly gesture, she patted his back before
joining Hakim. Salim and Hayat stayed back to clear the
table and clean it while Lamia was having fun with Souhila.
Her daughter knew how much Lamia wanted to have her
own grandchildren, but it made her happy to see that she
was making an effort to get to know Anas' daughter better.

In reality, it was a rather successful evening.

Anas looked at Hayat, who felt his gaze on her
back. She then turned to face him before smiling at him
and returning her attention to her father.

"Benti, would you like to go on a walk once we
finish this?" Salim asked while they were doing the dishes
together.

"Ok, I'll get dressed. Wait for me." They both smiled
before she ran upstairs and got something more modest. A
green kimono and a black hijab would be enough. It was
still a bit warm outside. Therefore, a light outfit was better
suited to the temperature. Once she finished dressing up,
she came down where her father was already waiting for
her at the entrance.

The sky was sublime tonight. No clouds or light too
bright to hide the stars. Even the moon was out. A cool,
gentle breeze hit their faces, adding to the coolness of the
night. Since they had set foot outside, no one had spoken,
enjoying each other's company. Salim with his hands

behind his back, and Hayat put her hand in the crook of his arm.

"I heard your mama last time, on the phone, when she asked you about you and Anas." His daughter's eyes widened while her cheeks flushed. Hayat was about to defend herself, but Salim stopped her by continuing. "I think that the discussion she and I had about her way of asking things wasn't enough," he paused to take her hand in his. "Semhili henunna." *Excuse me, my darling.* It was heartbreaking to see her father disappointed about something he was in no way responsible for.

"Baba, you don't have to apologize or be sorry, when you're not in the wrong. You did your best, and now we just need to wait. Sabr, baba. That's all we need to have right now." His daughter still remembered the anger she had felt during the discussion, but she kept it to herself. After a moment of silence, looking into each other's eyes, the two resumed their walk, still not knowing where they were going to end up. Nevertheless, at some point, they were going to make the return trip home.

"Is he treating you well?" The father was genuinely worried about his daughter. Salim knew some people could totally flip the coin after marriage and be a nightmare. Even if he didn't find anything about that, he was still worried. She chuckled a bit, finding Salim's attitude adorable and sweet.

"Yes, he is, baba. Don't trouble your mind too much." Hayat thought for a solid minute about what to add next. "In fact, I'm very surprised by the patience he's showing me. Probably because he already got married once, he had time to work on it. I don't know. But I'm glad I found a man like him, for now, I have nothing to complain about. It's only been a bit more than a week since we got married. We will see if anything comes up in the future.

However, I have faith in him and our relationship." She paused for a moment. "It's only the start, after all." Salim nodded, understanding where she was coming from. Her words made him feel a bit of relief about her situation. The father was glad to see her enjoying her relationship.

"You're right. Let's pray it stays that way until the end." Hayat tapped on the crook of his arm as if to tell him that he shouldn't worry too much. Nothing indicated that he was going to become the opposite of what he showed them.

Hayat had hopes.

After this very comforting discussion, Salim and Hayat retraced their steps back toward the house.

Little Souhila, as soon as they entered, ordered them to exceptionally watch a Disney movie with them, before bedtime. Of course, both were fans, so they were not going to refuse this moment of *Madeleine de Proust* to share together. When everything was on loan for the film Hercules, the little one was sitting on the sofa. Salim and Lamia on one side, and Anas and Hayat on the other, with Souhila between them. Barely a few minutes into the movie, then the little one fell asleep in her father's arms. It was adorable. But Anas was large enough to also have room for his wife, who eventually fell asleep on him too. He looked at them both with a massive smile on his face.

Anas was so happy.

I'm the most blessed man el hemdulliLlah.

Chapter 33

In a few days, they were going on their first trip together. Hayat was too occupied with her personal project to pay any attention to it. On her tablet, she played with colors to find the best possible combinations. With the most discretion, she had taken the measurements of the prayer room in order to transcribe them to a different scale, making a sketch on her white sheet. She wanted to marry the colors blue and green while keeping a certain brightness in the room. It was a complicated task, but in the end, she came up with a fairly conclusive sketch. While she was adding whatever decorations she imagined, she heard the office door open suddenly. Quickly, and in surprise, she closed the tab to open another and acted as if nothing had happened. Anas eyed her suspiciously, joining her at her desk.

"What were you doing?" A bead of sweat ran down her back under the sudden stress. To not blow her cover, she did as if she was too focused to notice him.

Hayat was as he had imagined.

The glasses at the tip of her nose, the strands of hair framing her chubby cheeks, her hazel eyes which juggled between his... In his mind, the question could hang around for a long time. As long as he could look at her.

Anas stared at her with lazy eyes. Finding her so attractive, he couldn't look at her another way. Everything was perfect at that moment, even if he was only putting his gaze on her. His ears started to get warm, exhibiting the effect she had on him.

"Nothing." She finally said, far too quickly. But her words brought back his attention to the main subject. She pursed her lips before giving him a fake smile, hoping it would convince him. He knew it wasn't genuine because when she smiled, her eyes were barely visible. Anas knew he had to try something else.

In one swift and efficient movement, he spun her chair around so that Hayat was facing him. Gently, he put his hands on the armrests, making every vein appear on his bare forearms, not breaking the gaze he held. Hayat had a lot of trouble keeping eye contact with the man standing in front of her. Anas was clearly turning her on. Her husband was the object of all her desires, and the more time passed, the more she wanted to taste him. Feeling his warmth and the way his muscles would effortlessly support her heavy body.

At this exact moment, she wanted to kiss him.

Unconsciously, her gaze drifted to his lips. She broke eye contact for half a second, making Anas smirk. He could see her cheeks tint with vivid red. He bent down to reach a few inches away from his wife's face. Forcing her to look up before she sat completely in her chair. For a moment, their breaths mingled in a burning silence of truth.

"Show me." He whispered. His hot breath hit her face, making her shiver. Hayat was getting into a state of neediness when he hadn't even touched her yet.

How is that even possible?

With difficulty, she replied in the same tone, "I can't." Anas arched an eyebrow, bringing his face closer.

Now their bodies shared the same heat, a little more, and their lips would caress. At first, the young man only wanted to extract information about his wife's activity, but he didn't realize that it would affect him too. The switch trapped him in a state of desire. This information no longer mattered when his wife was only millimeters away from his face. His eyes lingered far too long on Hayat's parted lips, begging to be kissed.

Short of breath, thoughts clouded with needs, he continued. "Why?" Her lips parted a bit more, but words couldn't escape them. He arched his brow again, and the simple action made it worse for Hayat.

Desire was slowly consuming her.

"Because." Hayat's words were no more audible than a breath. Therefore, Anas played his last card. He took off her glasses, tilting his head a little to the side. A little more, and they were finally going to kiss. They wanted to, but one was too shy to admit it, and the other was only waiting for a sign to finally taste her lips. His eyes still locked on hers, and the sound of their beating hearts completed the silence between them.

"Please, Hayat, show me." His plea made her melt on the spot, unable to respond to his request. Slowly, she shook her head. If even at this distance, with their lips touching with every word, she would rather not divulge anything about her activity. Anas gave up on getting an answer from her, so he walked away.

With a burst of courage, Hayat grabbed him by the t-shirt, pulling him back to the distance before his departure. Anas was a bit confused. Was she about to tell him the truth? Her trembling voice, completely needy, rang in his ears.

"Anas." She couldn't do anything but plead for his name. Her husband felt his heart skip a beat at the sound of his first name in such a distressed voice.

"Yes, Hayati?" His needs nailed him to the spot. The adrenaline made his heart beat fast and irregularly in an attempt to make him move faster, but he couldn't move an inch. Hayat was about to say something, but she stopped. Her brain completely blank, she didn't even notice the nickname Anas just gave her. He wanted her to go through with her idea, so he leaned forward a little more to push her a bit. And, this was enough. Enough for her to ask him to fulfill her needs.

"Anas, kiss me."

The request startled him and he froze in place for a second. Disconnecting his brain from any reaction. Hayat tugged his t-shirt, needy. *"Please."* The plea activated everything necessary for Anas to connect his lips to his wife's. In the heat of the moment, he put one hand in the hollow of her waist to bring her a little closer while the other firmly held the armrest to hold her in place. Hayat slid her hands around his neck to intensify the heated touch. It was magical. Both of them had imagined what it would be like, but nothing was comparable to the action itself. When they found themselves winded, they adorned themselves before resuming. After several minutes of making out, the heat of their bodies became unbearable.

They wanted *more.*

However, Souhila's call made its way up the stairs, and they instantly froze. As if they had been caught in the act, doing something forbidden. Even separated, they could still feel the burning sensation of the kiss on their lips. Cheeks red with desire, Anas went downstairs to join Souhila while Hayat returned to her sketch of the prayer room. Yet, with hazy thoughts, she ran her thumb over her lips, plumped up by the intimate moment they had shared. She giggled, before catching her breath, calming her racing heart.

Their thoughts were directed toward each other, even though they weren't around one another.

- ☾ -

The closet was wide open with the suitcase on the floor, while Hayat was standing in between them, imagining the outfits she might wear in the hot Malaysian sun. She had a color palette in front of her, with her clothes, her abayas, her khumurs, and her hijabs, but she didn't know which one to choose for the next ten days of vacation. While she was debating what was going in her suitcase, Anas entered the room with one too. She watched him pack his things, thobes, underwear, and shorts, put them in his suitcase, and close it as quickly as he opened it. Men never failed to surprise her. In the blink of an eye, they could pack their bags, without worrying about anything.

They have it too easy, she thought.

She saw him go into the bathroom and come back with a small toilet bag, which he put in the outside pocket before putting the suitcase in a corner of the room and sitting on the bed. Hayat blinked several times, puzzled by his quick decisions.

"And you're done? Just like that?" The confusion appeared on her husband's face.

"Yes," he looked at her empty one. "Not you, apparently."

"I can't choose what colors I want to wear." She paused, "They are all so pretty." Distraught, she sat down at his side, dropping her body on the mattress.

"You need my help?" Anas looked at her over his shoulder as she lied down. For a solid minute, they stared at each other.

"No," she paused. "I just need some time to decide." Her husband joined her, so he could face her on the bed.

"Ok, I will be here then. You still have a few days to finish packing." Hayat was fully aware of this, but her project was taking up too much of her time – on top of her work – so she had to finish this tonight. She put it entirely on her side before running her hand through Anas's hair. He wanted to snuggle up against her touch but restrained himself. Gradually, her hand slipped from his hair to then pass to his collarbone before passing to his chest.

Procuring him goosebumps on his skin.

He closed his eyes to appreciate this soft caress.

Just touching each other made them remember the kiss they had shared earlier. Beneath the palm of her hand, Hayat could feel Anas' heart racing, coming almost in sync with her own. She saw something slip in her husband's eyes, causing her to remove her hand from his chest. As she moved back and forth on it, she could clearly see the difference between her skin and his. It was mesmerizing at some point. They came from the same part of the world, and yet they looked so different. She was too focused to notice the shaky breath that broke the barrier of his lips as he held his wife's hand in place over his heart.

"Don't… Don't start something you can't finish." He said while opening his eyes, looking straight back at her. Hayat approached him. Slowly.

In a tone that wanted to be assured, but didn't sound more assured than hesitation, she stated, "What if I wanted to?" Her doe eyes gazed at him, the hazel orbs hiding a much deeper desire. With ease, he slid her under him before caging her between his two strong and muscular, arms. The surprise showed on her face. He started kissing her languidly in the crook of her neck, as she put her hand over her mouth to hide the little noises she was making. Anas stopped and looked into her eyes.

"Do you?" Silence. Then, he continued, trailing his way down while one of his hands started to slide under her oversized shirt. He stopped, and asked again, "Do you, Hayat?" Short breaths came out as a response. No opposition. So, he continued before one of his fingers slid on the side of her pants to take it down.

At that moment, Hayat grabbed his hand, gazing at him. Eyes glassy with desire, her hand hiding half of her completely red face. The action was enough to stop everything. She didn't need to say anything. Anas came back up and kissed her cheek before helping her to get up. The guilt of keeping him waiting was beginning to weigh on Hayat's shoulders. Even though Anas seemed patient, and didn't do anything to force her, the guilt remained present. Before getting married, she thought that the marriage had to be consummated as soon as possible. Some were even doing it without really wanting to.

But Hayat just couldn't do that.

Anas noticed the switch in the air as he got up to go to the bathroom, so he stopped and returned to the bed with her.

"What's troubling you?" Hayat looked at him, a tinge of sadness in her eyes.

"I feel guilty." Anas frowned.

"Why?" His wife sighed, collapsing in on herself under the weight of the confession she was about to make.

"Because, all I ever knew was to do it right after I get married, or all of this would be useless!" Hayat got up, angry at herself. "But, *I* can't." Several times, she tapped her fingertips on her chest. Anas came up to her, to ease her emotions. "Is there something wrong with me?" Hayat looked at him, still saddened by how she couldn't go forward in the relationship. Anas put his hands on her shoulder, with a kind expression on his face.

"No! No, nothing is wrong with you." He paused, sensing her muscles relaxing under his touch. "I did not marry for this. Yes, I want you because I'm attracted to you, but this is not the reason I chose you." He brought her a bit closer. "I chose you because when I look at you, my heart is at peace. All the emotions, and thoughts, that go through me during the day evaporate the instant I see you." Hayat felt hope blooming inside her chest.

"Really? You're not saying this to soothe me?" Her husband kissed her forehead and pecked her lips, holding her close to his chest.

"I meant every word." Hayat sensed all her worries falling from her shoulders. They stayed there, hugging until she felt better to get back to her suitcase.

After two hours of fighting with herself about what she wanted to wear on the trip, Hayat closed her suitcase.

Chapter 34

The wind breezed through the window, knocking on Hayat's face, keeping her awake till they got to the airport. The flight was very early, too early, even so, she had trouble staying awake. She also checked a few times to see if Souhila was still asleep, as the trip was going to be extremely long. At that time of the year, Anas had not found a direct flight. Thus, they will have to make a stopover for a few hours in Singapore before taking their second plane to Malaysia. Her husband seemed so focused on the road that he didn't notice the look she gave him.

While driving, every time he changed gears, Hayat could detail every vein on his hands as well as on his forearms. A thought crossed her mind, creating a feeling of jealousy. She cleared her throat, speaking loud enough only for him to hear.

"Wouldn't you like to put on more... Mastour clothes?" Anas glanced at her, keeping his attention mainly on the road.

"What do you mean?" Now, she felt a bit embarrassed. Until now, Hayat had no reason to be jealous, but only imagining a woman's eyes on her husband made her feel that way.

"I don't like knowing that another woman can see what I see." Only silence was a response to her worries. Then his castling voice came to make its way into the hollow of her ear.

"I will try." She was happy to see that he wasn't directly refusing her request and that he was at least going to try. The rest of the road was peacefully quiet. Nothing was wrong with that. Everyone was in a hurry to arrive at the villa they had reserved.

Gradually, the plane filled up, until it was almost full. Anas was between Souhila and Hayat. Once everyone was seated, Hayat began making du'aa for the departure flight and Anas did the same, telling Souhila to repeat each word after him.

"Allah is the Greatest. Allah is the Greatest. Allah is the Greatest. Glory is to Him, Who has provided this for us, though we could never have had it by our efforts. Surely, unto our Lord we are returning. O Allah, we ask You on our journey for goodness and piety, and for works that are pleasing to You. O Allah, lighten this journey for us and make its distance easy for us. O Allah, You are our Companion on the road and the One in Whose care we leave our family. O Allah, I seek refuge in You from this journey's hardships, and from the wicked sights in store, and from finding our family and property in misfortune upon returning."[10]

The youngest did a fantastic job, then once finished, he explained to her why he was doing a du'aa when traveling, and what every word in Arabic meant. Souhila listened attentively, appreciating the fact that her father always took the time to explain and teach her.

---

[10] Reference: Hisn al-Muslim 207

As the plane began taking off, he gave his daughter a book, so she could be entertained during the flight. His attention returned to Hayat, who was totally focused on her invocations, her hands over her ears, chewing on something. Anas was a little stressed because it was the first time they were going to fly since Souhila. Since her birth, Anas hadn't had the time or the opportunity to organize a trip or even take a vacation with his daughter, far from the city and the routine. Anas was about to take Hayat's hand during the take-off because he was anxious, but a shrill cry at his side nailed him to the spot.

Souhila was the source of it.

His daughter, who was totally focused on her book a few minutes ago, found herself yelling, probably in pain, at take-off. Panic started to take control of Anas. He did not know what to do. He felt helpless. Slowly, everything started to blur, and his heart started to echo in his ears. Anas just stood there, watching her scream and cry. Souhila asked for help by pulling on his sleeve, but he couldn't do anything.

"Anas!" Hayat's loud voice startled him. She handed him something, but so much panic consumed him that it took him a while to notice it was a pack of chewing gum. "Here, give her this. It can help, although if it won't solve the problem." He took the pack with a shaky hand, before giving her one. His wife was a little surprised to see his reaction. He was pale as if fear had taken over him. Worried, she put a hand on his shoulder to get his attention. "Anas, are you ok?" Her husband swallowed hard, running a hand through his hair, pretending nothing had happened, hearing her daughter's cries slowly disappear. He took her hand, before kissing it tenderly.

"Yes, I'm perfectly fine." Hayat looked at him suspiciously.

"Are you sure?" Anas hesitated but nodded since he didn't trust his voice. He was all shaken. A man like him, trembling like a leaf after his daughter screamed in pain. Hayat felt there was a reason behind it. The rest of the flight was rather quiet, turbulences waking them up at times, but she was able to go back to sleep. Anas had stolen the cushion she brought, so she turned him into her cushion and settled on his shoulder for the rest of the flight.

- ☾ -

Feet in the sand, with the gentle wind blowing from the ocean, moved the clothes of Anas and Hayat as they walked under the sun with Souhila. The transparency of the water was wonderful to see. The scene was similar to the ones we'd see in the movies. Blue sky, bright sun, fine white sand, and crystal clear water.

All the elements were there to promise a good vacation.

Even the little one had a good time by the sea.

At one point, Anas paused, forcing Hayat to do the same. She looked at him puzzled, not understanding what was about to happen. He pointed at a tree, not too far, with a big smile on his face.

"Race, you and me. The first to the tree wins." His wife instantly accepted the challenge, they called for Souhila to be the arbitrator and stand next to the tree. Since Anas was a bit more athletic, he allowed her two seconds before he started running. Hayat looked over her shoulder, thinking she was safe, but saw him arriving right behind her. She tried to speed up, but even so, she couldn't pass him.

Souhila noted the end of the race when her father arrived first. Exhausted, Hayat still wanted to start over.

The smallest jumped into the winner's arms, happy that her father had won. His wife did not accept the defeat and asked for a rematch. Anas kissed her forehead to both comfort her and distract her from racing again.

And it worked.

Her competitive spirit vanished instantly. The little family chuckled at the silliness of the whole thing. They continued their walk. Anas and Hayat were both so happy to be able to share this moment together. Occasionally, they exchanged knowing glances, meaning so many things for one another.

That night, Anas booked a fancy restaurant with a wonderful view of the sea. Fortunately, it wasn't too humid for the couple to be outside. For the occasion, Hayat and Souhila had decided to match their outfits. She knew how much their relationship meant to him, so with the simple action, she wanted to show him how great they were getting along. Anas had a huge smile on his face, seeing them matched when they came into the living room, ready to go. He came closer to them and took Hayat by the waist. Anas wanted to kiss her, but Souhila looked at them attentively. So, he resigned himself to just a peck on the cheek.

"Y'all be matching without me? I feel left out…" Anas displayed a falsely sad face that made the two girls laugh. He gasped dramatically, pretending to be touched by their mockery. In revenge, Anas took his daughter in his arms, before spinning her in the air, her soft laughter filling the room. Hayat looked at them, emotion shining in her eyes. She was happy to have come across a man like him. Seeing him like that, she had almost forgotten the reaction he had to her crying on the plane a few days prior. Hayat still wanted to know why he had reacted like that but didn't want to rush him either. She erased that thought from her head, before joining them on the doorstep.

The sea air did them so much good after the meal. Souhila was playing with a toy that one of the waiters gave her, while Anas and Hayat were enjoying the view beside them, holding hands. It was wonderful. At one point, Anas stopped looking at the sea, to concentrate on Hayat. This woman was sublime. He could stare at her for hours. But what made him the happiest was that he was one of the few men who could admire her true beauty – both physical and intellectual. Every day since they met, he prayed to Allah that this woman would be made for him. Now, here they are, married on a family vacation, enjoying the beach.

He felt complete.

Then Hayat caught him staring at her, making him feel embarrassed. She genuinely smiled at him. He instantly did the same. She could watch him smile for hours. The dimple that appeared on his face made her fall under his charm every single time. It was her weakness. She looked at him intensely, almost hypnotized by his gaze. Words formed in her head until her heart spit them out before she could stop herself, thinking it was much too soon.

"I love you, Anas." She didn't know why she said that, but it felt like the best time to say it. Taken aback, he didn't know what to answer. The awkward silence after that moment of vulnerability hurt her. The disappointment could be read on her face, making Anas regret his silence. He felt the same, and he wanted to tell her, but he couldn't. He just *couldn't*. Watching her push her chair, he could hear the sound of her heart shattering, after each step.

"Hayat, wait!" The surrounding crowd focused their attention on him, but he didn't really care. He just wanted to catch up with her, so he had a chance to explain himself.

Rushing, he took his daughter, paid the bill, and ran after his wife who was getting ready to get into a taxi to go back to the villa. He shouted her name, but she pretended to not hear it. For the first time in years, Anas was ready to pull out all the slander. Even the little one began to feel that something was happening under her nose.

"Baba, why did she leave without us?" Anas stroked her head, wanting to assure her, but all he was doing was reassuring himself.

"Don't worry, ghazaali, she was just feeling tired. We're going to join her now, ok?" He replied with a fake smile. He could already see himself losing her. The thought bruised him from within. Just like the first time. Panic got the best of him, though he was still trying to hide his emotions. Tears stung the corners of his eyes, but he couldn't afford to cry. Not outside, and even less, in front of his daughter. He had to make her feel like everything was fine and reassure her that Hayat wasn't going anywhere.

He would rather not put his treasure, and his heart, through this hell again.

Chapter 35

Running quickly, he entered the villa, he gently placed his daughter in her room, and gave her an extra toy to entertain herself while he found Hayat. He tripped on his thobe, hurrying to find her. He took it off and continued. Anas thought, by wearing one tonight, Hayat was going to notice that she was being listened to and that her opinion mattered. Indirectly establishing the feelings he got for her. Even though he couldn't say those words. He ran around, searching all the rooms hoping to see her sitting somewhere, or lying down, he didn't care. Anas just wanted to see her, he wanted to make things right, he needed to apologize and explain himself. His heart writhed in pain as he imagined the hurting he inflicted on her by remaining silent.

It's something he won't be able to forgive himself for.

After searching all around the house, he went into the garden and that's where he saw her. Standing by the pool, looking at her reflection in the water. With a voice that mixed relief and pain, he called out her name as he ran toward her. His heart broke again when he saw his wife's features crumpled and wet with sadness.

Hayat cried.

She had cried because of *him*.

He regretted it so much.

Once at her level, Anas took her arm wanting to make contact with her, but as if she had touched fire, she escaped. There was only sadness in her beautiful hazel eyes. Her voice, hoarse with tears, almost made him kneel as he was devastated by his failure.

"Don't touch me." The young man let his arm fall to his side, his fist clenched, as he was furious with himself. His tongue nudged his cheek, as he watched her turn her back to him.

"Please, Hayat, let me explain." She looked at him over her shoulder, before drifting her gaze back to the water.

"I know. What kills me is that I already know why you didn't say it back." Anas frowned, confused. It wasn't easy to understand, but he let her continue. "It's because of Zahia, right?" He nodded, still silent. She sniffled, breaking the crumbs of heart that remained in his chest. "I understand you can't say it because of her," Hayat paused. "But I still hoped to hear those words from you. Genuinely." She added, her voice breaking under the emotion. Anas wanted to take her in his arms, go back in time, and explain to her that he, *too*, felt this strong feeling of love. But it was already late. All he could do was stare at her, unable to do anything. Hayat looked at him, waiting for him to say something, anything. "Please say something…" She begged him, feeling her thoughts getting the best of her with every passing second. She felt her head sink into a haze of harsh questioning. Her rabbit hole slowly trapping her into a downfall surrounded by darkness. Hayat was just waiting for a word from him that would prevent her from sinking. Hayat sneered when nothing came from him. She turned to leave, while Anas stood there with fear and regret.

Once in the living room, Hayat felt her body being pulled around by her husband so that she faced him.

"Please listen to me." It was now his turn to plead his case. His wife, ironically, chuckled.

"I am, but all I can hear is silence!" She paused, trying to escape him one more time. "So, if you don't have anything to *actually* say, please leave me alone." The grip on her wrist was far too firm for her to flee. An ardent look was her only response.

"Could you please let me talk?" She didn't want to hear it, all she wanted was to be alone and cry until her tears were dry.

"I gave you numerous chances to explain, but all you do is stand there looking at me with a blank expression. I understand your struggles, that you think I'm going to vanish before you if you say it back. You also have to understand that I do get hurt if you say nothing after I opened up to you! I feel like I'm being taken for an idiot, I can't even look at you!" Her orbs were juggling between his. "On the plane. When you totally freaked out for Allah knows what, and you just brushed me off even if you were shaking like a leaf! At first, I thought it was because it was too personal, and you'd eventually share it with me when we'd be alone, but now, I'm seriously doubting that. I feel like you don't even trust me..." Her words suspended in the air, hesitant to add her final thought. "As if you don't *like* me." Hayat's voice broke on the last two words.

"I do!" His scream startled her. "It's true, I like you, Hayat. I thank Allah that he made you meet my daughter every day. I was calling your brother almost instantly after every muqabala to see you again. The moment I found myself at home, I realized that I missed your presence, your sight, your scent, your laugh, your voice. All of you. Your name appeared on each of my du'aa. Every night, I take you into my arms because I'm scared you won't be there the next morning!" Anas paused, taking deep breaths, trying to calm himself. "You're my nafs, my rooh, I can't leave without you." Heart pounding, he looked at her, hoping that those words might mend her broken heart. "I'm scared of my own feelings for you because, yes, every passing day I'm afraid that you could also disappear when my back is turned, or when my eyes are closed." Anas was about to add something, but a distant loud cry was heard from the stairs. Both surprised, they looked at each other, not understanding where it could come from.

Anas felt like his world was falling apart when he saw that his daughter was the one crying hot tears.

"Fuck." He breathed out. His emotions were clouding his judgment too much to take account of the word that had just come out of his mouth. Without thinking, Anas ran to scoop his daughter in his arms, who was babbling incomprehensible words between two sobs.

However, she escaped from her father's arms before running toward Hayat, screaming "Don't leave me! I'm a good girl, and I'm nice to you, please don't leave me!" These words destroyed Hayat. She didn't think for a moment that the argument would trigger such a reaction in her. Anas was on his knees, completely distraught. Hayat, after having dried her tears, put herself on the same level as the little girl, before she took her in her arms, gently stroking her back. When she saw that her sobs had subsided, she parted from her, showing her a breathing technique, to blow the candle. They counted together as they took each breath. Once her heart was serene, Hayat dried Souhila's tears.

"Do you want another hug?" The little one nodded, almost jumping into her arms. Hayat took the opportunity to move her on the sofa. Anas had not moved yet, he thought he had failed. Failed to protect his daughter, but also at protecting his wife's heart. The guilt was starting to gnaw at him so much, that he didn't even hear Hayat's repetitive calls. She came to him, a softer expression on her face, Souhila still in her arms, and led a hand for him to hold, and automatically, he did. Together, they sat down on the sofa, ready to finally settle down.

"You're not going to leave me?" The little girl asked, taking the words out of her father's mouth. Hayat looked at her, then Anas, who was also waiting for her answer.

"I'm not going anywhere." She responded by stroking her hair. Both had the same reaction; a breath of relief. Gradually, she saw the little girl's eyes closing under the calm she was feeling. Hayat laid her head on Anas' chest, feeling his heart pound. She bit her lip, feeling the guilt growing inside her. "I'm sorry, Anas." She whispered, looking at him. He cradled her face, caressing her cheek with a thumb, before kissing her softly.

"I'm sorry, too, Hayati." This nickname made her miss a beat. In his mouth, it sounded so unique. She smiled tenderly at him, before properly settling into the crook of his arms, taking advantage of this moment of calm and serenity to regain their senses. As they sat there, Hayat put Surat Al-Baqara, as a protection, so it would shield them from any evil that would cause them to argue once more.

- ☾ -

Anas placed his daughter under the covers, and Hayat was waiting for him in the door frame. He approached her slowly, Anas wrapping his strong arm around her waist, his other arm above Hayat's head, to bring her closer to him. Imprisoning her between his body, and the door frame. She loved it. Her curves married him to perfection.

"Are you trying to seduce me?" Hayat asked, forcing him to come closer by the collar.

"Maybe?" Her husband responded, inches away from her. "Is it working?" He added, leaving a trail of kisses from her cheek to her collarbone.

"Perhaps…" They both chuckled, before going back to their rooms hand in hand.

Once their routine was over, Anas and Hayat met in bed, half asleep. The sound of crickets filled the room, accompanied by the light of the moon streaming through the curtains. Anas was still thinking about Hayat's words, which were playing all over and over again in his head because she was right. He couldn't hide things from her and expected her not to be hurt by his behavior.

It wasn't fair.

He wanted to make it up to her. With a heavy heart, he settled on his wife's chest. She was surprised by the sudden gesture, but she accepted it by flicking his hair. The action relaxed him to sleep. But vivid memories of his daughter's tears kept him wide awake.

"She was two years old when it happened." Hayat didn't instantly recognize the subject of the discussion due to fatigue, then she quickly remembered. "Souhila was sick. *Deadly* sick. One night, me and Zahia were ready to go to bed when her shrill cry echoed throughout the house. At first, we thought it was a nightmare, but she was begging to turn off the light and her head was intensely hurting." He paused, pulling Hayat closer in his embrace. She stroked his hair, and back, to reassure him. "That's when we rushed to the ER…" A shaky breath left his body. "During the whole ride, all we could hear was her cries of pain, her tears, and her pleas. Of course, her mother tried to calm her down, but nothing worked. My ears still remember her cries. I felt useless." Another one. "That day, I thought I was going to lose my daughter. My *life*." His last words were no higher than a sigh. "El hemduliLlah, the infection wasn't too advanced, antibiotics were enough to heal her. But what could have happened if we arrived too late? Or if we had not seen the symptoms? Souhila…" Anas couldn't even utter those words, let alone imagine it. Hayat felt a bit silly for forcing him to divulge a new painful memory. She felt selfish.

"I'm so sorry, Anas, I always let my emotions cloud my judgment." He got up, before resting on one arm, stroking the face of his beloved with the other.

"Hayati, you don't have to feel guilty because you wanted to understand why I was hurting." He let his hand slide over her heart, making her blush. "On the contrary, it shows me that you are interested in me and that you want to understand me. *Know* me. We all have painful memories that we would like to forget, or even erase, but those are the ones that made us. Everything happens for a reason. If I didn't want to talk about it right away, I wouldn't have. But, I want to build something strong with you now. If I have to dive back into significant memories, I will." She took his hand in hers, before kissing his palm.

"Thank you for trusting me, 'omri." Anas' heart weakened after hearing that nickname. It felt as if every atom of sadness left his body, leaving him dizzy with satisfaction.

"How did you call me?" Anas bent to get closer to his wife's face.

"'Omri...?" She paused, unease by the silence, "You don't like it?"

Anas shrugged to her face, "Oh, I love it." Following these words, Anas plunged into her neck, making his wife laugh out loud. The father was blissful to know that his wife was feeling better, and felt more comfortable with him, even giving him an affectionate nickname.

The eventful day ended on a good note.

Chapter 36

The noises of the construction echoed in his eardrums. He had only been at work for a few hours, and yet he was already tired. Under the blazing sun of the last weeks of August, the workers were not making as much progress, and they were also making a lot more mistakes. It forced Anas to spend entire days monitoring them. Listening to their complaints, their hammers which struck constantly, the sound of the electric drills, their excuses and terrible solutions.

Since returning from Malaysia, he has been rethinking his plan as the people he hired were no longer able to achieve their work properly. For a few months now, everything was going well. Anas had a hard time understanding how from a good situation he could go to reviewing plans every day. Had he given his directions incorrectly? Did he not communicate the information correctly? Did he have to stay on their backs night and day to get what he wanted? With all these questions, he almost wanted to tear out all the hair on his scalp.

A little more and he would fire them all on the spot.

There were only a few details left for the house to be habitable, and for people to start living there. He glanced at his watch, checking the time, and his anger grew. He had a visitor today for the apartment that Hayat occupied.

And he forgot…

At full speed, his mind on two things at once, he grabbed his jacket. If he came back here later, and he saw another mistake on their part, Anas would sincerely fire this team. He took the time to remind the project manager who was responsible for the site before running to his car. Fortunately, the apartment was not too far from the house being renovated. Before getting out of the car, he brushed his hair and made sure his appearance was presentable before joining the couple waiting in front of the building.

This visit reminded him of the one he made months ago with Hayat and his friend Kamila. Only good memories. He still remembered her clothes, the way she walked, the shyness in her eyes and her voice.

Anas missed Hayat.

He missed his *wife*.

As soon as he opened the door to the apartment, he wanted to end it there and go home. Back to his wife, and his daughter. Put an end to this exasperating day. The responsibilities forced him to stay here and use his professionalism to finalize this rental. He hid his frustration perfectly by clearing his throat, not wanting potential tenants to take it home with them.

Once finished, Anas greeted them before returning to the torture.

The young man changed his mind by putting some Quran on the way home, feeling his anger gradually evaporate. He was still worried what they had messed up once more when he was away. When he arrived, he called the project manager to ask him for a report on the progress, and he was relieved to know that everything had gone well in his absence. He had nothing to report. Now

Anas had to stay here, watching them like an invigilator, to make sure everything was going well, while his mind just wanted to go back to his family.

- ☾ -

  The prayer room decorations and new furniture were due to arrive today, while Anas was still on his renovations. She had challenged herself to remodel the room before he came home today. This morning, as soon as Anas left for work, Hayat took the paint cans she had hidden to begin her renovations. She even asked for help from Souhila, who had fun painting too. Green and blue still managed to have consistently merged, even in real life, and especially dry. It was this result that Hayat was afraid of. Often, the colors could make pretty results wet, but once dry, nothing would be the same. But, this time it was *perfect*.

  Hayat removed the plastics, before bringing the new furniture into the room to assemble and arrange them in the right places. She had taken a small chest of drawers in brown wood, with a new white lamp. Occasionally, the fight they had last week flashed through her mind as she put the furniture sides together. Almost demotivating her to finish. Making her zone out. Slowing her progress as numerous questions crossed her mind.

  What if this happens again?
  Do I really need to hear these words from him?
  Is he going to hurt my feelings again?
  I'm scared.
  Why am I here?
  Why did I accept all these responsibilities?

  However, she forced herself to remember the words he said next, the only moment that really mattered.

That statement was far more important than a small argument. Shaking her head, she hoped to dispel all those unwanted questions obscuring her work. After assembling everything, Hayat took the mushaf with the Quran on top to put it on the brand-new furniture. Her chest swelling with pride, she looked at the final result.

Challenge succeeded. She thought, whipping her forehead, and staring at the surrounding walls.

Hayat was so happy that she didn't notice the time passing. Through the window of the room, she could see Anas' car parked in front of the house. She then hastened to go downstairs, in order to welcome him after his long day at work.

As soon as he set foot in the house, Anas was greeted by his wife's smile and his daughter's open arms. His hard gaze, after an exhausting day, softened once placed on Hayat and Souhila. This image warmed his heart. With joy on his features, he took his daughter with one arm before slipping his other arm around Hayat. The joy he perceived in their facial expressions and their laughter alleviated all the stress and complications he faced today.

"Salam a'leykoum my loves, did you have a good day?" The man noticed a stain of paint on his wife's neck when she turned her head.

She probably worked on something. Anas thought.

Hayat almost confessed what had taken her the entire day to prepare, but she let the smaller one answer before she revealed everything.

"Wa'leykoum salam baba!" His daughter's small voice captured his full attention. "We had a good day, Hayat and I painted!" She looked at her with wide eyes. For a second, she thought her surprise would die with her.

"Wa'leykoum salam 'omri, yes, we had." Hayat felt her husband's hand around her neck, his burning touch on her skin, it was pure delight. He watched her for a moment, before tilting her head to the side, giving him a better view of her milky skin. Anas touched a spot where the painting was. All the while he was looking her in the eye.

"I can see that." He said, drifting his gaze to his daughter. "What did you paint?" Souhila was about to respond, but she was cut off by her stepmother.

"Something that we will show him later. Right, Souhila?" The little one looked at her confused, before remembering that she had told her that it was a surprise. So, she just nodded. Anas watched his wife exhale in relief, sensing that there was something behind this. He looked at her suspiciously.

"Perfect, then. Let's see it now!" Hayat was going to protest, but Anas was already on the first step of the stairs, following his daughter's directions to where the surprise was. Before he could put his hand on the doorknob of the bedroom, his wife came to stand between them. Short of breath, she put a finger in front of his face to stop him and prevent him from entering.

"Stay there." Anas raised his eyebrows, smirking, showing his deep dimple.

"What are you hiding in there?" Her husband asked, towering over her from all of his height, forcing her to raise her head slightly.

Hayat sighed, defeated. Anas was already in front of their bedroom door, she couldn't just push him away and make him wait more."At least close your eyes…" With a suspicious look, he did. Hayat took her husband's hand, heart pounding. She didn't know what his reaction was going to be, or even if he was going to appreciate the renovation. It was two strong colors, it could not please everyone and on the top, he was the master of it.

After a few steps, she stopped in front of the door, closing it so that he would open it.

"Open your eyes." Anas saw in front of him a rather pretty closed door, he glanced at his wife, already with a joke in mind.

"Is that my surprise? The door is gorgeous, thank you." At first, Hayat was much too stressed to understand that it was a joke. But a few seconds later, she laughed. Once calmed down, Anas opened the door, letting a gasp escape his lips when he saw the new prayer room decoration.

"Wow! You made this all by yourself? It's amazing!" Hayat's features, once tense with stress, gave way to a big smile. Her heavy heart was relieved of all worries when she saw the light on her husband's face. He was sincere in his words, and that made her heart feel better. The woman pointed at her stepdaughter, a smile on her features.

"Souhila helped me, I wasn't alone." Under the loving eyes of his wife, Anas looked at his daughter before tickling her belly, filling the room with her laughter accompanied by praise coming from him. If Hayat had thought of immortalizing this moment with a video, she would have done it. Nevertheless, this memory will only remain etched in their memory to all three forever.

Anas noticed Hayat's withdrawal, refusing to leave her alone on her side, he held out his hand. She looked at it for a while, before taking it, and she felt herself tugged in one smooth motion. Now the three of them were celebrating this new space, with laughter and exclamations of joy.

- ☾ -

Anas was already on the bed with his chest bare from the heavy heat in the room, waiting for his wife to come out of the bathroom. The sound of the doorknob made him get up, just wanting to look at his wife before going to sleep. Hayat was sublime, her hair wet, and her floral shower gel filled the whole room and made way to Anas' nostrils. But he noticed that even after all this time, Hayat kept her clothes much larger for her, hiding every limb of her body. As if the insecurity she felt still wouldn't leave her. It stopped him from meeting the woman he felt when he pressed his body against hers. Having thick, baggy joggers and a long-sleeves t-shirt must not be pleasant with this temperature.

His burning, tired eyes were examining every inch of her hidden body as if he could already imagine every curve. The heavy look made her blush while forcing her to stand straight to her full length. She smiled shyly, approaching him. Taking his face between her hands, while she stood between his legs. He took the opportunity to put his hands around her waist before slipping them behind her knees. In silence, they only looked at each other, stroking one another with a thumb. The moment was so precious, just looking, without saying anything, without a sound.

Simply enjoying the sight before them.

While Anas looked at his wife with love, he remembered his call earlier in the day.

"My mom called today, she asked if you were ok." Hayat's features did not change, not even a little. She was still gazing at him with this special gleam in her eyes.

"Thanks for letting me know, pass her the salam next time." Unexpectedly, Hayat with a smile on her face, began to bombard him with kisses, causing him to burst out laughing. Without knowing how, his wife ended up sitting on his lap, his hands on her hips, still covering him with numerous affectionate gestures. Feeling the weight, and the warmth of Hayat, on his lap, closer to his body, Anas sensed the shift in his emotions. His heart began to race, almost louder than his wife's laughter. Her husband's large, veiny hands began to slide down her t-shirt, causing her to shiver. Desire crept into his eyes, while she was slowly coming back to kiss him once more.

Between two kisses, which became more and more carnal, she informed him that she was planning to do a picnic with Kamila tomorrow, his sisters, and Souhila – no men were allowed to come. It was the last days of summer, and the women wanted to share a little time together. Anas only responded with grunts, far too busy remembering the taste of his wife's lips. A squeal escaped Hayat when her husband carried her to put her astride him, without stopping what they were doing.

They wanted each other.

They were *hungry* for each other.

Anas placed her back gently on the mattress. For a second, Hayat was scared, but she also wanted to go on. He sensed her hesitation. Then, kissing her neck, her husband began the interrogation.

"What troubles your mind, Hayati?" A squeal escaped her before she could answer. She was afraid to chill the mood.

"I'm scared," she stopped, wanting to control her breathing, while Anas was teasing her. "You won't like my body." Without slowing down the pace, he continued.

"Why?" She wasn't thinking straight anymore, in her mind, nothing could make sense of this discussion. Seeing that she couldn't answer, Anas stopped, wanting to have a real conversation with her. It took her a few minutes to calm down. She looked at him with glassy eyes, which made Anas feel an electric shock throughout his body.

"Because I'm fat." Her husband frowned, not understanding where this was coming from.

"Who told you that?" He asked, holding her hand in his.

Hayat sighed, "I've always been defined that way…" She confessed, lowering her head. "I was told that I had to lose weight, eat less, that I had fat to lose. I tried diet after diet, yet nothing worked. And…" She paused, rolling her sleeves up, "I have these type of scares on my arms and thighs. So, I started to hide it at all times. If no one could see it, I wouldn't receive any comments." Anas took her arm, kissing each scare while looking straight into her eyes. They were barely visible, but he could feel them under his touch. It made his heart ache with sadness. Imagining Hayat lose against her demons, and freeing herself from her pain, was too much for him. Anas was grateful his wife was comfortable enough to show this part of her. Letting him understanding her a bit more. After a few more kisses, he took her chin, moving closer, so he could see the beautiful hazel eyes the man loved so much.

"Listen to me, Hayati, ok?" She nodded, with a slightly sad face. "I did not choose you for your body, I don't care what shape or form, or scares you have. I took *you* because I craved *you*. And, you don't need to care anymore, since *I* will be the only one to see you naked. I will assure you, you will be claimed as the woman you are and how you need me to." He paused for a second, seeing that his words were having an effect on her. Hayat knew he wasn't saying that in vain. He was sincere and ready to make her understand that. "And lastly, why do you think I go so much to the gym and lift heavy?" The woman almost gasped at the question, understanding his point indirectly. But, she needed to hear him say it

"I don't know, tell me." Hayat responded in a seductive tone, Anas smirked.

"To claim and praise a beautiful woman like you, Hayati." It was her turn to smile, before kissing him softly. "We are a team, if I do something wrong, or hurt you, just tell me. So, if you want us to do it tonight, we will. And I will make you feel wonderful while doing so, and if not, we could just kiss and cuddle until we sleep." Silence. For a solid minute, Hayat thought about this proposition. A part of her really wanted her husband, on the other, she was a bit scared to take the leap.

So, before giving her answer, Hayat went to lock the door, then returned to her husband's arms with a beating heart and eyes shining with desire. Without her even giving it to him yet, Anas had a smile that went from ear to ear. Welcoming her with hugs and kisses. On top of him, she admired her husband's features, letting her soft voice go through his ears.

"Let's do it then."

Chapter 37

The sun began to rise, and Anas and Hayat had already finished their morning routine. In complete silence, he combed his wife's hair, sometimes glancing at her through the mirror. Since their marriage, both Hayat and Anas' hair had grown. She enjoyed every stroke in her hair as he braided them. The couple took advantage of this moment when the little one was still asleep before getting ready for their day. Anas still had work to do, but, he was finally seeing an end to the horrible experience that had been going on for weeks now.

On the other hand, Hayat had to do the groceries to prepare everything for the picnic. Kamila had to join her around ten to put up the snacks together. Chirping sparrows filled the silence of the room as Hayat watched her husband put on a thobe. Just seeing him do that made her happy. She was aware that in such a society, going out in a mastour outfit from head to toe was not very well seen, and that people were very likely to stare at him. Nevertheless, she appreciated the effort her husband was making.

With a smile on her lips, she approached Anas putting her hands on his chest, while he welcomed her in the hollow of his arms. Hayat looked him up and down, her heart swelling with pride. There was no better beauty for a man than to wear modest clothes. Not tight, not transparent, simple.

It was beautiful.

He was beautiful.

Anas took advantage of the closeness he had with his wife to place a chaste kiss on her lips. He couldn't live without it – without *her*. His heart skipped a beat at the thought. Every time he tasted her lips, they tasted different. It was an inexplicable phenomenon that he particularly appreciated. Because with each kiss, he felt like kissing her for the first time all over again.

Hayat had to go shopping, giving Anas the opportunity to spend the short morning with his daughter. It had been a while since the two had spent time with just the two of them, it must have been weird for Souhila to go from the presence of a single parent to two in just a few months. So they arranged that Hayat would go shopping for the picnic by the time Souhila got up and finished her breakfast, allowing Anas and Souhila to spend some quality time together.

She had her hand on the doorknob when she was stopped by her husband, his large hand on her wrist, a hard expression on his face. Hayat was a bit confused, two minutes earlier his face was beaming, what was different now? She faced him, not really knowing what to expect.

"You can't go out like that." Anas said simply, analyzing her from head to toe. His wife arched an eyebrow, not quite getting his point. Hayat was literally covered from head to toe in large, non-transparent clothing. Was it the colors? Did he think women shouldn't go out with colors on their clothes? But if that was the case, her husband would have made a remark about her wardrobe a long time ago. So, why would the outfit only be a problem for him today? Too many questions concealed her judgment in just a few seconds, that she didn't even hear her husband's explanation about it.

She blinked several times, before getting back to her senses. "Excuse me?"

"You forgot your purse, you can't go out like that." Hayat nodded slowly, finally understanding when she saw that she was only holding the keys to her car in her hand.

"Oh…" She laughed weirdly, "Thank you!" Anas pulled her closer to him. Then kissed her cheek, clueless about his wife's thoughts.

"You're welcome, drive safe." He added another kiss, this time on her lips, sticking his forehead to hers, eyes closed under the weight of the statement he was going to make. "And come back to us. Please." This confession was barely stronger than her heartbeat when Anas tasted her lips one last time before letting her go.

Pain stung her heart.

Seeing your husband eaten up by his experiences, his *traumas*, touched her more than she thought it would. It was now her turn to reassure him. "I will, 'omri. I will, In Shaa Allah."

A sigh of relief escaped him before he let her slip through his fingers. With these words, Hayat waved at him, as his face had now become bright again. It was the only way she wanted to leave her husband.

While Hayat strolled through the aisles of the supermarket, the shopping cart in one hand and her note in the other, she felt her phone vibrate in her bag. She picked up the phone, thinking she'd see her friend's name appear on her screen, but it was Anas who was calling, who also had changed his name to "*my one and only*" in her contact list.

She laughed at the name, before answering.

"Yes, my one and only, what do you need? Do you want me to buy something?" She could hear her husband smiling on the other side of the phone.

"*I* don't need you, for now, but this little princess right here does. She asked for you when she didn't find you at home when she woke up, I told her you were at the store buying things for the picnic." He paused, sighing. "But she did not believe me. I called you, so you can tell her yourself." Hayat cracked a laugh, while her heart was melting. Knowing she had a place in her heart, already, was an honor for her.

"Give her the phone." Anas did.

"Hayat! Are you coming home?" The excitement was so present in Souhila's voice, that she almost screamed in Hayat's ears – and Anas' at the same time. She was heartwarming.

"Yes, I am coming home, sweetheart. I'll be there in around ten to fifteen minutes." This time it was really a scream, that resounded in the telephone. Hayat could only smile at this adorable reaction. Souhila seemed so happy to know that she would come back home. To thank her for this enthusiasm, her stepmother bought her a new toy. She didn't know if she already had too many or not, but it was nice to find something to share with her.

In the aisle of children's toys, Hayat found an erasable slate like the one she had when she was a child. It was perfect. That way, if one day Souhila wanted to draw while Hayat was working on her tablet, she could sit by her side and follow her. Hayat could already imagine it. With a smile on her face, she added it to her shopping cart before heading to the checkout.

Everything seemed perfect.

Just a foot in the house and Souhila came to hug Hayat, almost making her drop the bags on the ground. Anas instantly came to the rescue, taking away each one of them in only one hand. The woman took the opportunity to hug Souhila back, picking her up, with a smile.

"Darling, where do you want me to put the bags?" Her husband asked, looking around. Hayat pointed at the kitchen worktop. Hugging the little one tightly.

"Here," she pinched Souhila's nose, making her giggle loudly. "Plus, I already have my little chef with me!" Anas was so delighted by the view. Followed by Hayat, they were all in the kitchen. She placed Souhila in the children's chair so that the little girl could also cook with Hayat.

Once the groceries were put away, Hayat accompanied Anas to the door. Her husband took the opportunity to steal a last kiss from her before leaving for work. As he left, Kamila parked in front of the house. The two distantly greeted each other, before the friend literally jumped into Hayat's arms. All giggly and eager for the day ahead, they both directly got into the kitchen. The three of them washed their hands, ready to prepare the snacks.

After a few hours of preparation, the basket was full of different snacks; sandwiches, fruit in pieces, fruit salads, but also pancakes, ghrayef, and tamina. Hayat had picked out the little girl's dress in Souhila's room and explained to her that if she needed help, she could call her anytime.

When Hayat went to her room, a white bow caught her eye. She saw a small box on the edge of her bed, with a note on top. Her heart skipped a beat, seeing it. She took it between her fingers, before reading it.

"I told you I would make you one like Souhila's, here it is. Have a nice day, في أمان الله Hayati."

Hayat had an idea of what was inside it. With a wide smile on her face, she opened it to discover a beautiful summer dress. Without hesitation, she put it on to take a picture for Anas. As soon as she sent it, Hayat received a video call. Under Anas' gaze, she puts the phone on her vanity table. Her husband looked at her with particular emotion in his eyes, biting on his bottom lips as if he was about to say something, delighted to see that the dress suited her perfectly.

"Turn around, baby." She did, with a smile on her face. The dress was simply sublime. However, a question crossed her mind.

"How did you know my size?" Hayat eyed him suspiciously, the sounds of the renovation site filling the reflective silence he had.

"You think I can't measure your curves with my hands?" He winked and chuckled as she got red. "I took the measurements on one of your dresses." Said like that, it made sense. Hayat took the phone back in her hands to say goodbye. In a few minutes they had to leave to join Anas' sisters, so she didn't have much time to talk longer with him. She blew a kiss at him, before hanging up and joining the two girls in the living room.

Kamila was having a passionate conversation with Souhila on a cartoon that they both loved. In Kamila's defense it was Imran's favorite, therefore, to communicate with him sometimes, she needed to actively watch the show. It warmed her heart to see her friend having a good time with her stepdaughter.

- ☾ -

Given the weight of the picnic basket, Hayat and Kamila shared the handle of the basket, while Souhila insisted on carrying the blanket to put on the grass. After a few minutes of walking, the girls saw Anas' sisters already sitting on a blanket almost similar to theirs. They waved at them, with big smiles on their faces. The sounds of the park and the laughter of children added warmth inside their bodies. It only took a few discussions to arrive at the subject of the newlyweds.

"So tell us, Hayat, is our brother treating you well? Because if not, we will have a word with him." Hasfa said, waiting for any sign to scold her little brother. Hayat smiled at the question, delighted to see that his sisters had no bad intentions.

"He is," she pulled a little on the dress, in order to show the details of it. "In fact, he made this dress for me." The sisters exchanged a look of delight. They were happy to see what their little brother had become. In reality, Anas did not show this side of him too much, as he was usually mocked for being too feminine. Nevertheless, Houria and Hafsa always made sure to encourage his hobbies.

"I knew he would be fond of you, Hayat." She tilted her head to the side, not understanding the nature of this statement. Houria noticed it. "What I mean is that, in his first marriage, we could see he wasn't really himself, but rather the man that he was expected to be." The tone in her voice lowered. "With you, he seems to be more *himself*. It's good to witness that." Hayat was a bit surprised by the statement and welcomed it nonetheless. She looked at her friend, who was totally focused on helping the little one to not stain her beautiful dress with the food.

The young women continued the discussion as if they had known each other for years. During this beautiful moment, she discovered that Hafsa was in fact not married yet and wasn't looking for any partner in life. Hayat was impressed by her mentality. She knew what she wanted, it was amazing. Together, they had almost finished the two baskets, as all the snacks were delicious. The rest won't last long once brought home. The colors of the sky were slowly beginning to change, indicating the end of this wonderful afternoon. Everyone said goodbye happily, eager to see each other once again.

Upon entering the house, Anas was already sitting on the couch, patiently waiting for his wife and daughter to arrive, impatient to have dinner with them. Today, Anas seemed happier than usual. Hayat wonders why because the last few days he returned exhausted from work. As soon as he saw them, he greeted them with open arms, impatient to share the news with them.

"The house is finally done!" Anas exclaimed with joy. Hayat was surprised. With a smile on her lips, she jumped into his arms, before he could turn her around. She was reassured, that her husband will be home more often.

"That's amazing!" She stated, in his neck, before looking back at him in his eyes. "Are you going to rent it out directly?" He put her back on the ground before going to sit on the sofa with her. Like wanting to have a conversation at full comfort.

"Not now, I need to do some checks and make sure the house is up to current standards. It should take a few weeks." Hayat nodded, understanding that he still had a few steps to go before he was completely done with this project. Nevertheless, the young woman was as much at peace as her husband.

Anas was going to be able to spend more time with his family, that's all he wanted.

Chapter 38

Today was back to school for Souhila, unfortunately, Anas couldn't drop her off, so he let Hayat take care of her before she went to work herself. It was the first time that the stepmother was going to drop her off. Both were delighted to enjoy this moment together. The more time passed, the more we could see that Souhila grew visibly. Soon she will be seven years old, time passes so quickly. So much so that she didn't even need help to get out of the car, Souhila was able to do so without taking too much time or anyone's help.

Once in front of the school, Hayat let go of her hand before letting her run toward the entrance, seeing her disappear between her classmates. Even though she was more concerned about her stepdaughter, she still noticed the many stares she received from the other parents – who were in a group not far from the entrance whispering and talking among themselves – with their children. Hayat didn't appreciate this misplaced insistence. To let them know that she had seen their curious protruding eyes, she waved at them with a broad smile, making them feel embarrassed. Proud of her achievement, she quickly returned to her car, in a hurry to start her working day.

The meeting with Mister Lopez would soon begin, but he called her into his office before making the conference. Hayat did not really understand the reason for this express appointment with her superior. When her hand rested on the handle of the door, the other held her tablet, heart pounding, before signaling her presence behind the door.

"Come in." His hoarse voice allowing her to enter made her stress a little more. Hayat's heart resonated in her ears, she barely heard the greetings of her superior.

"Hello, you wanted to see me?" Mister Lopez nodded, inviting her to sit in front of his desk. Her heart did not stop beating, witnessing the heavy silence that was present in the room. Once she was seated, he sighed as if he was irritated by the information he just had this morning.

"I have terrible news…" At these words, Hayat could already feel the pity in his voice. "I'm not going to cut corners, someone sent us the same design as your last design." Her heart dropped. Why would someone do this to her? She was barely at the company, and she didn't speak to anyone at her job, given the treatment Hayat received the few times she was there. She could not believe her eyes, but she wondered how he had been able to find out.

"How?" In a simple movement, he turned his screen so that she had a vision of what was happening. Hayat gasped seeing the email on his screen.

"All the collaborators received this email, before your arrival, with your design attached." Mister Lopez explained, pointing to the email with his finger. "We know who sent it, but we have to prove that it was stolen, that it wasn't just a coincidence. Even if the two look identical, like two peas in a pod." Hayat froze. The meeting was soon to take place, but she had no design or even a backup for this conference.

Then, this point hit her like a flash.

She had a signature on every design she presented until now, hidden somewhere. Under the intrigued eye of her superior, Hayat took her tablet, to find the project in question in her drive. A few minutes later, she found it, looking for the signature in her design.

Once found, she zoomed in on it and pointed to it with her pen. "I sign all my designs just in case. Do you think it will be enough proof?" His superior nodded, surprised to see that Hayat had already considered this case – if it ever came to happen. In fact, this simple signature could actually prove that it was her model, if and only if the model received this morning also contained it. Turning her screen around, Mister Lopez looked in the same place for the signature she had just shown him. A smile appeared on his face. He showed it up on the screen, with his signature clearly visible on the zoom.

"Bingo," they nodded in agreement. "I'll call the collaborators, and the person who stole your design. A definite sanction will be applied, and the meeting will be postponed to tomorrow. Is it good for you?" Hayat agreed, but she still wanted to know who had stolen her work.

"Can I know their name?" Mister Lopez shook his head, turning back to his computer. A tint of deception colored her features.

"Sorry, Miss Mazari, I can't give it to you. It goes against the ethics of our company. What I can assure you, is that they will be fired and blacklisted. This is probably not their first time, and I hope it will be the last. And, I'll recommend everyone to change their passwords and add the two factors to their sessions." Relief washed over her, understanding it was a confidential thing she couldn't have access to, even if she was the main target. Before letting her go, they discussed the projects on her list for the next

few months, which were the busiest months of the year.
Especially with the arrival of Black Friday. Her work must
be finalized and presented at least one month in advance
in case there are major changes to be made.

Leaving the office, Hayat's shoulder struck
someone else's, who was going to her boss' office. Her
face told her something. Then it hit her. She was usually in
the room meeting when Hayat was explaining her projects.
Hayat was going to confront her, but she had already
disappeared behind Mister Lopez's door, with a mocking
smile on her face. She must have been unaware of this
little appointment, which pleased Hayat a little. This thief
was about to get fired, and blacklisted… For her, it was
only fair to face the consequences of her actions.

- ☾ -

Hayat waited outside Souhila's school, in front of
her car, spotting every movement behind the panes of the
door. A cluster of shadows began to move behind it,
indicating the impending arrival of many children. The bell
rang again while leaving the doors open, letting the crowd
of children joined their parents one by one. After a while,
Hayat could see Souhila running toward her car. Hayat
was ready to welcome the little one in her arms, but she
passed her by before getting into the car without even
greeting her. Confused, the stepmother got up, noticing
that a group of children – who were with the parents who
were watching her this morning – were laughing in her
direction.

They had probably heard the rags on her, to repeat
it to Souhila throughout the day. Her anger rose, she knew
very well that children could be abominably raw, especially
on sensitive subjects. Hayat experienced that. She was

about to explode on them, she barely restrained herself, not wanting to cause a scene without tangible proof. Hayat was going to have to speak with Souhila on the road, hoping to clarify things and speak to the headmaster about the matter.

"So, sweetheart, how was your day?" Hayat asked while bulking her belt, looking at her in the rearview mirror. Souhila turned her head, to avoid her stepmother's gaze. Silence. The little one seemed to be too upset to speak. Hayat was torn between asking her a new question and leaving her alone given the feelings she was going through. Hayat opted for the second option. She checked to see if the little girl had put her seat belt on and put on some Quran. She thought the ayas might soothe her a little. However, Hayat noticed that she kicked way too hard on her seat. Souhila was not about to calm down.

The stepmother didn't know what to do. She felt stuck, making the journey back home much longer and difficult, biting her cheeks from stress, sometimes glancing in the rearview mirror. Her heart was pounding when she arrived in front of the house, barely had she parked when the little girl jumped out of the car running toward the door. Souhila banged on the door, hoping that her father would open the door for her, but by no means did she want to cross paths with Hayat. Anas opened the door wide, hoping to see his daughter's sunny, smiling face, but all he saw was a sad one that ran straight into her room. His wife arrived a few steps later, helpless. Once back, he took her shoulders in his hands to reassure her.

"Hey, what happened?" Her sad gaze met her husband's brown eyes. It saddened him. At this sight, Anas hugged her tight. Hayat welcomed this gesture, feeling her heart calming down. This simple moment eased her worries.

"I think some kids at school bothered her because of me." Anas moved away from her a little, to take a better look at his wife, frowning.

"Why do you say that?" Hayat bit her lower lip, a little anxious to see her husband's reaction. He patted her back a little, wanting to ease the feelings that were blocking her words. It worked.

"This morning when I dropped her at school, a group of parents was weirdly looking at me with their children nearby." The longer she continued to explain herself, the more Anas felt his emotions getting the best of him. Slowly, the cadence of her speech quickened. "Then, when I picked her up later today, they were still looking at me all judgy. I don't want to make assumptions, but I'm pretty sure they have a role to play in this story. Kids could be really mean to one another, I know that." She paused for a second to breathe, still feeling his many caresses on her back, even though Anas' body was getting more and more tense with each of her words. As if each one of them were filled with sharp needles that gradually pierced his heart. "And I don't want her to suffer because of me..." Anas nodded, understanding her intention.

"It's ok. This is not your fault, I will talk to her while you wait for us here. Deal?" Hayat agreed with a nod, a little calmer but still saddened by what had just happened. Her husband kissed her forehead, before going upstairs, taking the stairs two by two. Coming near his daughter's room, he could hear sniffling behind her. With soft knocks on the door, he signaled his presence to his daughter.

"Go away!" Her little voice cracking with emotion broke his heart. The father knew she needed comfort in this situation, he pushed the door and then stuck his head into her room. Looking at her with doe eyes.

"Even me baba?" Souhila looked at him, her eyes shining. She stared at him for a few seconds, shook her head, waiting for her father to come give her a big hug. Anas sat down on the edge of her bed, opening her arms so that she could take refuge in them. When he was there, she felt invincible. Like he was the shield that protected her from all the evil of the world. When he felt that his daughter was relaxing little by little, he understood that he could finally start the discussion. "Tell me what happened at school today, ghazaali." For a moment, Souhila refused to speak, but after a few caresses on the top of her head, her tongue loosened.

"They were mean to me, baba." His pulse rose at her words.

"Who?" He keeps stroking her hair, wishing it could also help him remain calm.

"Kids in my class." Souhila said, moving away from her father to look him in the eye. "They said that Hayat wasn't going to love me because she isn't my real mama, and she will also leave me since my real mama did." The intense anger made him numb. At this point, Anas would be able to burn down the entire barn just so that his daughter wouldn't have to hear all of this nonsense anymore. Every muscle in his body was tense with rage. Finding no way not to release his anger while answering his daughter, he cracked his fingers before finding something sweet to say to her.

"You know what you can do?" The little one shook her head. "You're going to give me a list of every kid that said bad things to you, and I will take care of it. And I know you are upset, I understand that. It was a normal reaction after the day you got, but you can't be rude to people because of that. That's not the way to deal with it, and it's not an excuse, do you understand me?" Souhila nodded.

304

Anas kissed her several times, letting out that laugh he loved. He took her in his arms, before taking her downstairs to reconcile with Hayat.

Once downstairs, the pair saw Hayat on the sofa biting her nails, surely waiting for news from Souhila. Hayat was so worried that she hadn't even taken off her hijab yet. A feeling of relief passed through her when she saw the little one with a beaming smile. Souhila sat down beside her, ready to apologize for her behavior with her, but Hayat simply took her in her arms, glad to see that she was feeling better.

Anas watched them from a distance, relieved that everything was back to normal.

Chapter 39

Hearing children laugh in the hallway eased the tension in the principal's office. Anas and Hayat were waiting on their chairs, looking at every corner of the room, feeling their impatience gradually rise. Mister Johnson, we're nowhere to be found. It had already been fifteen minutes of waiting. Anas' leg wriggled in irritation. The father sucked on his teeth the moment the principal set a step into the office. Hayat and Anas got up in respect. He responded with a nod, inviting them to sit back.

"Thank you for your patience. I got caught up by a professor in the hallway." He also sat properly in his seat, under Anas' stern gaze. "To what do I owe the honor of this appointment?" Mister Johnson asked while crossing his fingers together above the desk. The father cleared his throat, wanting to dispel the tension that animated his body.

"We came today about Souhila." Anas paused a bit, looking straight back at him. "Yesterday, she came home, crying because of," he looked for the paper his daughter gave him, in his pocket. Then Anas started listing all the names on it; a total of six children were involved in this. "They said really harsh remarks to her." Mister Johnson genuinely nodded, concerned about every child's safety in his school. He marked their names down, wishing to be sure to call their parents and organize a meeting with all parties involved. The old man looked at them both, pinching his lips together, staying silent for a second.

"I understand. I will do my best to solve the matter as soon as possible, you will soon hear news about it." He sat back properly in his seat, wanting to add. "However, I would like the issue to remain discreet." Anas stared at him, sucking on his cheeks. For a few seconds, silence hovered in the room. Hayat began to feel her husband getting more hostile, so she took the situation into account and first put her hand on her husband's leg.

"We will do our best on that aspect too." She nodded, capturing his attention, a false smile on her face. By these words, the principal understood what she implied. To sign the end of this conversation, Mister Johnson tapped on the table before accompanying them to the exit.

"Thanks for coming in, I'm looking forward to meeting you again." As soon as the door closed behind them, the bell rang, allowing all the children to run in the corridors leading to the exit. By the time they also arrived outside, Souhila was already waiting for them outside, a slightly sad expression on her face. Anas called out her name to catch her attention and to make her look in his direction. The little girl ran into his arms for refuge, relieved to see her father present. They stayed like that for a while, when a few laughs rang in his ears. Anas' gaze drifted to the sound, his expression dropped dramatically. He made Souhila slip into Hayat's arms. She noticed a change in her husband's behavior but did not know what caused it. The child did not oppose it, also wishing to feel the comfort of her stepmother, as if it would make all the remarks disappear from her mind. Anas placed a hand in the crook of his wife's back, pushing her lightly toward the car. He leaned close to her ear, so only she could hear him.

"Get in the car, I will be with you in a few minutes." The tone in her husband's voice told her she shouldn't ask any more questions. As she walked to the car, she glanced in the direction of her husband, who was walking purposefully toward a group of parents. Which was, in fact, the same group as yesterday. That's when it clicked.

Anas was about to have some words with them.

Expression *closed*.

Jaw *clenched*.

Eyes *narrowed*.

Posture *straightened*.

The radiant anger from his body was enough to make them swallow their giggles. His imposing stature inspired a form of respect while making them instantly regret their actions. Hayat from the car, watched her husband act, hoping it didn't escalate into a heated argument. With a fake smile on his face, Anas was the first to engage in conversation.

"I would love to know what is funny when you look in our direction." One of the mothers – Miss Brown – cleared her throat, uncomfortable with his insistent stare, while the other parents looked away in shame.

"Oh…" She paused, looking at the other parent who had no courage to face him. "Nothing, we were-… We were just having a little *chat*, and we looked in your direction at the same moment." Miss Brown smiled at him, knowing her wrongs, hoping it would cover everything. "Your name is safe from our mouths." Anas nodded genuinely, understanding the meaning behind her words.

"Perfect." He remained silent for a second. "But it would be even more perfect if everybody here, and their children included, would keep my wife and daughter's name out of their silly mouths" Their eyes widened at his words. In order to ease the hostilities, Miss Brown chuckled in unease.

"What do you mean?" His *fake* smile changed into a hard expression.

"I know what your kids said to mine. And I'm pretty sure they didn't come up with it by themselves." The woman looked at her child, hiding behind her. "Therefore, it will be better for everyone if that stops right here." His eyes were expressive enough to convey all the warning in his words.

"Is that a threat?" One of the others was now bold enough to speak her mind. Anas' unbothered gaze drifted to her uptight expression.

"Take it as you wish, I'll just say that it would be better for you that their names remain out of your conversations." A simple nod as a response, and he left. With the same serene face he had left with, he got into the car, closing the door quietly behind him. A long, heavy breath escaped him under his wife's curious gaze, who was patiently waiting for an explanation. Anas gave her a side-eyed look, hesitant about telling her everything in front of Souhila. It wasn't the kind of behavior he wanted her to pick on. Therefore, he waited until his daughter would be home napping to explain to Hayat.

"I-" A notification cut him. In a smooth motion, he picked up his phone, seeing wonderful news on it. Someone, named Ghazoul, booked a visit for the house. However, it was this afternoon at five, and it was already past four… Anas didn't have enough time to drive home, and then go to the visit. He sucked on his cheeks, trying to find a solution.

Do I reschedule the visit? But what if they give up on the house because of that?

For a solid minute, he looked at his phone, thinking.

"Someone just asked for a visit to rent the house." Anas was interrupted by Hayat's gasp of joy. The young woman looked more excited by the news than him at the moment.

"It's good news!" With the look he gave her, every inch of her joyful emotion melted like ice under the bright sun. "There is a "but" right?" Her husband nodded, pinching his lips together.

"He is asking for a visit at five... today." She looked at him a bit puzzled, not seeing the problem.

"What's the matter, then?" Anas sighed.

"I'll have to let you wait in the car for at least twenty minutes, fifteen at best." Hayat raised her shoulders as if it were nothing.

"It's ok, you can go. We will find something to do while you're in," the stepmother turned to look at the little one in the back. "Right, Souhila?" The little girl nodded with a wide smile on her face. His wife's gaze got back on him, "See? We'll be fine. Don't worry about us." Eased by her words, Anas started the car, going straight to the brand-new house he just finished.

While driving, the young man was still thinking about the name of the client. It seemed familiar.

Ghazoul, Ghazoul, Ghazoul...

This name was going back and forth in his mind, while he vaguely listened to the discussion Hayat and Souhila were having. He knew this name was familiar, and it itched his brain not being able to connect the dots. It was as if the memory linked to this name was concealed by an opaque veil, and it only took a gust of wind to make it disappear to reveal the truth. His wife's tender hand on his shoulder brought him out of his thoughts. He turned his head slightly toward her, still focused on the road. Her features showed an expression so soft that the black fog that clouded his mind instantly vanished.

"Hey, what's on your mind?" Anas was about to answer when he saw a particularly familiar silhouette in front of the house. A woman in a veil standing before it, smirking at him as if she already won. This upright, well-assured look and piercing eyes could only be a person.

Ghazoul was the lawyer's name that signed his divorce paper.

Zahia.

Zahia was back in town.

His ex-wife was the one setting up a visit.

Chapter 40

Anas did not stop, on the contrary, he accelerated. He continued on his way as if he had seen nothing. Everything was starting to get confused in his head. Time. Speed. Feelings. It was just a gigantic knot that he had to untie by himself. His phone rang several times, but he didn't pick up.

He drove, only wishing to be home.

Far away from here.

From *her*.

Zahia was like an old scar that started burning when life got better. The stain on a white garment, wishing to make it vanish with some scrubbing. The simple fact of seeing her again got into his skin. She broke Souhila's heart. His family. *Him*. Leaving had destroyed him, but returning was worse. In three years, Anas and his daughter had time to change, grow, and *heal*, from her departure. However, to see her again today, unexpectedly, was like an earthquake destroying all the foundations previously built. He didn't want Souhila to see her. Zahia had no right to do this to her. His fingers were tapping on the steering wheel, needing to find a solution to save his daughter from seeing her mother again. Hayat's voice calling him numerous times wasn't even reaching him, it was only covered with emotions. He didn't even know what he felt anymore. Anger? Sadness? Sorrow? Everything was just a massive fog, creating a thick veil over all his senses.

He could just see the road, driving without interruption toward the house.

Hayat, noticing his lack of reaction, left him to his thoughts. Thinking they could talk about it calmly at home. She hadn't had time to see who was standing in front of the house, since her husband did pass in front of it so quickly. Only Anas had seen her. Even Souhila sensed the change in her father's behavior. No one had the strength to say anything, nonetheless.

They just all stayed silent, questions filling their minds, waiting to go back home.

Once parked, they all started to move, except Anas. Seeing him completely distant, Hayat tried to capture his attention, putting her hand on his shoulder. When his brown eyes met her hazel ones, they looked darker than usual, more glassy… He wasn't there. Hayat squeezed a bit of her grip on him, trying to touch a disconnected part inside of her husband. She didn't know what he saw, but it suddenly shook him in a way she couldn't understand.

"Anas, 'omri, let's go home." Hayat only had a soft expression on her face, praying it would be enough to wake him up from this state. However, it didn't work. No reaction from him. He simply slipped from her touch, as if it was burning him. Hayat retracted her hand, confused. Anas mumbled something inaudible under his breath, drifting his gaze to the house in front of him, forcing his wife to get closer to him. "What did you say?"

"You both, go home." Hayat frowned, not understanding what he meant.

"You're not coming with us?" Anas clenched his jaw, restraining his tongue from saying hurtful things under the emotion.

"Hayat, go home." His tone was harsher, turning the warm atmosphere into a freezing one.

"Anas-" He turned to face her, fire dancing in his eyes. Not the same fire she used to see. This one was more menacing. Dangerous. All of her words instantly got stuck in her throat, forming a knot in it.

"Go. Home." He stated between his teeth. Keeping his hard facade for a moment, before softening under the frightened gaze of his wife in the passenger seat. "Please," his supplication was quieter than a whisper. Without continuing to ask questions that could irritate him more, she got out of the car before taking Souhila and got home. Once they were out of sight, Anas let out a scream of frustration, filling the space. How could she show her face to him and his daughter? Gradually, he calmed down, wishing to find a solution to this problem. A new notification disturbed this restorative silence. He raised his phone to eye level, reading all the notifications he slid little by little.

Mr. Ghazoul

It's not kind of you to just pass by.

Mr. Ghazoul

I waited for you to come, and you didn't even greet me.

Mr. Ghazoul

I'm hurt... :(

Mr. Ghazoul

> Are you scared she will see me?

Mr. Ghazoul

> Your new wife.

Mr. Ghazoul

> Come meet me if you're a man.

His heart skipped a beat at the sight of the last message.

Mr. Ghazoul

> I want my daughter back.

All his thoughts started to spiral into a dark knot again.

Zahia wasn't here for him, to face him, or interfere in his brand-new life, but for *Souhila*.

Anas felt trapped. Was he in his right to deny her access to his daughter, since she left them for years? She even signed papers to waive her rights above Souhila. Zahia didn't know her. She didn't know her favorite color, her favorite food, or her school. Zahia had no place in her life. All these questions mixed up in his head, pushing him to flee to a place that can clear his mind; the masjid. Under Hayat's hopeful gaze, Anas left without looking behind him. Watching him drive further away, the hope of seeing him pass through their door gradually dwindled. Every muscle in her body relaxed, desperate. She stayed there, in front of the window, looking at the empty space in front of the garage's closed door. Hayat felt a light tug on her clothes, waking her from hypnosis. Souhila's questioning expression forced her to change hers. A smile took place on her features, hoping it would ease the daughter's worries – and hers too. Then she got an idea.

"Do you want to pray with me?" Hayat needed a little comfort in these moments. Souhila nodded, clinging to her as if she was also going to disappear in a blink of an eye. Slowly they got upstairs, their heart heavy. Somewhere in her mind, the little girl thought it was all because of her. Today they came to school just to deal with the bullying problem, and then her father changed his attitude the moment they were going home.

The rollercoaster they were in was only on its first loop.

- ☾ -

Anas was almost asleep in a quiet corner of the masjid, when a man told him it was time for him to go home. It was way past 'Ishaa, and he was still in here praying to Allah his ex-wife would just disappear from his and Souhila's lives forever. For the first time in years, he did not wish to go home. Anas couldn't. He was a mess. The man Hayat married, and the father of Souhila wasn't there. Anas shook his head at the thought of them seeing his face when he was so weak. Nothing persuaded him to come back. Not even the warm memories of the soft kisses from his wife, that he needed so much right now, were going to bring him home. He slightly sighed, before leaving for his car.

For a moment, he hesitated between staying in his car in front of the masjid, or coming back home and sleeping on the couch. As big as he is, Anas couldn't imagine sleeping in his car. So, he took the couch option. However, he didn't wish to be seen or heard by them. How was he about to enter in complete silence, and just sleep? Behind the steering wheel, he thought about it for a solid minute. After a while, he found the perfect solution; waiting until the lights in the house would all turn off and leave before Fajr. Anas wasn't pleased with his own behavior, but it was for him the only solution he had until the strength to face his ex-wife would fill him up. The anger was too strong to see her again. Anas wasn't going to give her any reaction. He wasn't going to give Zahia what she wanted.

Zahia wasn't worth it.

She left like a ghost, so he will treat her as it.

He needed some time to cool down and stay strong for his family. Once all the lights were out, he waited at least thirty minutes before taking his keys and entering the house. In the darkness and the silence of his house, Anas prepared himself to sleep, his heart heavy with guilt. His body landed in a silenced sound on the couch, trying his best to make no noise. He never thought once he would sneak up into his very own house just to sleep on the couch.

When he gave more thoughts about the situation, it was a bit ironic.

The day before, he was explaining how it was impolite to just ignore people when you were frustrated, and now Anas was doing the same thing to his wife and daughter.

Ignoring them because he was angry and frustrated.

This little scheme lasted for two weeks.

Every time, he prayed not to be caught while sleeping on the couch. However, tonight, Allah had other plans for him. As his new habit he was almost asleep on the sofa, so tired he could barely hear the steps coming from upstairs. A hard slap on his forehead startled Anas.

"Nod, nod qbel manahilek rasek." *Get up, get up before I rip your head off.* "You're lucky Souhila is sleeping because you can't imagine how much I want to scream at you right now." His wife's tense face, with her tongue, curled between her teeth, made him rise instantly.

"I can explain." Anas put his two hands before him, protecting himself from any object she could probably throw at him.

"What are you doing here?" Hayat whispered between her teeth, trying to hide her anger. Anas scratched the back of his neck, embarrassed by the fact he was caught red-handed. She was fuming. Her husband casually slept on the couch when she and his daughter were worried to death about him. "Since you're not dead, I'm about to kill you now," Hayat jumped on him ready to beat him up. Anas stopped her easily, sitting her on the sofa.

"Listen, I have a reason." His wife narrowed her eyes, "Kind of... I know I shouldn't have behaved like this." He explained in a softer tone, still holding her hands to hit him. "And I'm sorry." Anas was about to add something, but Hayat cut him.

"You know apologizing won't be enough, right? Because if I didn't catch you sleeping tonight, when were you going to talk to me?!" Her husband stayed silent, while she pinched her lips together. "Continue, so I can go back to sleep. And you'll stay here until we wake up, mazel makimiltsh m'ak." *I'm not done with you.* Her hand withdrew from his grip, before she slid it to his chin, looking at him sternly. Anas nodded approvingly to his words. He knew full well that this was only going to be the beginning.

Anas sighed, "Zahia was the one asking for a visit." Hayat's eyes widened, surprised by her confession, she blinked several times, hoping to have heard wrong.

"Excuse me?" His eyebrow arched while turning his head slightly to her right side.

"Zahia is here, and she wants Souhila back." Another shocking revelation. This news almost hit her as much as him. Confused, Hayat scratched her forehead hard enough to leave a red mark on her body.

"How? And why?" Anas pinched his lips together, raising his shoulder.

"That's what I'm trying to find out. I have been looking everywhere to understand how and why she came back now. But, I don't know…" He paused for a second, "She knew I was married when I didn't post anything about it, nor my family and I suppose you didn't either." Hayat shook her head. During the preparation, she specifically asked each guest not to post about their wedding on social media. And since only close friends, and family were gathered, someone must have spoken to her. For a moment, they both stayed silent, trying to figure out who could be behind this mess. Hayat started to list all her guests in her mind, checking on her phone if anything was posted anywhere.

When it actually clicked.

There was just one person who wanted to see Zahia come back into Anas' and Souhila's life.

"Oh, I think I know…" Anas frowned, clueless. "I can't tell you right now, I need evidence." She got up to go back to the bedroom. Hayat didn't want the little one to wake up in the middle of the night. Souhila had been sleeping with her for the past few days, as he couldn't

319

sleep alone at night. Anas held her arm, wishing to continue the conversation with his wife. She slipped between his fingers instantly, grading him sternly. Her index finger rose in front of his face, "Don't you dare touch me." She paused, a harsh expression on her features. "Just because I'm helping you, it doesn't mean I'm not mad at you. I am your wife, not some friend of yours, who you can cut off when something is wrong. Until you apologize correctly, don't expect me to forgive you." Hayat waited for a second, "Did I make myself clear?" Anas nodded, putting his hands on his thighs.

"Hayat, wAllahi I'm sorry. I regret everything." His wife smiled at him.

"Perfect. We'll have to talk tomorrow. And then you'll regret your behavior even more." She threw a pillow at his face, catching him off guard. He let a little sound come out of him, expressing his surprise. "Good night." Anas stared after her, wanting her to stay longer. Certainly, during these last two weeks, he longed to see them and settle this issue, he just couldn't face them. He just took the pillow, putting it under his head, apprehending tomorrow because his ears were going to suffer badly.

Chapter 41

Hayat woke up with Souhila half on top of her, she slipped out so as not to wake her up. It was still early, and she had to prepare breakfast and wake her husband up so that he could leave and come back when his daughter was gone, so he wouldn't disturb her before going to school today. Silently, she went downstairs, making sure the girl remained asleep on the bed. Seeing her small body under the heavy blanket made her smile before the apprehension of today's events came to her. Arriving almost at the bottom, she tilted her head to have a view of the sofa, Hayat was surprised when she saw it empty.

Anas had already left.

Hayat wandered around the house, wanting to make sure he wasn't there. No sign of him. So, she took her phone, ready to scold him, as he deserved. But the sounds of a key in the shoestring made her stop.

Oh, he did not leave.

Hayat crossed her arms together, waiting for him to enter. The anger she contained yesterday, just to not wake up the entire neighborhood, was slowly rising, making the veins in her neck pop. Anas opened the door, meeting a pair of hazel eyes burning with rage. A weird expression appeared on his face, trying to ease the tensions he felt in the room.

"So now you know how to open the door of your *own* house, huh?"

The cold voice she employed washed him, giving Anas shivers all over his body. He was used to the warm and welcoming Hayat. It felt unusual for he to hear her speak differently now. Shame spread in his chest. He wanted to hide again. However, as an adult, he needed to face the consequences of his actions.

"Salam a'leykoum, how are you?" His wife's expression didn't change.

"And now you remember I exist?" Anas' eyes narrowed, confused. Given his behavior, it would seem that yesterday's discussion had not taken place. Yet, it was genuine, but he wasn't going to point it out like an absolute idiot and buy himself more trouble than it was worth, so he kept his mouth shut. Hayat stood there, facing her husband's silence, while he was walking to the kitchen slowly. The fact that he did not play her little game, procured mixed feelings in her – it was irritating and seductive at the same time. Her harsh mask slipped for a second, but Hayat continued. "I'm fine, but I want you gone." Anas quickly turned his face, meeting her burning gaze, frowning.

"Why?" Like her, he crossed his arms as a way to protect himself. His heart sank, thinking that this time it was his wife who was going to kick him out of his house. Hayat approached a little closer to avoid getting louder, hoping that the little one was still asleep.

"Because Souhila will be awake soon, and I don't want her to see you. For now." Anas chuckled at her face, incapable of holding the sarcasm in any longer, especially if his daughter was mentioned.

"You're not going to forbid me to see my child, Hayat." As last night, her finger rose to explain her point.

"I am not…" She paused for a second, rewinding her words in her mind. "Well, I am, but it's not in the way you think." Anas raised his brows, waiting for her to continue. "If she sees you now, she won't focus at school because she'll be too busy asking herself where her dad was for the past two weeks. Neither you nor I want that, so this situation stays between us. Did I make myself clear?" She was right, his presence this morning was a disturbance for her. Her husband was about to respond, but a loud cry came from upstairs. Souhila. She woke up, alone. As if by reflex, Anas hastened to move toward the stairs, but Hayat caught up with him to get him out. "You get in your car, when I come back after dropping her off, we'll talk as we should." Guilty, her husband let her pass, watching her go to their room. He understood that his daughter had slept with his wife since he left. His heart broke even more at the realization. Slowly, he headed for the door, sad and unmotivated to continue this day. From his car, Anas could see their bedroom light on. Sitting in the driver's seat, he could only watch and wait.

Gently, Hayat stroked the back of the little one, reassuring her that everything was fine. The warmth offered by her stepmother's arms was precisely what Souhila needed after waking up to an empty place beside her this morning. For two weeks, Hayat had been making sure to finish breakfast before the little girl woke up to not lead to a similar situation. Her father was no longer at home, and he would rather not come back yet, this simple action brought back awful memories to the surface. With the back of her hand, Hayat wiped away her last tears, feeling that Souhila was breathing a little more regularly.

"Are you hungry, sweetheart?" Until now, they did not move from that embrace. In fact, Hayat realized she also necessitated some affection after being harsh to her husband – even if he deserved it. A few seconds passed before she could hear the voice of Souhila broken by her tears.

"When is baba coming back?" The sound of that provided a pinch in the heart of Hayat. Her breath after that question was so hot, it could burn her lungs. Her stepmother wanted to tell her that, in reality, her father was there, that he was waiting in the car in front of the house, and that he had never left the house.

That he had never abandoned her.

But that was not her role to play.

"I can't tell you…" She paused stroking her air, listening to Souhila's heavy sigh. "Soon, In Shaa Allah." Hayat placed a kiss on top of her head, intensifying the hug, wanting to stay like that a little longer. After a while, both decided it was time to eat and get ready for school – which started in less than an hour.

- ☾ -

Anas was stirring his spoon in his cup of coffee, Hayat with her piercing eyes who was just watching him adding more sugar into his cup. Under the weight of the embarrassment, Anas cleared his throat, wanting to ease the palpable tensions around them.

"So… are we going to talk, or…?" His uncertain voice only added irritation to Hayat's anger.

"I don't know if I should scream at you, or beat you at this exact moment." She paused, sucking her teeth, "Because every time I see your face I'm so mad that I want to rip your head off, but I also want to kiss you because I know that you're safe and alive." Hayat bit her lip, debating which of the two solutions was better for the situation. Anas smiled awkwardly, hoping it would help her decide the softest option.

"You can kiss me, and then we can solve the matter." Anas announced, in a humorous tone, wanting to lighten up the air. But that only added fuel to the fire, causing Hayat to explode like a hot teapot full of water.

"Don't you dare be joking around when you're in the wrong!" Anas was going to get burnt by the boiling water, "*Two weeks.* Two weeks of no calls, no messages, no info, no notes, no notes to say that you were ok, all the while you were sleeping on the couch? every night!" Hayat got close enough that Anas was forced to look down. Her finger hit his chest at every point she was making. "Do you know how many scenarios I have made up in my mind? Do you know how worried we were? Do you know how many tears I wiped on your daughter's face because her father wasn't there to kiss her in the morning? And then again before she went to sleep? For what? Huh?" Guilt muted him. "Even if you didn't physically leave, you left us." She paused, her hazel orbs tinted with sadness juggled between his dark pupils. "You left me..." His heart sank at her words. Her *facts*. Becoming aware of the damage caused by one's actions was not always easy. A knot formed in his throat, preventing him from replying. Anas tried to take her in his arms, but Hayat pushed him away. "No. You don't deserve it." His limbs joined his sides limply.

It was true.

I did not deserve it.

"Please, roohi, tell me how I can redeem myself." Hayat's heart skipped a beat at this new nickname, calling her his soul. She blinked several times, not wanting to show how much she missed him. Missed his warmth, touch, kisses, love, all of him. She missed her husband so much, it hurt. As best as she could, she suppressed this emotion that could bring down those walls she had built for him to climb by himself.

"It would be too easy for you if I simply told you straight away how you need to act." Reluctantly, she crossed her arms together. She needed to maintain the act, at least a little longer. "You will have to find out by yourself." Anas approached her again, wanting to feel her warmth, which he had missed so much. Just feeling her close to him, without even taking her in his arms, was enough for him. Her breath got heavier the instant he was millimeters away. Staying mad at her husband was by no means an easy thing, and Hayat understood that as she looked up and down at the man in front of her. Intuitively, her arms unbound, delicately rubbing Anas' chest at the same time, sending an electric shock down their spine.

Too close. He is too close.

"Hayati, tell me." His face leaned in, leaving nothing but their heavy breaths between them. A little more and he could kiss her, make her forget all the anger she had built during these two weeks. Reassure her that her husband was fine and that it was all over. "Please," this plea made her lean in too. They were like two magnets meant to be stuck together by the force of attraction; affection. At the last moment, Hayat came to her senses and walked away from him, her cheeks red with desire for her husband.

Hayat was about to answer, but someone knocked violently on the door. Both looked at each other, completely clueless about who it could be this early in the morning. Anas straightened up, clearing his throat before approaching the door, but a shrill voice sounded from the other side of it.

"Anas open the door! I know you're in here! And I hope your new wife is here too." It was Zahia. The young man turned to Hayat who was already looking at him with wide eyes. Both wanted to act as if they weren't there because they were far from having finished their discussion.

Panicked, her husband silently mouthed to her, "What do I do?" She responded the same way.

"I don't know!" Hayat tried to make a movement with her hands, but she was so taken aback that she didn't even know what to do with her body. The two remained silent, hoping that would make her go away. Hearing nothing for a few minutes, Anas and Hayat relaxed, thinking that she was finally gone. Anas' phone rang in the back pocket of his pants, ruining their little plan.

This day promised to be full of rebounds when it was only ten o'clock in the morning.

Chapter 42

Uncertain, Anas pulled his phone out of his back pocket. Confusion clouded his features when he saw his mother's name appear on his screen. Plenty of questions crossed his mind, not understanding the point of the call. Then, the realization hit Anas. To confirm his suspicions, he looked at his wife, who already seemed to have realized what was going on behind their backs. The anger started to rise, mixed with disappointment. He sincerely thought she had changed her mind and that she had finally accepted this situation since Zahia was a closed chapter.

"It's my mom." His wife suspiciously looked at him, was she about to have her answer? At least Hayat hoped so. Fast, she joined him, nudging him to respond. Anas nodded, "Salam a'leykoum, mama, ki daayra?" *How are you?* Her son could hear Faiza clearing her throat as if to check that no one else was listening.

"Better if you opened the door to Zahia." His grip on the phone intensified. All his muscles tensed, gradually realizing that his mother must have been in contact with her for a while now.

This weekend is about to be a disaster.

"What did you do?" Anas whispered, hopeless. Not wanting to hear more, he hung up before storming out of his house ready to blow on Zahia. In a few steps, he arrived at her height, seeing the sardonic features of his ex-wife. "How long have you been talking to my mom?" He paused himself, before changing his question. "You know what, this doesn't even matter. Why are you here?" Zahia chuckled at his face.

"See who finally decided to come talk to me, face to face." Nonchalantly, she pointed at the door, where Hayat was still standing, meeting her narrowed hazel eyes. "Did your new wife cut your balls off, since you lost all your nerve? I remember you being fiercer than that." Zahia looked back at him, sensing the fire dripping from his eyes. "Now, you flee from the consequences of your actions." She wore an expression of disgust as she added these words. At that exact moment, he wanted to destroy her. She was an unwanted visitor at their little nest. She deserved nothing more than his anger. "I want Souhila back. I want *my* daughter, she is *mine*."

"Zahia, you don't know me or even my daughter. *You* left. Being out of our life was *your* choice. I tried to make you come back, to find you-" The woman cut him off with a chuckle.

"Apparently you didn't look for me correctly, since your mother found me faster than you." Anas sucked on his teeth.

"I hope you're listening to me loud and clear." He got a step closer, making himself a bit more menacing. "You're not going to come back to *my* house, chasing after *my* daughter, and on top of that, talk bad about *my* wife. If I see you once again before my house, I will destroy you." Anas explained in a severe tone, hoping it would just make her leave forever. She put her hand on her chest dramatically, pretending to be shocked.

"Are you threatening me?" Anas chuckled knowingly.

"I, one hundred percent, am." He pointed at her car. "Now go away, I don't want to see you *ever* again." Zahia was about to reply, but she saw, in the eyes of the man she used to love, that he wasn't playing. He was literally ready to destroy the mother of his child to protect his new family.

Resigned, she backed down putting one foot back, "I will come back, and I will have my daughter. You can't stop me from seeing her. I am her mother!" Anas shrugged at her with an expression of victory. He knew that justice was protecting him. He couldn't physically stop her, but he could with the help of his lawyer.

As a last straw, he said, "You will never have this role for her. You left her when she was a baby, you never loved her like a mother, these are your own words. You will never come near my Souhila again. This role isn't only given by blood. You need to actively be her mother to earn that title. So don't you ever present yourself to me or anyone with the idea that you are a mother." Bothered by his words, Zahia left without adding anything. Anas knew she could possibly return one day and cause more trouble, but he stood straight on his feet, hoping he would look menacing enough for her to never come back. Shaken up, he got inside his house as a hollow of himself. This simple argument drained all his strength and energy to stand strong and tall. As soon as the door closed behind him, he wanted to let himself drop on the floor. When Hayat saw him, she decided to do a truce to comfort her husband. She opened her arms and her husband instantly dived into them. At this instance, he needed all the support he could receive. It surprised him at first, but he understood her gesture.

"It's going to be ok." These words were simple but still very efficient. With a few strokes on his back, Hayat could feel his heartbeat calm down, even his fast breaths were slowing.

"Does that mean you're not angry at me anymore?" The light laugh of his wife made Anas smile. Nothing was sweeter than her, laughing in his arms. Even in the middle of an argument, she still supported him. After a few seconds, he moved away a bit, maintaining her where she was. Anas looked her up and down, admitting to himself that she was the woman of his life. It didn't matter what situation they went through, he felt, deep inside him, that he had found his other half.

Love could make you do crazy things.

Hayat rearranged his hair, before escaping from his grip. "No, I'm just here when you need me to, and since you look better now, I'm back to being mad at you." In an instant, Hayat ran upstairs laughing at him. Shocked. He followed her, hoping it was a joke.

However, it wasn't.

Since Hayat would be here every time he needed her, he wanted to pull an act. He pointed at his pretending sad face, still following her to the room. "Look, I still need you, come hug me!" With a serious expression, his wife closed the door on him, so he couldn't follow her inside.

Forgiveness wasn't around the corner.

Defeated, Anas slid by the door, slowly sitting on the ground. He now needed to find a way to win her heart back. When he was about to find one, the door opened behind him, knocking Anas to the ground. He smiled at her as she passed over his body, completely ignoring him. She was dressed up, from head to toe, in her best abaya. Clueless about her whereabouts, Anas got up quickly, catching her right before she got to the door. She escaped in an instant, glaring at him with anger in her eyes.

"Where are you going?" Hayat's expression showed him the hesitation in her mind. She rearranged her khimar with the help of her reflection in the mirror.

"Souhila's classes will end soon, I need to get to her before she comes out." Anas smiled, looking at the clock, it was in fact soon time for her to be home.

"I can come with you." His wife looked at him, raising an eyebrow, certainly not letting him enter her car the day after his appearance. He was ready to put his shoes on, then got pushed away by gentle hands.

"No, you're not coming." She paused, looking at him up and down, "I don't want you with me." Hayat crossed her arms on her chest, trying to convince her husband that his presence was unwelcome – even if it was simply a lie. Anas planted his eyes in hers, seeing plenty of emotions going through them. Not really persuaded by her words or behavior, he straightened himself, towering over Hayat. Yet, a small distance was between them. With each step he took forward, she took one backward.

Until her back hit the door.

Hayat was now trapped between Anas' hard chest and the wooden door. All she could do was raise her head slightly to meet his darkened eyes. Hayat felt her heartbeat increase with every inch he decided to break. Their warmth mixed the moment Anas initiated his last step. An arm over her head, emphasizing their height difference. Anas looked down at her.

Hayat looked wonderful; half parted pumped lips, red tinting her cheeks, her heavy and fast breaths. He could feel her heart was about to burst, as much as his. Since he was the one initiating the move, Anas wanted to pretend that he was totally in control of his desires.

It was hard.

Extremely hard.

He resisted the urge to press his lips against hers, just to make her break first and admit, but it looked impossible. Teasing was his only weapon at the moment. So he used it as much as he pleased. His face was now mere inches away from hers. She looked at his lips, almost unable to resist, too. Anas smirked at this view.

"I know one thing about you, Hayati. You will never *not* want me." Hayat blew expectedly hard on Anas' face, forcing him to back down from her before she could slip through the door and close it to his face.

He lost again.

Anas sneered at the sight of himself in the mirror, his cheeks flushed with the heat, and his body filled with goosebumps. Amused, he peered out the living room curtain, scrutinizing every move his wife could make. He saw her driving her car, using her hand as a fan, with a slight smile on her face. Nothing was said yet, but it could be that she was already weakened by her husband's advances.

I will eventually catch you again, Hayati.

Souhila only set one foot into the house, and she was welcomed by a gigantic balloon and teddy bear, with a little note "I'm sorry, benti", between its arms. When the little girl instantly jumped on it, not actually reading the note, Anas pushed the plushy out of the way to take its place. He wanted to hug his daughter and smell her scent. He needed her to be in his arms. Souhila tripped over the teddy bear in excitement, landing directly in Anas' open arms. Once inside them, the girl giggled. She had missed her father, in a way that caused all the sadness she felt to magically vanish the instant her eyes met his. Hayat looked at them from afar, sincerely happy and relieved to see her react this way. The angry mask she wore faded for half a second before she resumed her cold and unwelcoming expression.

Once their emotions settled, Anas took Souhila's face between his large hands, almost covering her entirely, before spreading kisses all over it. During this tender gesture, he never once stopped saying how sorry he was.

"I'm so sorry, benti," he said between two kisses. "Will you forgive me?" Souhila's only response was laughter, accompanied by a nod and a hug. Every time his lips touched her face, it only increased them. Happiness. Hayat, from where she was, could almost draw it. It was a wonderful view. A father and a daughter reunited. Not wishing to disturb him, Hayat remained leaning against the wall, watching them unite again.

Soon it will be our turn.

Chapter 43

Anas was holding Souhila's hand in front of his parents' house. Soon to be a war zone. He wasn't here to have a good time and share good experiences he had with his wife. Anas was here to understand Faiza's motive and put an end to this nonsense. Since the wedding, Faiza has been making efforts to be nicer to her new daughter-in-law. However, now, he understood why. She was only distracting him to be more vicious.

His own mother.

It hurt.

Before knocking on the door, Anas sent a message to his sister, Houria, to confirm that Souhila was staying with her this weekend. The entire week, Hayat had still not spoken to him except for necessities. Anas decided that it was time for him to be forgiven and organized an intimate dinner. A romantic one at home should help his case – at least he hoped so. Just seconds passed before he received a positive answer from his sister. Content, he locked his phone, ready to finally enter his parents' house.

After knocking, Anas expected to see his mother first behind the door, but it was in fact his father who opened it. The old man welcomed his son with a wide smile and open arms, ready to hug him tight. It had been a really long time since Anas was home. Between finding a new routine with his wife, his work, his daughter, and the recent events, he didn't find any time to visit his parents.

However, today was about to be extremely hectic.

"Salam a'leykoum, weldi, ki daayr?" When planting his eyes into Hakim's ones, Anas couldn't see any recognition of remorse in them, as if he didn't know anything about the situation his son was going through. Then, he hugged him back, not wanting to punish him for something he wasn't aware of.

"Wa'leykoum salam, baba, mlih w enta?" Through the embrace, Anas could feel that his father missed him dearly. A first for many years. It was a pleasant feeling. This sensation of having love from his father filled his heart. Happiness overtook him before he remembered why he came all the way here. Anas took a step away, feeling a coldness replacing the warmth instead, Souhila instantly took her father's place to hug her grandfather.

"Baba, fin rahi mama?" *Where is mom?* Anas asked coldly. Not thinking twice about the tone he employed to ask this question, Hakim pointed to the living room, still holding Souhila tightly. Determined, he advanced with a tense face. The first person he met eyes with was Faiza. She instantly drifted her gaze away to escape the embarrassment she was feeling. Anas clenched his jaw, greeting everyone first before getting to his mother.

For a second, he hesitated to cause a scene or to speak to her alone about her disrespectful behavior. Did she deserve the discretion? He simply stood straight before her, questioning himself. A few minutes were enough to decide. Anas tilted his head, to show her the way.

"Aji, mama." Her son's imposing stature made her lower her head instantly. Faiza only felt shame right now. Luckily, her son didn't want to put her on a public trial. So, she followed him since he was already doing her that favor. Faiza wasn't in a powerful position. The only thing she could do was listen and obey.

Under everyone's confused look, they both got out to the garden. They were welcomed by the sunlight, warming their skin. Anas felt the appeasement sink into his veins gradually, calming his raw nerves. They sat down on the garden chairs. Faiza's words were stuck in her throat.

Shame engulfed her.

Anas looked her up and down, disappointed, "When?" Faiza pretended not to understand where her son was coming from since he hadn't yet established the direct subject. She couldn't even look back at him. He sucked on his teeth, waiting for her to speak.

"What do you mean weldi?" She chuckled in discomfort, wondering if it would help him change the subject. Before he could continue, Faiza went into the kitchen to get some traditional pastries, thinking he wouldn't follow her. But looking over her shoulder, she noticed the shadow of her son following her. The old woman quickened her pace to escape the consequences of her actions, but it was far too late.

The consequences were right behind her.

Faiza pretended to occupy herself with an empty tray, but that was by no means enough to dissuade Anas from staying behind her. He leaned against the door frame, looking at his mother with her back facing him. Her son cleared his throat.

"I asked you a question, mama. When did you start talking and plotting with Zahia?" The question sounded threatening, but his tone was so calm that even his mother couldn't believe it. Faiza turned to face him, but her eyes widened as she looked over her son's shoulder. Anas frowned, confused by her reaction. He looked over his shoulder, Houria was standing behind her, completely in shock.

The war was about to begin.

But not between him and his mother…

"With whom were you speaking, mama?" The middle child uncrossed his arms, ready to push his sister back into the living room, not wanting the screams of the two to draw any more attention. Houria didn't budge, nonetheless. She pointed at him severely, "Don't push me!" Her menacing look returned to her mother, who was trying to hide behind her son. Faiza was more afraid of her first daughter's anger than her first son. Since he was little, he had always been much calmer and more reserved than his sister, who was a bomb waiting to explode at any moment. Wanting to calm her down, Anas put his hands on her shoulders, redirecting her attention to him rather than Faiza.

"It's okay, I got this. Go back to the living room." For a second, the oldest tried to look over his shoulder to glare at her mother, but the youngest prevented her. They exchanged a knowing look before she could leave in peace. When she was far enough, Anas turned to his mother with disdain on his features. "She is gone. Now, are you going to answer my questions, or should I bring her back, so she could scream at you for a while?" Faiza shook her head instantly. Her shame was already reaching the top. Being screamed at by her daughter would take whatever respect was left among the group.

Following that, the two went back outside with a few biscuits, to accompany them. At first, when he came here, he wanted to yell at her and put her in her place. But seeing her fleeing and vulnerable, Anas only felt pity for his mother. So, his tactics changed. He opted for more gentleness while remaining firm in his choices and boundaries.

"I started talking to her almost a year after your divorce." She paused, biting her cheeks. Anas felt the anger return, but he did his best to control himself. "For me, Zahia was your perfect match. I took so much time choosing her for you, it was impossible to me that the marriage could be a disaster. So, after your divorce, I looked for her through friends and all. It took me months to find her, but I did." Faiza looked at him, sadness passed through her eyes. Anas stayed silent. He didn't want to cut her off, and let her continue to better understand her behavior. "When I did, I started to convince her to come back, for you and Souhila. She needed her mother, she was so young. At first, she didn't answer me, leaving me on read. I would send her pictures of you and Souhila too. Occasionally, I was receiving reactions, like hearts and all. It was only recently she started to respond more frequently." Faiza continued the story, as long as her son nodded through her words. Anas occupied himself with the biscuits in front of him. Sometimes his mother paused during her speech, wanting to see if he would react vocally to her story, but nothing. He remained stoic in the face of his mother's words. Once she was finished, Faiza obviously asked for forgiveness. Her voice was coated with emotions when she realized that her son wouldn't react, as if her storytelling did not impact him. In the silence outside, the mother grew impatient for her son's words.

"I can't forgive, since it doesn't only imply me. It involves my wife and daughter too. You know what?" Anas announced by sitting back properly in his seat, crossing his fingers above his legs. Faiza shook her head, patiently waiting for more. "You're going to call Hayat, and meet her to apologize." At first, the mother was going to protest, but either way, her son was right. She was the cause of all this, she had to take the initiative to apologize to his wife.

"I will do it as soon as possible." He got up, smiling at her, looking over his shoulder before leaving.

"Chokran mama, and don't forget to warn Zahia that she is not welcomed into our lives until I say so." With these words, Anas left, wanting to return home to find his wife and prepare for their romantic date. Passing through the living room, Anas stopped near his siblings, to quickly tell them what had happened. All were shocked by their mother's actions. He told them that everything was fine and that it was settled.

They didn't need to intervene.

On the doorstep, Anas kissed his daughter, leaving her with his sister and her cousins.

Anas went to his car with a smile on his face and a heart full of hope, he could finally return to his wife. Sitting in the driver's seat, he looked at himself in the mirror, combing his hair with his fingers, while checking that nothing was between his teeth.

He took a photo for his wife, before sending it with a message.

Anas

> Get ready for tonight, I bought you a beautiful dress. It's waiting for you on our bed, roohi.

Chapter 44

Hands full of shopping bags, Anas silently passed the door, checking if Hayat was anywhere near the kitchen. Fortunately, the way was clear. So he hurriedly put them on the counter, before emptying them individually. Busy with the preparations, he could hear Hayat moving upstairs, probably getting ready or still working on her tablet. Anas looked at the clock, to check on how much time he had left to prepare everything.

6:30 PM

While washing his hands, he calculated how long it would take to prepare a gastronomic dinner with two homemade dishes and a cheesecake he bought on the road. He set a timer for two hours in total. Anas noted the recipes on a sheet, before putting his apron on. For tonight, he chose to cook a *velouté* of wild mushrooms with hazelnut whipped cream, and some salmon ravioli accompanied by candied tomatoes and ricotta. The cook took out all the ingredients listed in the recipes, in order to have them at hand at all times. Anas wanted to be practical about everything tonight.

First, he started with the *velouté*, then moved on to the main course. The time passed at such speed that an hour later he had just finished the *velouté* and the candied tomatoes. Seeing that he might be running out of time, Anas accelerated. The commotion in the kitchen caught Hayat's attention, who poked her nose into the kitchen. When she saw her husband prepare dinner for tonight, her heart skipped a beat. In fact, Anas looked pretty seductive in his apron.

Hot, even.

Hayat closed her open – for too long – mouth before her husband could catch her staring. She approached him, still wanting to keep her distance, but curiosity took over her. Slowly, Hayat came up to him discreetly, just to stand by his side and watch him cook. It took Anas a solid minute to figure out his wife was standing inches away from him. The focus he had clouded his senses, making him unable to feel her warmth. He only noticed her presence once he stepped back and touched her unknowingly. She was still looking at him clueless.

"What are you cooking?" His wife asked, genuinely curious about the menu. Anas took a little spoon and made her open her mouth with a finger on her chin. First, Hayat's eyes were focused on the spoon, then they drifted to meet a pair of dark brown ones. His eyes were juggling between her opened lips and her shiny hazel eyes. She could actually see lust dripping from them. It made her knees weak. Hayat was about to fall to the ground due to the tension.

Heat made its way all over her body.

Every move from Anas seemed to be slowed down from her perspective. In fact, the simple contact on her chin caused her to have goosebumps and revived some memories. Hayat missed her husband. His touch, his scent, his kindness, the dimple on his cheek, and having *this* specific gaze only for her to see.

She *needed* him.

Hayat, totally focused on her husband's burning look, didn't even notice the spoon was already in her mouth. Gradually, she could feel all the aromas spreading on her tongue from this simple mouthful. She slowly swallowed the dish, teasing her husband a bit. Anas, still looking straight at her, took the spoon off of her mouth, waiting for a reaction from her. After a few seconds, Hayat felt an explosion of flavors invading her taste buds. It was delicious. Just by seeing her face, Anas could tell she was liking every bit of it.

"I'm making dinner for tonight." Hayat still did not realize the purpose of this evening. She looked around for Souhila, so she could taste it too. However, the little one was nowhere to be seen. Intrigued, she looked back at Anas.

"Where's Souhila? Is she in her room?" Her husband frowned at her question.

"No," he paused. "She's with my sister, so we could have the night together. Did you not receive my message?" Hayat shook her head, not seeing what he was talking about. Then, she realized. When she worked on big projects, Hayat put her phone on "Do not disturb". So she could focus correctly and not get distracted by anything.

"Oh, I was on "do not disturb" and I still haven't checked my notifications yet. Did I miss something?" Anas pinched his lips together, and sadness hit him too. Embarrassed, he cleared his throat.

"Yes," he was about to say something, but he changed his words at the last minute. "You know what?" Anas put his hands on her shoulder, and for the first time in a while, she let him touch her for more than one second. Three weeks to be exact. Hayat shook her head, looking at him puzzled. "You're going to take your phone, look at my beautiful picture and message and come back in less than an hour?" Intrigued, Hayat simply nodded, running to get her phone from her desk.

Hayat's heart raced, but she didn't know if it was the effort she had just put in or the excitement of having an evening alone with her husband. Probably a mix of the two. As she read the message on her screen, Hayat slowly walked to her room, wondering what type of dress was in the box. The presentation was a bit similar to the first time he offered her one. A white box, with a beautiful bow on the top of it and a note right in the middle.

"I know you would look wonderful in that dress."

A little reluctant to not know what kind of dress was in the box, Hayat slowly opened it, not knowing how to react when she saw the inside.

It was a simple black dress.

Very tight, with a slightly too low neckline and long sleeves to compensate. Though she was in awe at the sexy black dress, she was now hesitant. After her marriage, Hayat had gained a little more self-confidence, but the tight dress was still not in her clothing repertoire. It will show too much – even if he already has seen everything. Hayat put the dress on the bed, to have a better look at it.

Will I even fit in?

It looked so small compared to her.

While biting the inside of her cheeks, Hayat picked up the note between her fingers, re-reading it several times, wishing her husband's words were real. Not wanting to waste any more time, at the risk of wearing something else in the end, she headed for the shower to let the hot water run over her. It made all her tensed muscles, with the apprehension of the end result, relax. Hayat went to spruce up herself in just over half an hour; body lotion, hair, makeup, and perfume.

It was now time for the dress.

Hayat looked it up and down, wondering if it had been wise to get ready before putting it on. With a sigh, she took the clothing in her hands before slipping it on her body. The dress seemed to make her look perfect. A bit nervous, she looked at her reflection in the mirror. Relief washed over her. It was like putting on the perfect shoe. She embraced her curves hastily. Hayat liked it. Elegance and beauty were the only things present before her.

Anas was right.

I look wonderful.

She slid her hands down her body before a broad smile spread across her face. By discovering this new facet of her, Hayat had an immense confidence boost. Her body was actually beautiful in more than one type of clothing. She will, probably, add more of them after tonight. Walking toward the jewelry box, Hayat heard the bedroom door open. Anas couldn't believe his eyes. His wife was leaning slightly forward, arranging her earrings using the mirror on her vanity table, giving him a full display of every curve she had.

"Wow," he whispered, not being able to take his eyes off Hayat. With a smile that wanted to be arrogant, he stood behind her, towering above her. Hayat tried to hide the smile on her face, not wanting to give him this victory too quickly. She flipped her hair smoothly to face him, meeting a pair of eyes darkened by desire. Anas stepped forward, forcing his wife to raise her head. At this distance, he could smell the wonderful perfume she chose today. Her husband leaned in, "I love being right." Hayat chuckled at his words, resisting the urge to break the distance and kiss him. She kept her hands tingling with the desire to touch his chest.

"I can see that, sadly, you didn't make this one by yourself." Hayat looked down at herself, teasing him. It worked. He fell for it. Anas took another step in, mixing his warmth with hers. He rearranged a strand of her hair, to give him a better view of her breasts. He was delightfully looking at them. This simple action made his wife blush, who didn't really know how to react. She loved the effect she had on her husband; how he looked at her, touched her, caressed her skin with the tip of his fingers.

"Sadly, yes. I still don't know how to do perfect dresses like this one." He paused, leaving his face inches away from Hayat. His lips brushed hers every time he spoke. "But if I knew, I would give off all your indoor clothing and change them for that type of dress." Anas took a last look at her lips, before walking away and taking his place in the bathroom as well. Hayat sighed heavily, feeling all the tension disappear. She watches the door close behind him, wanting to completely cancel the meal and move on to reconciling. But Hayat was hungry, so she instantly gave up the idea.

- ☾ -

Anas arrived with the first dish, opening the ball with the *velouté*. Hayat's eyes were sparkling with happiness seeing all the efforts her husband had made, only for her, he had even added candles to make the room a little more subdued, more intimate. It worked. Hayat felt like in a cocoon made out of love enveloping her whole. A strange sensation bloomed inside her chest as she saw Anas sitting in the chair before her, his shirt raised to his elbow. It was simple but extremely seductive.

346

He was a delightful sight.

As time passed, both enjoyed the home-cooked meal. When he brought the dessert, Anas was hoping his last weapon would weaken her enough to make Hayat forgive his mistake. Compared to each day of the past week, Hayat actively responded to Anas' questions. Yet, she did not initiate conversation.

Only answers.

When she finished her plate, Hayat sat back on her chair, her stomach full. Without saying a word, she stared into her husband's gaze, patiently waiting for what was to come. Hayat knew for what purpose he had prepared his dinner and this dress. Therefore, she simply waited. Uncomfortable with the new look on him, Anas cleared his throat, ready to speak.

"I'm sorry, Hayat, I really am. I regret what I did. Leaving you for weeks without any warning or news is unacceptable. And I deserved the treatment you gave me afterward." He paused, not taking his eyes off her. "Can you forgive me?" Anas waited for a solid minute. The silence Hayat gave him was playing with his heart. With each second passing by, his chest felt pressure on it. In an instant, he could see mischief passing through her gaze. Hayat rested her elbows on the table, crossing her fingers, to rest her head on them.

"Only if you beg for it." She announced in a playful tone. Hayat, in reality, simply wanted to know how far Anas was able to go. Her eyes widened when she saw him kneel down next to her chair. Amused, she caressed her husband's face. He instantly leaned inside her touch. "You look cute from this angle."

Anas chuckled, "Please Hayati, forgive me." Hayat's eyes widened upon seeing Anas' distressed expression. She was about to respond, but Anas continued. "I regret everything. I miss you, my wife. Hayati. You mean so much to me. I want you back. Talking with you about anything, having you in my arms every now and then, feeling you close, praying with you. Taking your hand when I'm doing dhikr. I miss you. I'm sorry for letting you down. My point wasn't to hurt you or deceive you. I'm sorry. This choice clouded the part that deeply cares about you." Hayat didn't know what to say, so she simply listened to him. In one smooth motion, Anas took both of her hands before kissing them incessantly. "You bring out the best of me, Hayat, and I want to do the same with you." Another kiss, this time on her wrists, making her blush, *hard*. "You're my home, Hayati. I love you in this dunya and the akhira. Until Jennah reunites us."

Once he ended his little speech, Hayat forced him to get up with her. He looked at her with the most loving gaze. His wife took this occasion to rearrange a strand of hair behind his ear, then slid her hand on his hard chest. She could sense his heart accelerate beneath her touch. Feeling him react that way, made her feel special. With her free hand, she started to nervously play with the collar of his shirt.

"To be honest with you, I wanted to forgive you the moment I found you sleeping on the couch. The relief I felt at that moment, knowing you were okay and alive, surpassed my anger. But, if I did so, I would have felt taken for granted." Hayat sighed, finally confessing everything. The pressure on his chest vanished as she continued speaking. "Then, I just stood up and resisted the urge to forgive you for everything instantly. And, I would have missed this five-star meal." She kissed his cheek, while Anas' free hand slid to her waist, keeping her close. "Yes, I forgive you, 'ormi, and I would love to be your home again." This time it was Anas' turn to lean in and kiss his wife. She parted from him a bit before asking him a question that had been on her mind for a while. "Also, I wanted to ask you something." Her husband nodded.

"Tell me?" Her hand slid on his chest.

"In which way do you mean "Hayati"? As my life, or my Hayat?" He chuckled. In fact, he never really thought about it.

"I would say both." Anas pecked her lips. "Because you're my life, and my Hayat." It was now her turn to laugh. With her now in his arms, he realized how much he had missed her. She deserved nothing but love, warmth, and affection.

That's what Anas was about to give her tonight.

Chapter 45

Hayat was telling Kamila all about last week's adventures, while she was reacting to each plot twist as if she lived every single one of them. Her friend couldn't believe what happened to her only a few months into this marriage. An ex-wife poking their bubble of happiness, right at the start, was literally a hit-or-miss situation; either it would weaken them or make them stronger. Realizing that, Kamila pointed out to her friend that it was rather revealing about the future of their marriage. Hayat instantly agreed. When she was about to say how, and why this all happened, her phone rang, cutting her instantly. Faiza's name displayed on her screen. Hayat looked at it with an arched brow. She hesitated for a second before responding.

"Salam a'leykoum, Hayat. How are you?" Her mother-in-law said instantly after answering. The tone she employed was a bit too joyful, for what she had made her go through.

"Wa'leykoum salam, Faiza. I'm good, el hemduliLlah, and you?" To have some comfort in this situation right now, the youngest looked at her friend. The simple sight of her, made her feel at ease.

"El hemduliLlah." Her mother-in-law said instantly after answering. Hayat didn't add anything, she remained silent, adding nervousness to Faiza's shoulders. But she didn't even care. Her mother-in-law cleared her throat, "I want to invite you for a coffee, at my house, next Thursday. Are you free?" Hayat did not answer immediately, leaving some doubt. Hayat knew full well that she was free, nevertheless, she wanted to choose the appointment date herself.

"I can't on Thursday, can we meet on Friday or Monday? I know you always have family meetings on the weekend." She paused, "Because we clearly need to talk." The silence present on the other side of the line was quite revealing about the response that the young woman was about to receive. Hayat could hear her grumble something without being able to understand it. "Excuse me?" Again, Faiza cleared her throat as if nothing happened.

"Nothing, we can do it on Monday." Her mother-in-law sighed, "It's perfect." She added in an ironic tone. Faiza already sensed that the discussion was going to be hectic. If she wanted to have a good relationship with her son, she would have to get along with his wife. Anas had made that clear. After some greetings, Faiza hung up. Hayat sighed loudly under the curious eye of Kamila.

"Why did your mother-in-law call you?" She asked, leaning forward, her cup of hot tea in her hands. Hayat looked at her, desperate.

"She was the one who called Zahia." Kamila gasped, surprised by her words. She knew that people could be capable of everything, but she thought that mothers-in-law were only vicious in series or Disney movies. She approached her friend before coming to snuggle up against her.

"But why?" Hayat shook her head, as clueless as Kamila was. Her knowledge on that matter was limited, and the next meeting was a way to answer all her questions. Plus, Hayat will take the opportunity to reaffirm her boundaries since she had already crossed the limits. Kamila took her by the shoulders to comfort her.

The rest of the afternoon was reserved for them after she had told Kamila all her last adventures and how she settled them with her husband. The two of them continued to discuss everything and anything until Anas returned home, accompanied by Souhila. The reunion between Kamila and Souhila was most adorable. They behaved like old friends who met after years of being apart.

Seeing the sky changing, Hayat begged her friend to stay longer and eat. She didn't want to let her go on an empty stomach. At first, Kamila refused, but once the request came from the mouth of the sweetest little girl, she couldn't anymore. Together, they prepared dinner in a mood that was intended to be family and friendly. Hayat, watching this moment from the outside, could only smile.

Joy always came after the storm.

- ☾ -

Monday arrived in the blink of an eye. Hayat, under the last rays of the summer sun, rearranged her hijab one last time, thinking she was ready to face her mother-in-law. Her marriage was directly impacted by this relationship, she had to find a way to soften it, or Faiza ended up accepting their limits. Those were the only viable solutions. Therefore, Hayat had to find a way to achieve one of those ends without breaking their whole relationship. It made her nervous. Her heart pounding, her palms clammy, she decided to knock at the door. In a few seconds, it opened, revealing an expression half kind and half cold in the opening of it.

"Salam a'leykoum, Hayat. Dkhli, dkhli!" *Come in, come in.* Faiza said, welcoming her by stepping aside, so she could enter easily. Her daughter-in-law smiled back at her, walking straight in.

"Wa'leykoum salam, Faiza." The hostess led the way to the living room, where tea, coffee, and pastries were already waiting for them. Being the first day of the week, no one was at the family home. Faiza and Hayat had the house to themselves today. Still just as nervous, she sat down on the sofa facing her mother-in-law. Her expression still hadn't changed, even after they both sat. This was always a mixture of two opposing emotions.

Was she trying? Or was it just fake?

Hayat couldn't tell. This made her feel strange, but she kept her cool and waited. While they poured themselves their drinks, the two of them remained in an awkward silence. They sometimes glanced at one another, curious of each other's reaction to this. Hayat didn't want to be the one to start first. After all, Faiza invited her. She drank her tea while Faiza took a biscuit in her mouth, avoiding engaging in the hot topic. Hayat stared at her mother-in-law, forcing her to spill everything out of embarrassment.

After a few minutes of resistance, the lady weakened and began to speak. "Smhili benti… 'afak." *Forgive me, my daughter… Please.* "I wronged you, and I did something very cruel because I only thought about myself in this situation. It was selfish and vicious." She paused, waiting for a reaction, but nothing came from Hayat as she sensed Faiza was about to add more. "I'm not saying this because it's the right thing to say, I'm saying this because I mean it. When I heard the hurt and disappointment in my son's voice, I realized how far I had gone." Faiza looked down, shameful. "By doing this, I did not only wrong both of you, but I wronged myself too. It was a low blow. Everyone is now in the loop of what I did, and seeing their judging gaze made me regret my mistake even more." Her mother-in-law looked back at her, sincerity in her eyes. Hayat stayed silent, thinking about what was appropriate to say in this situation. Nervous, she tried to get some out with a sigh, so her thoughts won't be fogged by it.

"First, I want to thank you for the gesture. But, I want to know something, to understand where this is all coming from." She paused, getting a bit closer. "Why did you do this to us? To your son?" Faiza sighed in return before getting up and sitting by her side. Hayat was still keeping her distance from her, but at least she did not flee from the sudden approach. Still, with their hot drink in hand, Hayat listened intently to the story of why Faiza had done all this. Certainly, it was not going to help her to forgive her more quickly, but at least to understand her actions. During her speech, Hayat actively nodded, not leaving out a bite.

Once Faiza ended, Hayat continued, feeling her heart free from weight. "Thank you for explaining your vision." The guest sat back correctly on the sofa, "To be honest, it was only a way for me to understand your behavior and why you were so reluctant for your son to marry again to someone who wasn't Zahia." The oldest nodded, genuinely interested in what she was about to say, as Hayat sipped from her cup. "I do accept your apology, but I still can't forgive you. Because I'm not sure whether you won't do it again or change with time. Just like Anas, I will need to see you making a real effort in our relationship to forgive your mistakes." This time, Hayat tried to initiate something on her behalf, hoping it would help with the situation. She took Faiza's hand and squeezed it a bit. "I need you to at least try to accept our marriage. Or this won't turn out the way you think." Without adding anything, the hostess directly understood the meaning behind her words. In return, Faiza took her hand in hers, smiling at Hayat – a sincere one this time.

"I will do my best, benti. Thank you for understanding me." Following this discussion, the two of them felt better. After all that happened, the tensions necessitated it just to be settled at least. In their hearts, Hayat, as much as Faiza, hoped their relationship would improve.

Returning from this meeting, Hayat found a tense and on-edge husband sitting on the couch, arms, and legs wide open. Clueless about what caused this reaction, she came up to him, sitting beside her husband. Seeing her, Anas intentionally changed position to rest his head on his wife's thighs. Slowly, she brushed his hair with a hand, sensing all his tenseness coming out of him. Hayat kissed his forehead, his nose, then his lips, waiting for him to speak up.

But it didn't work.

"What happened?" She asked, still passing her hand through his hair. Anas sighed loudly, feeling his soul leaving with it.

"Zahia came back today, Souhila saw her." Shocked, Hayat lowered the cadence of her stroking. Anas put his arm on his eyes as if he was about to sleep through the problem.

"How did she react?" For a solid minute, he stayed silent, wondering how he could word her response.

"It was a mix between shock and happiness, I think?" He paused, "She froze when she saw her in front of the house, and then she ran toward her to hug her." Anas sat up, the better to sit on the sofa and face his wife. "What should I do? Zahia looked really happy to see Souhila, but I don't – and I can't – leave my daughter alone with her, since she is not legally Souhila's parent anymore. And now, I can't keep her away from her mother since she saw her." He relaxed limply on the sofa, desperate. Hayat slipped into her husband's arms before stroking his chest to soothe him. Anas closed his grip around her, feeling all his anger and frustration vanish once he had her there.

She is my peace.

"Do what you think is best for you both. If you don't want her in your life, you have the right to. If you think having her back will be good for Souhila, you need to set your boundaries with her." She looked up at him, "For example, she can see her only if you're present, like in a park or something. What do you think?" Anas nodded, holding her tight. Now happy, he kissed her multiple times, feeling a boost of love every time their lips touched. Her giggles made his heart melt.

"Thank you, Hayati." Her husband rearranged a strand of hair behind her ear, looking at her with such a tender gaze that only love could be seen. "I'm happy to know that you will be my wife in Jennah."

Epilogue

2 years later

The loud noises of machines were almost covering the sound of laughter and screams of happiness in the place. The familiar music of arcade games echoed in their ears while Anas and Hayat bought their tickets to play the various games present. As soon as they set foot in the arcade room, their competitive spirit swallowed them up. Nevertheless, one of the two was going to have their ego bruised tonight. Hayat and Anas exchanged a knowing look before engaging on the first machine: Mario Kart.

Luigi, for Anas, and Yoshi, for Hayat, lined up at the finish line, carefully watching the countdown before their eyes.

1...

They exchanged a look.

2...

Their feet pressed lightly on the pedal.

3...

They were now completely focused.

GO!

The starting signal was established, leaving the preheated karts to launch on the track. Three rounds and the better of the two had won. Thanks to the various assets, Anas took advantage, followed shortly by Hayat. Since he was totally focused, he did not see the arrival of a blue shell, which changed the faith of the race.

Hayat won.

Anas sat back in the seat, disappointed by his defeat. "Let's do another one. It was a lucky win." He pointed at the screen with his hand, unhappy with the result. "I was number one during the whole thing! That's unfair." Hayat sneered, seeing how much her husband hated to lose.

"This is how you talk to your wife? And it's a bit sexist to assume that I only won by luck. I won't give you another chance!" She stood up before pulling him by the arm to straighten him up. "Let's play another game. You will probably have enough luck to beat me." Her provocative tone made her husband laugh, who had well deserved it. Hand in hand, Anas and Hayat headed for a new machine to challenge each other once again.

This little circle lasted all night. As soon as one has lost, they demanded a rematch of the said game. Even if the competitive spirit was present, there was only good humor that radiated from them. They had had very little opportunity to be just the two of them for a few months, so it was always a pleasure to be together.

Before leaving, Hayat came across a UFO catcher to get a small stuffed animal. They looked adorable behind the glass. She needed at least two of them. One for her and one for Souhila. The little girl was staying at Hafsa's house for the weekend, so both of them could enjoy a bit of alone time together. Hayat still wanted to bring her a little soft toy, and if she couldn't catch one, she would just buy it nearby.

Under the eye of her husband, Hayat inserted the coin, ready to win. "Bismillāh," she whispered before moving the grappling hook using the joystick in front of her. Thanks to her technique, Hayat arrived easily on the plush, but nothing was certain yet. After pressing the button, she saw the small silver grappling hook go down slowly. Every inch of its descent only made Hayat's heartbeat quicken and focus intensify. She actively wanted something to bring back home from this date.

Yet, the first try was obviously a failure.

Motivated, Hayat tried several times without success. Mentally defeated, she headed for the exit to buy a small stuffed animal, which happened to be much less pretty than the one in the UFO catcher. Seeing her annoyed, Anas put in a last coin, hoping to catch two at once. He failed. So, when no one was watching, Anas kicked the machine quite hard, causing more than one stuffed animal to fall.

After all, he had put plenty of money into this machine to have enough for everyone.

With a smile on his lips, he caught up with his wife, who was still choosing which one to buy. He patted her shoulder before handing it to her once she turned around.

"I got them for you." Just seeing her face light up with joy was enough to end the evening on a high note. Hayat instantly jumped into his arms. Her heart relieved to be able to bring something home. Anas automatically welcomed this gesture by holding her tight and inhaling the beautiful scent he loved so much.

"Thank you 'omri!" Before detaching herself from him, she kissed his cheek while taking one of the stuffed animals. Anas had nothing but love in his eyes as he watched his wife skipping away as if she had just received the most wonderful news.

- ☾ -

Coming out of the bathroom with his towel on his hips, Anas could only admire his wife, who was already waiting for him under the sheets. Hayat, with a smirk, patted the empty place beside her. Her husband chuckled a bit before directly slipping in with her. She adjusted to face him while resting a hand on his chest. Due to fatigue, Anas closed his eyes, enjoying the caresses. The soft voice of his wife called him back and made him open them again to meet a pair of hazel eyes, which shone with gratitude.

"I can't wait to have a night like this again." Anas smiled at her, caressing her face in return.

"Me too." He confessed before kissing her forehead with the most tender of kisses. Happy, Hayat laid her head on his chest. Instinctively, Anas put his hand on her back, stroking her hair. At that moment, the relief they could feel was endless. The silence surrounding them was enough to speak about how much they loved each other. "Hayati?"

She raised her head to meet his eyes while he rearranged a strand of her hair behind her ear. "Yes?" For a second, he found himself bewitched by her eyes, which reminded him of the first time he had seen them.

"I need to tell you something." His wife could hear his heart racing in his chest, wondering what he was about to say that made him so nervous. Hayat simply nodded, waiting.

"Tell me," Anas opened his mouth and closed it. Then he gave himself a second before admitting what he felt deep inside.

"You're my other half, Hayati. Even if I had chosen different paths, Allah knew I was going to end up with you.

For eternity," he confessed, hoping it wasn't the wrong timing to open up on his feelings. She smiled at him before coming up to him and kissing him tenderly. He answered her automatically, intensifying the kiss by placing his hand in the crook of her neck. After a few seconds, she looked at him, giving Anas his last kiss.

"I love you too." Both satisfied, they laid back down on the bed, their chest filled with a unique and indescribable emotion. Only five minutes passed for Hayat to ask a question in return. She wanted to hear more about how much her husband loved her. "How much do you love me?" She propped herself up on one of her elbows, wanting the answer as she looked him in the eye. He gave her a gaze that said enough before letting his rocky voice roll down his mouth.

"أحبك في الله."

The End…

Or not.

Bonus

Night had fallen for several hours already when Anas had just parked in front of his house. It was so dark that he had to turn on his flashlight to see the lock. He checked his phone, hoping it wasn't too late.

1:56 AM

A breath of fatigue was the only sound that filled the living room once he got home. All the lights were off, no one was waiting for him. The thought that his wife and daughter might have waited until very late for him made him feel sad. After he did his evening routine, in the downstairs bathroom, Anas silently climbed the stairs so as not to wake anyone. Arriving at his daughter's door, he opened it gently, making as little noise as possible. Nevertheless, the father found the bed empty. Anas frowned at this sight.

Is she sleeping with Hayat?

The two had been inseparable for five years now. Anas wouldn't even be shocked if he found out one day that his daughter loved Hayat more than him. So, still, silently, Anas went to his room, finding the door half open as an invitation to join them once he was home. He, after this exhausting day, could almost cry at the sight of the peacefully sleeping faces of Hayat and Souhila. All his struggles were worth it for their calm expressions, he couldn't wake them up.

So, Anas stayed like that for a while, looking at them before taking a seat on the sofa to disturb them. It reminded him of the first time he had decided to fall asleep on the couch, however, this time, he hadn't decided to disappear.

After only two hours of sleep, Anas was awakened by a hand on his chest. His gaze was welcomed by a beautiful pair of hazel ones, almost hiding behind round cheeks. Still tired, he simply put his hand on hers, his eyes full of love.

"Why didn't you come to bed?" Hayat asked, stroking her husband's fingers softly. "I left the door open on purpose, so you could join us." Anas smiled, realizing that he hadn't misinterpreted the signal his wife had left him.

"You and Souhila looked so peaceful, I didn't want to bother." Hayat tugged his hand lightly, so he could get up, stealing a soft kiss from his lips. Anas gave another one in return, enjoying this little act of affection. Getting up from the sofa, Hayat pulled him with him.

"You never bother us, and the bed feels empty without you." His wife whispered, before adding another – longer – kiss to his lips, almost tiptoeing to reach them. Anas smiled, feeling finally complete. Hand in hand, they went back to bed, happy to be reunited.

- ☾ -

Screams of frustration, accompanied by constant clicks of the mouse, filled the room. Anas and Hayat, in front of their computer screens, glasses on, in one versus one, fighting to see who was the best – for the umpteenth time since their wedding. Anas, completely losing, sometimes looked at his wife's screen, stealing information on her position. Hayat knew he was cheating, as always, and still managed to predict where he would come from.

His gameplay was simply too obvious to her.

After seven defeats and one victory – by cheating, Anas decided to stop there. As a reward, Hayat stretched herself on her chair while listening to her husband whining on her left.

"See? I almost always win against you." She paused, smirking at him. "I can teach you if you want." Anas, totally irritated by his wife's comments, wanted revenge in another way. Her husband was not very good at video games against her, but he beat his wife in another area: teasing her. Advancing toward her like his prey, Anas caged her between his arms, giving her the most burning gaze over his glasses. Hayat, still sitting on her chair, was expecting a reaction from him; it made her smile even more when she saw that her provocation had worked. Clenching the armchairs progressively to make her come closer made his forearm's veins pop up, distracting his wife for a split second.

"You can, and I think you would look extremely hot as my teacher." And there he was, Anas in all his glory. He knew exactly how to speak to her, so Hayat could melt on the spot. Just with his words, he could see the instant effect he had on his wife. In this burning gaze game, Anas and Hayat teased each other just to see who would break first, and today Anas wasn't going to lose.

Now their faces were merely a few inches away from one another. Between their burning and unbearable gaze, their beating heart, and the desires they fought to win, nothing made sense in their mind. At the slightest weakness, he had won. To guarantee his chances of winning, Anas took off Hayat's glasses while keeping his own, as if creating an imbalance between the two will help him.

Hayat had a hard time resisting.

Her husband loved breaking her walls one by one until she folded between his arms. He waited for another second, feeling the built-up tension almost ready to explode. When Anas saw desire slip into his woman's eyes, he knew he had won. In an instant, their bodies became one, enjoying each other's warmth.

Between two kisses, Anas whipped to her lips, "I love you, roohi." With a smile on her face, she intently responded.

"I love you too, nefsi."

THE END

About the Author

Neya B is a new indie author who used to write fiction on Wattpad when she was younger. At 20 years old, she decided to start real projects with "new ideas" that could bring some fresh air to the different genres. Today, as an indie author, she tries her best to capture your heart and make you dream about a different life through her stories. While adding a part of her into the literature. As an Algerian and Muslim author, she wanted her debut novel to represent her at best.

Connect with me

Instagram: **@author.neyab** & **@kozukidbasma**
TikTok: **@authorneyab** & **@kozukidbasma**
Goodreads: Neya_B_

Join my Facebook group: Neya's darlings

Acknowledgments

First, let's say El HemduliLlah, I finally finished this project. I want to express my sincerest gratitude to my family and friends for following me into that kind of crazy project. This book would probably never have seen the light because of all my insecurities. It's my first time writing a whole book in English. To everyone reading this, you need to know that I'm an Algerian born and raised in France, with my mother's and father's culture. As you guessed, English isn't my first language. I hope it wasn't too noticeable through the process of reading, and I apologize if it was. Since I'm a very indecisive person, this book will probably be rewritten with added or deleted parts until it could fall into your hands.

I want to dedicate this part to my siblings. I know I'm not the best speaker, but each of the characters here has a part of you that I absolutely love. When I wrote all of them, I couldn't *not* include you all in this. You are my role models, and as the youngest, I will always admire you even if we can sometimes fight, but that's what siblings do.

It's my way to say I love you.

Mama, baba, I will never be grateful enough for everything you have done for me. All of this work, in fact, for the major part, was for you. I hope you are proud of your daughter.

To my friends. I think that Allah سبحانه وتعالى always puts people in your way for a reason. They all bring you something, good or bad, for a period of time – or forever. If I had to choose you, I'll choose you all over again. Meeting you changed me into a better version of myself. Especially some little souls for which I couldn't even be grateful enough. This work is also dedicated to you guys, you pushed me (hard enough) to go through my ideas, and it's only the start of this journey.

I want to say El HemduliLlah again because if I wasn't Muslimah this book wouldn't be here today. Islam plays a big part in my life, and I think that love in Islam is not explored enough. We have a special way to love, and I wanted to honor it in my very first published novel, but I also wanted to give a new face to my culture. My North African culture. I was so tired of seeing the lack of *good* representation in romance or books in general. I hope this book will give you a new look at our people, our welcoming and loving people. We all have flaws, but this degrading image needed to stop.

I needed to recognize myself a bit more in books.

Now, to my lovely betas, ARC and readers.

Thank you, thank you, and thank YOU! Your feedback, notes, and reviews helped me to get better and to give more emotions, descriptions, and all to my stories. Without you, I can't see the problems in my writing or in the consistency of the whole. Your work is very dear to me because it's a necessity – for me – to understand if something is wrong.

So, thank you again for giving this book – and me – a chance. I know it's only a romance with no plot, but that was the point of this one. Don't worry. I will come back with different themes, In Shaa Allah.

For my Muslim readers, who felt that Islam wasn't welcoming in terms of love. I know this book is a very romanticized version and is less difficult, too, compared to real life. Nothing is easy in this world, but I wanted to show you that it was still possible to have halal love, even in our society.

Don't lose hope. You got this.

And last but not least, for my non-Muslim readers. My point was to show you how we do love in Islam and how we pursue love in Islam. Muslims are romantics. There are plenty of actions or ways to show our love and interest in someone. However, we don't show it in public. We, as Muslims, are very private and modest with demonstrations of affection outside. That's how we are. I hope you have a new vision of Islam, Muslim, and our North African culture in general.

Thank you all for being with me on that journey.

See you soon!

Translation

'Amou: 'Amou is the brother of my father.

'Amtou: 'Amou is the sister of my father.

Aah: Yes in the Moroccan dialect.

Abaya: A full-length outer garment worn by some Muslim women.

Adhaan: Call to prayer.

Akhira: Refers to the hereafter.

Akhy/kho: Brother.

AstaghfiruLlah (أَسْتَغْفِرُ اللَّه): AstaghfiruLlah is a phrase in Arabic meaning "I seek forgiveness in God."

Atay: Tea.

A'udubiLlah (أَعُوذُ بِاللَّهِ): A'udubiLlah is a phrase in Arabic meaning "I seek refuge in Allah."

A'udubiLlah mina sh-shaytani r-rajim (أعوذ بالله من الشيطان الرجيم): A'udubiLlah mina sh-shaytani r-rajim is a phrase in Arabic meaning "I seek refuge in Allah from the outcast Shaitan."

Aya: A verse of the Quran

Barak'Allahu fik (masculine) or fiki (feminine) (بارك الله فيك): Barak'Allahu fik is a phrase in Arabic meaning "May Allah's Blessings be Upon You."

Baraka: Blessing(s).

Baba: Father/dad/daddy (it's also an affectionate nickname for children.)

Bent: Daughter

Bismillāh (بِسْمِ اللَّ): Bismillah is a phrase in Arabic meaning "in the name of Allah" that occurs at the very start of the Qur'an and opens the Basmala.

Dhikr: It's the remembrance of Allah.

Duaa (اَلدُّعَاء): Dua means invocation – to call out – and is an act of supplication, meaning asking or begging for something earnestly or humbly.

Dublah: An engagement ring.

Dunya: Refers to this temporary world.

El hemduliLlah (اَلْحَمْدُ لله): It means "all praise and thanks be to Allah."

Ghazaal: Ghazaal means deer.

Hayaa: Shyness / Modesty

Hennaya: A hennaya is a woman performing henna for events.

Hbiba/hbibi/habibti/habibi: My love.

Henunna: My darling in the Algerian dialect.

Imam: Islamic leadership position.

In Shaa Allah (إِنْ شَاءَ اَللّٰه): If God wills.

Jennah: Paradise.

Jumu'ah: Jumu'ah is a congregational prayer that Muslims hold every Friday, just after noon, in the place of dohr.

Khalou: Khalou is the brother of my mother.

Khaltou: Khaltou is the sister of my mother.

Kheir: Good

Khimar/kumur: A head covering or veil worn in public by some Muslim women, typically covering the head, neck, and shoulders.

Mahram: In Islam, a mahram is a family member with whom marriage would be considered permanently unlawful (haram).

Mama: Mother/mom/mommy (it's also an affectionate nickname for children.)

Masjid: Mosque.

Mulaqat: A visit.

Muqabala: One or more interview to get to know each other with chaperon(s).

Na'am: Na'am means yes in Arabic.

Qibla: The direction of the Kaaba (the sacred building at Mecca), to which Muslims turn for prayer.

Salam a'leykoum (أَلسَّلَامُ عَلَيْكُمْ): "As-Salaam-Alaikum," the Arabic greeting meaning "Peace be unto you," was the standard salutation among members of the Nation of Islam.

Salat: Salat means prayer.

Salat Fajr: Prayer of the sunrise.

Salat Dohr: Prayer of the zenith.

Salat 'Asr: Prayer of the afternoon.

Salat Maghrib: Prayer of the sunset.

Salat Ishaa: Prayer of the evening/night.

Subhaan'Allah (سُبْحَانَ ٱللهِ): Subhaan'Allah can be translated to mean, both "God is perfect" and "Glory to God."

Sujood: The act of low bowing or prostration to Allah.

Weld: Son

Wudu: Ablution / a form of purification that Muslims complete before praying

Ya: Ya means "O", "hey" or "you", and is a vocative particle preceding a noun used in direct address.

أَحبك في الله: I love you in Allah or I love you for the sake of Allah.

في أمان الله : Fi AmaniLLAH is an invocation which means "In Allah's Protection".

<u>Grammar</u>

The suffix "i" can mean the possessive of the first person, for example, Benti = my daughter, Weldi = my son, Hayati = my Hayat or my life…

The suffix "k" can mean the possessive of the second person, for example, mamak = your mom, babek = your father…

To be continued.

Made in United States
Troutdale, OR
10/25/2023

13987406R00219